MAKE ME BEG

RICH DEMONS OF DARKWOOD BOOK 2

C.R. JANE

MAY DAWSON

Make Me Beg Copyright © 2022 by C. R. Jane and May Dawson

Photograph: Wander Aguiar

Cover by Eve Graphic Design

Formatted by: The Nutty Formatter

All rights reserved.

No portion of this book may be reproduced in any form or by any electronic or mechanical means, including information storage and retrieval systems, without written permission from the author, except for the use of brief quotations in a book review, and except as permitted by U.S. copyright law.

For permissions contact:

crjaneauthor@gmail.com

maydawsonauthor@gmail.com

This book is a work of fiction. Names, characters, businesses, places, events, locales, and incidents are either the products of the author's imagination or used in a fictitious manner. Any resemblance to actual persons, living or dead, or actual events is purely coincidental.

Proof: Jasmine Jordan

Make Me Beg

THE RICH DEMONS OF DARKWOOD SERIES BOOK 2

C.R. JANE
MAY DAWSON

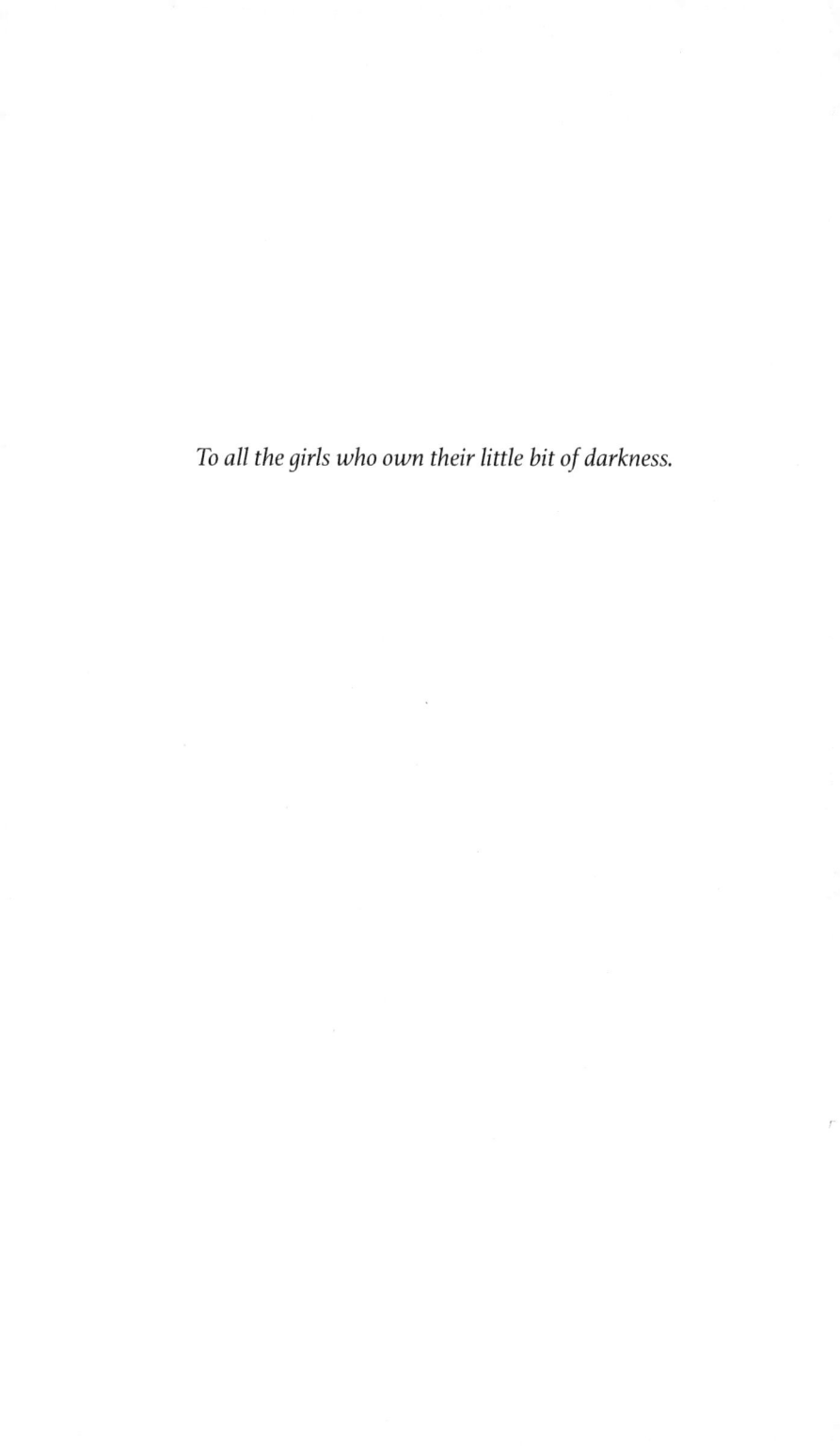

To all the girls who own their little bit of darkness.

JOIN OUR READERS' GROUPS

Stay up to date with C.R. Jane by joining her Facebook readers' group, C.R.'s Fated Realm. Ask questions, get first looks at new books/series, and have fun with other book lovers!

Join C.R. Jane's Group

Join May Dawson's Wild Angels to chat directly with May and other readers about her books, enter giveaways, and generally just have fun!

Join May's Group
Subscribe to May Dawson's Newsletter to receive exclusive content, latest updates, and giveaways.
Join May Dawson's Wild Angels on Facebook

Goddess
Jaira Burns

Bad Kind of Butterflies
Camila Cabello

you should see me in a crown
Billie Eilish

Take It Out On Me
Bohnes

I Feel Like I'm Drowning
Two Feet

Sail
AWOLNATION

Horns
Bryce Fox

Killer
Valerie Broussard

How To Be a Heartbreaker
MARINA

Watercolor Eyes
Lana Del Ray

Miss America & The Heartbreak Prince
Taylor Swift

Need to Know
Doja Cat

What Goes Around.../Comes Around...
Justin Timberlake

Needed Me
Rihanna

Savage
Megan Thee Stallion

Stay High-Habits Remix
Tove Lo, Hippie Sabotoge

Get the SPOTIFY playlist HERE

MAKE ME BEG

The monsters almost made me love them.

And now I'm paying the price.

But so are they.

Stellan, Cain, Remington, Paxton and I are locked together in a war that I refuse to lose.

They've taken my freedom, my money, my reputation... but they can't take my soul.

They keep forgetting I was forged in fire by a demon. Monsters don't scare me.

They think I'm trapped in their mansion with them. They think every time I seek their mouths, their hands, it means something.

They think they can break me with their punishments... and their pleasures.

But I'm only playing their game to win our war.

One by one, I'll find their secrets, however bloody they are, and make them think I'm saving them...only to use those dark secrets against them.

Death. Bloodshed, Betrayal...and now Sex. That's all my

life will ever be. Now it's time to welcome these men into my nightmares.

These monsters think they're the kings of the world.

But the king always falls without the queen.

And the kings in this game...are going to burn.

RICH DEMONS OF DARKWOOD SERIES

Make Me Lie
Make Me Beg
Make Me Wild

This is a college bully reverse harem series which means the main character will end up with multiple love interests. It may have triggers for some as this is a dark romance with scenes of intense bullying, murder and mayhem, and sexual scenes.

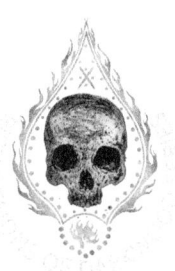

PROLOGUE
AURORA

Nine Years Old

The first week that I lived with my father was pure magic. I had no idea that he'd become even more of a monster than the family he'd saved me from.

We moved into a big, rambling house out in the country. The house had been sold with some of its furniture and books, and there were two dozen rooms to explore. I went through every musty-smelling book in the library, poked into every dusty corner, stepped into the enormous stone fireplace that was big enough for me to stand up in, and looked up to see if I could glimpse the blue sky through the flue.

The house backed to an endless fairy-tale forest. The only break in the greenery was the edge of a cliff, overlooking a long silver river that wound through the trees, with rocks breaking through the surface.

I'd stand at the edge and throw rocks and sticks into the river, watching them get dragged under the rushing water.

"Delilah," the Demon said quietly.

I spun to face him, my heart beating fast. He must have seen the terror on my face because he knelt in the fallen leaves. One orange leaf landed in his dark hair, but he was too focused on me to notice. "Delilah, it's all right. I just came out to check on you and found you standing here with your toes all but hanging off the cliff."

"I'm sorry," I said.

"Don't be sorry. You're a brave, fearless girl. I'm proud of every bit of you." He smiled at me, his deep blue eyes creasing at the corners.

The warm glow in my chest felt like life. He looked at me like no one had ever before, as if he were pleased by me, delighted, even.

He straightened. "I thought we could go shopping today."

"Shopping for what?"

"Whatever we find."

We walked hand in hand back to the house, and he opened the back door for me, as if I were a princess and he was the coachman.

It was a long drive down the steep, wooded driveway before we turned onto a country road, then took the ramp for the highway.

When the two of us were at the mall, I kept stealing glances at another man and his daughter. She was a little younger than me, but she was gripping his hand and skipping. I eavesdropped, unable to stop myself or even hide the way I watched them. They were going to the movies. She looked as if she were a little older than me, but she still called him *daddy*.

I could tell from the look on my father's face that he'd caught me watching them. There was a knowing glint in his eyes. Embarrassment flooded my cheeks red.

I felt a little silly even wishing I could hold his hand; I hadn't held anyone's hand since I was five years old. I wasn't a little girl anymore.

"You know, I'm just learning how to be a dad," he said. "I'm sad I missed out on all the years when you were little. Sometimes it helps me to watch other people to know how I'm supposed to act." In a quiet, confidential voice, he added, "I've been doing that all my life."

"I feel like I have too," I admitted.

He held out his hand, and feeling a little bit silly—but also warm and cared-for—I reached out and took his hand. It was okay that I felt shaky about how to be a normal girl, that I'd never fit in at school, because he did too.

"Can we go to the movies too?" I asked. I almost said *dad*, but my tongue tripped over the words.

"Another day. We don't have much time today."

Disappointment flooded me. I'd never been to a movie that I could remember. "I wonder if my mom ever took me to a movie before she gave me up."

He stilled. "You know your mother gave you up?"

I nodded.

"What do you remember about her?" His voice had taken on a cold, dark tone, and I shivered, wondering what I'd done wrong to make him mad. Maybe he didn't like it when I talked about my mom.

"Nothing," I lied, my voice coming out in a whisper.

Everyone said my memories of my mother, the stories she'd told me, were lies I'd made up for attention. People got mad at me when I talked about how my mom and I had been on the run. They just talked about the last part, the part where she'd smiled at me as I picked out a Coca-Cola and a Snickers bar at the gas station, where she'd kissed me and reminded me to use my new name and told me to sit on the bench. It was a chilly, damp night and she'd taken off her hoodie and put it on me.

Then she backed out of the parking lot, waving and smiling at me through the windshield. She'd turned onto the highway, and her headlights had faded into the night.

"I'll take you to the movies, Delilah," he said. "I'll give you everything you've ever wanted. I'll never leave you, I promise. I'll always be with you. Always be watching over you."

At the time, those words had sounded comforting.

He bought me toys and books and a new stuffed animal to replace the one that my foster brother had thrown into a mud puddle. He bought me pretty dresses, and shoes, and the jeans I wanted.

"Go change into this one," he told me, holding out a bag with a lacy dress. "I want you to dress up for dinner tonight. I'm taking you somewhere special."

My heart swelled as I took the bag from him. He was so handsome, I wanted to look like a pretty girl.

I changed in the bathroom, frowning as I squeezed myself into the dress. It was too small, and I felt as if everyone could practically see my panties. I debated pulling my jeans on too, but I didn't want him to think I wasn't happy with all his gifts. He'd really liked this dress.

I went out and he smiled approvingly, so maybe I was just too used to wearing jeans. He took me into a nice restaurant, where the room was dark and there were big cloth napkins to smooth into my lap, and he ordered three different desserts when I couldn't decide.

"I can spoil my little girl," he said, smiling at me across the table as I alternated bites of chocolate cake and ice cream. "You're pretty perfect right now; a bit of spoiling won't hurt you."

The waitress smiled at us. "Your little girl is just too cute."

But her gaze lingered on him, like she meant *he* was just too cute.

He smiled back at her, looking thoughtful, but all he said was that he thought so too, and I felt myself blush again.

Afterward, we walked around the mall. He stopped at a bench and the two of us sat down.

"Delilah, my darling," he said. "There's a man following us."

My gaze snapped up to his, but he looked calm, relaxed, in control.

Not like I remembered my mom. I didn't remember what she'd told me. I only remembered the fear, the sense we were running away from a relentless monster. She'd been wild-eyed sometimes, and I'd learned to sleep lightly, never sure when she'd pull me out of bed and we'd run.

"It's all right," the Demon promised, jerking me back to the present. "He's not going to hurt you; I'm not going to let him. Do you see him? Over there, watching you? Don't let him see you look."

I looked around, pointing to the pretzel shop behind him as if I were begging for one, but I saw the man he was talking about. He was watching me in a way that made my skin crawl, but his gaze jerked away when he saw me. "I see him."

"You are such a clever girl," he said admiringly. "I'm so glad you're my daughter."

"Why's he watching us?"

"He's watching *you*." He wrapped an arm around my shoulders, pulling me close, his lips next to my ear so he could speak to me quietly. "I know that man. He's taken a lot of little girls home with him, and he hurts them, and they never go back to their mommies and daddies."

I shivered and he hugged me tighter. "It's all right. I would never let him get you. But if you're willing to be very brave, I can get *him*. I can keep him from ever hurting anyone again."

"How?"

"I'm going to pretend to leave you in the car, in the parking lot, and I'll run back in. I bet he'll come to get you, but I'll get him instead."

My eyes welled with sudden tears. I could just imagine him leaving me forever.

"Oh, Delilah, I'm not going to do it if you don't want me to. I'm sure he probably won't hurt anyone else tonight, even if I don't stop him. You don't have to do anything you don't want to."

No one had ever said that to me before.

"I can do it," I said. "We won't let him hurt anyone else."

My stomach ached with the thought that maybe my father would leave me there, that he didn't really want me after all, but I wanted to try to trust him. If he came back, I'd know he was really my dad. He was really always going to look after me.

"Good girl," he said approvingly. The two of us went out into the parking lot. The cold sank through my too-small dress immediately, and I rubbed my goose-pimpled arms. Dad smiled at me as he opened my car door like I was a lady, then he threw the bags into the trunk. "Oh, I forgot I needed to grab milk!"

He glanced toward the drug store at the side of the mall.

"Can I stay here and read my books?" I begged.

"Oh, all right. But keep the doors locked, okay?" He got

my bag from the bookstore out from the trunk and gave it to me.

He closed the door and left it unlocked, then walked away through the shiny sea of cars. I watched him with my heart in my throat.

I was more scared he would abandon me than I was of the strange man.

My car door opened suddenly and a strange man loomed there. "Hey, honey. Are you okay? You looked scared."

"I'm fine," I said, sliding across the seat, toward the opposite door.

"Your dad got held up. There was an accident in the store; a man fell and he's helping him. I've got my daughter with me too, so I said I'd come check on you."

He hadn't had a daughter with him before.

My fingers wrapped around the door handle. The man's gaze flickered toward me, then abruptly, he jumped toward me.

My father loomed behind him. He had a needle in his hand, which he drove into the man's neck. The man cursed, turned to fight him–then the man went boneless. The Demon shoved him into the backseat, where he fell. His head almost landed in my lap. He tried to raise his hands, and they looked twisted like claws as he reached toward me, his eyes wide and horrified. Then his hands fell as if he'd lost the last of his power.

I scrambled out of the car.

"It's all right," the Demon said. "You'll ride up front with me this time. Like a big girl."

He smiled at me brightly as he bundled the man's legs into the seats, then slammed the doors shut.

The monster was coming home with us.

1

CAIN

The fire alarms started to go off in the middle of the party.

I'd been drinking with Stellan, who seemed like he was in pouty bitch mode, even though we were tormenting Aurora for *him*. He was the one who needed revenge, like Pax had needed it for his mom. We just had to wring a confession from the bitch first.

It seemed like a waste to punish her, to be honest. She made the world a much more interesting place. The thought of a world without Aurora in it seemed like a drab, boring one, like the world felt to me most of the time until she strolled into my life.

"Here's to you turning that frown upside down, asshole," I said, clinking glasses with him. "You think Aurora murdered your sister. Now she's crying because people hurt her feelings. You're bringing her down and it took *nothing*. We *Carried* her ass and she crumbled."

I was disappointed Aurora had crumbled, to be honest. I'd expected more of a challenge from her.

Then the alarms went off.

Remington winced. "Hope that doesn't hit the sprinklers and—oh fuck."

The ceiling seemed to open up as water rained down on all of us. Girls scattered, shrieking, and the men were hardly any better. Remington pulled off his tux jacket and held it over his head. Too bad I'd taken mine off a while ago. Stellan's white shirt was already half-transparent and clinging to his chest.

"Let's find out who ruined our party and go kill them, shall we?" I suggested to my friends.

I turned to find a wide-eyed pledge standing in front of me. He managed to say, "There's been an, ah, incident…"

"I can see that," I said helpfully. I hated it when they acted scared of me. So pathetic.

But then, I also hated it when they weren't.

"It's with your McLaren, sir…and a bunch of other cars," he finished awkwardly.

"I see," I said, my voice coming out like ice.

Pax and Stellan exchanged a look, and Remington whistled. "Someone is definitely going to die tonight."

I pushed my soaking-wet sleeves up my biceps as the four of us hustled down the stairs to the garage. The acrid scent of a fire hit my nose as soon as I pushed open the doors, all gasoline, burnt plastic and metal.

The McLaren was nothing but a burnt-up shell. Stellan cursed as he saw his own car with paint peeling and a shattered windshield. Dozens of the cars were damaged, but the McLaren was obviously the center of the chaos. Someone had been trying to get my attention… they wouldn't enjoy their victory, though.

"Security footage," I ground out just as our cell phones pinged. Remington had his head down over his phone; he must have just sent it out to all of us.

Aurora came up on the video. She swaggered into the garage carrying a bottle of my booze and my cigar case. She flashed a big smile and a special finger at the camera.

And she lit my goddamn car on fire.

I didn't know what the fuck to do with myself.

I should kill her.

If she'd done that to someone else, though, it'd be so fucking hot.

"Let's not rush to punishment," Pax said.

"We don't need to rush the punishment," I said, purposefully reinterpreting him. "Anyway, I'm sure she's run halfway across the state by now. She knows how to hide. By the time we've caught up to her, I'll have decided what to do with her."

"Do you want me to release the internet on her again?" Remington asked. "I'm sure the sightings will start rolling in, track her movement for us."

"No, she's ours," I said, and I didn't even know what I meant by that. Ours to punish, definitely. Ours to hurt. Ours to...

The alarms got shut off and a clean-up crew came to deal with the McLaren and the rest of the damaged cars. My jaw tightened as I left the disaster.

That car had been one of my favorite toys, and I hated when anyone played with my toys but me.

I walked into my bedroom, already peeling off my wet shirt.

Aurora was on my bed.

"What the fuck?" I growled. The surprise racing through my blood felt like coming to life.

She was never fucking boring.

"Hi, Cain," she purred. She was laying back on my pillows, and as I watched, she took a handful of popcorn from the paper bag and tossed it into her mouth. She'd helped herself to my television; it was playing some kind of rom-com.

"What do you think you're doing? Do you have a death wish?" My voice came out cold and clear and...curious.

A wise girl would've run.

"I'm eating popcorn," she said, as if I were a bit stupid. "The party got boring."

"You didn't seem bored the last time I saw you. You looked like you were going to cry."

She tilted her chin, her gaze meeting mine frankly. "I was disappointed in you. Now I know who you are, though, so there's no reason for me to be upset."

"There's no reason for you to be upset?" I was about to give her one. "I didn't expect you to stay here."

"Where else would I go?" she asked innocently.

"Somewhere safer than my bed when you've just pissed me off."

"You're not going to kill me," she said confidently. "You want answers about Stellan's sister. You're all too stupid to see the truth, to believe I wouldn't have let the Demon hurt her. And until you get answers, you can't hurt me."

She was right, but I was stunned by her courage in coming back here. "I can hurt you *plenty* without killing you. Burning my car was a very foolish move, Aurora."

She sat up on the bed, her violet eyes flashing. "Throwing a lavish ball to humiliate me was a foolish move, Cain." Then she laid back against my headboard, pulling my blanket over her lap, looking cozy and comfortable. No one reacted that way in the face of my anger. "But you need me here. And more than that, you *want* me here, don't you?"

I wasn't going to answer that question. She looked at me too knowingly, as if she'd realized how much I wanted her near me. Especially now, when my cock was hard, when I was so furious and wanted to punish her, to make her beg...

"You're going to have to pay for your sins."

"And so are you."

"You first." I grabbed the end of the blanket and pulled it away from her. She wore a crop top, exposing a flash of her taut belly above her sleep shorts. "I've been wanting to do this for a while."

"Oh? What's that?"

"Spank your wicked ass." I dropped my wet shirt in a ball at my feet, Then I unbuckled my belt and slid it through the loops of my tuxedo pants.

Her eyes widened in surprise for a second, then she couldn't resist smiling. "You have to know, deep down, that I would never have hurt her. Otherwise, you'd never play with me."

"I'm not playing," I assured her.

She knocked her popcorn across my bed as she made a sudden move to escape. I caught her and dragged her across my lap, landing a smack across her ass that stung my palm. Her ass was firm and tantalizing, and my cock jumped; she had to feel it against her thighs.

I pushed my hand under the waistband of her sleep shorts, palming the delicious curve of her bare ass, and she moaned. She certainly didn't seem to mind the spanking.

I pushed her shorts down the rest of the way. I'd seen her perfect ass before, but there was something special about having her at my mercy like this, seeing the curve of her taut ass and the red where my hand had marked the pale skin. I was only getting started. My fingers wanted to toy with the pink of the most perfect pussy I'd ever seen when she was so vulnerable over my lap, but I resisted the impulse, landing more smacks across her ass.

She wriggled across my lap, protesting, but I wasn't sure she was trying to get away.

I had a feeling she liked being punished, judging from the way her pussy flushed and grew shiny with her desire. I rubbed my hand across her reddened ass, then teased my fingers across her clit. She gasped in response, her back arching, and I found the cadence that made her writhe.

When she was on the very edge of coming, her thighs tensing with the power of her growing orgasm, I pulled my fingers away and landed several more smacks against her ass. She moaned as if she might just come from the spanking.

"I'm going to make you wet," I told her quietly, "and I'm going to leave you tied to my bedposts all night."

She moaned, then looked over her shoulder at me. There was mischief in her eyes. "You don't have bedposts. And you want me just as much as I want you. More, probably. Almost certainly."

She might be wicked, but she was definitely entertaining.

"Mm." I caught one of her wrists and reached over her, grabbing the restraints that were hidden at the sides of the bed. She realized what I was doing just as I clicked the cuff on and began to fight me in earnest, but I pushed her off my lap, grabbing her other wrist and pulling it up.

"Cain," she protested, then fell silent, as if she'd been trying to figure out what argument would make me see reason and then realized there was no argument. I would do what I wanted to her.

One day, I wanted to make her come over and over again.

But not tonight.

Her shorts and panties had fallen down around her

calves and I pulled them off completely, standing back and enjoying the sight of her. She was so beautiful, especially in a moment like now when she was very pissed off at me. Her eyes narrowed, her beautiful lips pressing together.

"You knew I'd punish you," I chided. "You didn't even try to hide what you were doing."

"I'd hate for someone else to take my glory."

"No, it's all yours." I folded the belt over, curious how much the pain-pleasure line could blur for Aurora.

Certainly, bringing her pain would be all pleasure for me.

I grabbed her wrists and reached under the mattress for the leather restraints. I'd tie her down on her stomach, where I could enjoy looking at my handiwork all night; her ass was red, marked all over by my hand, and I couldn't wait to rake my fingernails over her skin and leave more red fingerprints across her curvy ass.

As I tied her ankles, she almost nailed me with one foot in the crotch, but I twisted and she kicked my thigh instead. I stood over her, just watching her for a moment. She'd gone still, accepting that she was at my mercy physically, at least. But she had that cunning look in her eyes as if she was figuring out her next move. My cock was so hard that I could barely stand it. But Aurora certainly didn't deserve my cock tonight.

I spanked her ass with the belt. Her whole body stiffened for a second, as if shock were rushing through her.

"Cain," she said, a desperate edge in her voice. That sound, combined with the sight of her shapely ass marked with my belt, made me even harder. I was about to come right in my pants from how much I wanted her–but I'd rather deny us both than satisfy her.

She writhed in the sheets, as far as she could move, as I went on spanking her.

"Want to tell me that you're sorry?" I taunted. I wouldn't care anyway.

"No," she said into the sheets. "Definitely not sorry."

She gasped at that next stroke of the belt.

"Good," I said. "Because I don't care,"

I was curious if she was still turned on, and I ran my fingertips across the curve of her ass. When I teased my fingertips over her clit, she was wetter than ever, and her thighs tightened around my hand, trying to hold me there as I stroked her clit rhythmically.

With my other hand, I toyed briefly with her rosebud. Her hips ground down against the bed, her slit tightening against my fingertips as she neared orgasm. No matter how red and sore her ass was, she moaned, trying to guide me back as I pulled away.

I ran my hand over her hair, gentle and comforting, then sank my fingers deep into her hair to hold her still as I whipped her ass. Her moans could've been pain or pleasure--it was all the same to me right now. One day, I'd turn every bit of pain into pleasure, but tonight...she owed me a debt and this was just one small part of what she owed.

I dropped the belt and delved between her thighs again, teasing her until she was on the very verge before standing back off the bed. She rolled onto her side as much as she could manage to keep an eye on me as I picked up her panties and dropped my trousers down my thighs.

I wrapped her panties around my cock and began to work myself back and forth. I could smell the faint tang of her arousal in the air, and it just made me want her even more.

"You don't deserve this," I told her. My cum sprayed

across the curve of her back and her ass. She glared up at me but didn't protest, and I leaned over and pressed a kiss to her forehead. "You look good wearing my cum. Soak in it all night."

I loved the idea of having marked her with my cum.

"You're a fucking psychopath," she said.

"And you knew who you were playing with." I got into bed beside her, my cock still hard.

Maybe she'd try to strangle me tonight with her chains, but I didn't think I'd left enough play in them.

The threat didn't keep me from falling into a deep sleep, sweeter than it had ever been before without Aurora by my side.

2

STELLAN

Aurora had to be a thousand miles away by now, but when I thought I heard her voice in the hall, my heart jolted.

I rolled over and stared at the alarm clock. It was early morning, too early for Cain's low rumble of a voice to be outside my door. I'd heard Cain fucking around last night, taking out his anger on some eager co-ed who was happy to have his touch, no matter how rough it was.

I pulled open the door, was startled to see Aurora wearing sleep shorts, a crop top and a guilty expression as her gaze met mine. Her cheeks had gone pink, and I wondered what the hell made the Demon's daughter blush.

Cain stood behind her, a massive wall of tattooed muscle, wearing nothing but his boxers.

"What the fuck," I asked eloquently.

"She can't quit being our roommate," Cain said pleasantly. "She's going to pay us back for the damage to our cars."

Aurora laughed. "Good luck with that."

"Don't fucking backtalk me." Cain's hand dropped to her

ass, squeezing the curve of her ass hard. She bit her lower lip, and I couldn't tell if it hurt or turned her on. "Go take a shower. You're filthy."

She waited until she reached the doorway to her room before she turned around and mocked Cain, "Because *you're* filthy."

Cain took a step toward her, and the door swung shut in a hurry. Cain's lips twitched, closer to a genuine smile then I thought I'd ever seen from him before.

"Why is she here? And what are you doing with her?"

Cain shrugged. "Who knows? But it's going to be interesting."

AURORA

I sat up in bed with a gasp, my gaze dancing across the room, wondering what had woken me up.

Everything looked normal. The door to my room was still closed, and my closet door was still cracked open, light pouring into the room.

A loud bang crashed, like the sound of someone dropping a metal pan on a tile floor, and I jerked in surprise. Where had that come from?

And then there was something else.

It took me a moment to realize what I was hearing.

Screaming.

Nearby.

Like an animal dying.

I froze for a second, and then I hesitantly got out of the bed, shivering as my feet touched the cold wooden floor.

It was okay to leave my room. Nothing was going to happen to me. I was safe now. I was with my dad.

Even though I was telling myself that, I still opened the door as quietly as I could and then stood there for several long moments, seeing if I heard anything else.

It happened again and I flinched.

It took me a minute to figure it out.

It didn't sound like it was coming from outside. It sounded like it was coming from...below.

I took one step out of my room, and then another. And then I walked down the dark hallway until I got to the living room, not seeing my dad anywhere. I wandered into the kitchen, thinking maybe I was just imagining it. Maybe it was wind going through the pipes or the water heater...or something.

That happened, right?

Just as I was getting a drink of water, I heard it again. The glass slipped out of my hand and shattered onto the floor. I was shaking as I stood there, not sure what to do. Finally, I tiptoed over to where the butcher's block was on the counter and slid out one of the largest knives.

I knew where the sound was coming from now. The basement.

Everything inside of me was screaming not to go, that I should immediately crawl back into bed and put my head under the covers. But I moved forward, like I didn't have control of my body anymore. Until I was standing in front of the basement door.

The one door of the house that I'd never opened.

I jumped as another loud scream shot through the air. It was definitely coming from down there.

My dad had warned me about the basement. He'd told me that there were boxes and broken things he hadn't had time to get rid of and that if I went down there, I'd probably end up hurting myself.

And like daddy's good little girl, I hadn't tried to go down there...until now.

The scream sounded familiar. I'd heard that voice scream happily, when she threw her arms around my neck and hugged me, when she watched her big brother's soccer games and cheered.

My hand was shaking as I turned the door knob, trying to be as quiet as possible. My breathing was coming out in gasps, and it sounded too loud.

I got the door opened and I paused, sure that whoever was downstairs had heard me and would be storming through the second door at the bottom of the stairs.

But no one came. There was just a muffled groan that sounded like when she'd cut her foot when we were running through the grass by the river.

I started to go down the stairs. When I stepped on the third step, there was a loud creak, and I paused, waiting to see if I'd been heard.

As I got closer to the bottom of the stairs, I realized why no one was rushing out. Along with the screams, there was music playing. Classical music.

I'd never been a big fan of music like that, but my dad had always loved it. The music was blaring so loudly that by the time I finally made it to the bottom of the stairs, it felt like my eardrums were going to burst.

I stood there, trying to convince myself to run back upstairs, to pretend like none of this had ever happened.

But I finally opened the door, just as slowly as I'd opened all the others.

And when I finally got the door cracked open, and I peered into the room...I saw them.

My best friend was laying on a long metal table, her eyes

wild and crazy as she thrashed her head around, moaning. Drool was sliding down her chin. And every once in a while, she screamed.

She wasn't tied to the table, but her body wasn't moving, just her head. Like the rest of her was paralyzed or something.

He was there, leaning over her and holding her hand with a big smile on his face like he always got when I did something he was proud of.

Bile filled my throat when I realized he was popping her fingernails off, like they were acrylics and not her real nails attached to her hands.

I only watched one more minute before I went into action. Lifting my knife, I let out the long scream I'd been holding inside, and I burst through the door, running towards my father as fast as I could.

He stared at me, shock plastered all over his face. I'd somehow managed to catch him so off guard that he didn't even move until I was right in front of him. At the last second, he tried to dart away, but my knife still slid forward, slicing right down his chest like butter.

I knew in that moment that my father wasn't a man.

He was a demon.

And demons had to be killed.

STELLAN

I WAS GOING THROUGH HER JOURNALS AGAIN. MY SISTER LOVED to write. She'd fill pages and pages with everything from her random thoughts about pop culture to the boys who paid attention to her at school.

She also wrote about *her*.

Delilah.

The girl I was trying to forget.

It was hard to hate someone when you were reading your little sister's thoughts about how much she loved Aurora.

My sister had a secret. She hadn't just loved Aurora as a friend.

She'd *loved* her.

She'd wanted her.

My cheeks burned as I read about her coming to terms with the fact that she was in love with her best friend. She wrote about being desperate to kiss her. Thinking that she was the most beautiful girl in the whole world.

And then her thoughts would go dark. She'd write pages and pages about how Delilah would never love her back. And that it was so hard to be around her without telling her how she felt.

In one of her entries, a few weeks before Delilah had disappeared, she wrote in detail about Delilah's body when she'd changed in front of her.

To say it was uncomfortable reading about my little sister lusting over Delilah's body, was the understatement of the century.

Because my sister and I both had a similar appreciation for Delilah's assets. Except she'd been more of an ass girl. And fucking Delilah's tits was what kept me going.

Okay, this was getting creepy.

I snapped the journal shut, frustrated, and feeling a little bit guilty. I'd taken these books from my parent's house without them knowing, and even though she'd been gone for years, it felt like a huge invasion of her privacy.

I honestly could have gone without knowing that my sister had been in love with a girl whose virginity I took.

To add to everything, I couldn't get her out of my head. Delilah. Aurora. They mixed together. And I couldn't connect in my mind how the girl that melted in my arms at the sight of a cupcake, was the same girl who could've participated in my sister's demise.

Watching those videos of her and the Demon, it felt like they featured a completely different person. I'd start to come up with fantastical ideas like Aurora was actually someone's twin, and her twin was the one who was the raging psychopath.

Obviously wishful thinking.

I went over what I knew about the Demon. He was like Ted Bundy, handsome and charming, with a voice like silk. He'd lured his victims in, or he'd used Aurora to lure them in.

And then his mask would come off, and the monster inside of him would appear.

I guess when I put it in that context, she'd had years of learning at his hand; it would make sense that she could be two people at once.

Hating her was the hardest thing I'd ever done.

Having here in this place, so close, was like torture. I swore her scent was coming in through the air ducts, or maybe it had just saturated everything in my room that night.

I heard movement outside my door just then, which normally wouldn't have been a big deal, but I'd already gotten up once to find Aurora and Cain engaged in something that was weird even by Cain's standards. I had a weird feeling. And whoever it was had stopped right outside.

If one of the guys was playing a fucking joke, I was going to murder them.

My door wasn't locked, and just as I stood up to see who it was, I saw the doorknob slowly turning.

It felt a little bit like I'd stepped into a horror movie, where the trembling victim was watching her doorknob turn, and the killer was right outside. Except, in this case, I was the killer...or about to be, because seriously, those assholes were about to die.

Fuck. I needed some sleep.

There was a long silence, until the door opened just a crack, and I could hear the sound of heavy breathing.

So heavy it almost sounded like whoever was standing out there was...terrified.

They obviously should be, if they were trying to come into my room and do something at this time of night...or did this count as morning already? But that fear meant it couldn't be Pax, Remy, or Cain...because those fuckers weren't scared of anything.

I was really interested in what was going to happen next.

The door opened in tiny increments, until I could finally see who was standing there.

It was *her*.

Aurora.

She'd left Cain, then come to me, and that sent a jolt of pleasure and pride warming my chest, before I remembered that I didn't want her.

She was still wearing a pair of what had to be the tiniest sleep shorts in existence. I was pretty sure that their sole purpose was to ruin me. And her loose white cotton shirt that slid off her bare shoulder wasn't any better...because it was obvious she wasn't wearing anything underneath. Judging by the fact that I could see her perfect breasts clearly outlined through the shirt.

I shook myself out of my lust fog only to see that she also had something else.

A huge ass butcher's knife. She was gripping it so hard next to her that her knuckles were white.

What the fuck.

She'd officially lost it.

I went to open my mouth, but then I realized something. She was here, but she wasn't.

Her eyes were wide open, her pupils blown up, but she was staring straight ahead, at the wall to the right of me, like she was watching a movie.

There was no sign that she even knew I was in the room.

Was she...sleepwalking?

I tried to remember if I'd ever heard about her sleepwalking while she was growing up. Something nudged my brain, but I couldn't quite grasp it.

"Delilah," I whispered, not wanting to startle her.

Fuck. I really needed to stop calling her that.

I'd been right about what her breathing had sounded like. Whatever she was seeing right now terrified her. Her breath was coming out in gasps, and she was biting her bottom lip so hard that she broke the skin, and I watched as a drop of blood dribbled down her chin.

She actually looked kind of scary. Kind of like a sexy scary...serial killer.

How fitting.

She took a hesitant step forward, and then another. And then she paused again, like she was listening for something. She took a few more hesitant steps and then paused. All of a sudden, she raised the knife in the air, took a deep breath, and then lunged forward. Not to the wall.

But right at me.

I dove out of the way of the knife, and her knife lodged

into my mattress. She yanked it forward, cutting into the mattress in a downwards line.

Okay. This was getting weird. "Aurora," I barked.

But she still showed no sign of hearing me.

She crept around the bed, her gaze intent on mine but still blank, and then she lunged. This time, I was a little too slow, mostly because of the nightstand directly behind me. She managed to catch my arm in a long slice. I growled and stumbled backward, the lamp on my nightstand crashing to the ground.

But still, she kept on.

"How could you?" she screamed abruptly, but it wasn't her low, sexy voice. It was more high-pitched, more child-like. Whatever she was dreaming, she was years younger in it.

"You monster," she whimpered, as she swung the knife. I dove on the ground, because sleepwalking or not, the girl had a wicked arm.

Darting across the room, I yelled her name, trying to plot how I was going to stop this.

She ran at me, swinging so hard that she lost her balance, and I tried to grab her, but her stupid fucking ninja skills were out in full force, and she elbowed me in the stomach. I also narrowly missed a kick to the balls, which would've been painful, and likely life-threatening under the current circumstances.

Aurora was coming at me slowly now, her face scrunched up in concentration. "I'm going to kill you. Make sure that you're never able to do anything like this again."

She stalked me like I was prey, until my legs hit my mattress behind me, because of course I'd backed away from the door.

Forgive me if I wasn't thinking clearly first thing in the

morning with a raging psychopath trying to attempt murder while sleepwalking.

"Aurora," I roared.

Still, she showed no signs of hearing me. Aurora sprung forward and I fell backward, the knife literally stabbing the air right where I'd been. She would've stabbed me in the fucking heart.

Which was actually kind of fitting considering what she'd done in real life.

I shuffled backward on the bed as she started to climb on it, somehow still managing to look graceful, while she held on to the butcher knife like a maniac.

After this, I was either going to have nightmares or wet dreams. Possibly a combination.

If anyone could manage to bring that out in a guy, it was her.

"You're trapped now," she taunted in that high-pitched voice, which was a little terrifying.

Okay, new game plan. Jump off the bed and run to the fucking door.

I went to move as her knife was swinging, and this time she didn't miss. The knife scraped my fucking cheek, and now I had blood dripping down my face and down my arm. She raised her knife again, and I realized I was possibly going to die.

Right before the knife sank into my chest, I lost my mind.

That's the only explanation for why kissing her was what I came up with to try and wake her up.

I caught her wrist and then forced it out to the side while yanking her body towards me. Then I leaned down...and I pressed a kiss on her full, fucking perfect lips.

Her eyes flew open mid-kiss, and a shocked cry ripped

out of her mouth as she yanked her lips away from me. Her eyes were wild--wild and afraid. Her gaze was darting all over the room as she tried to figure out what was happening. It took her a minute to notice the knife, and when she did, she quickly dropped it with a small whimper before she stumbled off the bed, staring at me in confusion and fear.

"Well, that was interesting," I threw out, wondering if I needed stitches. Maybe this would help with my pretty boy image, give me a little toughness, because I was positive that it was going to leave a scar if I didn't get it looked at.

An absurd part of me wanted to leave it there, as a visible reminder of where she'd been.

"I'm so sorry," she whispered, before she ran out of the room like the devil himself was chasing her.

And maybe he was. That had to be what she'd been dreaming about...who she'd been trying to kill.

I guess she could have been dreaming about killing us too.

I shook my head and slid off the bed to check myself out in the mirror, feeling strangely horny.

I didn't think I was going to be getting any more sleep tonight.

AURORA

My pulse was pounding in my chest as I ran out of Stellan's room, and it felt like my lips were burning from that stupid fucking kiss.

It had been a long time since I'd done that, reenacted a nightmare in my dreams.

But usually my dreams were from memories that had

actually happened, and seeing Sophia strapped down on the Demon's "fun" table was not something that actually occurred. Right?

I mean, you didn't just forget something like that. And I didn't remember ever attacking the Demon, because I knew I would never win. I'd had to work behind the scenes to turn him in, not go after him directly.

So why was my skin crawling? Why did I feel like I was about to puke all over this pretentious fucking hallway?

Why did I feel like I was forgetting something?

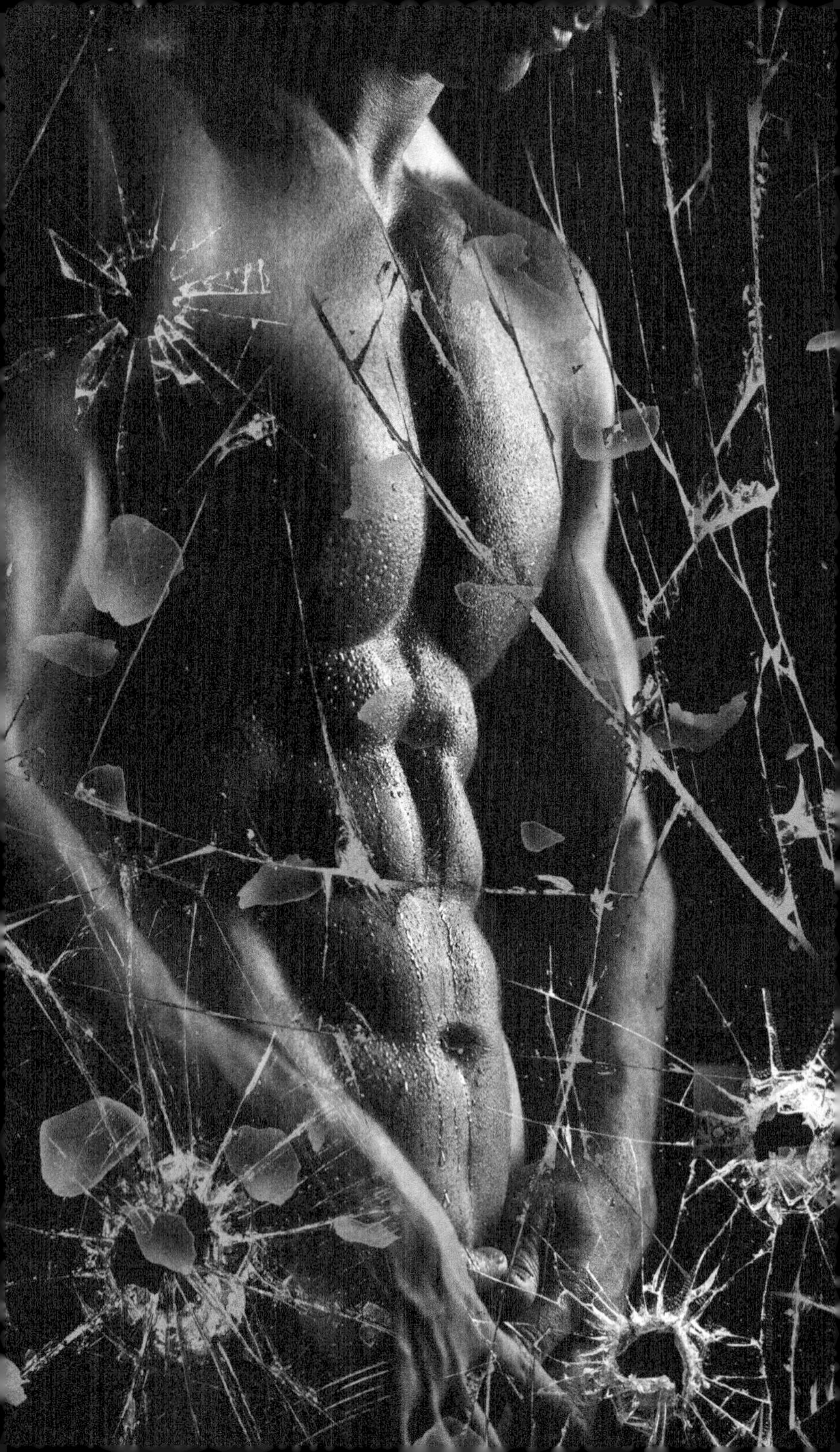

3

AURORA

I had to get out of that house. I hurriedly dressed in leggings and a hoodie, then dashed down the stairs.

One of the first-years who scraped and groveled in front of our friendly neighborhood psychopaths stepped in front of me at the door. "Where do you think you're going?"

"Out," my voice came, cold as ice. Maybe Cain and I were soul mates after all, because I was about two seconds from trying to gut this guy if he didn't step out of my way. I didn't think very highly of the boys who hung around Cain and company.

"I don't think so." He took a step closer to me, then another, so close that it forced me to look up at him as he towered above me.

He was trying to dominate me with his size, but I had plenty of experience with Cain, Stellan, Pax, and Remy dominating me–any way they could–and every other man seemed like a joke in comparison.

"You're not under their protection anymore," he said. "They want to hurt you just as much as the rest of the world does. No one's going to stop me from doing anything I want to you."

Icy fingers sunk into my stomach. Not because I was afraid of this tool; I could deal with him myself. But if he was right, then Remy had probably already shared my location and every other detail about me with the internet. All those attack sites that had been tracking my movements and plotting 'revenge'—really, just bullying--would be up and running again.

That sure made last night's spanking seem like it wasn't much punishment at all.

He leaned forward, his eyes glinting wickedly. "And I know what I want to do with you right now."

He grabbed my arms, his grip bruisingly tight, yanking me toward him. He tried to plant a kiss on my lips, although I had the feeling that a kiss wasn't his end goal.

I let him pull me close.

And I used that momentum to knee him in the balls.

He doubled over, cursing. I jumped up and kicked him in the face, knocking him into the air until he fell on his ass, then I headed for the door.

He fell on me from behind. I grabbed his arm and started to throw him, but as I squatted to get momentum, another guy tackled me. The two of them managed to pin me on the ground.

"I'm going to give you something those guys couldn't," the one snarled. Blood dripped steadily from his nose, soaking into my hoodie, and I tried to kick him off. "You're not theirs anymore. I'm going to–"

"She's always ours." Stellan's low, cold voice sent a wave of panic washing over the bloodied face of the man who was trying to get on top of us. "What were you going to do to her?"

"Nothing," the second man stuttered. "We were just going to return her to you. Make sure she didn't get away."

"We have her under control," Stellan said. "And I don't appreciate you touching what we've specifically said is ours alone. You need to learn a lesson in respect."

The two men backed away from him. One of them cast a wide-eyed, desperate look at me, as if I were going to help. I gave them a shrug and a smile instead.

Play stupid games, win stupid prizes.

Part of me was surprised Stellan had stopped them, especially after I'd just attacked him with a knife. There was an angry cut across his cheek, but he seemed completely focused on these two men—and furious.

Stellan and the others were more attached to me than they wanted to admit–although I wasn't sure if they were attached to hurting me or desiring me.

Or both.

Stellan suddenly burst into motion. One of the guys grabbed me as if he were going to push me into Stellan to distract him, but I ducked him and gave him a shove in Stellan's direction instead. Stellan caught him and punched him across the face, then moved on to his friend. He beat the two of them bloody, then opened the door I'd been trying to leave through and shoved them outside.

"No, you don't," I said.

He cocked his head to one side, as if he had to think for a second before he realized what I was responding to. He'd said *we have her under control.* Then understanding dawned on his face.

He leaned in the doorway to talk to the two bleeding, cursing first years. "You're done here. You'll never be our brothers."

Then he shut the door, locking the two of them out...

forever. He turned to face me, his wavy hair flopping into his face from the fight, but he barely looked as if he'd broken a sweat. Blood was pouring down his cheek now though, and he stopped and stemmed it with the back of his hand pressed to his cheek. The desire to press myself against him and tend his wound was a sudden, strong temptation... but I was too ashamed of my sleepwalking to take a step forward.

"How long were you there, watching me like a creep?" I asked.

"Long enough. I was enjoying watching while you were still putting up a fight." His words dripped with condescension, but I had a feeling he was just baiting me and knew his words weren't true.

I never stopped fighting, even if sometimes that fight looked like compliance to the stupid.

"Thanks for the rescue," I said, baiting him right back.

He scoffed. "I don't want them to ruin our fun."

He gripped the nape of my neck and guided me away from the door, back further into their castle.

"You said I'm yours. It's touching."

"Our trash," he said.

I shrugged. "Still."

His hand was heavy on the nape of my neck, firm and commanding. It sent a ripple down my spine that was complicated–a little bit of fear, a little bit of lust, a decent amount of sizzling fury.

Suddenly, he dropped his hand, as if he'd realized he was touching me.

Or as if he'd remembered that he hated me.

Stellan's feelings seemed complicated. There was a part of me that felt sorry for him. The best parts of Stellan had been destroyed by his sister's death, and I mourned her too.

But he still needed to pay for hurting me. I didn't feel

that sorry for him.

"Where are we going?"

"Cain will want to see you for breakfast."

"So you're Cain's personal manservant now? That must be fun. Maybe *manservant* is too dignified for you, and you're more of a minion..."

He leaned close over my shoulder, his breath a huff. "It's cute that you're trying to fuck with me, but my ties to Cain aren't going to be that easy for you to pick apart. Even with those sharp claws of yours."

You'll see how sharp my claws are, Stellan.

I walked into the dining room ahead of Stellan. Remy, Cain, and Pax were already waiting. Remy was kicked back in his chair, fiddling on his phone. Pax looked sullen, almost upset; then he saw me, and rapidly shifting emotions seemed to chase across his face.

Remy sat up suddenly. "She's still here? Why didn't you tell me?"

"She's crazy," Cain said.

"Takes one to know one." I took my seat at the table, smoothing my napkin on my lap. God, I'd take whatever punishment they dished out–for the chance to deliver my own–but I just hoped they didn't mess with my food. I was hungry. Whip my ass, fine, but give me my waffles.

Cain smiled at me pleasantly and laid the newspaper aside on the breakfast table. "How are you doing this morning, sweetheart?"

"That word sounds very odd on your lips."

"I just realize now that we all misjudged you," he said.

"That's a quicker epiphany than I'd expect from any of you," I shot back.

"What do you want for breakfast?" Stellan asked.

"Are you taking breakfast orders too?" I turned to Cain

with wide eyes. "You're really getting him trained!"

Maybe I should've taken my waffles, not potshots, but I couldn't resist.

"I was going to put your order in with the kitchen," Stellan said, his voice so mild-mannered that I was sure he'd spit in my breakfast.

But I told him what I wanted anyway. Stellan melted away, then came and sat down across from me.

They obviously had some game they were playing, something fun waiting for me. There was no point in asking. Cain was already eating his eggs.

Remy gave me a long, troubled look, then glanced at Cain and Stellan as if he were trying to read them. Finally, he turned to Pax, apparently deciding to just forge on as if I weren't trapped in this circle of hell with them. "Ready for tonight's match?"

"Yeah." Pax didn't sound very interested.

"You were up late studying for that Physics test." Cain leaned back in his chair, drumming his fingers absently on the tabletop as he looked at Remy. "I thought the great Remington didn't have to study."

Remington shrugged. "I never said that. Just like the rest of you, I wasn't born understanding the Dirac equation and how it describes all spin-half mass particles. But unlike the rest of you, I know now."

Remington was so smart he gave me a headache, and based on the way Cain rolled his eyes before he sipped his coffee, Cain felt the same way.

"Good luck," Stellan told Remington. "Not that you need it."

Stellan's obvious pride in his friend was a little bit endearing.

One of the servants brought in my breakfast. I inhaled

the scent of the sugary waffles, crisp bacon, and coffee. I dove into my food with enjoyment.

If these men weren't all psychos, this life of extravagance and wealth, sex and power and banter, might be... enticing.

Too bad about their personalities.

"I'm sure you're wondering why I'm feeling so forgiving this morning," Cain said.

"I'm sure you can't wait to tell me." I couldn't stop whatever was coming, but I could steal the fun from it if I didn't react.

"You're just so generous. I'm very impressed." He gestured to Remy, who reluctantly pulled up something on his phone and broadcast it to the television hanging above the fireplace.

I caught a glimpse of one of my false names in the corner of the screen, then a bank logo. Ice water washed through my stomach.

Remy kept loading more and more screens, all showing my various bank accounts where I'd stashed my money.

They all had a zero balance now.

"Donating all that money to a fund for sexual assault victims was so generous!" Cain said.

My vision went red. Without that money, it would be hard to escape them—or anyone else.

For now.

I could rebuild. I always did.

But I was going to have to be far more careful how I got my revenge, because it might be best for me to stay close to them until I was ready to move.

I didn't plan to stop this time with burning down some cars.

I was going to burn down this cursed house and the whole secret society that enabled these pricks.

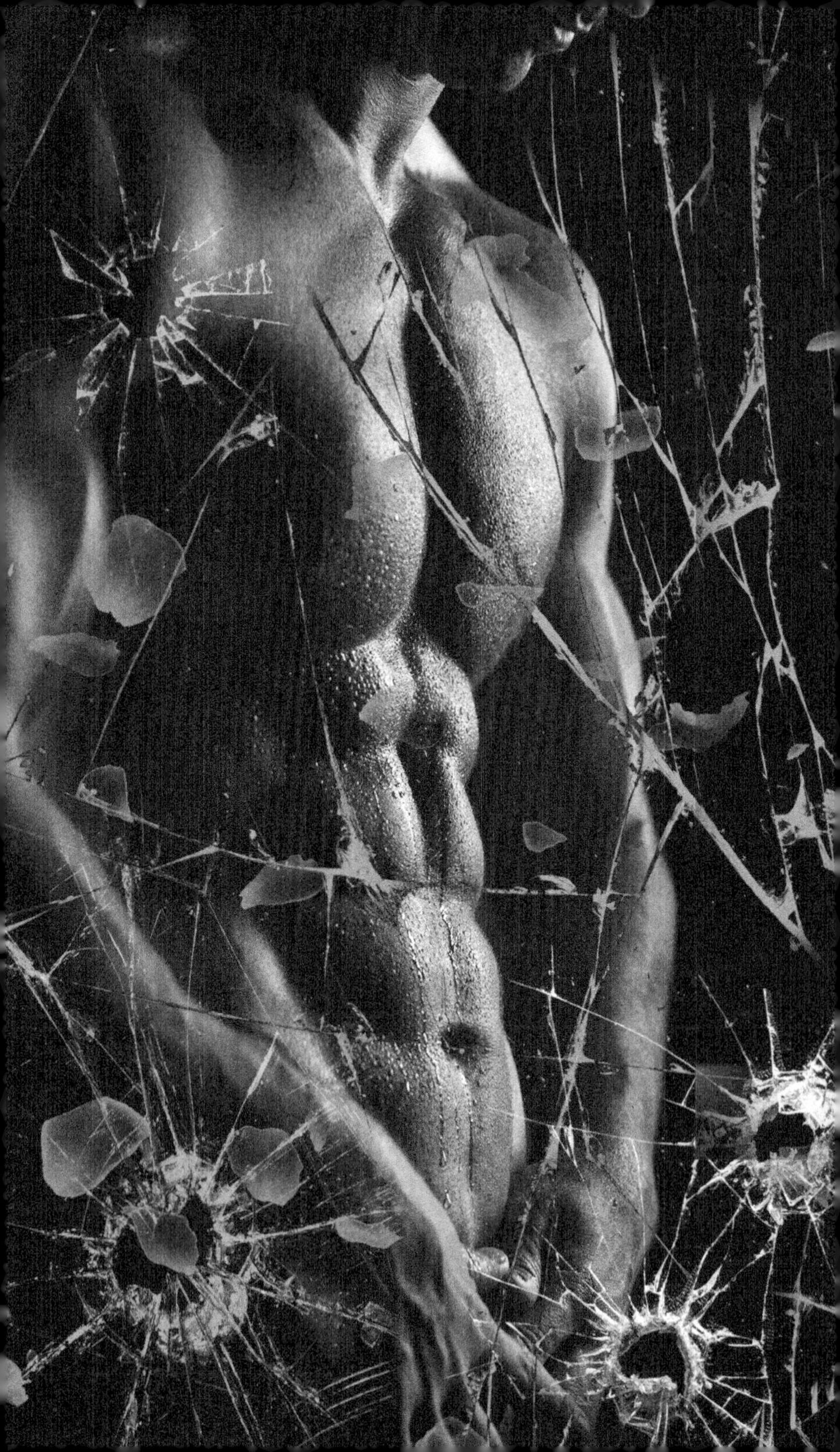

4

AURORA

Only Fans. That's what I was thinking about right now as I crossed the green and headed to the library. I was trying to think of any way to refill my coffers. My skin felt uncomfortably tight and the back of my neck was burning. Getting my own money had been the first thing that I'd worked on after getting away from the Demon. When I was growing up, he controlled everything. I obviously hadn't been allowed to have a job, I couldn't babysit, I couldn't even get my own money in exchange for doing chores.

Not that I'd ever have offered to do chores. The Demon would've tasked me with things like cleaning the blood off of his tools, mixing up the neurotoxins he used on his victims, and helping to bury body parts.

And he already made me do those things for free anyway.

So once I'd gotten him locked behind bars, I'd wanted my own money. Desperately. I was lucky I had a friend who was a hacker, Nena, because she'd helped me get the money from his accounts and hide it from the government. Money was the safety net I couldn't live without.

And now it was gone.

I could see what the guys were doing. They were trying to tear my defenses down in any way they could. Psychologically, academically, financially. I guess the next thing was probably physically, although they'd already kind of done that...my thoughts went to Cain whipping my ass with a belt—and now my panties were somehow fucking drenched.

Stupid fucking hormones.

Hence why I was walking angrily and thinking about *Only Fans*. Maybe I could wear a mask, and then I'd have some level of protection. There were people out there who were into that, right?

I shook my head. What I really needed was to get that money back, by taking it from them. But I'd have to think about how to do that. My thoughts drifted back to the hacker friend that I'd met online a few years ago, Nena. Maybe she'd still be willing to help.

Although, it would get tedious if the guys and I were just constantly stealing money from each other over and over again. Of course, I could just take it all out of the bank and bury it somewhere that they couldn't find it. That would be a way to end the game rather quickly.

I sighed as I entered the library. When I'd first come to campus, and someone had left me notes, I'd wanted to spend as little time as I could in here even though I loved libraries.

But it felt like something was happening to me. It felt like I was shedding my fears and all my insecurities the longer I was in this place. It's like it was somehow doing what I'd never been able to do under the Demon's thumb; it was stripping off my layers until I became a new person.

Which felt a little fitting since I already had a new face. Maybe this new "me" would match my new face much better than my old one.

In the back of the library, there was a dark room where they kept old newspapers. I wasn't really interested in those, but I was interested in the computer there that I'd never seen anyone use before. I wanted to look up news about Sophia's death, because it was driving me crazy thinking about it after that dream I'd had.

I'd almost made it to the back room when I heard my name whisper-shouted from down one of the rows of books. I stopped, immediately recognizing who it was. Jenna.

My insides were all twisted up when it came to her. She'd dropped me like a bag of dog shit when news about my real identity had leaked out, but then, at one of my weakest moments, she'd been there.

I was pretty sure that put her friendship balance at zero currently since her negative and positive actions canceled each other out.

She was walking towards me quickly, a timid look on her face like she wasn't sure if I was going to talk to her today. I gave her what I hoped looked like a warm smile so she would feel more at ease.

"How are you?" she asked as soon as she'd gotten close to me, looking concerned.

I read the meaning in her words. I'm sure that news of what had happened at the "Kings" masquerade had spread like wildfire through campus. I wouldn't be surprised if it had spread all over the northern hemisphere by this point.

I hoped the news of Cain losing his beloved McLaren had spread around too.

Fucker.

I thought about how to answer her question. I was

penniless, forced to live with my enemies, and everyone hated me, but on the bright side, I was still alive. Count your blessings and all that.

"You know what, I'm doing okay," I finally said. She looked so unabashedly impressed at my answer, it was a little unsettling.

"Are you here to study? Is it all right if I sit with you?" she asked hopefully. I studied her, wondering if I could trust her with what I'd come to the library to do. I decided I might as well bring her along. It's not like the guys didn't already think I was responsible for Sophia's death. It wouldn't be shocking for them to find out that I was looking up her disappearance.

"I'm here for a little research project. I'm pretty sure Remington is some master hacker and tracking whatever I'm doing on my laptop, so until I get some software to protect it, I thought I'd use the computers here."

"Sounds good. What are you researching?" she asked curiously as I led her towards the room. After making sure no one was in there with us, hiding behind the rows of newspapers, I closed the door and locked it so I could at least let my guard down for one fucking minute.

"Stellan's little sister. We used to be best friends. I was neighbors with them and we hung out all the time, but sometime after my father forced us to move, she disappeared, and no one really knows what happened to her. I've never read anything about it, so I wanted to see what I could find," I explained to her as I fired up the computer.

"They think you had something to do with it," Jenna said softly.

I nodded, not looking at her. I didn't want to see if she believed it too.

Once the computer turned on, I went to work. There was

just a small newspaper in the town where we'd lived, so it was easy to find stories about her, because there really wasn't very much that ever happened there.

The stories talked about how she'd disappeared sometime in the night. She'd said goodnight to her parents, and then gone into her room. Her dad had checked on her to see if she'd actually gone to bed and wasn't on her phone at around ten p.m., and she'd seemed to be sleeping soundly. But the next morning she hadn't come out of her room to eat breakfast. And when her parents went into her room, she wasn't there. There hadn't been any clues. The window had been closed, and there weren't any unusual fingerprints.

Sophia and Stellan's family had cameras around the house, so assumedly they would've caught anyone going in or out. Except the cameras were only turned on at night after Sophia's dad went to bed. And he'd gone to bed around midnight that night. So that meant that most likely the only way she could've left the house would've been between the time when her dad checked on her at ten and when he'd gone to bed at midnight.

It was like the JonBenet Ramsey story all over again. There was no sign of her. No clues. No people claiming that they had seen her. There was just nothing.

Jenna had pulled a chair beside me, and she was reading the articles avidly, making small noises when she got to different parts of the stories.

"If you had already moved away, why did they think that you had something to do with that?" she asked.

I hesitated before I answered, not sure how much I could trust her. "He... Dad...the Demon didn't like it when I grew close to anyone. Obviously, the closer someone got to me, the likelier it was for them to realize something was off about us. He'd...threatened me before we left about her, that's why I'd moved away with him so willingly."

"Okay...so there's a chance that he went back. But that doesn't mean that you went back with him," she said adamantly.

Something warm wiggled around in my chest. She sounded so confident that I hadn't been involved. There was no one on this planet that was confident in me about *anything*. I side-eyed her, trying to see if I could find any hints of ulterior motives, but I didn't see anything there.

Shaking the fleeting feelings of happiness away, I went back to my search. Sophia's story had never been national news, although a few of the bigger local news stations had picked it up. But they didn't add anything new. I was scrolling down one story and came across a picture of Stellan standing with his parents, his shoulders hunched and a look of complete devastation all over his face. My heart ached just looking at the picture. Because I knew what he'd been feeling in that moment. It was the same feeling I'd felt every time I let myself think about Sophia's disappearance.

I wiped a hand down my face. "None of this has been helpful," I growled.

"Let's go get something to eat, and then you can come back to look for more. It's already been three hours," Jenna commented, stretching her arms above her head. I stared at the time in shock. Had it really been three hours? It had gone by so fast.

I wanted to agree with her, before I remembered that I had no money. The only place that I could eat now was on campus where I could use my meal card, unless they'd drained that too. I pulled out my phone and quickly logged into my school account, breathing a sigh of relief when I saw the balance was still there on my cafeteria plan. That would've fucking sucked if I'd had to start scavenging around for food...or stealing.

"Let's go to the Collis Center," I threw out. The Collis Center was the smallest of the eateries on campus, and it was also the least popular. Maybe there was a chance I could get away with not running into anyone who was actively stalking me there.

Jenna agreed easily, and after I'd erased the history on the computer, we left the room. The library had filled up in the time that we'd been in there. I could feel their eyes crawling along my skin as we walked, and I swore that the whispers of people talking about me had risen to a small roar.

These people needed to get a fucking life.

As we walked out of the library, I noticed a group standing out on the green with signs.

"What's going on over there?" I mused. "Looks like some kind of protest?"

"Huh, why are they all wearing white?" she asked as we walked closer. You had to go past that area of the green to get to the Collis Center. As we got closer, and I could actually make out the signs the people were holding, cold sweat drenched my skin.

"Fuck. Fuck. Fuck." I hissed, grabbing Jenna's arm and yanking her in the opposite direction of the group.

"I thought you said you wanted to go to the Collis Center? What's going on?"

My heart was pounding so loudly I swore I could hear it beating in my eardrums. The Demon, being the internationally famous figure that he was, had a lot of people interested in him.

There were hundreds, maybe thousands of groups

around the world whose sole focus in life seemed to be following him. Some of them were dedicated to solving the mysteries of his kills. Others liked to come together and write scathing articles about what a terrible person he was, and what a terrible person I was.

And then there were others who worshiped the ground he walked on. These were the nut jobs who wrote letters to him in prison, confessing their love for him and sending him marriage proposals. They were also the groups most likely to breed copycat killers.

So basically, they were all psychos. And because they were so obsessed with the Demon, by extension they were also kind of obsessed with me.

Some of the groups thought that I was the heir apparent to carry on the family tradition. Some even believed I'd helped put my father away in prison as part of some elaborate scheme of the Demon's.

Others didn't quite see it in such a nice light. They considered me a traitor, and there were countless websites and chat groups you could find on the Internet dedicated to cursing my name.

And that group we'd just seen on the green, the ones all creepily dressed in white and holding signs, they were the worst of those groups.

It was really amazing that campus security hadn't come out to put a stop to their protest yet, because there were all kinds of creepy things on those signs: some pictures of the demonic-looking Lucifer, my father's smiling mugshot, a pentagram, a few skulls. What really creeped me out though, was that someone had actually put a screenshot of one of the videos that had been released showing my father at work.

They'd probably been searching for me for the last year, and now that my identity was out, they'd come to get me.

They'd have to get in line.

"If you ever see any of those people dressed like that, you run away. Do you hear me?" I barked at Jenna when we walked around the library and were hidden from sight. She looked at me, nodding, her lips slightly trembling in fear.

I sighed and pushed my hair out of my face. When had I started feeling like protecting Jenna was my responsibility? I didn't have room for that in my life.

"Those people are obsessed with my father, and they hate me. They're probably here to try and kill me or something."

"Should we call the police?" she asked. I snorted, thinking of the police ever wanting to help me. I'd had to basically make the FBI sign in blood, to work out the deal I'd made to turn the Demon in and keep my freedom. They'd looked at me the same way that everyone on campus did, their eyes full of distrust and loathing.

My stomach grumbled just then, and I groaned, knowing that we were going to have to go to the main cafeteria. For a moment, I longed for a fancy dinner back at the Sphinx, and then I pushed that thought away. At least I would know I wasn't at risk for poisoning in the cafeteria.

At least I probably wasn't.

Jenna was quiet as we walked, looking as if she were the one who was haunted. I felt a little bad, but any harsh realities I spilled to her were necessary. If she was going to be my friend, and obviously this was a huge *if*, she'd have to come down from the ivory tower she'd grown up in.

I didn't want that for her. Jenna hadn't told me tons about her family, but she'd told me enough that comparing our lives was like comparing a Disney princess to a street rat. Her family loved her. She'd always been warm, happy, and loved. Bodies and blood were not a thought she'd had growing up.

As much as I didn't want to bring her into my world...it also would be nice to have a friend. A ride or die that I could depend on to break me out of coffins and stab people if need be.

I sighed. I was obviously a selfish bitch.

Hopefully Disney princesses could learn to be badasses.

I tensed as we got closer to the eating hall. This was where I'd first seen the "kings", my first step into the descent to hell that I'd found myself in. Although I was hoping that they'd be eating at the Sphinx, I was again reminded that hoping was for fools.

Cain, Stellan, and Remington were holding court with guys that I assumed were on the football and soccer teams. They immediately began to track me as soon as we stepped into the dining area, and I felt like a gazelle being stalked by a lion hiding in the bushes. I was tempted to take Jenna's hand and run, but that wouldn't be very badass of me, so I soldiered on.

I was also really, really hungry, so that trumped trying to avoid their bullshit.

Jenna and I got in line for the grill, and I did my best not to fidget or look behind me. It didn't matter, though, that I wasn't watching them...I could feel them.

I knew Cain had walked up behind me before I'd even turned around. His Big Dick Energy was so powerful I could feel it sliding over my skin, trying to take over.

"Do you need something, Cain?" I asked, annoyed. Jenna had turned around, obviously not wanting to have her back to a predator, but I pretended I was avidly interested in the grill in front of me that held stacks of hamburger patties.

He was standing so close that his breath was brushing against my neck, and it was a struggle not to shiver.

"Personal space, bud," I chided as I took a step closer to Jenna, but he just followed me.

"Bring your tray over to our table when you're done," he ordered in a silky, scary as fuck voice.

"I have a dinner buddy. Thanks though."

"That wasn't a suggestion, little devil," Cain murmured.

"You're not going to like it if I sit with you," I warned him.

"Oh, I'm sure I'll be all right."

I didn't know who had sprung up in my brain, but she was indeed a little devil and had already come up with a million ways to get back at Cain.

"Grab me a Coke before you come over," he ordered before he walked away.

My shoulders dropped as soon as he was gone, feeling like I'd just waged a war.

"How are you surviving living with them? I would just be a melted puddle of goo every second I was with them. Am I goo right now? Are you going to have to scrape me off the floor, because he's fucking beautiful?" Jenna whisper-yelled in my ear.

I scoffed, because he was an asshole, but I couldn't argue with her. He was beautiful. Like a poisonous tree frog that lured you in and then killed you the second you touched it.

We got our food and then I headed over to grab a drink, mixing up my soda concoction...and then grabbing a Coke. Just in case.

"What are you doing?" Jenna hissed as I led her to a table on the opposite side from where Cain, Stellan, and Remington were sitting.

"I'm not a dog, Jenna. He can't just tell me what to do and expect I'll obey."

"Okay well, there's a difference between being a dog, and having a bit of self-preservation," she retorted, throwing a fearful look in the guys' direction.

I didn't bother answering her. I'd already begun the countdown in my head for when one of them would walk over to try and enforce Cain's order.

5...4...3...2...1.

"Did you lose your way, sweetheart?" purred Cain, and suddenly his hand was wrapped around my neck as he stood behind me, squeezing just enough to let me know he was in charge.

I calmly picked up my burger and took a bite, very aware of Jenna sitting across from me and looking like she was about to shit her pants.

"I have an excellent sense of direction, Cain. Did you lose your way? Your table's over there."

His hand tightened and my bite of hamburger got caught in my throat, forcing me to cough or choke.

He didn't loosen his grip to let me recover. Asshole.

"I'm going to ask you one more time to get up and walk your pretty little ass over to our table."

I sighed deeply before I answered. "No need," I hissed through my teeth, and then I picked up the Coke that I'd gotten him, and I splashed it all over his face so he was dripping wet with the sticky sweet soda.

He immediately let go of my throat, and I used his momentary distraction to leap from my seat and start running towards the exit.

"Come on, Jenna," I yelled, a hysterical giggle slipping out, because fuck, had I really just done that?

She had obviously read my mind, or she'd correctly

predicted that Cain was most likely going to try and kill me, because she was behind me in a second.

We burst through the doors into the night air, aware that the room behind us had gone completely quiet.

"I can't believe you just did that," she crowed, a manic smile on her face.

She obviously hadn't heard that I'd burned a million-dollar car and damaged a bunch of others.

I was obviously capable of a whole lot of crazy.

"He's going to come after you," Jenna told me, a hint of fear in her voice.

I just smiled wickedly back at her. "I can't wait."

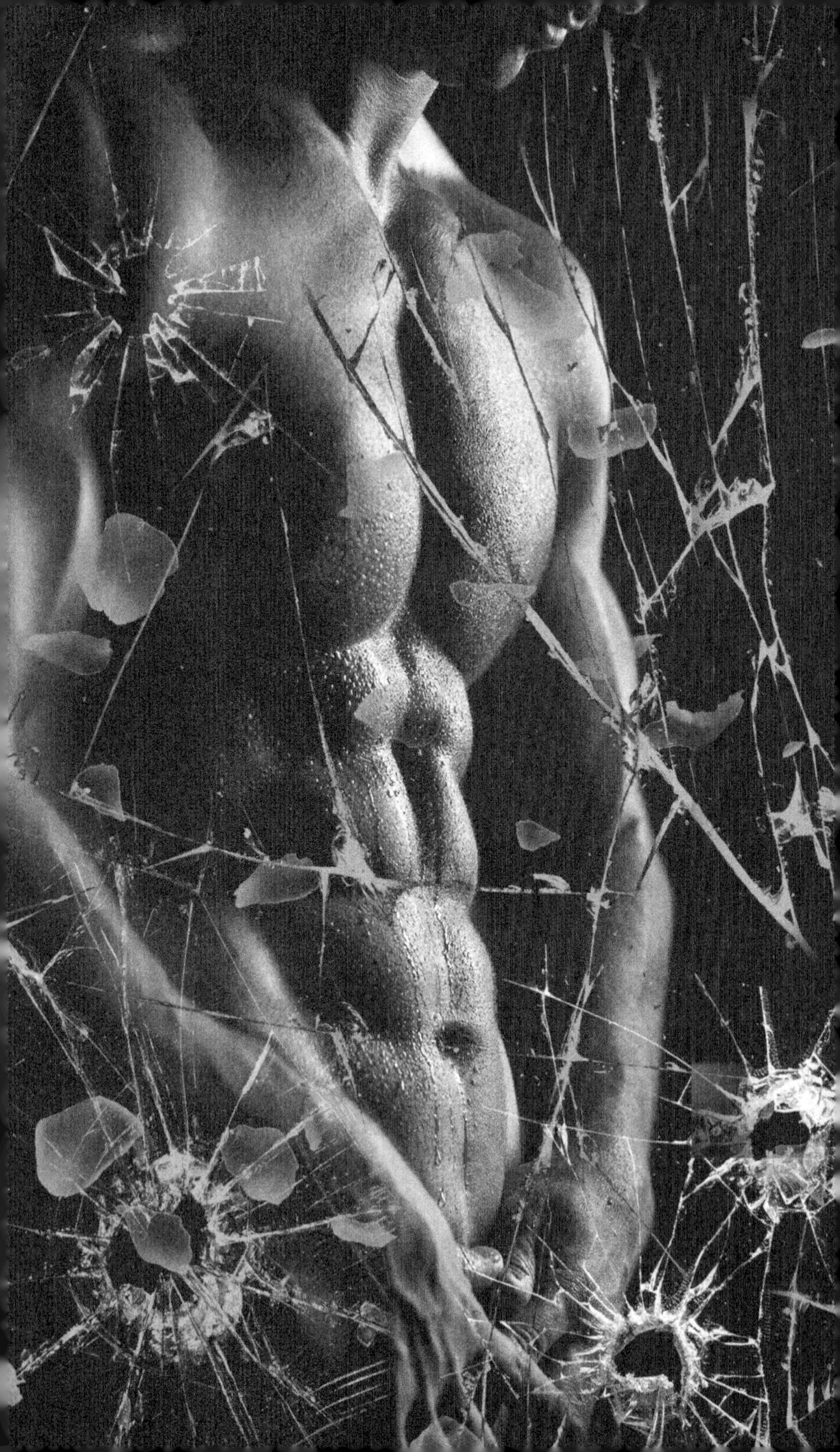

5

AURORA

It had been quiet, too quiet. I'd expected immediate payback after that cafeteria scene, but so far there'd been nothing. I hadn't even seen any of the guys over the last two days.

I was on edge, half-expecting Cain to appear around the corner with a chainsaw at any moment. I was hovering outside of the dining room, wondering if I could sneak in and grab something to eat from the kitchens without having to sit at the table with them. All of a sudden, I felt a hand on my back. I jumped and swung around. It took a lot to creep up on me. But obviously, Remington had ninja-like skills because I hadn't heard him walking at all.

I wondered where he'd learned that skill.

And why.

"Princess, what are you doing out here? Plotting your next world domination plan?" Remington asked silkily. One of his hands had slid to my hip, and his thumb was making my brain go numb as it stroked the skin in between my shirt and my jeans. It took far longer than I wanted to admit to pull myself away. And, of course, the asshole just smirked at me knowingly.

"I was about to go in. Correction, I was about to figure out a way to go in without sitting next to any of you," I answered sarcastically.

He hummed and put his hand back on my lower back and pushed me around the corner and through the door. I sighed when I saw that the other fools were sitting at the table already. None of them looked up when I entered. Remington kept his hand on my back all the way to the table, and I was sincerely regretting my choice of a crop top today because it felt like the heat of his hand was branding my skin.

"Make sure not to give her anything to drink," drawled Cain, and I flashed my teeth at him, thrilled that days later he was still thinking about it.

One of the staff came out carrying trays of food, and I grimaced when a bowl of bran flakes was set in front of me.

"Sorry, do you have any eggs..." My voice trailed off as she ignored me and practically sprinted back to the kitchen.

The guys were all suspiciously talking about Paxton's fight tonight, none of them paying attention to me. I noticed that *their* favorite breakfast foods were set out in front of them. Just like normal.

Evidently, this was the next stage of their plan.

Sighing, I grabbed my spoon and put a tiny bit of the cereal on it, and reluctantly brought it up to my mouth.

I immediately gagged as soon as I tasted it. Not only was it bran flakes, but instead of regular milk, they had put buttermilk in it. Buttermilk.

"Enjoying breakfast?" asked Paxton, an evil little grin on his perfect face that made me want to punch him and ruin the image.

I schooled my face and scooped up another large bite, holding his gaze as I forced myself to chew it.

This was Stellan's doing. Without a doubt.

In one of the foster homes that I'd been in, all my foster mom had given me was bran flakes. Breakfast, lunch, and dinner. I'd sworn to myself after I got out of there that I'd never eat it again, yet here I was.

Pride was a stupid thing.

I shoveled the bites in, shooting daggers at Stellan while I did so. It had been a story that I'd once told him, obviously very vaguely. But he'd known that on my least-favorite foods list, this was number one.

The buttermilk was almost helping me eat it, though. My foster mom had at least served it with milk so I wasn't getting quite the same trip down memory lane with every bite.

After they realized they weren't going to get anything out of me, they went back to talking about tonight's fight. I listened closely, noting every detail I could. Tonight's fight was a big one; it was bigger than the one that I'd already attended.

Paxton's challenger was aptly named Scarface, and evidently, like his name, he was incredibly scarred from a car accident he'd been in a few years ago. He channeled all his rage from being disfigured into fighting, and he'd been tearing up his opponents left and right. The guys were all discussing the bets that they were putting down, and I was doing my best not to get up and start taking victory laps around the room, because oh, did I have plans for tonight.

It was going to be a two-for-one kind of night, and I'd always loved when that happened.

Paxton was going to lose tonight, and they were all going to forfeit their bets.

"A hundred thousand dollars? You must not think Paxton's going to win," I murmured as I slid my last bite of crap into my mouth.

Remington glanced at me. "Care to put down more? Oh, wait. You can't really afford that now, can you?"

My insides burned at the reminder that my safety net was gone. I was still waiting to hear from my hacker friend. I'd been logging in every night at the library to see if she was on, but she hadn't popped up yet.

"Nope. I can't. But I'm still willing to bet something tonight," I said calmly, wishing I had some orange juice, or a sip of water to wash down the terrible taste in my mouth.

"What's that?" Paxton asked, looking intrigued.

"I'm willing to bet that Paxton loses tonight. And if he doesn't, I'll let you know where Carrie Hayward's body is buried."

They all sat up straighter at that.

Carrie had been the man in the video that went viral and turned the world against me for good. He was a state senator who had a penchant for little kids. My father had kidnapped him and tortured him slowly before killing him. The Demon had strapped him down to a table and made him pay.

Obviously, he'd forced me to assist.

Although the Demon had confessed to the murder, he'd never told anyone where he was buried. Or rather, the five different places parts of him were buried.

I was the only person who knew that.

Cain sat back in his chair, calmly folding his arms in front of him. "I'm intrigued, little devil. Go on," he drawled.

"I'm sure it would look good if you guys managed to unearth the secret somehow. Maybe you could give the info to your father, Remington. For a little political capital. Isn't he all about that?" I asked. Remington's face was suspiciously blank. I wondered if that was because I was talking about knowing where the Demon had buried bodies...or was it because of his father? I made a note to look into that later on.

"The question is, what are you asking for if you win?" Cain pressed, examining me closer. I had to pull out all of my tricks when it came to Cain. The Demon had taught me how to hide my emotions well, but it always felt like Cain could see under my skin. He and the Demon had that in common.

"If I win, you all have to apologize to me on the green in the middle of campus. On your knees."

Remington snorted and shook his head, a small smirk on his lips. It was funny to me too, thinking about them on their knees.

If I had my way though, that would be a common occurrence from here on out.

"Take the bet," Paxton said in a bored voice. "There's no way I'm losing to Scarface."

What was that saying? *Pride cometh before the fall.* That seemed fitting in this situation. I wondered how long it would take for them to stop underestimating me. For the kings to see that there was a queen in their midst.

I guess we would find out. The guys got up from the table and started to walk away. Cain paused and looked back at me when he'd made it halfway to the door. "We're leaving at nine. Be ready," he said in a tone that brokered no argument.

I held in my scoff. "Actually, I'll be going separately tonight. Jenna and I are going together," I told him.

A slight grimace ran across his face as he debated

whether to force me on this one. But I knew he wasn't going to offer to bring Jenna with us.

"Whatever," he finally said before leaving the room. I took a deep breath and exhaled, glad that I'd managed to win that particular battle.

But now to figure out the rest of the plan. Or how to implement the plan, I should say.

I'd been coming up with ideas for Paxton's fights almost since the moment I'd blown up Cain's car.

I texted Jenna. "Want to go to Paxton's fight with me tonight?" I asked.

It took less than a minute for her to reply:

Only if you're promising mischief and mayhem. I'm starting to enjoy running for my life.

A laugh slipped out of me. Who knew Jenna had that in her?

I'll come to your room at eight, I typed out, a little sadness leaking into my gut over the "your room" part of the text. It hadn't been that long ago when it had been *our room*, but why did it feel like a lifetime had passed? I pushed the feeling away and slipped out of the room, not bothering to try and scrounge up scraps from the kitchen. The bran flakes had done their job, and I had absolutely no appetite left.

It had taken me a minute to come up with the plan. I couldn't drug Paxton. Drugging him would've taken the fun out of the whole thing. I wanted him fully alert for his downfall. That was the only way that it would hurt enough.

After making a few calls, I'd found out Scarface's glove size. I'd heard them talking about this fight for the last couple of weeks. There was a special type of boxing glove that you could buy. Basically a boxing glove for cheaters. He'd never be able to get away with them in the UFC or one of those Pay-Per-View fights, but for this kind of thing, it would work.

The specialness of the glove wasn't noticeable right off the bat. But the glove was an inch or two longer than a normal one. And in that space was the equivalent of brass knuckles, meaning that every hit packed more than a punch.

That in itself wouldn't be enough to beat Paxton–he was just too good. But with a little distraction...the right hit could be enough to win.

Thank goodness I'd bought everything that I needed before the whole *taking all my money* thing. That would definitely have made things infinitely harder. It had been work to get the gloves to Scarface's trainer, but after giving him some money, he'd agreed to make sure Scarface used them whenever he fought Paxton.

I hated having to depend on people for my plans, but I'd also made sure he knew that I was the Demon's daughter. Hopefully that would prevent him from reneging from the deal.

The day dragged on. I went to one class, and then I spent the rest of the time holed up in my room, working on the "distraction" part of the night. It had taken a whole lot of trial and error in Photoshop, but I'd finally nailed it. I couldn't wait to see the look on Paxton's face when I showed him my work of art.

Finally, it was time to start getting ready. I got dressed in what I considered to be my dominatrix outfit. I'd also bought this online before the whole money stealing thing, and I rather liked what I'd come up with. The outfit consisted of a red leather corset top that made my boobs look incredible, and a pair of skintight leather pants that did the same for my ass. They were some kind of fake leather material, so I could still bend and stretch...and run if the need called for it. I did my hair in long beach waves and gave myself a dark smokey eye that Jenna would most likely have to fix.

Red lipstick completed the look. Maybe that was a new thing I would do. Wear red lipstick all the time.

It certainly seemed to work for Taylor Swift.

Although the outfit would've looked better with high heels, again I chose to be practical and put on a pair of flat boots. I eyed my chucks longingly for a moment, but I was going for sex kitten tonight, and the chucks didn't quite match that look.

I shivered as I walked across the green to Jenna's dorm. I'd put on a leather jacket so my top was hidden, since I was sure you didn't see a girl dressed like a dominatrix walking around campus every day. Especially not a girl as infamous as me. But judgmental looks still followed me as I walked.

Maybe they were jealous of how good my ass looked.

I felt that annoying pang in my heart again when I finally got to Jenna's dorm. For a second I was back on the first day of school, looking up hopefully at this building and thinking that I'd have a fresh start.

I wanted to go back in time and slap myself, because I should've known that fresh starts don't happen to girls like me, girls who are stained to the point of no return.

We don't get second chances, we just got new regrets.

I shook off the morose thoughts, because I definitely didn't have time to feel sorry for myself in my plot for revenge, and I forced myself into the building. The hallway was busy; girls were flitting in and out of each other's rooms, I'm sure getting ready for a party, or for the fight tonight if they were lucky enough to have been invited.

They cast me wary stares as I walked by, and their whispers felt like loud roars in my ears. The sound was almost comforting. The Sphinx was completely quiet most of the time, and the quiet gave me too much time to think…too much time to remember.

This was much better.

I lifted my hand to knock on the door, but Jenna threw it open before I could do anything.

"Wow. You look amazing," she said excitedly, pulling me inside and heading straight towards her makeup area where she went to work on my smokey eye makeup…just as I had predicted. I kept my eyes away from my old bed and decided this had been a terrible idea to come over here.

It just reminded me of how I'd believed in a second chance, and I'd lost it.

"You don't have a new roommate yet?" I asked quietly, and she paused in brushing what looked like black glitter on my eye for a long moment, a look of shame crossing her features.

"I don't think I'm getting one," she finally said, just as quietly, before resuming her work.

I let the awkward silence sit for a moment, because hell, she had been awful, and I was petty like that.

And then I started talking about the fight. "At some point, we're going to have to run," I warned her, and she smiled nervously.

"I'm ready."

I went over the plan and showed her my "artwork", and she gasped when she saw it.

"Um…is that real? Because I'm not sure what to think right now, but I'm getting a little horny."

"It looks pretty real, doesn't it?" I said proudly as I looked over my handiwork. "I think it will definitely get Paxton's attention."

"What will you do if he doesn't notice...or doesn't care?" she asked curiously.

There was no way that he wasn't going to notice. He'd been very much aware of exactly where I was at all times during the last fight.

He could say he hated me, but that wasn't going to stop him from acting almost the same exact way tonight...with the exception that I didn't expect that he would be dedicating his fight to me.

But that was fine. I didn't want someone to dedicate a fight to me. I wanted someone to actually fight *for* me. And that was clearly not Paxton Jones.

"That's not gonna be a problem," I told her confidently.

I glanced at my phone. It was time to go. Butterflies shot off like rockets in my stomach as I prepared myself for what was to come. Up to this point, Paxton hadn't really been my enemy. He'd just been there, following the rest of them. But that was definitely about to change.

I'd told Jenna I would drive–we were likely to be leaving in a hurry–but when we reached my car, all four tires had been slashed. I stared at the deflated tires, which looked as if they'd melted into the pavement.

"Do you think the guys did this?" Jenna asked.

"No. I think this is the work of regular old assholes who are bored with their own lives so they bully me and pretend they're some kind of great vigilantes. It's sad." I crossed my arms, genuinely feeling sad no matter how little I thought of those people. "The guys would've come up with something more exciting. Like blowing up my car in front of me."

Jenna took a stutter step back. Then she asked, "Want to take my car?"

We decided to take Jenna's practical little red Honda rather than call for an Uber. The drive was silent except for the sound of Jenna nervously tapping against the steering wheel. I resisted the urge to reach out and silence her hand.

"Are you sure you want to do this?" I checked again. Actively participating in this was a whole lot different than just being my friend.

She gripped the steering wheel tightly and then unclenched her hands before answering. "I want to do this."

Jenna took a breath. "I still owe you so many apologies for what happened when I learned who you were. I was scared. And I was weak. And you didn't deserve that."

Something that felt way too much like tears welled up in my eyes, and I blinked rapidly to push them away.

"I forgive you. It's a lot to ask someone to look past," I told her softly. "But you should know...not all the rumors about me are false." I heard the sharp intake of her breath.

"Which ones are true?" she finally asked.

"Maybe someday I'll tell you," I answered. "I'm not ready yet."

We didn't talk for the rest of the drive.

THE FIGHT WAS IN A DIFFERENT WAREHOUSE THAN THE LAST time. I assumed that they had to move around quite often to try and prevent raids like the one that happened during the last fight.

I wasn't even sure how everyone found out about it. I'd heard people whispering about it in one of my classes, and Jenna had heard the same thing. Probably the smart thing would've been to ask Cain where the fight was, but I doubted he would tell me. He probably would've just tried to force me into his car again, or perhaps it would be his trunk this time.

As we approached the line of dilapidated-looking warehouses, I saw a guy in a red hoodie leaning against one of the buildings. When he saw our car approaching, he straightened up and then signaled with his hand for us to turn left. Jenna nodded at him then went in the direction he pointed. Sure enough, we rounded the corner and there were rows of cars parked. We got out of the car and made our way out onto the road where the hoodie guy was still lurking. Without saying a word, he pointed down the street to another warehouse, and we both nodded and began to walk. The longer we walked, the louder it got. People finally came into view. They were being pushed inside the warehouse as fast as they could get through, burly bouncer-type guys keeping a watchful eye as they rushed people through to try and avoid suspicion. I had so much adrenaline coursing through me, it was practically choking me.

We made our way inside, and my mouth dropped. There were twice as many people here tonight as there were at the other fight.

Twice as many people to see one of the kings fall.

As if pulled by a string, my attention went upwards to where I could see the kings and their posse up on the higher balcony. It must've been a prerequisite for them while scouting locations, that they had a special viewing place they could lord over their people.

Stellan was by himself, leaning over the balcony...and staring right at me. And he didn't bother to pretend like he wasn't watching me. When the intensity between us became too much, I ripped my gaze away from his and marched forward. Jenna followed silently behind me. She grabbed one of my hands and squeezed it, and I could feel her trembling against my skin. I squeezed back, trying to make her feel better. Who knew, maybe she'd get a little taste for danger and begin to like it.

We pushed our way to the ring where there were already two fighters tearing into each other. Their form was sloppy, nothing like the artistry that Paxton displayed. But they were knocking the shit out of each other, which was always fun to watch. I almost took an elbow to the head at least ten times as I walked through the crowd, but finally, we made it to the front.

The smaller fight seemed to drag on. Paxton's fight was, of course, at the end, and the warehouse just kept filling up. A couple of times I found myself staring up at the balcony when the guys would make an appearance, only grimacing slightly when a girl would be wrapped around them. Cain had three around him, obviously ready to suck his dick, and Remington was keeping some busy as well, but Stellan was standing off by himself, looking completely depressed.

For a moment, that night and how I'd felt broke through my carefully constructed barrier and washed over me. As much as I didn't want to admit it, he'd taken something from me that night, and it hadn't just been my virginity.

It took far too much to push that thought away.

The crowd noise level went from a roar to an ear splitting decibel, and I threw my full attention back to the ring where the same announcer as last time—Jack if I was remembering his name correctly—was pumping a fist in the air and prompting the crowd to get louder. His Mohawk wasn't green tonight, it was a dark purple, and his blazer was a garish orange color that somehow he made look cool. As his gaze drifted across the crowd, he noticed me standing outside the ring, and he winked.

"And now, for the fight all you cocksuckers have been fucking waiting for..." he crowed, which bizarrely only made the crowd get louder. "Facing off for the first time, Scarface and...Paxton Jones," he screamed into his sparkly microphone.

The music changed to a dark song that I vaguely recognized as one of Marilyn Manson's. The lyrics about devils and demons spun through the air as the crowd parted.

Scarface made his way towards the ring. I sighed in relief when I saw that he was wearing the dark red gloves that I'd given his trainer. He looked even more scarred than he had in his pictures, and I felt even more vindicated for what I was doing tonight.

He would win a shitload of money when he won this fight.

The crowd went crazy as he walked to the ring and slid inside before holding up one fist in the air, obviously not one for dramatics.

Scarface's song melted into "Nine Inch Nails". Energy pulsed in the air, and the crowd seemed to tremble with excitement, like they were all holding their collective breath until Paxton made an appearance. The minutes seemed to drag on before he appeared through a door and started to make his way through the crowd. I had to cover up my ears at this point because it was so loud, and the girls next to me were literally sobbing as they watched him reverently.

Here, Paxton was more than a king–he was a God. And these people all recognized it.

I wondered how everyone was going to react when they saw their hero fall.

He didn't notice me until he slipped into the ring, and then his gaze caught mine and his usually impenetrable stare slipped for a second as he gave me a cocky wink before schooling his face once more. Asshole.

Drumbeats started to blare out of the speakers, and the

announcer looked like he was about to die in ecstasy as the crowd's roar built around him.

"I'll give you one more second to get your bets in," he called to the crowd, and I looked behind me to see guys dressed in black spreading through the crowd collecting bets as they went. Didn't seem very technical. I wondered how they kept track of it all. Because I was pretty sure the guys had placed their bets earlier.

Finally, the fight was about to begin, and my heart was about to beat out of my chest.

"Is this going to be a bloodbath?" Jenna yelled into my ear, and I winced before giving her a bland shrug. She rolled her eyes at me and jumped up and down excitedly.

The announcer had his hand up, and then a bell rang and he jumped out of the ring as the fighters began to circle each other.

A bead of sweat trailed down Scarface's back. He was obviously nervous, rightfully so, but I was counting on him to have his shit together. Paxton moved in first, leveling a hook shot at Scarface's jaw, who just managed to drop back before getting his cheekbone caved in. That seemed to wake him up, because he began to come at Paxton, swinging at him ferociously a few times, but never making contact. Paxton made it look far too easy to move out of the way.

Another minute passed before Paxton got a hit in, and I realized that Paxton had been playing with him this whole time, which was not good. He needed a distraction. I turned my poster around and held it up, screaming Paxton's name.

The sound of my voice somehow drew his attention even through the raging of the crowd, and his gaze flashed over to me. When he saw the expertly photoshopped poster of Cain on his knees sucking Paxton's cock, his steps faltered, allowing Scarface to get in a hit to the side of his head that had Paxton reeling from Scarface's suped-up gloves. The crowd went quiet as Paxton stumbled, and I knew I had a manic grin on my face as my gaze flicked up to the balcony where Cain, Remington, and Stellan were all staring stonily down at the ring...and at me. Clearly unimpressed.

The cheers returned when Paxton shook his head and darted forward. Several hits in and Scarface was backing up, on the retreat.

That wouldn't work. I held up the sign again and yelled, "Can I watch the next time Cain fucks you?" and I knew Paxton heard me because his eyes flicked over to me once more, allowing Scarface to get another hit in. I set the poster down, and then I pulled the strings of my top to loosen it before pulling it down and displaying the tan strapless bra that at first glance would look like I wasn't wearing anything.

I heard Paxton's "what the" as he saw what I was doing, and that was just what Scarface needed, because the next hit from him was so loud that the sound of it rattled through the warehouse and Paxton's blood flew everywhere.

Paxton sunk to his knees, and right before Scarface was going to knock him out, the announcer jumped in, obviously getting a signal from Cain or one of the others to stop the fight since I'd seen lots of other guys get knocked out tonight. The announcer looked super confused, and a little worried, as he screamed into his microphone that Scarface was the winner. Showing the first signs of life in his deadened eyes, he pranced around the ring, obviously in complete shock and disbelief that he'd won.

Now Paxton was the one who looked dead inside as he stayed on his knees, blankly watching Scarface strut around and yell to the crowd. His mask slipped when he looked over at me, and pure rage shone in his eyes, promising me that I would pay for what I'd done.

Perversely, a flicker of excitement flitted through my insides just imagining what he would come up with. I winked at him and then looked up at the balcony. Cain was the only one still standing there, looking down at the crowd. As I watched, he slid a finger across his throat like he couldn't wait to slice mine open, and then he turned and walked away.

I heard a loud crack, and the crowd roared again. Jenna dug her nails into my arm excitedly, dragging my attention back to the ring. Paxton had gotten up, and even though the fight was over and there wasn't anything he could do to change the result, he'd just knocked Scarface out.

Paxton ripped off his gloves and held up his middle fingers to the crowd. Then he jumped out of the ring...right in front of where I was standing. He grabbed my arm and began to walk, yanking me after him.

"Aurora!" Jenna yelled, panicked, and I looked back at her with wide eyes. Looks like my judgment day was coming faster than anticipated. Well, it had been a good run.

I was hoping that his brain had been rattled at least a little bit in the fight, but Paxton didn't seem to be any worse for the wear except for the fact that there was blood all over him. I pulled hard against his grip, trying to test how far he would go in front of everyone, but he seemed perfectly fine with holding me so tightly that I knew I was going to have bruises embedded in my skin.

Paxton dragged me through the door that he'd come out of to start the fight, and I found myself in a dimly lit hallway. It kind of resembled something out of a B-horror flick as the tube lights flickered off and on. The hallway was completely empty, and I saw a bench a few feet away that had some tape and some folded clothes on it. Apparently, this was Paxton's makeshift locker room for tonight.

"You think you're clever, little devil? Do you think losing some fight is going to destroy me?" he asked.

My gaze got caught on the beads of sweat on his perfectly chiseled chest, and I honestly had to stop myself from licking right down the center of it. His hair was sexily mussed from the fight, and the blood all over him just did it for me.

I obviously had issues. A lot of issues.

"Mmmh. I didn't think it would destroy you, but I knew it would make you mad. The fact that your buddies all lost tons of money was a bonus too," I responded with a smirk.

He moved in closer to me until I was plastered against the wall. His strong forearms were caging me in as his head dipped forward.

Paxton dragged his stubbled face across my skin as his nose moved into my hair and he breathed me in.

"There's nothing you can do that could hurt me, Aurora. I don't have anything left inside me to break," he whispered in my ear, and tingles sliced down my skin.

"Get away from me," I growled, ignoring the little pang in my heart that was calling for him.

Broken always attracted broken, and Paxton...he was the poster boy for messed up.

Just like me.

"Make me," he taunted, his tongue trailing down my ear.

"Fuck," I murmured, shaking my head to ward off the lusty whore inside of me that was desperate to tear Paxton's clothes off.

Paxton stepped back with an amused chuckle, and for some reason that annoyed me.

Without thinking, I reared back and punched him in the

face, knocking his head back and reopening the cut on his eyebrow.

He stumbled back a few steps, and then looked at me in shock.

"I don't know why you look so surprised, Paxton. You've seen me in action."

He rubbed his jaw with two fingers while he looked at me, something undecipherable burning in his gaze.

"Why don't you try that again?" he asked silkily.

And honestly, it was like someone had possessed me, because I rushed at him again, and he didn't try to fight back as I began to pummel him in his chest, his face...his hard stomach.

I only stopped when I realized he was laughing, the sound a bit crazed. I took a step back.

"I—" I began to say, not sure whether I was going to apologize to him or scream at him, but he cut me off.

"My turn," he grinned before I was suddenly against the wall, his hand wrapped around my throat.

Before I could ask what he meant, his lips crashed against mine, coaxing my mouth open with desperate, hard licks. His tongue pushed into my mouth as he kissed me deeper. I found myself moaning at the feel of his tongue licking into my mouth. My breasts were swelling and my nipples hardened, and I swear my vagina was pulsing in need.

That made me furious, so when he began to move away, I made sure to bite his lip, adding another cut to his already beat-up mouth so that I could taste the iron tang of his blood.

He growled and with his free hand, grabbed my leather leggings and yanked on them so hard that the leather completely split in front, showcasing the fact that I wasn't wearing any underwear under the pants. They were so skintight, I hadn't wanted panty lines, but I was really regretting that choice now.

"Fuck," he moaned as his hand around my neck tightened until it was hard to breathe. But I was completely distracted from that when he abruptly slammed two thick fingers into me. I gasped and my head fell back against the wall as my core tightened around the intruding digits.

"I hate you," I said through gritted teeth as he began to work his fingers in and out of me.

"The feeling's mutual, sweetheart," he said with a dark chuckle that sent searing arousal coursing through my veins.

Suddenly, he ripped his fingers out of me and let go of my throat before spinning me around until my cheek was plastered against the cold, rough wall.

"Put your hands on the wall," he ordered, and my breath hitched as I found myself obeying.

Paxton abruptly slid my pants beneath my butt, exposing my ass to the cold air, and then I heard the sound of the elastic of his shorts as his hot breath brushed against my skin.

I felt like I was in an alternate reality as I felt his fucking huge length slide against the folds of my sex.

"Tell me you want me to fuck you, little devil," he rasped. My whole body shook, the command in his voice just doing something to me. It was like his voice held the key to my body, and he'd unlocked something inside of me that made it to where he could get whatever he wanted out of me.

I bit my lip in an effort to not say anything. Because the needy bitch inside of me was desperate to beg him for some relief.

"Give me what I want," he said in a low, smooth voice as

he continued to slide through my folds with long sweeps. I'm sure he could tell that I was just dripping for him.

"I can't say I had any intention of fucking you when I came to the fight tonight," I gasped.

He chuckled as the thick head of his cock rubbed against my clit. I squeezed my eyes tight as a shiver slid down my spine. One of his hands moved around my hip and then trailed down until he'd gotten to my clit, and then he was working it from the front and the back.

My body felt feverish and my breath was coming out in gasps. I was starting to get lightheaded from all the sensations coursing through my body.

"Did you dress like this for me? Or were you so desperate you just wanted to have any guy look at you tonight?"

Before I could snap at him, he reared back, and then he pushed into me, his groan long and loud as he bottomed out inside of me, forcing a scream from my throat.

He was big, so fucking big. And I didn't even know how I'd gotten here. I lost my breath as my body struggled to accommodate his size. Stellan had been big...but this was a whole other level.

A fleeting image of Cain's dick outlined in those sweatpants flicked through my mind, and I wondered if he would feel like this...or would it somehow be even tighter?

"Bet you spent hours on that sign, little devil. Didn't you? You probably had to take breaks so that you could get yourself off thinking of Cain sucking my big fat cock," Paxton purred, and I moaned, because fuck...it was hot to think about.

I was gushing, so much that every time he slid back into me, it made a squelching sound that I would have been embarrassed about in any other situation. My legs shifted wider and my hips pressed back, my body desperate to give him as much access as he wanted. He was pounding into me so roughly that I was whimpering with every thrust. His hand had slipped from my clit back to my hip, and his fingers were digging into me. The edge of pain just added to the whole thing though, and I moaned again...loudly.

"You like it rough, don't you? Fucked once, and you're desperate for cock, aren't you?" he growled into my ear. The hand that wasn't on my hip moved to my hair, and he gathered it in his fist as he yanked my head to the side before biting down savagely on my neck.

For whatever reason, that immediately sent me spiraling into an orgasm, and I choked on the scream that ripped out of me.

"Fuck, that's hot," he hissed as he slammed in and out of me. Our breath sounded through the hallway.\

Paxton growled, and his hips began thrusting faster until his rhythm abruptly faltered and I felt the warm, liquid heat inside of me as he came with an erotic groan that was going to be starring in my vibrator sessions from now on.

He pressed his cheek against my hair and I realized then how sweaty I'd gotten. My hair was plastered against my neck, and the leather felt sticky against my skin. He gripped my hips as he slid out of me, and there was an ache left behind, a dull desire for more of him.

Wet slick slid down my thigh.

"Fuck," I murmured as the full weight of my predicament came slicing through me. Here I was, my ass and pussy out for anyone to see, and my pants ripped so fuck knows how I was going to get out of here without the whole world seeing everything I had to offer.

And his cum was literally dripping down my leg. I bit my lip, feeling his hot gaze tracing down my back. I took a deep breath and then slid my hands down the wall and slowly turned around, reluctantly looking up at him.

Which was a mistake.

His eyes burned into me, and when my gaze dipped down...because how could it not when I hadn't seen his dick yet, I gasped when I realized that he was somehow still hard.

And fuck, he was huge.

I shifted as more cum dripped down my leg, and I forced my gaze back to his face which was now eerily blank.

"Well, that was..." I began.

"That was nothing. You saved me from having to work off my adrenaline with one of the dirty bitches panting for me out there," he said casually, tucking himself back into his tight shorts.

Anger...and embarrassment flushed through me, and I awkwardly pulled at my pants, trying to hold the front together so my vagina wasn't at risk of flapping in the breeze.

"Have you been checked recently?" I snapped, waving my hand at his dick.

"You really should ask those questions before you let someone fuck you bare," he said with a smile, and then he walked over to the bench and stuffed his clothes and gloves into a bag before grabbing it and walking off down the hall without a look back while I stood there frozen, shell-shocked.

When the fuck had this night gone so off course?

I was supposed to be fucking up their lives, and here I was, somehow thoroughly the one who'd been fucked.

The door we'd come through from the main room abruptly flew open, and I flinched as I pulled at my pants more, trying to keep myself covered.

Jenna's face popped into view, her anxious expression turning wide-eyed as she caught sight of me.

"I'm not sure I even want to know," she gasped.

"Please don't," I said with a groan, waddling towards her while I tried to keep my pants together.

Jenna opened up the purse she'd brought with her and pulled out...some duct tape.

"Here. You can use this to hold your pants together," she said, a giggle ripping out of her.

"Why the fuck did you bring duct tape?" I asked her incredulously.

"I didn't know if we'd need it."

"Need it for what?"

"I don't know...to tape someone up...like in the movies?"

I grabbed the duct tape and then laughter ripped out of me, and then we were both laughing hysterically in the hallway as I tried to tape my pants together.

When we finally pulled ourselves together and my pants weren't in danger of falling off, we took off down the hallway and out through another door that led to the outside. The cool air felt like heaven against my flushed skin, and I took a deep gulp of the fresh air.

We turned the corner and my steps faltered as I saw Paxton surrounded by a pack of girls. I kept my face blank as we walked past him, and it didn't hurt at all when they slid their hands all over his still bare chest.

It didn't hurt at all.

6

AURORA

The next morning, even the sunlight streaming through my window seemed out-of-place in this dark mansion. A bird landed on a tree outside my window and sang insistently. I tried to open the window, only to find it had been nailed shut.

Funny that these monsters thought they were so different from my father when they employed so many of the same tactics in my direction.

"Wrong address," I told the bird through the planes of glass. "Your princess is not in this tower."

The bird cocked its head at me then flew off. Maybe I should never have changed my name to Aurora; Delilah had suited me better. After all, Delilah humbled the men around her. First I'd sent the Demon to prison; now I was going to give these men of the Sphinx some of the worst days of their lives.

Even if it was painful for me too.

I opened my laptop, entered the code, and was thrilled to see a message had popped up from my hacker friend, Nena. I'd just swept my laptop for bugs and keyboard trackers from a program I'd stolen from the IT Department, so I didn't have to walk all the way across campus. I checked the time stamp, hoping she was still on.

Hey, are you doing okay, Dee? I saw that someone scrubbed the internet of all mentions of you... who is the white knight?

Ha, not a white knight, I typed in reply. I thought for a second, hating to sound ungrateful, then admitted, *I didn't know it was possible to scrub the internet like that.*

If I had, I would've asked my friend to help me with that a long time ago, although given how often new stuff had to pop up about me, it would've been a big ask.

I would've if I could've, baby girl. It takes big bucks–bigger money than either of us has.

She understood what I meant. I chewed my lower lip, wondering if *she* was really a *she* at all. We'd never met, and I felt I was taking a crazy gamble feeling like she was my friend. Did internet friends ever really count? For all I knew, she could be anyone.

In fact, a crazy idea occurred to me...maybe she was really Remington.

The next second, I was typing again. *I don't have any money anymore. Mr. Not-So-White-Knight might've taken me off the internet, but he also stole all my money.*

Do you need help burying the body?

No. I'm an expert on that.

The weirdest thing, perhaps, was that in all the years I'd 'known' her, she'd never pried into my past. She always wanted to know how I was doing, but she never pushed the conversation. Normally everyone wanted something from me, just like these men did; they needed to know the truth about what happened to Stellan's sister.

There was something odd about my old friend.

Tell me how to help.

And that right there–the willingness to help me when I needed it–was the weirdest. I racked my brain, thinking about something Remington would never do, something that would hit him where it hurt.

He was so proud that he was so smart. Was it possible to alter his grades in a way that wouldn't just be fixed quickly and easily, with a little of his hacking knowledge and/or daddy's money?

Could you change someone's grades? And could I have copies of both the before and after that make it look like the GOOD grades were the doctored ones?

I held my breath at the blinking cursor, wondering if I was really talking to Remington. If I was, he would find some way to turn this all around and make my life even more miserable. But then, it didn't make sense Remy would have contacted me all those years ago...unless Stellan had somehow put him up to it.

I added yet another item to my to-do list: set up a meeting with my old friend, no matter how unwilling she was. She'd always told me she was far better on the web than IRL. She claimed she was socially awkward to the ninth degree.

As if I'd judge someone for that. I was the queen of awkward.

I can do that, she promised. *Who are we going to hurt?*

I grinned.

My day was looking up as I strolled into breakfast with the boys. The same boring bowl of bran flakes waited for me, along with four stone-eyed psychos.

"You're so considerate," I purred. "I've been meaning to go on a diet."

I plopped myself down with one leg slung over the arm of the chair, grabbed my bowl, and began to slurp the cereal down. With the sour tang of the buttermilk blocking the familiar taste, I could appreciate the crunch of the bran flakes. I was a pro at making the most of a bad situation, and I managed an appreciative moan–even over cereal–which made Cain look annoyed.

I dropped the spoon in the bowl and stood, strutting over to stand above him.

His cold eyes rose to meet mine. "What's up?"

He had an enormous hard-on. He could be as big of a dick as he wanted, but the man got hard when I made the slightest sexy noise. It's funny that men think they rule the world when they're so weak.

I glanced down at his hard-on derisively, then met his gaze. "Nothing interesting."

He scoffed as I started to sashay away.

"Don't turn your back on me," he warned, and the next second, he was out of his chair, his big hand circling the back of my neck, hard and possessive. He spun me to face him.

His gaze had come alive. God, this man loved to play games with me, and my body responded with a rush of heat.

I loved to play with him too.

The next second, he'd dragged me across his lap. His hard thighs pressed up against my stomach, his cock jabbing me as hard and steely as if he'd misplaced his handgun. He flipped my skirt up, then rough fingers yanked my panties down, tracing over my ass. Maybe I should've been embarrassed, angry, scared, but I was just turned on, especially when I caught a glimpse of Stellan, Pax, and Remington watching. But I barely had the time to register their expressions before Cain's hand smacked hard against my ass, marking me as his, sending fire racing across my skin. I let out a gasp, my hair tossing in the air as I kicked out.

But there was no escaping Cain. He kept spanking me, his hand branding my ass over and over, each spank sending a rush of heat not only across my skin but straight to my pussy. It was so intense that my core squeezed as if I was going to come right there over his lap.

Then suddenly, he pulled me up, his hand roughly in my hair. He growled into my ear, "Don't you ever walk away from me like I'm nothing to you."

As if that spanking had been a deterrent at all. I was breathing hard, but so was he, and I couldn't wait to provoke him again. He was losing control even more than I was, and I'd just almost come across his lap.

Cain could punish me like this any day he wanted. I worried the beating he'd given me with his belt had awoken some of my memories of the Demon's punishment, even though those had been nothing but endless, unrelenting pain, so different from my time with Cain. But having Cain's heavy hands marking my skin...That was completely different, and all it awoke in me was desire.

"Be a good girl and sit there nicely," Cain demanded, his hard arm wrapped around my waist, holding me as I straddled his thigh. One hand played with my hair, his fingers tracing up my neck in a way that could have been soothing and sexy in equal measure. My still bare ass throbbed, his jeans rough against my naked, wet sex.

Pax's chair was on its side as if he'd been mad and had stormed out, furious, during the spanking. That must not be the kind of punishment he'd imagined after what I did to him last night... or was it because he wanted to be the one touching me like Cain was?

Remington, on the other hand, seemed amused as he

propped his chin in his hand and stared at the two of us. "So, Aurora. Any big plans for the day?"

"Wait and see," I told him.

"Oh, are you going to get 'revenge' on me too?" Remington made air quotes. He still looked amused. "You are so very out-classed, little girl."

I grinned back at Remington, and despite himself, there was something bright in his smile back at me.

"Did you sleep well?" Stellan drawled, pushing his plate away. He leaned back in his chair. "You didn't try to murder anyone in your sleep last night."

"What?" Cain asked flatly, his arm tightening around my waist. *Fuck.* He glanced suspiciously at the red cut on Stellan's face.

"She has nightmares at night. Haven't you heard them? Yells threats like she's going to kill someone."

Why the hell was Stellan covering for me? If Cain knew that I'd almost stabbed Stellan to death, I was pretty sure he'd chain me up at night, and not in a fun way. I frowned at Stellan, struggling to understand him.

"She doesn't have nightmares when she sleeps in my bed, covered in my cum," Cain purred, resting his hand on my inner thigh, so intimately close that my clit throbbed in response. "Do you, little devil?"

I shrugged nonchalantly in response. I'd slept for a while next to Cain, but I'd begged him to let me up early in the morning because I had to pee. He'd seemed to enjoy tormenting me until I threatened to pee in his bed, and then I'd earned myself a few more smacks and being unchained. Now I wish I'd let him keep me tied up all night, because I was scared of how I'd hurt Stellan.

"Answer me." Cain's hand wrapped my throat.

"Doubtful. If there's anyone I'd accidentally murder in my sleep, it's probably you, Cain."

He huffed a laugh and dragged my face down to his to press a kiss to my forehead, his fingers pressing hard into my throat. My vision danced with stars, but the blood that left my head seemed to flow straight to my clit.

"I knew you liked me best," he said, then suddenly released his grip on my throat and pushed me away.

I rose from his lap with all the dignity I could muster, given my bare ass and the way my legs were shaky from how near I'd come to orgasm.

"I hate you the most," I told him, "but tell yourself that's a special bond."

I didn't bother to fix my clothes as I swaggered toward the doorway. I could feel the tension rise behind me as if they didn't like the idea of me bared for anyone but them, and I smiled to myself as I heard a chair push back, as one of them acted. Possessive bastards.

I was just opening the door when a hand slammed into it, closing it hard. A familiar scent enveloped me as hard muscle pressed my back, and I knew who he was without looking.

Stellan pressed against me from behind. His hands stroked down my skin, raising sparks everywhere they touched, yanking my shirt back into place, pulling down my skirt, drawing my underwear back up my thighs. His warm touch on my skin so intimately, almost taking care of me, sent fresh heat flowing through my body.

"You're ours," he muttered into my ear. "No one else gets to see you. To touch you."

His jaw ran against the side of my forehead, then his lips, as if he couldn't stop touching me. His hands wrapped around my hips, and he inhaled deeply, as if he were drinking me in, as if he couldn't get enough of my scent just as I couldn't get enough of his.

Maybe I should have sex with someone else. I knew it would hurt them all but Stellan most of all.

I couldn't do that, though.

I had no doubt they would kill anyone who touched me.

"You're a bunch of psychopaths," I whispered.

"Don't forget that," he said, and then his hands were sliding around my thighs, drawing me back against his hard cock. Even through all those layers of fabric between us, I could feel how hot his cock was, how he throbbed for me. His lips pressed against my throat.

"I can smell how wet you are," he murmured. His hand slid up my thigh, his fingers brushing my panties, which were soaking wet. "Even if I couldn't feel it."

What could I say? I'd just discovered I had a kinky side I'd never known existed. I'd come close to orgasming over Cain's lap, and now as Stellan began to tease me over my panties, my thighs trembled as if I'd come right here from his lightest touch.

I ground down against his fingers, and he indulged me, rubbing my needy clit eagerly. His lips teased against my ear, the side of my face, as if he were about to kiss me, but he restrained himself.

"You want me so badly," he whispered, withdrawing his hand now that I was at the brink.

"No," I whispered, sure that only he could hear. "I want Cain."

He suddenly released me. I didn't have to look over my shoulder to know how hurt and angry he would look.

This time when I pulled the door open to go, he didn't stop me.

7

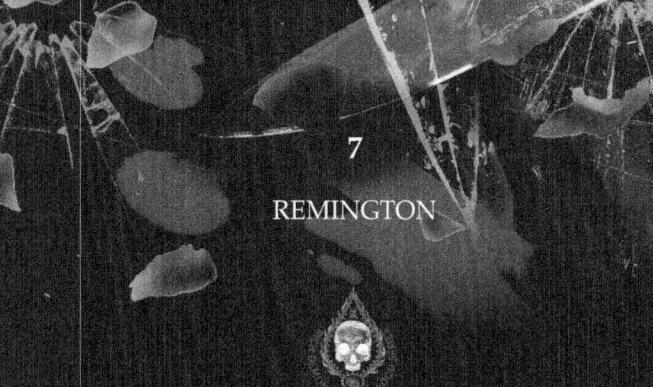

REMINGTON

I was supposed to be studying on the quad while I waited for Aurora to emerge from her class. Stellan had quietly suggested that we should keep an eye on her, day and night. I would ferret out why later, but for now, I was humoring him.

It was hard to concentrate, though, on my textbook, with tits in my face and polished red fingernails on my shoulder. Presley Harper seemed intent on sitting in my lap. Normally I wouldn't exactly push away a pretty girl who wanted to make me happy, but every girl seemed like a shallow imitation of Aurora Kane at the moment.

I looked up at Presley, studying her, her hair highlighted by the sunlight as she stood over me smiling. Maybe I should let her suck my cock. Maybe it would help me get over the ridiculous, uncontrolled attraction I felt to Aurora. I had obligations to my friends and, most of all, to my younger siblings that were counting on me to get them out of my asshole father's tender care. Nothing else mattered.

But when I looked up at Presley for a second, I could've sworn I saw Aurora's violet eyes. As if she were haunting me.

Then I blinked and she was gone, and it was just Presley's plastic face and empty eyes.

"Take a fucking hint, Presley," I said, hefting my book between us. She gave me a hurt look, then flounced off, as if she wouldn't be back tomorrow, smiling and pretending I'd never scorned her.

Aurora had more dignity with a smacked ass and rumpled skirt, her hair wild around her face, arousal tinting her cheeks pink.

The memory made my cock stiff in an instant, in a way Presley never could.

I started to read–finally–but something pulled my attention away after a few pages. I looked up to see Aurora walking down the steps of her building. She was talking to that mousy friend of hers. I frowned, trying to remember her name. The girl was pretty enough, but she'd dropped Aurora like she was infected with a skin disease when Aurora's identity surfaced. I didn't like the idea of Aurora being a doormat and being friends with her anyway just because she was desperate. Aurora never seemed to take abuse without a fight, and as much as we liked to punish her, I loved her spirit.

Several white-wearing weirdos rushed toward Aurora. Without hesitation, she shoved her friend behind her, yelling at her to run, and turned to face them.

I threw down my book and was across the yard in an instant. One of them had gotten in Aurora's face, yelling at her. I grabbed his shoulder and threw him away from her before his words even registered.

He'd been yelling that she was betraying...the Demon?

"And I'd do it again in a heartbeat," she said, high color in her cheeks. "He was a monster, and you're an idiot for idolizing him. He loved people like you that he could use!"

"You've thrown away his legacy," the man shouted at her from the ground. Spittle flew out of his mouth, and I frowned at him in disgust.

I turned to face Aurora, not afraid the crazy man would attack me from behind. I could take him easily, and right now I wouldn't mind an excuse to beat him into a pulp. "What the hell is going on?"

"My father has a fan club," she said crisply.

I'd have to go back through the files I'd deleted from the web about Aurora. I had my bots at work every time she was mentioned, attacking each site to take it down for a day or two as punishment for daring to say our girl's name, but every occasion was archived. Crazy always made me curious.

"You shouldn't be seen with me," Aurora told her friend.

Her friend looked torn but finally said, "Aurora, I'm not just going to abandon you. Again."

Hey, she was self-aware. I almost liked her.

I turned to look at the man who was getting back up, helped by his friend. They tried to brush off his robes, but they would never be quite so white again. What was wrong with these weirdos?

"What do you want from her?" I demanded, and my voice sounded rough, intense. Not like myself.

"We want her to–" the man met my eyes, and something he saw there made him shrink back. "Nothing. We just wanted to talk to her about her father. To hear what he had to say from her mouth. She was the closest to him."

I was on top of him in a second. His friend seemed as if he wasn't sure whether to run or hit me as I wrestled inside his jacket, searching for his wallet. I yanked it out just as the friend made up his mind and went to deck me, but Aurora was there, catching his arm. She yanked him around, then punched him in the face. He landed with a crash on his ass, and I stepped on his arm to hold him steady while I grabbed his wallet too.

I flipped through the wallets and found their IDs. "John Wakofski. Peter Leonard." I threw what was left of their wallets at their feet, but pocketed their IDs. "If I were you, I'd get out of town."

"Or what?"

I fixed them with a smile and they backed off, though they shot threatening backward glances at Aurora.

"Thanks for the help there, blondie," I told Aurora.

She looked at me dead in the eyes, her violet gaze steely. "United front in a fight. Even if I would like to watch someone punch you...but not as much as I want to punch you myself."

Why did I find that strangely touching?

"Jenna, go home," Aurora said, touching her friend's arm, her voice kinder than it ever was with me. "We can text...I don't think you should be seen with me though."

"I'll be careful," Jenna promised. "You deserve to have friends, Aurora."

Aurora smiled at that. "We don't always get what we deserve."

Then her eyes slid up to me, hardening, as if she was thinking just how true that was.

"Let's walk Jenna home," I said. "Being seen with me should help dispel some of the... danger."

I couldn't pretend as if some of the people who hated Aurora might take that anger out on Jenna or anyone else seen as being kind to her. But at least on this campus, everyone was either scared of me or in love with me. Or both.

When we'd dropped Jenna off at her dorm, Aurora said, "That was nice."

She said it with a tone as if she couldn't quite make sense of me. Well, that was mutual. I didn't understand Aurora, and I didn't understand how I felt about her.

"That's me. Nicest guy in the Sphinx." I fixed her with a bright smile.

"Low bar," she shot back.

"You'd be an expert." I rubbed my hand across my face, suppressing a laugh as I remembered Stellan's put-out face as he stormed out of breakfast this morning. "You let Stellan finger-fuck you with bacon grease still on his hands. No standards."

"But I wouldn't let you finger-fuck me at all," she said with an equally sunny smile. "So I guess even a girl with no standards still wants something better than you."

"I hope Cain spanks you again at dinner." I'd enjoyed the show. Cain usually acted as if he were a robot doing a halfway decent but glitchy imitation of a human; Aurora brought out something new in him and I was fucking intrigued.

"I hope he does too," she said brightly.

Even if the two of us were ripping each other apart, it still felt like teasing banter, and there was something strange and light in my chest that I hadn't felt since...well, ever.

But when I walked into the Sphinx, one of the boots looked at me with something like pity, then scurried away as if he worried I'd hit him.

Then Stellan stepped into the room, and he had a look on his face too.

A pit opened in my stomach. Something was wrong.

"It's your grades," he told me.

Fuck, if something was wrong with my grades...my

father always felt I was an embarrassment, but as he told people, I might not have "any fucking common sense but he's book smart as hell." He used to punish me whenever he thought I wasn't trying hard enough.

Now, it was my little siblings he punished for any misdeeds, although now those sins were never about my grades. If I were perfect, I could protect them.

"What about my grades?" I ground out, turning to face Aurora, who looked wide-eyed, innocent, and completely unconvincing.

8

AURORA

The moment Remington saw his grades splashed across social media and the internet, his eyes went clear and steely. He looked up and his eyes met mine, pure, unadulterated rage icy in his gaze.

"They were obviously doctored," Stellan said. "You'll get them off the internet."

"Of course," Remington said, his voice dark. It didn't matter to Remington. My friend made it look as if his *real* grades, the ones he'd worked for, the ones he was proud of, were the ones that had been doctored.

Remington could fix the trail on the internet–but for him, many of the people who mattered would already think he cheated. He couldn't undo the loss of his reputation and pride.

The next second, his hand was in my hair, his fingers twining into it at the base of my skull. "What is wrong with you?" he said, his voice flat. "I was almost starting to like you...are you really going to try to fuck with all of us?"

"I still don't like you, Remington."

"Stellan must be next," Cain said from the doorway.

Stellan already lost his sister.

"What are you going to do with her?" Cain asked as Remington tightened his grip on my hair, dragging me against his body. My eyes watered as he pulled me tightly against his hard-muscled frame, but I smiled up at him like I didn't give a damn.

I'd hurt him, and he could hurt me back, but I had a lot more practice taking damage. These boys would never outlast me.

Remington took so long to answer that I thought he didn't even know. Then he said, "Since Aurora loves playing games so much...I think Aurora and I are going to play a little game."

He dragged me toward the door. I had to rise onto my tiptoes as my scalp ached under his rough touch, and he yanked me along without acting as if he cared if he ripped my hair out.

"Remy," Cain said. There was a note in his voice that almost seemed like concern, and when Remington turned to face him, I caught a glimpse of his face too. Cain was almost frowning. "Don't make her ugly."

"I'll make sure all the ugly stays on the inside," Remington promised, but his grip on my scalp relaxed...just slightly. His gaze met mine again, the promise of pain glinting in his eyes. "After all, you're very pretty, Aurora. Like Nerium Oleander. Do you know anything about flowers?"

He answered his own question, muttering, "No, of course you don't. Everyone in this house except me is an uneducated moron."

He was wrong, though. I'd learned all about poisonous plants when I was a kid and I first considered killing the Demon.

"Why the fuck are you talking about flowers right now?" Cain looked bored.

Remington must have decided he was bored too, because he dragged me toward the stairs down to the basement. I tried to fight, afraid he was going to imprison me in one of those crypts, that he would leave me there to die.

Remington looked toward Cain, and Cain suddenly grabbed my ankles. Remington whipped his belt off, the leather whispering through his trouser loops. If this was just going to be another spanking, I was *so* ready for my punishment, but I didn't get the feeling it was going to be that fun this time.

I kicked Cain, breaking his grip on my ankles, and flipped up to my feet. Had they forgotten who the fuck I was?

Remington slipped his belt around my throat and reeled me in close to him, cutting off my airway as I slammed against his chest. I was trapped against the hard length of his body, his cock jutting hard against my ass, as he held me there. The edges of my vision faded to black the more I struggled, the two of us locked together and breathing hard.

"Tie her hands," Remington ordered Cain.

"My pleasure." Cain was wearing a tie today, and he ripped it off. His grip was bruisingly hard as he gathered my wrists in one hand and looped the silky fabric around them before knotting it. The soft material and hard fingers against the inside of my wrists sent an unexpected shiver of pleasure through me. My body was endlessly confused by these men...by these monsters.

"Not too tight," Remington said. "I want her to be able to get loose."

Cain looked at Remington, and he smiled the darkest, scariest smile I'd seen from the man yet.

Remy dropped his grip so he was carrying me under my arms, and no matter how much I struggled, the two of them carried me, kicking and swaying, down the stairs. I caught glimpses of their grim faces as we descended into the darkness.

I stopped struggling, trying to make sense of where we were, when we stepped through the door into the tunnels. "Hold her a second," Remington told Cain, and he dropped me with one hand so he could use his phone. He typed quickly with one thumb.

Then he tucked his phone back into his jacket and scooped to grab me again. "All the doors are open," he told Cain.

"I see," Cain said. "I'm intrigued."

I was not fucking intrigued. "You guys are monsters!"

"And you like to play with monsters, little devil," Cain chided me, and that word *play* was doused in sex and danger. His hands had slid slightly as I thrashed around, and his big hands encircled my calves, his fingers pressing into the back of my calves. Remington's hands under my arms left his fingers pressing the curve of my breast.

The two of them were still carrying me through endless twisting stone corridors, through doors that had just snapped open in the wall that I was pretty sure had once blended in. I tried to memorize the order we were going through–even though I was upside down, which made it harder to remember left and right and make a map in my head.

Then abruptly, we stepped into another room.

"Cool our vengeful little pixie off," Remington said.

Cain dropped my feet and I caught glimpses of something stone he was drawing a long lid from. Another crypt? He set the lid on the ground with a *thunk*.

An enormous cistern.

I began to struggle harder, thinking they were going to drown me, but Cain grabbed my ankles and Remington grabbed my arms, and the two of them slung me onto the edge of the cistern. Dark water, deep and frightening, seemed as if it absorbed what little light was in the stone room.

I lashed out to kick, trying to escape. Remington seized my wrists, his tall body leaning into mine, as Cain pulled a knife loose. Cain slashed upward, and his tie ripped with a screech of silk.

The next second, I was tumbling forward, pushed by hard hands.

I slammed into the icy cold water.

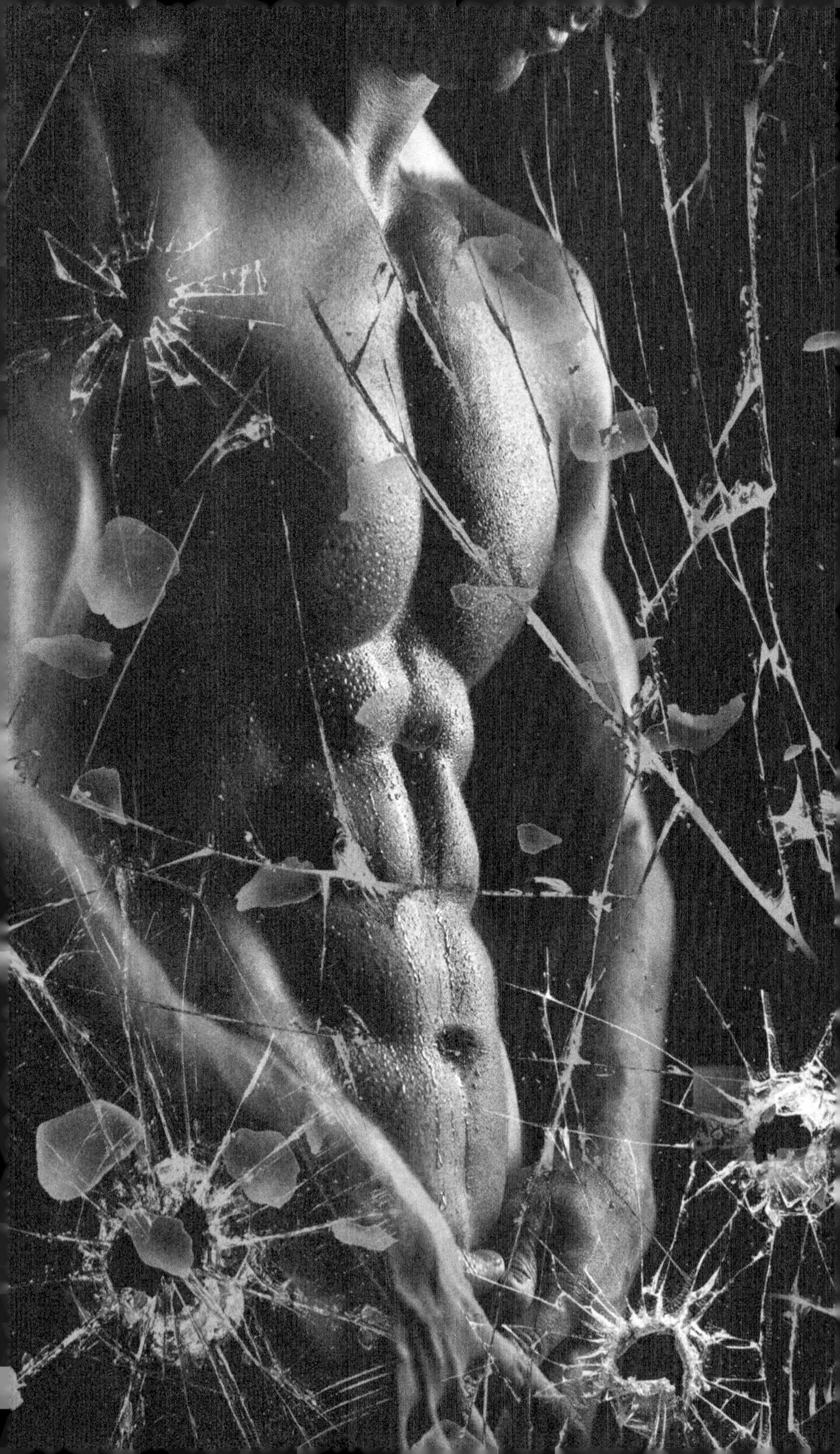

9

AURORA

For a few terrifying seconds, I didn't know which way was up or down in the black water. I couldn't see anything in the darkness. The water was so cold I could barely breathe. My shoes made it hard to kick, so I stopped and yanked them off. They disappeared into the dark as soon as I released them.

I kicked out, swimming for what I hoped was the surface, my lungs beginning to ache.

Then my fingertips painfully slammed into the rough bottom. The shock of hitting the bottom forcefully made my lips part, and some more air slipped out, leaving my lungs hollow. Even as I thought *don't breathe,* icy water stung my sinuses and burned through my lungs. Panic surged through my body. I turned and launched myself off the bottom, swimming frantically through the black water, hoping I was aiming upward and wasn't going to slam into one of the cistern walls. I'd been close to drowning before and I'd survived. *Stay calm, Delilah.*

I broke out of the water into the gloom of the empty stone room and drew a desperate gasp of a breath. My broken, half-sobbing hyperventilating breaths seemed to echo in the room as I fought my way to the side of the cistern. The wall around the water was tall, and it took me multiple attempts to fling myself out of the water enough to catch the stone edge. I broke two of my nails before I finally managed to straddle the side and roll out, landing hard on the stone floor. I lay there on my back for a few long seconds, trying to get my breathing under control.

I was in shock.

Dangerously cold.

But I was *alone*.

Remington and Cain were gone. I sat up and stared around the dimly lit room, which was illuminated by the light leaking in from the hallway. The room was eerie, with elaborately carved stone sculptures of human monsters facing the cistern. I wondered what the hell the purpose of this room was, and if it had anything to do with the Sphinx's ridiculous water bills.

Rich people are so unendingly *weird*.

Not that I'd reject the chance to be all rich and weird.

I climbed gingerly to my feet, my clothes drenched to my body. The stone floors were slick under my bare feet.

This couldn't be this easy, could it? I stepped into the hallway, wondering how far it would be back, and if I'd be locked out of the Sphinx. Was being wet, cold, and lost down here my punishment from Remington? How boring. I actually felt a little disappointed in him–I thought Remington was more interesting than that. He might burn me up, but I didn't think he'd just freeze me out.

Blue emergency lights illuminated the long hallway, giving it an eerie glow. I closed my eyes, trying to remember which way we'd come from.

When I opened my eyes again, I knew which way to go.

But I was also submerged in darkness.

Someone had turned the lights out while my eyes were closed.

The feeling that they—or at least Remington—were watching solidified in my chest. I could feel their gazes between my shoulder blades, even if I didn't know how they were watching me or from where.

I raised my hand and gave Remington the finger. I wasn't exactly afraid of the dark.

I reached out to my right, expecting my fingertips to graze the rough stone wall so I could trace it along my path.

Instead, my hand collided with a solid, warm wall of muscle.

I jumped back, but I was too late. I was caged by strong male arms, and I breathed in the scent of spicy cologne and male musk. I lashed out blindly, slamming my elbow into his hard abs, but he barely seemed to feel the hard blow.

A dark voice murmured in my ear, "Let's get you out of those wet clothes, sweetheart."

I flung myself out of his grip, but he had the hem of my shirt. There was a loud ripping sound. I couldn't be sure if he'd used a knife that close to my bare skin to cut the shirt. Cold air teased against my skin as my shirt flapped in tatters around me.

I caught the faintest glow of two eyes in the darkness—*night vision goggles*—and then it was gone. I ran as fast as I could down the hallway, my hands held in front of me to keep me from slamming into any walls. I hated knowing they were watching me and probably laughing.

A low, wicked male chuckle seemed to echo through the hall.

Yep. Definitely laughing.

I needed to get my hands on those night vision goggles.

"Left, right," I muttered to myself, afraid I'd lose track of where I was supposed to be going.

Then suddenly, strong hands seized my upper arms and pushed me against the wall. I threw my weight backward against the stone wall, raising my legs to kick out at my new attacker. But thighs slammed into my feet, taking the force out of the blow. I was pinned by a hard wall of muscle.

Hands slid down my waist, pushing my leggings down, as I struggled. "Be a good girl for once or I'll cut these off you." The voice was a hot whisper, and I frowned, trying to decipher the voice, trying to be sure it was Remington. There were so many hands sliding across my thighs, my exposed lower abs, that I couldn't be entirely sure it was just one of these men pressing against me.

There was a tearing sound as my leggings were pulled off my body and the cold edge of a knife slid against my skin–the back, not the blade. I knew the icy feeling of being cut too well. I froze, my heart in my throat, making sure they didn't cut me by accident.

"Good girl." The voice was a hot breath against the shell of my ear, and his hands were in my hair. This time, the way he tugged my hair commandingly sent an unexpected jolt of pleasure through my body.

He tilted my head back against the stone, his lips plundering my throat, his hands gliding down my thighs, lighting fire everywhere he touched. He touched me as if he owned me, his lips alternately sucking a bruise, then kissing it away. An involuntary moan escaped from the back of my throat, and I yanked away from him, humiliated by the telltale reaction of my body. Something was so broken in me because I loved these games, and it was my desire that I ran from, not Remington, as I pushed off the wall and fled.

I careened through the hallways, trying to get away

before Remington could keep on stripping me. I had no doubt he meant to continue. I'd peeled away his guise of careless brilliance, and he wanted to strip me and leave me feeling just as vulnerable.

What a joke that was. These were just clothes.

I stopped and turned, raising my chin high. "You want me naked? You know I'm twice the badass you are, even wet, cold, and naked."

I could feel hard gazes on me, even if I couldn't catch the telltale flash of night vision goggles right now. I didn't have to see their responses to know they wanted me, though. I ran my hands up my bare sides, putting on a show for them, cupping my breasts momentarily over the silky material of my bra before I released the latch and let the cups fall off my breasts. I dangled the bra from two fingers, then dropped it on the floor.

I pulled the waistband of my panties away from my taut waist and rolled them down my thighs slowly, doing a little striptease.

I knew he was close before I felt his touch, as if I could feel his power in the air, and my nipples pebbled.

Fingers wrapped my throat, and he dragged me close. This time, his touch was firm but not painful, just commanding.

"The next time I catch you," he whispered, "I'm going to hurt you."

"Not if I hurt you first." My voice came out ragged, not as strong as I wanted. I ran my hands up his hard chest, up his throat to his stubble-covered jaw. I managed to get my fingers around the edges of his goggles and tried to yank them away.

He let go of my throat with one hand to catch my wrists in his other hand, his grip bruisingly hard. "Always plotting." His lips grazed my throat, his hot breath seeming to go straight to my core. I wasn't cold anymore; adrenaline flooding my body had filled me with heat.

He let out a laugh, then suddenly released my throat. "Run."

I ran.

"Right, left, left," I whispered under my breath, taking the turns at a dangerous speed when I couldn't even see. I was so close to escaping them, back to the comparative safety of the Sphinx.

Not that these men couldn't drag me right back down here, but I had the gut feeling we'd all honor the spirit of these twisted games. They might come up with something even crueler to throw at me next, but they wouldn't repeat the same ruse.

Then there was a stone wall in front of me. Before I could turn, a body slammed into mine, forcing me up against the wall. A hard cock jutted against the curve of my ass, and I struggled to escape, but there was no moving the big, muscular man who pressed against me.

His hand wrapped my thigh, his thumb teasing between the seam of my legs, brushing against my clit.

"Leave me alone," I gasped, the weight of his body pressing me against the stone painfully. My exposed nipples were being pressed against the rough wall, and the only give was between his hips and mine so he could rub his fingers hard and mercilessly through my wet heat. Despite myself, my core squeezed painfully, wanting more of his rough touch.

"Never," he promised me, his voice dark. "You'll never escape us."

Was Cain here in the dark, or even Stellan and Pax too, surrounding us? I couldn't be sure–his hands seemed to be everywhere in the dark as he dragged me back slightly away from the wall. Hands stroked over my body, palming my nipples, pinching and toying with them, rubbing against my clit, teasing the curve of my ass. In the darkness, it was as if he took over all my senses.

He kept his merciless tempo up between my thighs, driving me toward orgasm, his cock teasing steadily between the curve of my ass. I struggled to get away, which seemed to just make his cock harder and bigger, his tip gliding against the curve of my ass and across my wet folds.

Despite how much I struggled, I also couldn't help grinding down on his fingers, seeking release there. My knees went weak, my thighs beginning to tremble, but it didn't matter that my legs were turning boneless. His lips teased against the curve of my throat, and the gentleness of the kiss he pressed there surprised me so much I stopped struggling for a second.

"I told you I'd hurt you," he warned, and the next second, his teeth sank into my skin. Pain seared into my throat. I let out a gasp and arched back at the pain, which pushed my hips into the stone wall, trapping his hand. I couldn't believe he'd just bitten me so hard, and he sucked now, marking me, drawing my blood into his mouth.

Then suddenly, he released me, and I fell to my knees in the darkness.

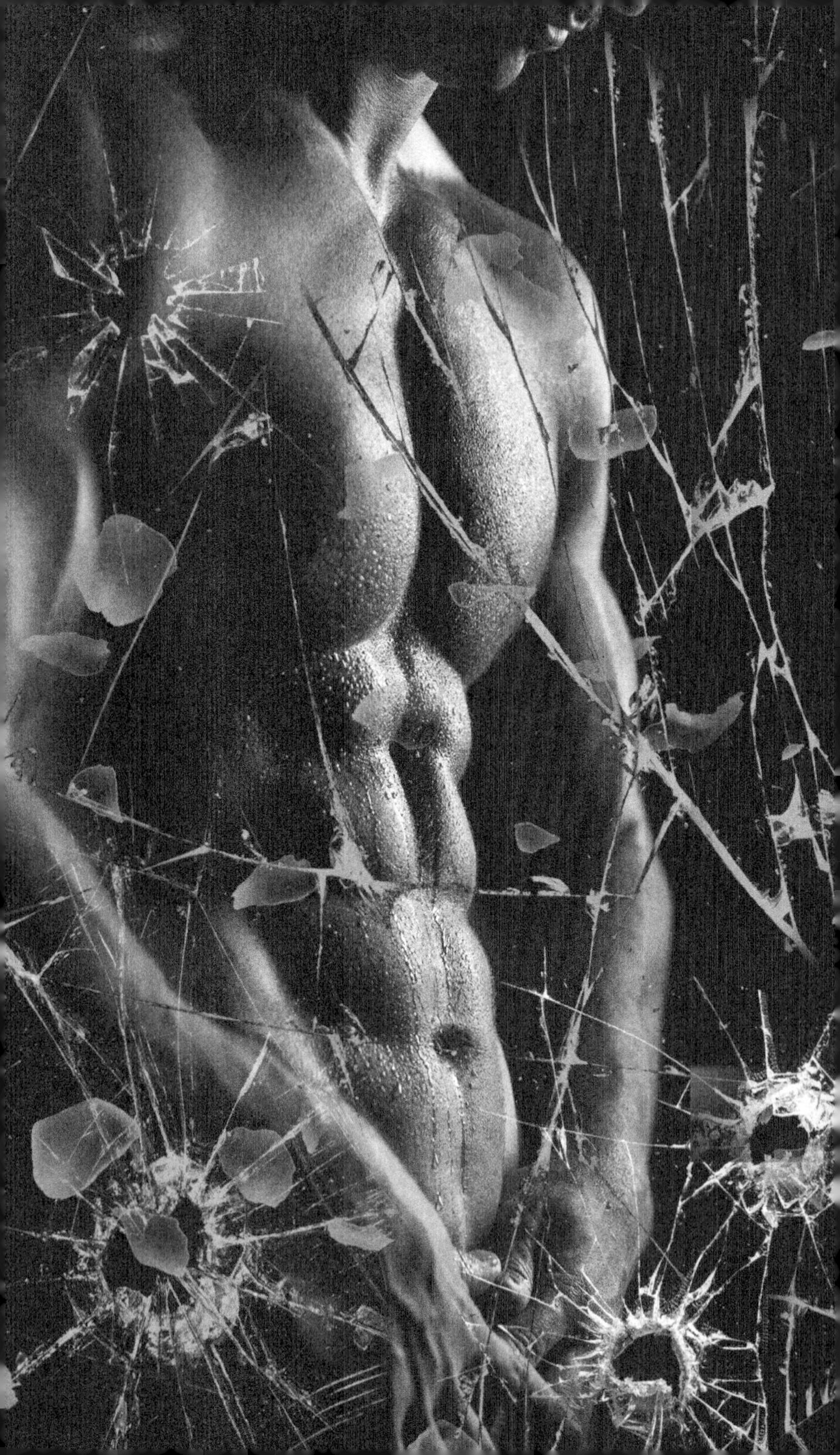

10

AURORA

I climbed to my feet, my clit throbbing even though I was furious. I started moving again, preparing myself for the next attack. I wanted to find a way to turn on the lights, which would temporarily blind them in their night vision goggles. I hadn't known there were so many doors and hallways down here; apparently there were hidden doors that were only known by certain depraved men of the Sphinx.

I could feel him coming after me. A thin stream of blood trickled down my throat, down my shoulder, even wetter than the feeling between my thighs as I ran. My breath came in short gasps, a mix of desire and rage and fear, and as much as I tried to calm myself down and think clearly, I was losing myself to something more animalistic.

I wanted to tear him apart. I wanted to rip my teeth into his skin too. I wanted to hurt him...and I wanted his fingers in my hair, his lips on my throat. I wanted to make him nice to me again so I could hurt him all over again.

Everything between us was broken and jagged, and so were we.

I stepped on something soft and almost slipped. I was several feet beyond it when I realized what it was.

My bra.

I'd gone in a circle. Fuck. Panic hammered in my chest. I couldn't get away from him.

This time, when he caught me, I didn't fight.

His lips claimed mine, his hands sliding into my hair, pushing me against the wall so hard the stone scraped my bare skin.

"Please," I begged him, all to distract him, to slow him down, as I reached into his pocket for his phone. "You're scaring me."

"You should be scared to fuck with us," he said, just before he kissed me so hard it left me breathless, as if he were stealing the last of the air from my lungs. I drowned in him worse than I had in any cistern, any well. His tongue plundered my mouth, thrusting against my tongue in long, powerful strokes, his hips swaying against mine over and over. He drove me into the wall, and my fingernails sank deep into his shoulders, trying to push him away.

He ducked his head, his mouth capturing my nipple. Fear darted through my chest, but his tongue teased against my nipple just the way I liked, his mouth hot and wet, his tongue licking me over and over. He drew my nipple deeper into his mouth then bit down, just hard enough to wrench a cry from my lips.

"Next time I catch you," he whispered against the hot ache of my breast, and he palmed my aching clit. He didn't finish the threat. He didn't need to.

I ran and found myself smelling saltwater. *The cistern.*

I ducked hard to the left and scrabbled to find the door, then slammed the door shut behind me, sealing me into the darkness. Remington had probably already realized I had his precious phone. The screen lit up, and I squinted in the darkness at the square of blue light, which was painful to see now.

Remington had apps that controlled everything in the Sphinx and below it, and probably across the whole campus. I turned on the lights with a sense of triumph, squeezing my eyes shut, knowing it would hurt to adjust to the light but not like it would hurt for them with their night vision goggles.

The grunt of pain I heard was close. In the room with me. Adrenaline shot through every muscle.

In front of me, Remington ripped his night vision goggles off and tossed them onto the ground, before pressing the heels of his hands into his eyes. Somehow he'd gotten ahead of me.

I used the opportunity to kick him in the balls.

He doubled over, but he also lunged forward, grabbing me around the waist. The two of us slammed into the ground together, fighting to get on top of each other, and I landed several vicious punches into the hard muscle of his side. But he managed to pin me with all his weight on top of me.

"I told you that you better not let me catch you again." His fingers were in my hair, and he dragged me up to my feet. "But you want me to catch you, don't you? You provoke us and stay around for our punishments."

He pushed me against the cistern, my hips meeting the stone. His hips ground against my ass as he bent me forward, and I caught a glimpse of the two of us reflected in the dark water. His eyes looked black and fathomless in his god-like face, his hand deep in my hair. My face looked alive, my lips parted, my eyes bright, as if I only found myself awake in my nightmares.

"Deep down, you must know you deserve every punishment," he ground out into my ear.

He kept one hand pressing down on my lower back, holding me against the edge of the cistern, as he pulled his cock out with his other hand. The hard tip of his cock jutted into my wet heat before I tried to jerk my hips away, twisting to each side.

His hand circled my throat, his fingers pressing hard into my skin, almost cutting off my airway. Black edges burst at my vision even as all the blood seemed to flow straight to my aching clit.

"Stop," I gasped, my voice ragged.

"I don't want to." His voice was dark. "And you don't want me to either. You know you want me to hurt you."

He plunged deep inside me, fast and hard. I let out a gasp as he set up a punishing pace, his hand still on my throat.

My fingernails curled against the edge of the stone, trying to keep myself from plunging forward into the cistern again. My legs ached from adrenaline and from being pushed close to orgasm again and again, and they were already shaking again from the power of him filling me over and over. I wasn't sure I had the strength to swim if I had to again. I'd come so close to winning this last round when I stole his phone, but he'd successfully run me down like I was prey and he was the cruelest hunter.

The world faded to nothing but him and me and our cursed reflection staring up at us, as my lips parted, as my eyes went heavy-lidded. His face was as cold and beautiful as a marble statue of a god.

Then I was coming around his cock, shaking and trembling. He didn't stop, even though my clit was sore and aching from the power of that orgasm, plunging himself into me over and over again until he exploded too. He filled me, and when he abruptly pulled out, his cum spilled down my thighs.

He was still gripping my throat. He reeled me back against the hard muscle of his body, his hand dropping to the base of my throat.

"You could have gotten away," he murmured into my ear, his deep voice seeming to reverberate through my bones. "But you wanted me to catch you."

"No," I said in a gasp.

"Don't say no to me." He turned us both around, dragging me around to see where Cain towered inside the doorway.

Cain's hands were folded behind his back, and his lips were tilted up. Cain smiling was always truly terrifying.

"You were there too, the whole time," I gasped. "In the dark."

"Always," Cain promised me.

"Time to thank Cain for punishing you too." Remington's fingers curled into my shoulders, pushing me down. "Suck his cock. Then you can go upstairs and sleep off all the...excitement."

He sounded almost...caring. As if I'd really brought this on myself and they'd only been doling out what I owed them.

Cain stood off the wall, bringing his arm out from behind his back, and I caught a glimpse of his belt once again dangling from his fingers. "Feel free to defy us," he said mildly, but his jutting cock belied his disinterest.

Remington forced me to my knees, the stone cold underneath them.

"If you bite me," Cain promised, "the punishment won't

be an ass-whipping. You'll be spending the night in that cistern. With the cover on. Do you hear me?"

"She would never." Remington looked down at me almost fondly, his fingers resting in my hair. "She's in a nice submissive mood now, aren't you, Aurora?"

His fingers in my hair pulled my head back, angling my jaw up for Cain. Cain drew himself out of his pants, revealing that enormous snake of a cock. He ran his tip over my lower lip.

"You talked a good game about how well you can suck a cock," Cain said. "Are you a liar?"

His voice was taunting, but there was no hiding the desire and intrigue in his eyes, the way his face lit up when he looked at me.

Even on my knees, I had so much power over these men.

I leaned forward and licked up his cock. His eyes widened in surprise as I reached his hard lower abs and licked around him, pressing my face against his cock so my tongue could tease against his ballsack. I licked along the underside back to the tip, and he couldn't suppress the way tension shivered through his body, the way his eyelids went heavy.

He was too big to take all the way into my mouth, but I made up for that with pure wild desire. I set up my own merciless pace, licking and sucking him, channeling all my anger and desire into sucking him off like my life depended on it. Cain's thighs began to shake, and I smiled around his cock.

"Hold her head," Cain commanded, then Remington's fingers were hard, gripping my face, and Cain began to fuck my mouth. He plunged in too deep every time, making me gag, and drool started to run from the corner of my mouth.

Then he exploded, hot cum shooting against the back of

my throat. I gagged again, but Remington held me there as I swallowed Cain's cum, some of it leaking down my chin. Cain bent down, a smile on his face, and wiped my lips with his fingers before shoving them into my mouth, forcing me to take in all his salty cum.

He straightened, and Remington suddenly released me. My legs were boneless from orgasm and exhaustion, and I couldn't help sinking even further to my knees as the two towered above me.

"Too bad we know you won't learn any lessons," Cain said, his voice amused. "You'll just have to keep being taught, won't you?"

Cain adjusted his pants, tucking himself back inside, zipping himself up. Then the two of them left me there, in the brightly lit stone room that smelled of salt from cum and the cistern.

I stumbled up to my feet, determined to get out of there before I was abandoned in the dark again. I'd rather they chased me through the dark than be alone–and when I realized that, it hit me like a ton of bricks.

I felt lonely that they'd gone, even though they were my tormentors. They also wanted me intensely, in a way no one had ever wanted me before.

I stumbled into the hall, trying to remember the path I'd memorized, but I was so exhausted I found myself sinking to my knees. The darkness weighed on me heavily, and I knew it wasn't safe, but I was so tempted to curl up and sleep in the darkness.

Then someone lifted me up, wrapped me in something soft–a blanket–and warm arms. I couldn't even open my eyes.

But I felt warm and safe as someone carried me.

"I think I'm falling in love with you, Aurora." The voice was a whisper that might've been a dream.

I tried to open my eyes and found myself in my own bed, the room empty.

I didn't know if I'd just dreamt the voice.

11

HIM

I watched her move around the room. She spent quite a bit of time looking out the window like a trapped bird that was begging to be eaten. Next was my favorite part. I unbuttoned the top of my jeans and slid the zipper down as I pulled out my cock, already hard from just the anticipation of what I was about to see. I had cameras all over the room, even in her closet, so I wouldn't miss a thing. Maybe she'd feel like taking care of herself tonight; there was nothing I liked more than watching her bring herself to orgasm in her bed. I had to squeeze the tip of my dick to stop from coming, and the show hadn't even begun.

She finally slid off her shirt, and I panted at the sight of her rosy nipples peeking through the lace of her bra. She was perfect, and someday she was going to be all mine. I knew everything about her. Delilah. Aurora. They were the same to me. I began to slowly stroke my shaft up and down as she pulled down her jeans, showcasing that luscious ass that I wanted more than anything to bite.

Soon. That's what I kept telling myself every time I was tempted to move in too fast. Soon I'd get to mark every part of her smooth flesh. There wouldn't be a part of her that I didn't touch.

I lost it when she unsnapped her bra. The sight of her tits was too much for me even though I saw them every night when she changed into her sleeping clothes. I threw back my head and came all over my hand.

It wouldn't be too long now until I was coming in her.

The devil's daughter belonged to me. She always would, and she always had. And soon, she would know that too.

AURORA

"There's a party tonight," Jenna told me as soon as I saw her in the cafeteria.

"Yeah, and?" I asked her absentmindedly as I looked over the deal of the day. Hamburgers. Not bad. The grill actually made a good one here.

"Well, I think we should go," she said hesitantly.

I winced before she even finished the sentence and turned to look at her. It was crazy to me to think about what life had been like when I thought I'd been looking forward to a normal college experience. Bits and pieces of that party...and Cain splashed through my mind, and I had to grit my teeth at the imagery.

"Who's throwing the party? I highly doubt that anyone on this campus is going to let me in."

"Oh, I feel like they'll all be creaming their pants to get you through the door of any party, because they'll think that the kings will make an appearance."

"Hmm, they must be missing the reality of the situation."

"Did I not see you looking very well-fucked at Paxton's fight?" she teased.

I tensed, biting my lip as I thought about all the other times she didn't know about. Like the tunnels. I still wasn't sure how I felt about that, even if just thinking about it turned me on.

"One hit wonder," I responded, trying to ignore how wet my panties were all of a sudden.

"This frat makes this special drink, and they have this game they play there. It's like ping pong but they rip off the handles of the paddles."

"That sounds the opposite of a good time," I told her with a lifted eyebrow as I finally got to the grill where I could place my order.

"Please. It's my birthday," she pleaded as she put her food on her tray.

Guilt flooded my insides. "It's your birthday?"

"Well. In like a month. But who knows what those guys will do to you between then and now, so I need to cash in my party time with you before things escalate too much."

I snickered and rolled my eyes. Little did she know how much it had already escalated.

"I'm not drinking," I told her. "I can't afford for them to catch me off guard."

She nodded eagerly, obviously sensing she had me right where she wanted me.

"I won't drink either," she promised.

"You don't have to do that."

"Well, I'm pretty sure that I need to be ready to step in if something happens. Keep your head on a swivel and all that."

I laughed, shaking my head. Jenna got funnier every time we hung out. I'm not sure where she got her information about evil, but it seemed a whole lot better than the evil I'd come across.

"Well, just make sure to bring your duct tape," I teased.

And she nodded, a serious expression on her face like she was making up a list in her head right that very minute of everything she was going to need for the party.

I grabbed my food before following her to a table in the blissfully *king* free room.

"So...what are you going to wear?" asked Jenna.

I sighed and shook my head, nervous anticipation building up inside of me. I'd have to find something to cover the teeth marks on my neck. I could only imagine the rumors that would spread around campus if people saw them.

Not that any of the rumors could come close to matching the craziness of the truth of how I'd gotten them.

Why was it that I could handle shaving the skin off someone with almost no issues, but the thought of attending a college party was almost more than I could take?

Definitely something to discuss with a therapist.

If I ever had one.

IT WAS COLD. AND I WAS WEARING FAR TOO LITTLE CLOTHING. I'd tried to bring a coat, but Jenna had insisted I leave it behind, saying there would be nowhere to put it at the frat. Which made sense. Throngs of drunk girls throwing their coats everywhere was probably not an ideal situation for taking home the same coat that you'd arrived at the party in.

And I liked my coat.

"So what's this frat's thing?" I asked as we walked towards Frat Row.

"Thing?"

"Yeah, like are they a particular sports house? Are they the nerd house? Don't they all have like themes...or reputations, I guess?"

"You think I would take us to a party at the nerd frat?" she exclaimed, putting her hand over her heart dramatically like I'd offended her.

I snorted and nudged her shoulder with mine.

"This one's the hockey house. Think the movie *Animal House*, but with hockey sticks."

I nodded like I understood what she was saying. I'd never seen *Animal House*. I'd never seen most movies. But I didn't want to tell her that. Our friendship was a fragile thing, and although she was the one who had hurt me, the needy part inside of me that was desperate for a friend didn't want to show her what a freak I really was.

We got to Frat Row, and there was a mass of giggling girls herding down the street like sheep. I tried to imagine what it would be like to have lived the kind of life where I could giggle like that so effortlessly. I couldn't even picture it. I'd have to ask Jenna what that was like someday.

It looked like there were a few parties happening in various frats, but it was obvious what the big party of the night was. The enormous white house was at the end of the street, and loud music was booming from the open windows. There was a long line of people stretching down the sidewalk, and like that first party, there were guys with clipboards manning the door like this was an exclusive club or something. Not a college party filled with cheap beer and stinky basements.

Jenna took my hand and led me around the crowd and straight up to the entrance.

"What are you doing?" I hissed, hating all the eyes glaring at me from behind us.

"If those assholes are going to make you infamous on campus, we might as well use your celebrity status to get things."

"I don't think you understand what 'infamous' means. It doesn't quite mean the same thing as famous," I commented dryly as she stopped in front of the pretentious prick in a popped collar carrying a clipboard.

"The party has arrived," she said calmly.

"You can get in line," he drawled, not looking up from his list.

Jenna just cleared her throat. She was a persistent little thing.

He finally looked up, annoyed. His gaze flicked across hers, unrecognizing. But then he spotted me and his eyes widened. He took a step backward as if I was going to lunge at him and slice his throat.

"Go right in," he said, stepping aside and not looking at us as we passed. Disgust curdled in my stomach. I hated that reaction. He wasn't scared of Aurora. He was scared of the Demon's daughter. And that was someone I had never wanted to be.

"Told ya," Jenna said excitedly, missing my mood.

We stepped through the doors and I saw that this house had the same basic setup the first party had. I wondered if the guys were holding court at the top of this house too.

"Do you want to leave?" Jenna asked suddenly, and I came back from memory lane to see her staring at me worriedly.

I immediately felt guilty because here I was being a killjoy, and we were supposed to be celebrating her birthday. Her birthday that was a month away.

Although she had a point, with the rate my life was going, who knew if I would be around to celebrate it.

"Nope. This is great," I said cheerfully, and she smirked at me, because evidently, I was easy to see through.

As we walked through the long front entryway that was packed with people, I tried to ignore everyone who was looking at us.

"Maybe we should get one drink," I muttered to Jenna.

"Really?"

"It might be necessary," I answered as a group of girls started to whisper to each other...loudly as we passed by.

I didn't miss the "demon slut" slurs they were throwing around.

How original.

Jenna seemed to have a tracker for the frat's special drink, and she headed straight back through another room where a DJ was pumping music through enormous speakers to where buckets of clear liquid were stashed along the wall.

I stared at them dubiously.

"The last time the drink was red. What the hell are they putting in this that keeps it perfectly clear...except for straight vodka?"

Jenna was humming along to a *Backstreet Boys* song while girls screamed and danced nearby, because there was nothing a group of college coeds liked more than some throwback boy band songs.

"It's fine. There's so much alcohol in this that it kills off anything bad that could be in it," she explained calmly as she took a ladle and scooped some of the drink into two red solo cups.

I put it up to my nose and took a big sniff. Nothing. It might as well have been water, because I couldn't smell anything.

I watched as some frat bros went up to one of the other buckets and scooped some of the drink into cups. They guzzled it back and laughed uproariously.

Well then, at least it didn't kill you right away.

Jenna was watching me, amused, as she sipped her drink. "Just taste it," she scoffed.

I scrunched up my nose and then hesitantly took a sip.

Hmm.

"I can't taste anything," I told her quizzically.

She just smirked at me, taking another long sip out of her own cup.

I took another sip, and then another, confused. Unlike the punch at the first party, which had just been delicious, this literally tasted like water. I'd even go so far as to say that water had more flavor than this did.

Whatever was in this must be powerful though, because the people crowding the room all were drunk as fuck.

I could see a group gathered in the next room around a giant ping pong table. "Is that the 'pong' game you were talking about?" I asked as I watched four guys playing against each other. One of the guys was covered in tattoos. And I wasn't talking just tattoo sleeves--he had tattoos going up over his jaw, and I could see some interwoven in his hairline.

"Yep," she said, popping her 'p'. "That guy right there, Tyson, he's the president of this frat. He's a little addicted to tattoos as you can see. But evidently, he's actually done most of the ones on his body. He's really talented."

I watched the ball fly back and forth across the table until it landed in one of the cups of punch, and then Jenna was pulling me into the crowd to dance. I pretended not to notice when people immediately moved away from us as soon as they saw me.

I could already feel the alcohol relaxing my muscles and I let myself just...have fun.

Or as close to fun as someone like me could have.

Jenna was grinding against me like I was a pole and she was a stripper, and I threw my head back and laughed when she shimmied all the way to the floor.

And that's when I saw him.

Cain.

Heading up the stairs with two girls following close behind him, giggling nervously with each other. One of them had two fingers hooked in the back of his jeans.

Maybe another person could have looked at the situation calmly and rationalized the situation. They just happened to be going in the same direction as he was. The rest of the guys were probably all upstairs and Cain was just headed up there to join them. They were desperate for him, and he probably didn't even notice them.

But in this moment, I was definitely not a rational person. In my mind, I could still feel the cold rough stone underneath my knees as he'd fucked my mouth. I could still taste his cum in the back of my throat. I could still feel the fear battering around in my chest as they'd chased me around in the dark like animals.

A bite was still seared into my neck like he was a fucking wolf who'd just marked me for eternity.

They'd all made it clear over and over that I belonged to them. That my body belonged to them. My soul belonged to them. Everything about me belonged to them.

And here was Cain fucking Hamilton, thinking I didn't own him right back.

He was in for the biggest fucking wake-up call of his life.

The best way to explain what happened to me then was that I'd lost my grip on humanity. The girl that the Demon had carefully crafted from the desolate misery of my childhood came fully to the surface, pushing away any remnant of the girl I'd been trying so hard to be when I'd first started my new life. Ice leached through my veins, freezing any feelings that could possibly be classified as good.

I grabbed Jenna's hand. "I'm about to do something completely bat shit crazy. Are you in?"

Jenna's mouth opened and closed like a fish as she tried to adjust from the whiplash of dancing to *Everybody* and then me going all *Exorcist* on her.

"Um...yes?" she responded hesitantly.

"Perfect," I told her calmly as I began to stride through the crowd towards the door.

"Where are we going? What happened? Are you okay?" Jenna whispered urgently as she trotted along beside me.

"You know what's wrong with men like Cain, Jenna?"

"Ummm...everything?"

"That no one has ever held them accountable for anything. Men like Cain take and they take until you have nothing left to give. And when they're finally done with you—there's nothing left of you but a dried-out husk of a person. A corpse."

"I feel like I'm missing so much," she mused as we pushed through the front door, out to the porch where a long line was still stretched out down the sidewalk.

It didn't feel cold anymore. There was so much blind rage flaring through my bloodstream that I probably could have survived walking through Antarctica butt naked if I needed to.

I began to jog down the street, and Jenna huffed as she tried to catch up. "Wait a second," she called out as she stopped and pulled off the wedges she'd been sporting. She winced as she began to hustle down the sidewalk.

"Just wait here. Or go back to the party. I have to get some...supplies," I told her, not wanting to be slowed down at all. Not when the need to get back at him was a blinding pulse in my head.

"Is this something I should talk you out of?" she called after me as I sprinted away.

"You couldn't if you tried," I responded over my shoulder.

It was like the universe was behind my plan, because one of the Sphinx guys was coming out as I got to the door and I was able to slip in.

I might have had to knock him out in order to stop him from giving me a hard time, but sometimes a little violence was necessary.

The Demon had been a genius. Spawned by the devil for sure. But still a genius. The poison that he'd created that kept his victims awake but paralyzed had taken years to perfect, and I happened to have stolen some before I'd gotten him locked away.

I walked into my closet and reached behind some of the hung clothes, to the back corner, where I'd cut into the thick carpet and the wood underneath to create a little hiding spot. I cackled a bit like a freaking witch from Snow White as I grabbed the vial of the poison and tucked it into my bra. The line separating me from villain status had already been crossed a million times in my life, but I'd felt like I'd done a good job of keeping the evil inside of me tucked away.

Clearly, the box I'd been storing my crazy in had burst right open, because I could feel it rolling across my skin.

At the end of this, only one of us would be standing. The kings or me. But I wondered, if I was the winner, would there be anything left to make the victory even worth it?

I stared at the small bottle in my hand. I didn't really

have a plan; I was kind of just going with whatever popped in my head at the moment, but even if I didn't come up with anything else, this poison would at least have him feeling helpless for a moment. I wanted him to feel the blind panic that I'd experienced. I wanted him to feel like I held his existence in my hand for just a second.

Yes, I was fully aware of how crazy that all sounded.

I shrugged off the self-doubt as I left the Sphinx and headed back to the party. I was surprised to see Jenna still waiting practically where I'd left her, looking a little blue-tinted from the cold.

"Why didn't you go back in?" I asked as I rushed towards her.

Her teeth were chattering and she wrapped an arm through mine as we headed back to the party.

"I wanted to make sure you didn't slip in without me seeing you. Someone has to keep you alive."

I barked out a laugh as we rushed past the bouncers, not even bothering to ask if they'd let me back in. Maybe they could sense the crazy emanating from my pores, because none of them said a word.

The party had only gotten crazier since we'd left. There was literally someone passed out in the middle of the dance floor, and everyone was just dancing around him like he was a piece of furniture and not an actual fucking person.

Hmm. Not my problem.

We walked up the stairs, and the rage that had cooled just a tad on my walk came rushing back as I began to throw open the doors in my quest to find Cain.

I saw a lot of things in those rooms...but not Cain.

"Where the fuck is he?" I hissed under my breath.

I was at the last door of the floor, and I threw it open, not expecting to see him in there at that point.

And there he was.

Cain was sprawled out in an armchair, a glass snifter in his hand that he was sipping slowly as he watched the show in front of him.

The two girls were clothed just in their underwear, and they were dancing against one another, their tongues down each other's throats.

And I saw red.

"Get the fuck out of here before I kill you," I murmured silkily. The girls both froze and turned towards me with identical looks of horror all over their faces.

One of them looked back at Cain, and honestly, it burned a little bit that they would still deign to ask permission from him when I was threatening to end their lives.

"I'm just going to wait in the hallway," Jenna whispered behind me, and I heard her retreating out of the room. Smart of her.

Cain looked bemused as he sat there, his gaze locked on mine. It was ridiculous of me, but I did glance at his pants and didn't see any evidence of an erection...and there was no missing Cain's erection, no matter what he was wearing.

Had he not been turned on?

"I probably would listen to her if I were you, ladies. Aurora doesn't say things lightly, and she does have a body count a mile high at this point." His tone was light and mocking, but it sent the girls scrambling for their clothes nonetheless. As the girls passed, I popped my foot out, sending one of them sprawling awkwardly to the floor like the petty bitch I was.

Cain chuckled darkly, and the girl scrambled off the floor, her tits flapping as she struggled past me.

"I must say, little devil, I don't appreciate having my

evening entertainment ruined. Unless you're going to replace it," he drawled.

I smiled at him, I'm sure looking a little manic because his eyes began to glimmer like the games were about to begin.

And they were.

Just not the games I'm sure he was anticipating.

I turned and closed the door, smiling at Jenna reassuringly in the hallway as I did so. I paused in front of the closed door, steeling myself before I slowly turned around.

Cain was still just sitting there, a small smirk on his lips...his enormous dick now out as he slowly stroked it up and down.

He was definitely hard now.

"You know, it's a bit alarming how far you're willing to fall to try and prove you aren't obsessed with me, Cain," I murmured as I slowly walked towards him.

His smirk only widened. "Obsessed. That's quite a big word, Aurora."

"It is, isn't it," I whispered as I stopped right in front of him. His hand was still moving up and down, a small bead of pre-cum dotting his slit.

And now I knew exactly what it tasted like.

Just because, I gave in and licked the drop away, and he growled as my mouth moved off his dick. I slid forward onto his lap until I was straddling him, my dress sliding up on my thighs so that the only thing separating my pussy from his huge dick was my damp pair of underwear.

Cain's pupils were blown out, and I watched as his tongue slipped out and he licked the bottom of his lip.

I leaned in close to his ear and his breath hitched. "I'm going to make this the most memorable night you've ever had in your life," I whispered.

And then I stabbed him in the neck with the syringe loaded down with the poison.

He growled and ripped me off him, throwing me to the floor. Cain tried to come after me, but the poison worked almost instantaneously, so he was able to lurch forward, and then his limbs stopped working and he just kind of... toppled over, his hard cock still hanging out.

I got to my feet and smoothed down my dress.

"Wha tha fu—" he garbled as the muscles in his throat stopped working.

I crouched down in front of him and smoothed a piece of his gold hair off his face. It was incredible how someone so incredibly fucked up...could look so perfect. I tucked his cock back into his pants—because I wasn't a monster.

"How does this feel, Cain? Being powerless. Does it feel good to have all your free will taken from you?" I murmured silkily as I stroked his face and looked into his eyes which were panicked and full of hate.

If I hadn't been accustomed to staring into someone's eyes and seeing pure evil, I might have been scared by the look in Cain's gaze.

Jenna burst through the door right then, her eyes wide and panicked. She came to a screeching halt when she saw me leaning over Cain.

"Wow. Is this some kind of weird sex thing? Because I can come back," she murmured, taking a step backward.

I shook my head at her. "Close that door and lock it," I hissed. I didn't want anyone to barge in until I was done with him.

Although what I was going to do to him, I hadn't quite decided yet.

Jenna closed it, and I heard the click of the lock. "Um,

not that I'm not 100% supportive of whatever this is...but what exactly is this?"

"I poisoned him," I said calmly, standing up and looking around the room for ideas as I heard her gasp.

Wait a minute...

"Do you know whose room this is?" I asked, walking over to a desk on the far side of the room that was loaded down with equipment. I sifted through stuff and almost screamed with delight when I realized what it was. It was tattoo equipment. There was a tattoo gun, and there were pots of ink.

"I bet this is that Tyson guy's room," I said out loud before Jenna could answer.

"This is where you get crazy, isn't it?" she asked, coming up beside me and looking at all the equipment.

"Any chance you can go make sure Tyson doesn't decide to come up here while I...play?" I asked Jenna.

"Um, are you going to do what I think you're going to do?"

I shrugged, already picking up the gun and selecting some black and pink ink. "YouTube can teach you anything, right?" I said.

As I walked back towards Cain with my supplies, it was definitely eerie that he was just lying there, perfectly still, his eyes moving around the room tracking my movements.

"Don't do anything you can't come back from," Jenna said softly before leaving the room, the door closing behind her with a soft click.

I strode over and locked it behind her before going back over to Cain.

"Let's see, what design should I do? I have to tell you that I almost failed art class, so let's just hope a miracle has happened and my skills have suddenly improved."

I laughed when his gaze flared in pure panic.

I pulled up my phone and found a video for the tattoo gun brand and watched it for about two minutes before I got bored and decided to just wing it.

I'd come up with a brilliant idea.

"Cain, you're constantly telling me that I belong to you. I've never heard the word 'mine' so much in my entire life until coming here. But everyone on this campus must not have gotten the memo that you belong to me as well. So I say, let's make sure it's obvious to them anytime they feel tempted to touch what's mine. What do you say to that?"

He was screaming at me so hard in his head right now I could almost hear it, and a giggle slipped from my lips.

I didn't really recognize myself in that moment, but I felt...wonderful.

I hummed as I pulled his pants down until the area right above his dick was showing, then I doused his skin with rubbing alcohol. I didn't know anything about tattooing, but making sure everything was clean seemed to make sense.

I didn't want to kill him.

I just wanted to make sure that for the rest of his life, no matter where our paths took us, he would always know that a piece of him belonged to me...just like a piece of me would always belong to him.

I took the tattoo gun and touched it to the skin. His eyes flashed with pain, and I pulled the gun away. "Oh, I'm sorry. Did that hurt? I wonder if it felt as bad as being chased in the dark butt naked and then forced to suck your cock? Does it hurt that bad?" I asked mockingly as I pressed the gun to his skin again and went to work.

In sprawling cursive, I wrote "Property of the Demon's Daughter" in black and hot pink across his skin so that anyone who came close to his dick wouldn't be able to miss it.

It took a while...and it kind of looked like a kindergartner had done it, but I was pretty proud.

I'd learned a new skill.

I set the gun down and picked up my phone to take a picture. For posterity's sake, of course.

"Smile," I said wickedly before snapping a picture. And a few more just for good measure.

"No smile. That's bold. Makes you look super mysterious. I like it," I joked, cracking myself up because I'd obviously lost my mind.

I was taking some closeups of the tattoo when I heard Jenna's voice through the door. "Aurora, I lost Tyson," she whisper yelled.

I stood up and lazily stretched before grabbing the equipment and putting it back on the desk. Then I walked over and let Jenna in. She was sweating and looked like she was the one who'd just temporarily paralyzed someone and given them a tattoo. "What did you end up—" Her words abruptly dropped off as she looked down and saw Cain's tattoo.

It was hilarious to see her gaze go back and forth between Cain and me, her mouth gaped open in complete shock.

"I mean, I told you 'bat shit crazy', did I not?" I asked lightly as I kneeled down to pull Cain's pants up higher before patting his cheek. His eyes were literally staring daggers at me. It was kind of an amazing thing how much just the eyes could tell you. The rest of his face was completely relaxed and serene.

"I'm going to definitely start thinking bigger when it

comes to you," she murmured. She crossed her arms in front of her and shifted uneasily. "So what do we do next?"

"We go back to the party. The stuff will wear off in a couple of hours, and then he'll try and kill me. So we might as well have fun in the meantime." I moved Cain's head so that it was facing the door. I wanted him to watch me walk away.

She gaped at me. "You are on a whole other level. And I'm not sure I'm capable of this kind of creativity."

I snickered and then took her arm and headed towards the door. I stopped at the threshold and looked back over my shoulder. "If I forget to tell you tonight...I had a really good time," I told him, blowing him a kiss.

"You just quoted *Pretty Woman*," said Jenna dryly.

"Name a better movie," I said as I closed the door behind us.

"I mean, the list is long."

We both burst into hysterics as we started down the stairs, stepping over the pile of vomit that someone had left in the middle of the stairs.

When we got to the main floor, it was like stepping into a sauna. The cold air coming in the still open front door combined with the humid air from the sweaty masses of people dancing made the room look almost hazy.

I was running high on adrenaline from what I'd done upstairs, almost like I was drunk, and Jenna didn't even have to cajole me into jumping right into the fray. In that moment, I didn't care about the dirty looks, I didn't care about the smell, I didn't care about the people knocking into me. All I cared about was that upstairs, the king of this college had been marked by me. And even if he tried to get it removed, the memory of laying there on the floor while I did whatever I wanted to him...it would stay in his mind forever.

And that was the best fucking thing I'd ever heard.

Jenna and I danced and sang along to *Mr. Brightside*. Evidently, the whole party was throwback night because every song was from grade school. It was awesome.

Even though I was well aware of the clock ticking down in my head to when the poison would wear off, I was still surprised at how quickly an hour had passed. And I had to pee. Badly.

"I'll be right back," I told Jenna who had a pretty cute guy grinding up on her. She winked at me and gave me a thumbs-up, and I had a little flashback to that first party once again.

My, how things had changed.

The bathrooms were upstairs, and I trotted up the stairs, noting that there was another vomit pile added to the first. It was only a matter of time before some drunk person slid on the vomit all the way down the stairs.

The bathrooms were just down the hall from the room I'd left Cain in, so of course, I glanced at the door as I passed.

It was ajar.

I bit my lip, wondering if Tyson had wandered in, and then sighed as a suspicious emotion inside of me that I refused to acknowledge forced me to check it out.

I walked to the door and pushed it all the way open.

And a fucking red haze filled my vision.

That girl who'd had her hand in his back pocket was straddling him and palming his cock as he stared up at her in horror, still unable to move.

I sprang into the room and grabbed her by the hair before throwing her off Cain. She screamed as I pulled on her long locks so hard I was surprised her hair didn't all rip out.

I pulled up Cain's pants so his dick was tucked back in and only my tattoo peeked from his pants. I yanked her head so it was just a few inches away from the marking.

"Do you see this, bitch?" I hissed, shaking her head forcibly as she cried and screamed. "Or can you not read?" I smashed her head against the ground and her nose burst open as it broke, spraying blood everywhere. "I want you to tell all your little friends that you tried to touch something that wasn't yours. And if I ever see your face again, I'm going to cut out your eyes and feed them to you," I said calmly before smashing her face against the floor once more for good measure before letting her go.

She staggered to her feet, sobbing hysterically and mumbling nonsensically. The girl tried to make it to the door, but she was definitely not capable of walking in a straight line after the concussion I'd just given her, so it took a minute.

She was lucky I hadn't cut off her hands. I must have been feeling charitable today.

After she'd finally disappeared through the door, I pulled out my phone and texted Remington:

Pick up for you at the hockey house. And you might want to hurry...

He immediately texted back:

What did you do, little devil?

I just had a little craft time after the party got boring, I typed back before locking the door and pocketing my phone.

I glanced down at Cain who was staring up at me... looking confused.

"I told you that you belonged to me, Cain," I whispered,

wiping some of the blood on my hand off on his shirt before standing up.

I left the room again, locking the door behind me this time, which, let's face it...I should have done the first time. I blamed the fact that I'd been a little too intoxicated with power to think straight at that moment.

Happened to the best of us.

Finally peeing, I tried my best to get rid of at least some of the blood spray covering my skin with some paper towels and water from the sink. Thank goodness for black dresses. At least you couldn't tell by my clothes I was soaked in blood.

After cleaning up, I casually walked down the stairs and back out into the mass of people. There was no sign of the girl I'd destroyed, and no one looked like they'd just seen a bloody, broken girl running by. But maybe these people were used to those things.

A flashback of the red punch being thrown all over me at that party crashed through my mind.

Yeah, maybe they just didn't care about things like that.

I looked over to the dance floor and immediately locked eyes with Jenna who was still dancing with the same guy. "Everything okay?" she mouthed, and I nodded before moving, melting into the crowd and situating myself against the wall so I had a view of the front door...and the staircase.

It only took about five minutes for Remington, Paxton, and Stellan to come through the doors and silence the whole crowd. At least they had taken me seriously. They'd been very timely in their response. Maybe they were finally starting to learn that I didn't fuck around.

Although they definitely didn't fuck around either.

I briefly wondered why Cain had been by himself tonight before I got distracted by them looking around the crowd, I assumed for me. I slipped behind one of the fancy, pretentious Corinthian columns in the room and watched as they moved through the room towards where the drink buckets were. People were panting as they watched them, their faces lighting up with hope as they approached, thinking they might speak to them. The girls would push out their boobs, the guys would stiffen their shoulders and try their best to look cool.

It was all pathetic looking, really.

When would they realize that men like the kings considered everyone else to be sheep? They were nothing to them.

It kind of turned me on to watch the guys cut through the crowd like a pack of predators. They moved like a unit, totally in sync with each other. They didn't spend very much time in that room before they were heading back towards me. I braced for them to search the crowd where I was standing, but they headed up the stairs without a glance.

I was kind of wishing for a camera as I pictured them searching the rooms for the surprise I'd left them. They would probably think Cain was dead at first when they saw him, with all the blood and whatnot.

People went back to partying after the guys disappeared upstairs, although I did notice a high number of people suddenly having a need to go upstairs. The bathroom was probably a happening place right about now.

I was getting bored as I waited for them to come downstairs, and I was tempted just to leave. Maybe they were going to wait it out in that room until Cain "came back to life." That probably made the most sense. Or maybe they were going to call an ambulance.

I was about to give up and leave when Paxton came pounding down the stairs, his face a completely blank mask. I watched in confusion as he walked over to the large room where everyone was dancing, and he raised his fist. "Let's get wasted," he yelled before he began to walk through the crowd who once again parted like the Red Sea as he passed through until he got to the buckets. I snorted as everyone began to offer him red cups filled to the brim with the house drink.

My attention was so focused on Paxton that I almost missed Remington and Stellan walking down the stairs with Cain in between them. Which would have been the point of Paxton's little show, to distract from Cain. It looked like the poison was wearing off. He just looked really, really drunk as he struggled to help Remington and Stellan get him out the door. You had to be looking closely, or know Cain really well to notice that his eyes were completely alert...and enraged.

Giddy anticipation surged through me as they disappeared through the front door that had somehow miraculously cleared.

I pulled out my phone. *You good?* I texted Jenna, not wanting to go into the same room where Paxton was holding court, suddenly the most gregarious person I'd ever seen. She responded a few seconds later:

This guy is so fucking cute. I'm getting lucky.

I smiled, feeling a dash of wistfulness that I wished I didn't. What would it be like to meet a guy, a normal guy, and get butterflies that didn't end up in spankings, bloodshed, and being hunted down like an animal in the dark?

Probably completely boring.

Or at least that's what the crazy part inside of me whispered.

Let me know when you're back at your dorm, I texted back before heading towards the front door.

I'd just gotten to the door when I felt Paxton's gaze

slicing across my back. I turned and looked back, not surprised at all when I saw him standing in the middle of the room, his eyes definitely on me.

I waggled two fingers at him and then winked before turning and striding out into the night.

All in all, a great fucking night.

And the fun was just beginning. Whatever Cain came up with to punish me was guaranteed to be good.

I couldn't wait.

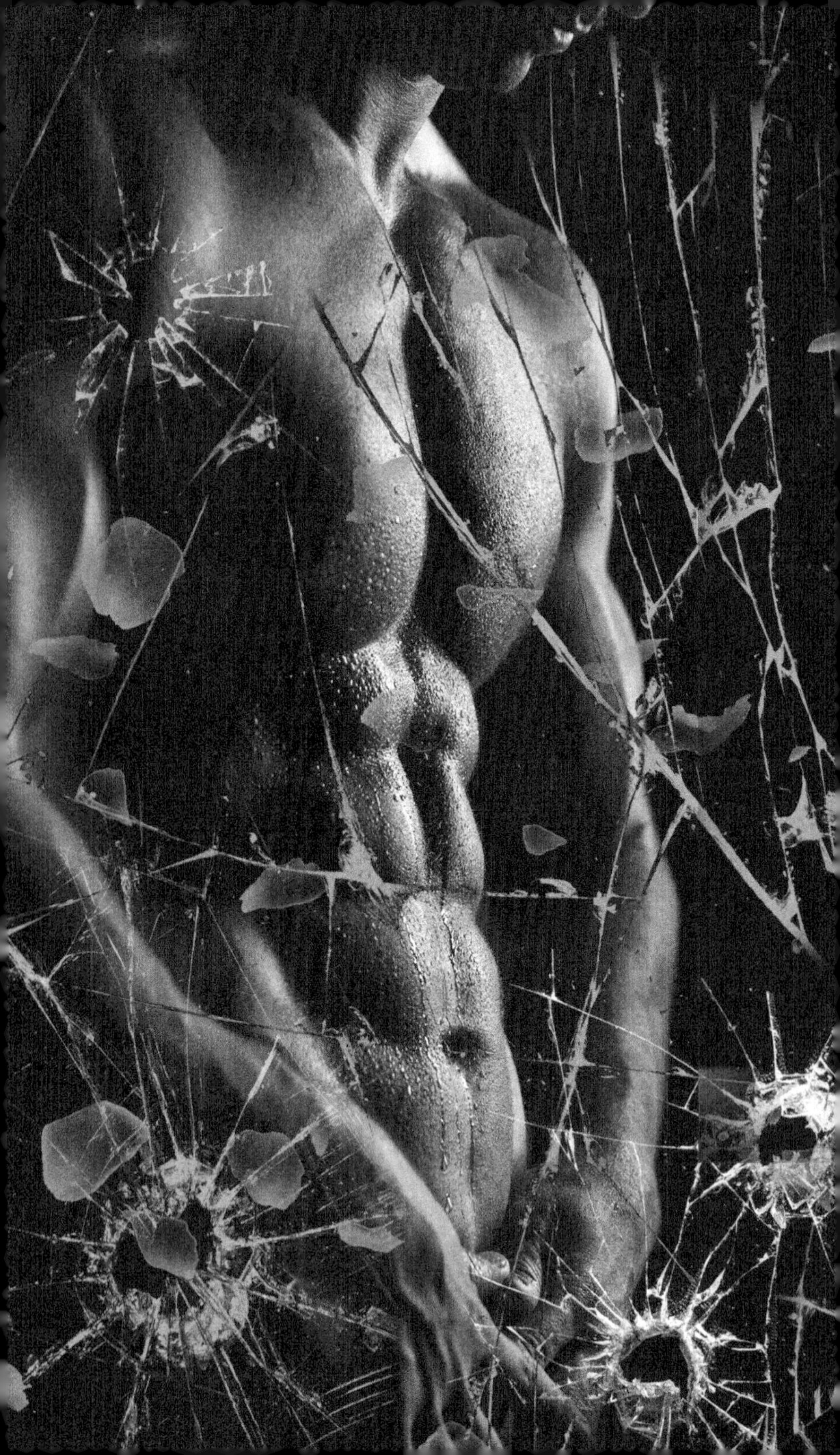

12

AURORA

I woke up in the morning in the quiet of my room and smiled to myself as I gazed up at the ceiling. I'd *slept* last night, as well as I'd slept in Pax's arms before he betrayed me. But I didn't need Paxton. I didn't need any of these men.

I rolled onto my side. It was still early; I slept with the curtains wide open because it made me feel a little less trapped—even if the windows were nailed shut—and for now, the world outside the Sphinx was as dark as it was inside.

That was why I caught the faintest light emanating from the electric outlet opposite my bed. I frowned and rolled out of bed, staring at it.

It was a camera.

Suddenly keenly aware someone might be watching me as I watched *them,* I forced myself to yawn and rub my hands across my face sleepily, pretending to be casual when my heart was beating a wild tattoo against my ribs. If the guys were watching me, well, maybe I would give them a show. I could definitely have the chance to use this against them. I could use this to feed them misinformation on where I was going and what I was up to. I couldn't wait to send them running off in the wrong direction.

But like every weapon I could employ against these men, I'd get one shot and one shot only. I had to make it count.

I quickly got dressed, then pretended to be reading a message on my cell phone. "Jenna," I whispered as I shook my head and grinned, hoping the watcher would think I was heading off for an early morning study session.

I headed out of the room, wondering what other cameras might be watching me. I hid inside the house behind the door of an empty room in the hallway and watched as Cain stumbled out of his room, looking pissed as hell.

He banged on Remington's door until a sleepy-looking Remington yanked it open. "What?" Remington demanded.

"What the fuck," Cain said. "Can you believe what your little devil did?"

"She's mine now?" Remington sounded amused as he crossed his arms over his chest, leaning in the doorway, which earned him a glower from Cain. "I guess she was extra naughty this time."

"I assume this is because *you* fucked with her and now she's out for blood. Christ." Cain sounded so genuinely grouchy and upset that I had to press my hand over my lips to smother my laugh. God, these men were a delight.

Cain turned around and kicked open my bedroom door. It splintered under the force of the impact, swinging wildly off the hinges before it slammed to the floor. He stepped on the door as he stormed into my room. I wrenched down on my lower lip, trying to keep from laughing, but I was dying. He was so big and scary and throwing such a tantrum, it was hilarious. The look on his face was a memory I was going to tuck away to bring out whenever I had a bad day.

Thinking about being a thousand miles away from these men and having only memories was odd, and it felt like a strange tugging inside my chest. It already felt as if we'd been tied together for years.

Time flies when you're having...well, not fun exactly. Time flies when you have psychopaths?

"She's gone." Cain seemed even more put-out as he stepped back over the groaning shards of the door.

"I hope she didn't leave forever," Remington said mildly.

"Never mind that. Come with me," Cain ordered.

Remington rolled his eyes. "Save the dominant routine for Aurora. *She* thinks it's cute."

The two of them left together anyway, though.

I took the opportunity to slip down the hall and into Cain's room. It would be no surprise to me if he wanted a constant video feed of my room. He brought *possessive bastard* to new and previously uncharted levels.

I sat down at his long wooden desk–trying to push down the memories of touching myself on this desk–and opened his laptop. I searched it thoroughly but didn't find any sign of a camera feed. Frowning, I moved to the doorway and listened carefully before rushing down the hall to Remington's room.

His door was locked–what an untrusting bastard–and it took me a few long seconds to work my lockpicks. Then I slid inside his room and looked around.

Cain had one sleek Macbook, but Remington had multiple computers and half-a-dozen monitors; his custom-made L-shaped desk took up a big portion of his oversized room. His room was full of bookshelves stuffed with books, and I was curious to see what the titles were if I hadn't had a mission.

I needed to know which one of them was watching me so I could plan my attack. I might even be able to change their feed when I needed to so they wouldn't know I was gone.

But I couldn't access the feed from anywhere on Remington's computer. I frowned at the screen, tugging at the end of my hair absently.

I opened his email and began to look through his messages.

One of them had the subject line PRESENT FOR YOU, and I would've thought it was a random porn email except that it was starred automatically, as if the sender was important to Remington. I opened it.

Inside was nothing but a photograph.

It showed a little boy, his face twisted and tear tracks down his cheeks, crying so hard it looked as if he couldn't catch his breath. It was so upsetting and shocking that I clicked X to exit.

I took a deep, steadying breath. My father used to make me watch the most awful videos where kids were being tortured, hurt, raped when I was a child myself. He said that I had to understand the men who were hurting them in those videos, because they were our prey. Then I'd helped him to lure those men off the streets so my father and I could torture them.

The things I'd seen were seared into my brain, but I'd almost managed to forget them. Now I had to press my hand over my mouth and breathe slowly through my nose as I tried to fight down the bile rising up my throat.

Remington.

Involved in hurting kids.

I thought he was a monster in so many ways, and yet I was shocked he could hurt kids. Remington wasn't that kind of man...I'd thought.

Did this mean they were all like this? Remington, Pax, Cain, even Stellan? Stellan seemed so caring about his sister...but then, Carrie Hayward had turned into a serial killer as he grew up in the shadow of his missing, kidnapped brother. His family pain hadn't prevented him from turning into a monster; maybe it had helped make him one.

I forced myself to open the email again, to take a better look at the photo. This time, I memorized the background. This time, I noticed that his tiny wrists were bound with a wide leather strap–something to prevent bruising, something that took a lot of premeditation. This time, I searched for any clues about who he was and where. It had been sent early this morning, after Remington went out with Cain. He hadn't seen it yet.

I was going to save this kid.

And I was going to kill Remington.

If nothing else, I should be able to follow Remington if he went to meet this child himself. Or maybe he was directing films, just for money, and he wouldn't be going anywhere. The dark possibilities swirled through my mind, and they included not just how I'd protect this boy like no one ever protected me, but how I'd torture Remington. I had the skills.

Maybe I should stop denying my potential.

His email chimed as another email came in. Same address.

We both want to see you today. Noon.

Relief flooded me. Remington was going to go, and I was going to follow him.

I had my way forward to rescue this kid.

I quickly made it look as if all Remington's emails were unread. Then I heard a sound in the hallway, just outside the door, and I froze with my fingers over the keys.

There was the scrape of a key over a lock.

Remington was home.

13

AURORA

I got down on my belly and squirmed under Remington's bed. Luckily, someone kept his room so clean that it smelled like pine under his bed. Someone else, because I was sure Remington had never touched a mop. I didn't know why these guys were such assholes when they'd lived such perfect lives.

My bare feet touched the cool wall opposite me. I made it completely under the bed and twitched the rumpled blankets that hung from the bed just before the door opened.

Remington walked in and threw his keys on top of his dresser, then turned to face whoever was outside the door. "I don't know, Cain. Maybe you should tell her that you're sorry."

Cain stepped into his room, scoffing at that suggestion. Then Cain's nostrils flared. "Did you have Aurora in your room?"

"No. I leave the cuddling to Pax."

"Well, it smells like her."

"Oh, really?" Remington looked amused. "Okay, Mr. Bloodhound. What exactly does she smell like?"

"You know," Cain said.

"I don't. I apparently don't have your skills–you're like a fucking sommelier and that girl is a fine wine."

Cain scoffed. "She's Smirnoff Ice, at best."

"You don't believe that for a second."

Cain crossed his arms and stared him down. "She smells like coconut. You seriously don't smell it on her? I couldn't find her perfume in her room."

That asshole had searched my room.

Well, I would've felt violated if I hadn't been hiding under Remington's bed.

"Were you going to make the next girl you fuck wear her perfume?" Remington asked with a laugh.

"Give me a break. I'm not like Stellan; I can fuck another girl."

What? Stellan couldn't stand to be with anyone but me?

"And yet, you haven't." Remington threw himself into his chair and grinned at his friend. His fingers danced over the keyboard.

"I'm going to breakfast," Cain said.

Remington went still, staring at the screen ahead of him. "Okay." His voice sounded flat and dead. "I'll be right there."

Maybe he didn't like what he was involved in. I chewed my lip, wondering if there was any way he could be an unwilling participant. But I couldn't let myself turn stupid and weak for these guys. I'd been too trusting with them already…and that was how I'd ended up covered in blood. I'd fallen for their bullshit once. Never again.

My version of Occam's Razor: the worst answer is probably the right one.

Cain cocked his head to one side. "You all right?"

"Golden."

Cain looked unconvinced, but he left. Remington buried his face in his hands, then got up. He quickly dressed in jeans and a dark t-shirt that clung over his shoulders, then tucked a handgun into a holster at the small of his back before he pulled on a thick wool sweater that hid the gun. Then he went out.

Fuck. *Fuck.* Remington was going to be armed. Ideally, I'd have to get the kid away without him seeing me at all.

I crawled out from under the bed and went to the safe in the closet where Remington had taken his gun, but it was locked. It would be nice if the man were a bit more careless; I could pick my way through a lot of doors, but I couldn't beat the safe.

I headed into the hallway and made my way down the hall, trying to move quietly, because I needed to get out of the house without the guys seeing me.

Just as I walked past Stellan's door, it opened.

Fuck my life.

"Delilah?" Stellan stood there with rumpled hair and a look I couldn't quite make sense of. He looked like he was the one who had the nightmares.

"What?" I put all my disdain into my voice, but worse, all my boredom.

Stellan hurt me the worst when he betrayed me.

But why couldn't I stand to punish him?

I saw his sister's face when I looked at him. That's what I kept telling myself.

Stellan winced, then raked his hand through his hair, as if my tone had actually bothered him. "Come in here."

He stepped back from the door. I shouldn't be as much of my own curiosity's bitch as I am, but I walked inside.

"I haven't been in here since we slept together," I observed as I walked inside, because my life had sucked too much for me to feel the need to filter my thoughts. "Oh, the memories."

Stellan sighed. "You're not going to make this easy."

"I'm not going to make this easy? What exactly do you want from me, Stellan?"

"I want to make a deal with you."

This should be good. "What, exactly, is your deal?"

"Just tell me where she's buried." His voice was calm, the same Stellan I'd grown up with who was the cool, unshakeable tall athlete that every girl worshiped. But there was something feral and dangerous in his eyes. "That's all I need to know, Aurora. Just help me bring her home."

"I don't know where she is, Stellan."

I moved to go around him, and he grabbed my shoulders, pushing me against the wall. His big body dominated me, but no matter how hard his fingers bit into my shoulders, his eyes gave away how lost he was.

"Our mother spends every night in Sophia's bed," Stellan ground out. "She can't move on. Can't sleep. My mom just lays there under her blankets, watching the window...as if she can make Sophia climb back through it."

I winced at the thought. Stellan's mom had been so cheerful and teasing, just like Stellan's sister. It was painful to imagine her forever devastated. My mother had walked away from me at that gas station with a smile on her face; I wondered if she ever even thought about me.

"Delilah," he said, the way he used to say my name. The way he changed what name he called me every time made me feel as if we both changed, over and over, flip-flopping between who he'd been in the past when we were innocent and the jaded assholes we'd turned into. "Please."

His *please* was jagged enough to cut us both.

"If I could, I'd give you what you wanted," I said.

"I can fix everything," he said. "Just tell me where she is. I'll get you out of this house, I'll get you money. I'll give you everything you need."

He sounded so desperate–it made me hurt for him, but it also made something painful tighten in my chest.

I reached up and tapped his cheek, ever so lightly. His bright eyes watched me greedily.

"I don't need you to give me back my money and my freedom," I said. "I need you to stop being a fucking idiot and see what's right in front of you. See that I never would have hurt her. I loved her."

His eyes flared in a way that didn't make sense. She was my best friend; of course I'd loved her.

"You did?" he asked.

God, he just kept cutting me and I kept letting him, as if I were the one holding myself down on my father's operating table.

"I'm sorry for your loss and for how your family is suffering, Stellan. I'd do anything to fix it if I could," I said. "But also, fuck you."

I flashed him a smile and a wave and headed out.

Time to ruin Remington's life.

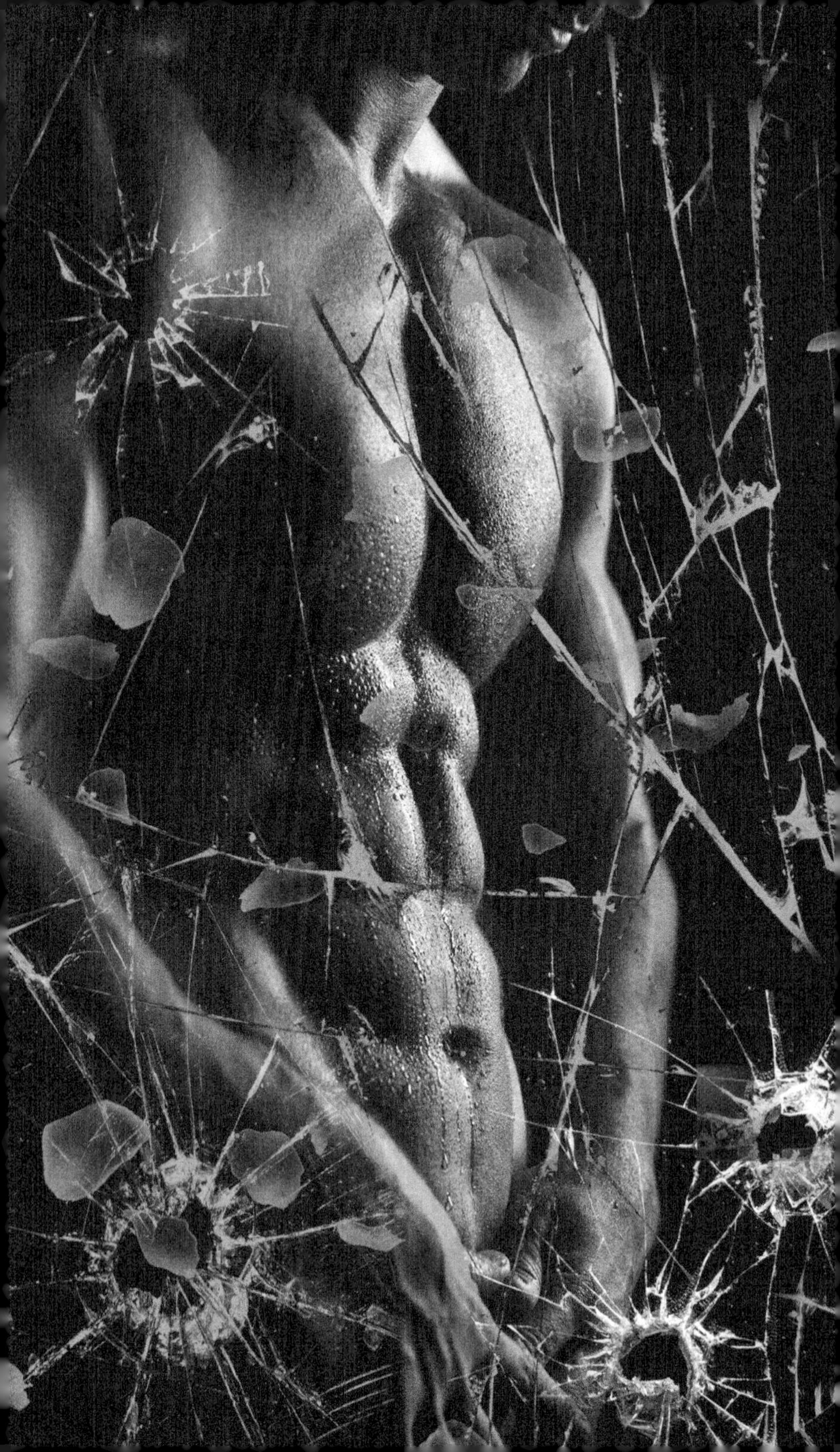

14

AURORA

Following Remington was going to be a real pain in my ass. I wasn't eager to commit a felony. I'd done enough of those to last a girl a lifetime. But I needed a way to follow Remington, my car's tires were still in ribbons, and I didn't think Uber was going to do it for me.

The Demon had made sure I was an excellent lock pick and car thief by the time I hit middle school. He hadn't been the best father, but I had to admit he taught me some useful skills.

I stole a Honda Civic out of one of the student lots, hoping that the owner would stay nice and hungover from a good time the night before.

Maybe I shouldn't have burned Cain's McLaren. It was rude of me. And that also meant that I couldn't use it. He would probably have been my first choice to steal from. I bet it would be fun to drive his McLaren and know it made him furious, to be the one controlling that stick he claimed women rode to masturbate for his amusement.

I followed Remington. Despite all of his skills, he probably didn't know very much about avoiding a tail.

At least not a tail that had as much practice as I had. I'd spent a lot of time casing our future victims.

I followed Remington to an enormous brick mansion on the edge of the city. He sped, of course. His muscle car taking the corners so quickly I had to let more space grow between the two of us. There was no surprise there. It's not like these men seemed like the type to have much respect for speed limits.

When I got there, he was pulling through the gates toward the house that was barely visible around the curve and the tall trees that lined the drive. The gate was closing behind him, but that was okay. I wasn't too worried about the gate.

I palmed the tiny fraction of poison that I still carried and had a little left behind. I wanted Remington to understand what was happening to him. God, it hurt even more because I'd cared about him; I had let myself call them *monsters* almost affectionately, I could see that now. I'd believed they were dangerous and ruthless but nothing like the Demon.

Remington had ruined all the games. I felt a strange sense of loss about that. For a brief moment, I hadn't even wanted to truly escape these men. I'd wanted to keep playing with them.

Stupid, I muttered to myself. And that wasn't directed towards Remington. That was all me. Monsters are what they are.

I tried to make them too complicated. I scaled the fence and climbed and dropped down on the other side, then I made my way toward the bushes around the house.

I caught a glimpse of Remington, his posture perfect, his hands stuffed into his pockets, sauntering toward the house. He looked so relaxed that I felt a jolt of fury, although I knew how much that could be a mask for him sometimes. I watched him enter the house without knocking, then I crept along, bent over between the hedges and the house, keeping my head beneath the level of the windows. I had to find Remy in the house.

When I was hiding in the hedge, a dog came barreling straight toward me. Fear jolted my heart into my mouth. It had always made me feel worse to take someone when they had a dog, both because I was afraid of being bitten and because dogs loved their people, even the evil ones, so fiercely. I'd always been afraid of dogs and wished for one at the same time. But I'd never have dared to bring a pet into the Demon's house. He wouldn't have tolerated me having anyone but him.

The dog was baying fiercely, then slammed through the hedges and stared me down as if I were captured prey.

From inside the house, I heard someone ask, "What's that goddamn dog hunting down now?"

Great. I never wanted to hurt an animal, but this was not a complication that I needed right now.

I stared the dog down as it snapped at me. Rottweiler, black with brown patches, ropey with muscle, and a face that might've been cute if it weren't growling. It stopped just a few feet away from me and growled again, obviously ready to pounce. Its black ears were flattened back and its teeth flashed menacingly.

I dug in my pocket and pulled out the last bit of poison. It wouldn't hurt the dog, not permanently. I had to hope this was the only vicious attack dog that the house had besides Remington himself, of course.

I threw the poison into the dog's mouth as he jumped at me, knowing I only had one shot. His mouth snapped shut in shock. He lunged forward to attack me but collapsed in the dirt at my feet.

As soon as I was sure the dog wasn't going to attack me, I dragged it into the bushes, hiding it behind the hedge along the wall. From here, I could hear a man pacing around inside, talking on his cell phone.

Abruptly, he said, "I've got to go. Remington is here."

I petted the dog absently as I listened. One of its big brown eyes rolled up to watch me as I gently stroked its coat.

"Good afternoon," the man said.

"What do you want?" Remington demanded, his voice curt. Strained, almost.

"You've been lying to me." The man's fury sounded as if it were tightly lashed down but there right under the surface, and it made my stomach knot as if it were my own father. "You know that's unacceptable. It's one thing for you to manipulate, to lie, to *them*. But I have to know the full truth so I am prepared when you fuck up...as usual."

The sense that maybe I'd misread the whole situation prickled at the back of my neck. Something about Remington in this situation made me feel uneasy.

"There are consequences, Remington."

"It looks as if there already *were* consequences."

"That was just to get you here. I knew you'd be too much of a coward to face up to consequences without some...motivation."

Remington heaved a sigh. "Let me get him out of there first. Then you can do whatever you called me here for."

Him? Was Remington here to rescue the kid? Was this the opposite of what I'd thought?

"No. I think that ridiculous secret society of yours has made you arrogant. But this family made you who you are, and you might live outside it, but you'll never leave it."

"I guess you've never seen those refrigerator magnets that say *friends are the family you choose*," Remington said mildly.

"Why are you always such a fucking idiot?"

"A question that I ask myself every day."

"Always making everything into a joke. Well, make this into a joke, Remington."

I couldn't see whatever made Remington go silent. I tried to move into position to see through the window, but decided the voices were too close to the window and it was too dangerous. My curiosity wasn't as important as protecting the kid inside.

I decided I had to go in and get him while Remington and this asshole distracted each other. Worst case scenario, at least I was able to help the kid.

I made it to the front door and got in, knowing there were video cameras watching me–Remington's kind loved cameras–but the footage wouldn't matter until later. The mansion wasn't quite grand enough to suggest it had its own human security twenty-four-seven.

When I let myself into the grand two-story foyer, with dark tiled floors underfoot, I heard someone vacuuming on the second floor, but there were no housekeepers in sight. I moved quietly and swiftly down the hall, briefly taking in lots of framed paintings on the walls and expensive furniture.

The door to the room Remington and the man were in was open, so I hesitated for a second to one side of the doorway, then moved swiftly and silently across the opening. Speed was my friend here.

And curiosity was my enemy, yet I glanced to the right as I stepped. I caught the briefest glimpse of Remington's gaze meeting mine, Remington's bare chest, the man behind him. For just a second, Remington's gaze seared into mine.

Then I was on the other side, and I couldn't see either of them anymore. My breath had frozen in my chest, and now it seemed my heart beat impossibly fast. I expected Remington to yell.

The house was eerily silent.

Then there was the sound of leather meeting flesh—a loud crack of a sound, more dramatic than Cain's belt. By a lot.

What the hell? Were all the rich people beating each other behind the walls of their fancy mansions? Did money re-wire people's brains so they all went a little bit Caligula?

Shaking my head, I kept moving to try to rescue the kid. I searched the house as quickly as I could, ignoring the jolt and shiver that went up my spine every time the lash landed. The vacuum cleaner shut off on the second floor, and I hid behind a doorway as a woman left the house. She went out the backdoor and drove away in a battered little Honda. Could that possibly be his mom? Or was it a housekeeper?

What the fuck was going on here?

At least she'd given me the chance to search the house. Even upstairs, I could hear it; the vacuum cleaner was abandoned in one of the bedrooms upstairs. Had she left the house because even over the vacuum cleaner, she could hear—or just because she knew what was happening? A disquieting thought wiggled into my brain...did she love Remington? Was it all hard for her to bear?

I'd thought Remington was here for a business matter. But maybe it was a family matter instead.

I quickly searched the bedrooms, and the closets too, but all I saw were a lot of fancy brands I'd never owned and no sign of criminal misdeeds. The house was eerily clean and quiet.

Then I reached the master bedroom, and walked into a room where a woman was lying on the bed. I froze, afraid she'd seen me, but she was staring in my direction with glazed eyes. I thought at first she was dead, then realized she was just drugged.

What the hell was happening in this house?

I stopped and stared at the painting that hung at the top of the grand stairs down to the first floor.

A man, a woman, a young ruddy-cheeked version of Remington...and two dark-haired younger children.

One of them was the boy in the photo, the one in Remington's email.

Fuck.

The feeling I'd fucked this up burnt in my gut. I hurried down the stairs, replaying that flash when Remington saw me. He'd looked...relieved.

As if I were going to rescue him.

His hands hadn't been bound. He'd come here willingly.

So the only way to help him was to help his siblings.

I headed for the basement stairs. There'd been a lock on the door that led down. It was just a little suspicious.

It took me a long minute to unlock the door. Every time that jolt cracked through the house, I bit my lower lip. It took me right back to the Demon's earlier tortures. By the time Remington let out a broken gasp of a cry, my lower lip had started to bleed.

I hustled down the basement stairs, turning on lights. Most of the basement seemed fun, a lot more fun than the basements I was used to. The basement was divided into several rooms with light gray floors and bright white walls that made it feel inviting; there was a full-sized wet bar, a round poker table, and Foozball. I could picture Remington with his friends, hanging out.

Then I turned the corner and found the cages.

Suddenly, I could picture Remington spending his childhood years here.

They were both in dog cages, the dark-haired little boy from the photo and his twin sister. I hurried to unlock the cages, but then they refused to come out.

"Remington is waiting for you. He just sent me to help," I said, hoping like hell that actually made them feel more comfortable. I didn't want to think Remington was that kind of monster.

The little girl looked at me skeptically. "Are you Remington's girlfriend?"

If that would get her out of the cage... "Yes."

"He says you're crazy," she said.

"Probably true," I admitted, but also, holy shit, what was Remington saying about me? "But I'm also a good friend, and Remington wanted me to bring you out to the car."

The boy brightened, even though his speech came out a rasp. "He's finally taking us to live with him?"

Ugh, my heart.

"Yeah," I said. I held out my arms, trying to urge them out of there, afraid of what would happen if we didn't escape *now*. "But we've got to go."

I said it cheerfully, managing to hide all my horror.

I finally got them to come out, but the little boy seemed unsteady on his feet. I scooped him up to carry him, hating that now I'd be slower in a fight. The three of us steered toward the front entryway. When I could see the green trees out the windows near the front trees, I almost dared to breathe.

Then that awful sound again, and the boy in my arms jumped.

"Remington," the little girl said, and she went straight back into the house.

"Get back here," I whispered, but I didn't exactly ever have a part-time job babysitting; I didn't know the first thing about how to talk to kids. I didn't even know when I was a kid. She was already gone.

Reluctantly, I moved back into the house after her.

"We've got to get out of here," I whispered when I reached her, my voice barely audible. She had stopped just outside the room where Remington was. "Then I'll come back and rescue him."

"Is that so?" a mocking voice asked, and a man with a gun moved into view, stepping into the hall.

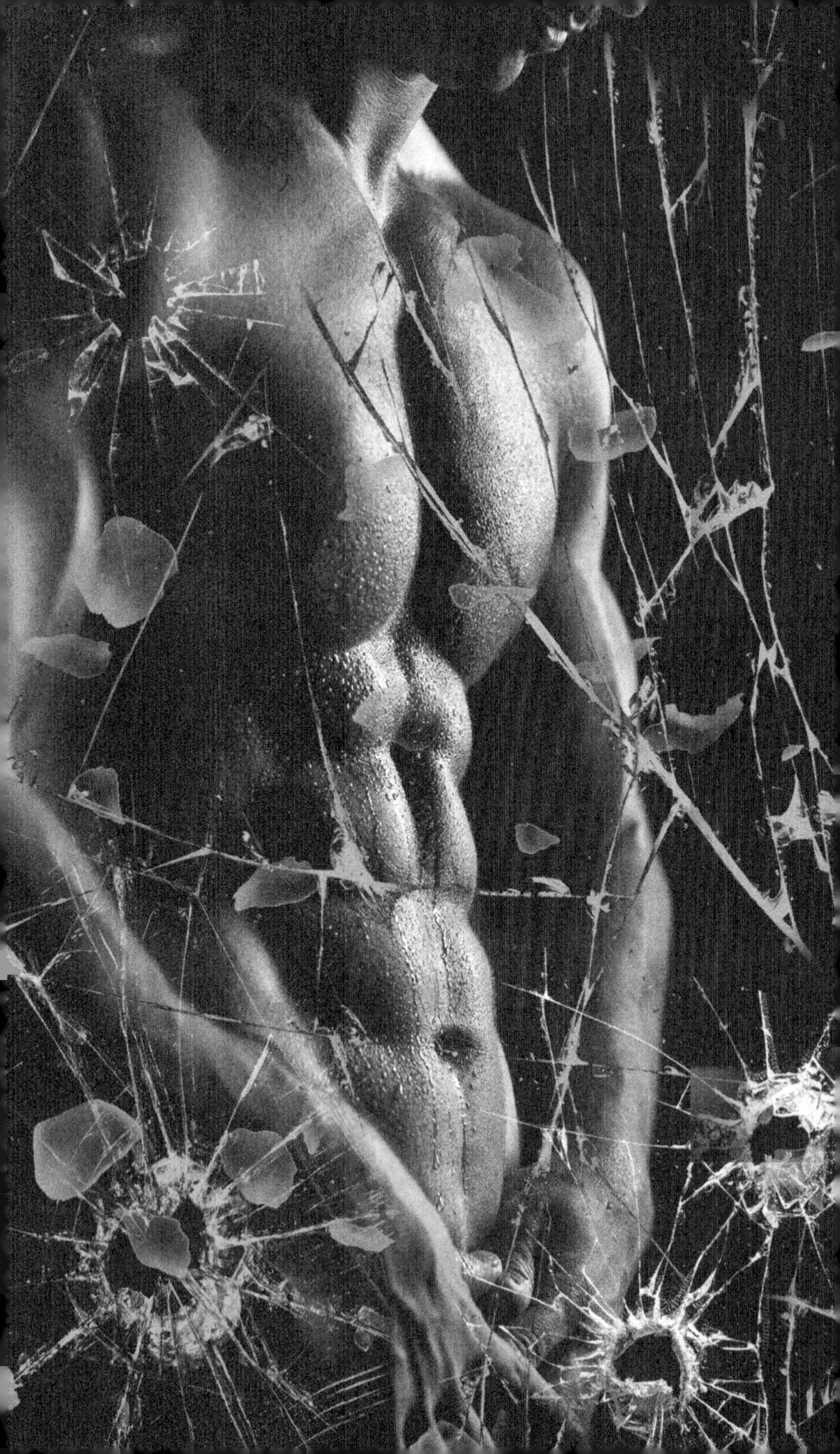

15

AURORA

My mind raced, and the kid in my arms froze, his arms looped tightly around my neck. Where was Remington's gun? Was it the one in the man's hand?

I was holding this guy's son. Would he really shoot through him to get to me?

Given what I had just seen, I had to assume this guy didn't give a damn about his kids.

Remington was pale, sweat beading along his hairline, and I realized he was dripping blood into the carpet. His gaze met mine, and I couldn't quite read his expression. Concern? Disappointment? Exasperation? Light-hearted Remington wasn't as easy-breezy as usual.

"What are you doing here?" the man demanded.

"I came to help these kids." I flashed him a tight smile. "I have ways of dealing with monsters."

I sounded pretty cocky, I realized, for someone on the wrong end of a gun. But I did have a lot of experience with being terrified.

"And who are you?" he demanded.

"I'm a friend of Remington's."

Remington gave the briefest shake of his head, warning me off, but it was too late.

The man huffed a laugh. "Oh, I know who you are, *Aurora*. I know I told my son to stay far away from you, but he couldn't follow a simple order any more than he could keep from lying about his grades."

"Remington's not lying about his grades. He pissed me off. So I set him up." I cocked my head to one side, studying Remington's father. "You didn't realize Remington's good grades were correct? He must get his intelligence from his mother's side."

Remington looked tensely coiled, but he glanced at me, his eyes widening faintly and his lips quirking in surprise. He didn't deserve for me to take his side, but here we were.

"Aurora, I can have the police here in two minutes," the man said. "If I were you, I'd get away from my children...and stay very far away."

"You'd really want the police here with the cages in the basement?" I asked.

"Let the kids go," Remington said. "Then let's talk this out."

The man hesitated. "Go upstairs to your mother," he told the kids, and they scattered, running up the stairs.

I breathed a sigh of relief once the kids were out of the direct line of fire. Now I just needed to keep Remington and myself alive.

"You can't keep doing this," Remington said. "You can't keep hurting them."

"You're the one hurting them, Remington. All you had to do was what I asked."

God, this guy reminded me of the Demon, and I felt both a twitch of irrational fear in my stomach and a deep desire to disembowel him because of it. "Why don't you put the gun down?"

Instead, he called, "Hey, King!"

"You named your dog King?" I asked, crossing my arms. "Not very imaginative."

Remington looked nervous. This guy must set the dog on people, and I wondered what Remington had seen before. But his dog wasn't coming.

"Listen," I told the guy, "I happen to have a cult of fanatic fans of my father watching my every move. They love nothing so much as torturing evil men to death and burying the bodies where no one will ever find them. If you ever touch those kids again, I'll set them on you."

"You can't control them," he scoffed, but he'd gone pale.

Color was returning to Remington's face, even though blood had pooled by his feet.

"You're going to get out of this house and leave them alone," I told him. "Your wife, your kids. And if you don't... well. I am the Demon's legacy."

"I could just shoot you now and the police would side with me over the daughter of a serial killer," he scoffed.

"You could," Remington said, then slammed into his father from behind. I dove forward, getting control of his gun hand. The gun discharged into the floor, the noise so loud it blew my eardrums out.

Then I had the gun in my hand.

Remington smiled at his father. "We'll wait while you pack a bag...Warren."

Warren. That was the perfect name for the asshole.

His father fled, but from the look we shared, Remington

knew as well as I did that beating his father wouldn't be that easy. This was just the first step in my plan.

"Why was he hurting you?" I asked Remington.

"My grades," he said. "Well, the scandal, really. Bringing bad attention to the family." His gaze flickered to my eyes, then fell to my lips, before he admitted, "and seeing you."

The thought of his father hurting these kids–and him–because of me rankled. "You don't have a choice in seeing me. I'm living in the Sphinx."

"You know what I mean." Remington frowned at me, looking confused. "After everything I did...why did you come to help me? How did you even know?"

"I saw your email." I debated telling him what I thought he'd done, but decided against it.

"How?"

"A girl has to have her secrets, Remington."

"Were you serious about the cult?"

"I hate them," I said. "But I wasn't joking that I could probably successfully set them on your father." I mused it over. "The only thing I wasn't serious about? *Waiting.*"

This man was a threat, and I intended to eliminate him.

Remington scrubbed a hand over his face. "Aurora. I don't get it."

"I'm not a monster, Remington. Simple as that." I also wasn't a girl who forgave that easily, no matter that I'd be on Remington's side against his father. "Hey, I had an idea. I think it's about time your father started passing some of the family assets on to you, hmm?"

A grin spread across Remington's face. "Nothing would make him crazier. He's always controlled the money in this house with an iron fist."

"We'll fix that together," I said. "You and I can work together to get the money out of his accounts."

Much of it would go to Remington's family. I wanted to make sure his little siblings had everything they needed.

The rest?

Well, Remington owed me.

In every way.

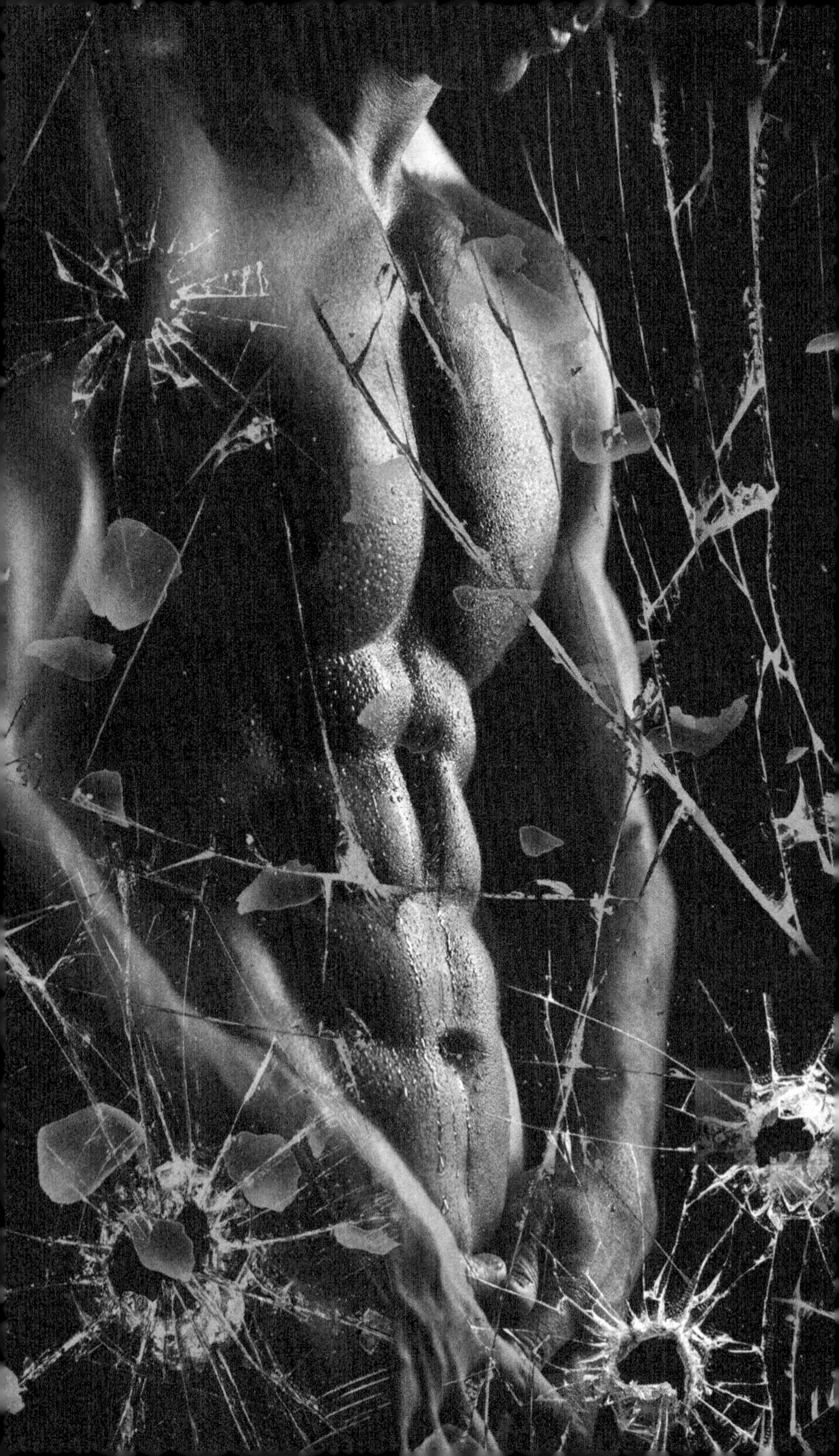

16

REMINGTON

My mother was flying high as always. Once my father was out of the house–off to his vacation house, he wasn't exactly flirting with homelessness–I called my aunt. It was up to my mom if she was going to rehab; it wasn't as if I could force her to leave the stupor my father had encouraged/forced for the past few years. But the twins could stay with my aunt until I could take over as their guardian if my mom wasn't able.

I couldn't exactly bring them into the Sphinx.

They clung to me when we said goodbye. I hated having Aurora see such a sensitive family moment. I would've hated anyone seeing my weaknesses like that though.

I'd wanted to save my little brother and sister for years. When I still lived in that house, I'd wanted to save them even more than I wanted to save myself. They'd been born way smaller than they should have been, thanks to my mother continuing to abuse substances throughout her pregnancy. My dad hadn't wanted her to get pregnant in the first place after me, so he'd hated them the moment they'd come into existence.

But me? I'd seen their two squirming, tiny bodies.

And I'd fallen in love with them instantly, promising myself that I'd do whatever it took to keep them safe.

A promise I'd broken over and over again despite my best intentions.

So how come Aurora had been able to come in and do what I couldn't accomplish in all that time? I knew it wasn't going to be that simple, and I needed to prepare for my father's counter-attack. But for now, they were safe.

I shifted in my seat and winced.

"We need to get you to a doctor." Aurora glanced toward me sideways, her brow furrowed.

"I'll be fine," I promised, and when she looked unconvinced, I added, "It's not the first time."

Her lips pursed. It was the first time anyone had been protective of me at all. Paxton and Stellan cared, but we weren't exactly warm and cuddly with each other, either. We had each other's backs, and if I'd asked them to help me kill my dad, I was sure they'd be there. Cain too, with a sledgehammer and a smile. But Aurora radiated protective warmth that wasn't like anything I'd ever had before, and it made something unknot in my chest.

Just a little.

It bothered me.

When we walked into the house, the pledges looked up from their chores. Cain, Pax, and Stellan were in our den on the first floor. Cain leaned back in his chair, gripping a sweating glass of whiskey in one hand and his Chem book in the other, not that I had the feeling the booze was going to help him master Organic Chem. Stellan was on his laptop, and Pax frowned down at his phone.

When Cain saw Aurora, his eyes sparked with interest. "Where the hell have you been all day?"

"Saving Remington's ass," Aurora said brightly.

Apparently we weren't keeping *that* between the two of us. I could see that; if I were her, I'd be doing everything I could to show us that she was one of the good guys. Not that we were exactly white knights ourselves.

Unfortunately, that sent doubt wiggling through my gut. Maybe she'd set me up.

"Do tell," Cain drawled. He patted his knee. "Come here, little devil."

"I'm not in the mood for your bullshit today," she told him. "I'm going to my room."

"Not an option." Cain's lips tilted just faintly at her defiance, as if he were thrilled to have an excuse to punish her.

And as amusing as I found it, I was exhausted from the pain and the adrenaline let-down of everything we'd just been through. I wasn't interested in dealing with Cain, and I didn't think she should have to deal with him either.

"Leave her alone, Cain," I said.

Cain's fingers tightened just faintly around the glass, then relaxed. "Oh, fine. You heard Remington, little devil. No one wants to play with you tonight."

"Great."

"Dinner's at seven," he called after her as she headed for the door. "Try to look presentable. You've got someone's blood on your shirt. Again."

She didn't bother to answer him.

I moved to close the elaborately carved wooden door behind her, shutting out the curious pledges, because I knew Cain would want to say something to me. "What?"

Stellan leaned forward before Cain could say anything. "Was it your father again?"

"Yes."

Cain unfurled back into his seat, relaxing, and I hadn't

realized how much he seemed poised to strike until he pulled back.

"You said you'd tell us," Pax said quietly. "He's got to be dealt with."

"I'm working on it," I promised. It's not as if any of them came crying to me with their problems. We worked together when we had to, but we tried to keep our shit private. I didn't exactly run to comfort Pax when he screamed at night, and I backed away the time I found Stellan with his shoulders heaving on his sister's birthday.

"With Aurora?" There was a hook in Cain's voice. "After we just chased her through the tunnels and fucked with her completely? I wouldn't trust her, Remy."

"I don't," I said.

"What did you two do to Aurora?" Paxton demanded, frowning. "I thought we agreed we'd decide on punishments together."

"Spur of the moment thing," I dismissed it with a wave of my hand. "She liked it. You saw how wet she was...she wants to play the games as much as we do."

Maybe that was true, but that didn't mean those games wouldn't have consequences.

Cain scoffed a laugh and took another sip of his whiskey.

He was always hard to lie to.

AURORA

THE KNOCK ON MY DOOR CAME JUST AFTER SIX O'CLOCK. I'D taken a shower–Cain was right; I'd ruined yet another t-shirt with blood, but this time it was Remington's–and dressed in one of the many cocktail gowns that now adorned my closet even though I wasn't exactly invited to many cocktail parties. At least I felt pretty in the Ted Baker London black sheath dress, even if *pretty* was going to be wasted on those assholes.

My freshly curled white-blond hair hung down my back as I pulled the door open to find Cain filling my doorway.

"What do you want?" I asked curiously. "I'm not in the mood."

"I didn't come for a fight. Or a punishment," he added, as if he could tell what I was thinking. "I came to offer you a cocktail before dinner."

"Oh really?" I crossed my arms skeptically. "You've *offered me a cocktail* before, Cain, and I think I'm going to pass."

"Don't be pouty," he said. "This time it's just a drink with some friends."

"Some friends?"

"I thought you and I and a few girls from Kappa Kappa Tau could sit down and have some drinks and conversation." Cain's eyes were bright. "It would be good for you to make some friends, Aurora."

"I have all the friends I can handle right now, thanks." I had to keep Jenna alive despite her loyalty, optimism, and the duct tape in her purse. "You boys are just so much fun."

He cocked his head to one side. "So you don't mind if I go have a few drinks with the girls."

"I thought I made myself clear, Cain."

His icy blue eyes glinted. He looked awfully self-satisfied by the idea of my bloodthirsty cock-blocking. Did Cain *like* that I had claimed him? It was so hard to figure out what went on in the man's terrifying brain.

"If you won't let anyone else satisfy my needs, little devil," his voice had gone heavy, as heavy as the hand that he rested on my shoulder then traced slowly down my back, "then I guess you'd better do it yourself."

His touch seemed to spread through me like warmth, ending with a throb between my thighs.

"I don't owe you anything."

"Mm, but I still owe you something." His tone was amused, but his cock was hard already, as if he were imagining my next punishment.

"Is that what you came to collect tonight?" For some reason, I replayed the memory of being forced to my knees, of Remington's hard grip on my jaw, of Cain thrusting in and out of my mouth–and the need low in my belly pulsed.

"Just a drink. We'll see where things go from there."

I had to assume there was a distinct possibility my drink was going to be drugged. After all, I'd done it to him. But I shrugged and walked across the hallway toward his room.

"Down in our den," Cain corrected, his big hand wrapping around the back of my neck. His grip was gentle, but everything about that touch was still commanding, and I felt it ripple all the way down my spine. His fingers stroked lazily down the side of my throat as the two of us went down the stairs together and into the empty den.

"Don't worry," Cain drawled as he moved to the bar at the edge of the room. "I wouldn't lower myself to being a copycat. I'll come up with something interesting for you."

"I'm filled with anticipation."

He came back to me carrying two crystal glasses, filled with a heavy red liquid. I stared down at it, letting my annoyance show across my face.

"What the fuck is this, Cain?"

"It's delicious. I don't intend to stop drinking my favorite, *Delilah,* just because it comes with some bad memories."

"For me," I said flatly. "The bad memories are all mine."

"Is that true?" he asked, his voice mocking. He held out the glass to me. "Do you want to throw a drink at me? Would that make you feel better?"

"About what you did? Only if I throw the drink to break the glass and use the shards to cut you open."

"That's what we did to you? Cut you open. How interesting." Cain was still studying me, his blue eyes alive. "You cared about what we thought."

He was right, and I hated that.

"You're a fucking idiot." I turned to go.

"Aurora," he said, his voice laced with that authority that made everyone stop in their tracks. I turned but kept walking backward toward the door; morbid curiosity always compelled me when it came to Cain. He waggled the glass at me. "One chance."

"Fine. It doesn't make us even." I held out my hand for the glass; if he was so desperate to be doused in cocktail, let's go.

"Hell no, we won't be," he said. "You haven't yet begun to pay, little devil."

Those words should've made me squirm, so why did they heat me up instead? I gripped the crystal glass tightly, thinking how insufficient this was if it was his attempt to make up with me. And slowly, as I watched his expectant face, the hurt I felt inside crystallized into understanding.

"You know what I think, Cain? You're right. You got inside my defenses and hurt me," I said, and he looked self-satisfied before I went on. "I felt stupid that I trusted you, and you betrayed me. But you could never do what I did. You're not strong like me. After everything I've lived through, everything I've seen, *I've* still clung to hope and friendship and kept trying instead of turning cold."

Cain had frozen, even before I spat out, "You want to break me because you can't stand that I'm better than you."

For a few long seconds, dangerous heat seemed to crackle between Cain and me. His eyes had gone icy as ever.

Then he leaned forward. "I want to break you because you hurt one of my best friends, Aurora, so don't lecture me that I don't understand *friendship*. Those friends are all I have."

"How sad. You barely even talk to each other." I stared up at Cain with a smile, no matter how intimidating he was. "You could never love me, Cain. It's all empty inside you, and you pretend like that's strength. *You don't have the power.*"

Cain moved abruptly, grabbing my wrists. The drink went flying in the air, soaking his shirt red to his body, as he propelled me across the room to the wall. He slammed me into it, and the reminder of how he'd pushed me into the wall in the labyrinth was a jolt of need to go with the sudden surge of fear.

But once he had me against the wall, his lips crashed into mine. He kissed me mercilessly, stealing every bit of air from my lungs, crushing me against the wall. His body dominated mine completely, his hands pinning mine against the wall. He ground against me, pushing me into the wall so hard it hurt–but it was a good hurt.

I smiled against his lips in the barest space between us, because Cain's desire for me pulsed from every pore.

He pulled himself away from me just enough to yank up the hem of my dress, his hands sliding over the curve of my ass before he yanked my thigh up to wrap around his. The two of us ground together like that, his cock rubbing against me through both his jeans and the thin, damp fabric of my panties. His lips seared my skin over and over.

"I like these bruises on your skin," he said, rubbing his thumb over the bruised bite marks on my throat. The pressure against the bruises was a dull ache that rode the border between pain and pleasure, just like when we all press a bruise to see if it still hurts.

"I like seeing my mark on you," I retorted, pulling at the hem of his shirt. He pulled his red-stained shirt over his head in one smooth motion, revealing the hard angles of his chest and abs, and just the faintest line of my tattoo that peeked over his waistband.

His skin smelled like the liquor in my cocktail, and I leaned forward and licked his shoulder, then traced my way down his hard abs as he groaned. Cain looked as if he were covered in blood, but he tasted delicious. My hands slid down his denim thighs as I knelt to lick along the lowest hard ridges of his abs, and I looked up at him.

"You didn't have to force me, you know," I said, my voice threaded with meaning.

His fingers sank into my hair. "But that's half the fun, little devil."

I'd never had a boyfriend before–Stellan was as close as I'd come–but I'd read a whole lot on the internet.

I yanked his zipper down and pulled him out. Seeing my handiwork would always make me smile, those pink letters standing out against his chiseled lower abs. The skin was still angry from my tattoo, but I didn't bother to kiss it better. I just wrapped my mouth around his cock and went to work, grabbing his balls in one hand as if they belonged to me. He let out a gasp that was half pleasure, half shock, as I manhandled his balls roughly.

He groaned, his thighs shaking, then shattered into my mouth. He'd come even harder, faster, than when he'd fucked my mouth.

I was still trying to swallow him down when he bent over and grabbed me off my knees, throwing me over his shoulder. I let out a squeal of surprise as he carried me toward the bar and all but threw me down on the edge. The next second, he ripped my panties off and forced me flat on the bar, spreading my legs for him.

"You could ask," I gasped.

"But I don't give a fuck if you say no," he said, as pleasantly as Cain could, right before he pressed his head between my thighs. He licked the length of my pussy, and my core pulsed, my legs trying to squeeze shut. His hands braced my thighs, pushing me down hard against the cool wooden surface, just before he began to eat me out like the effort would earn him another million dollars.

The door opened behind him, then Pax said, "Oh shit."

"Stay," Cain murmured. "We're almost done with cocktails. Dinner's in a few minutes."

He sounded like such a posh bastard even though my cum was on his lips, and then he dove back in, his tongue thrusting inside me. He moved one hand to thumb my clit, and my hips jerked. My hands tangled in his blond curls, although I wasn't sure if I was trying to pull him closer to my clit or push him away. I never knew with Cain.

Pax did his best to make himself a drink around me as I panted and arched. I was still pulsing with the power of my orgasm when Cain pressed his lips to mine in a long, demanding kiss, and I tasted the smokiness of my own cum on his lips.

"You two have an odd definition of cocktails," Pax said drily as Cain stepped back abruptly, leaving me exposed and reeling with pleasure.

I sat up with all the dignity I could muster and yanked my dress down to cover myself. I looked around but couldn't find my panties, then realized Cain was stuffing them into his pocket.

"You don't need these," he said. "I want to think about your bare pussy grinding against the chair during dinner."

"You're ridiculous. I love food too much to think about sex during dinner. Especially if it's just sex with you."

Pax was watching me with a look that I couldn't quite make sense of.

"What?" I demanded.

He shrugged, his eyes shuttering.

I swept into dinner, expecting to have to act excited about another bowl of Bran Flakes, but a hot dinner was waiting for me. The scent of grilled meat and freshly baked bread filled the air, and my stomach growled.

I wondered which one of them had ended that particular bit of torture as I chowed down on my steak. It was delicious and perfect.

And every time I shifted in my chair, I knew I'd lied to Cain.

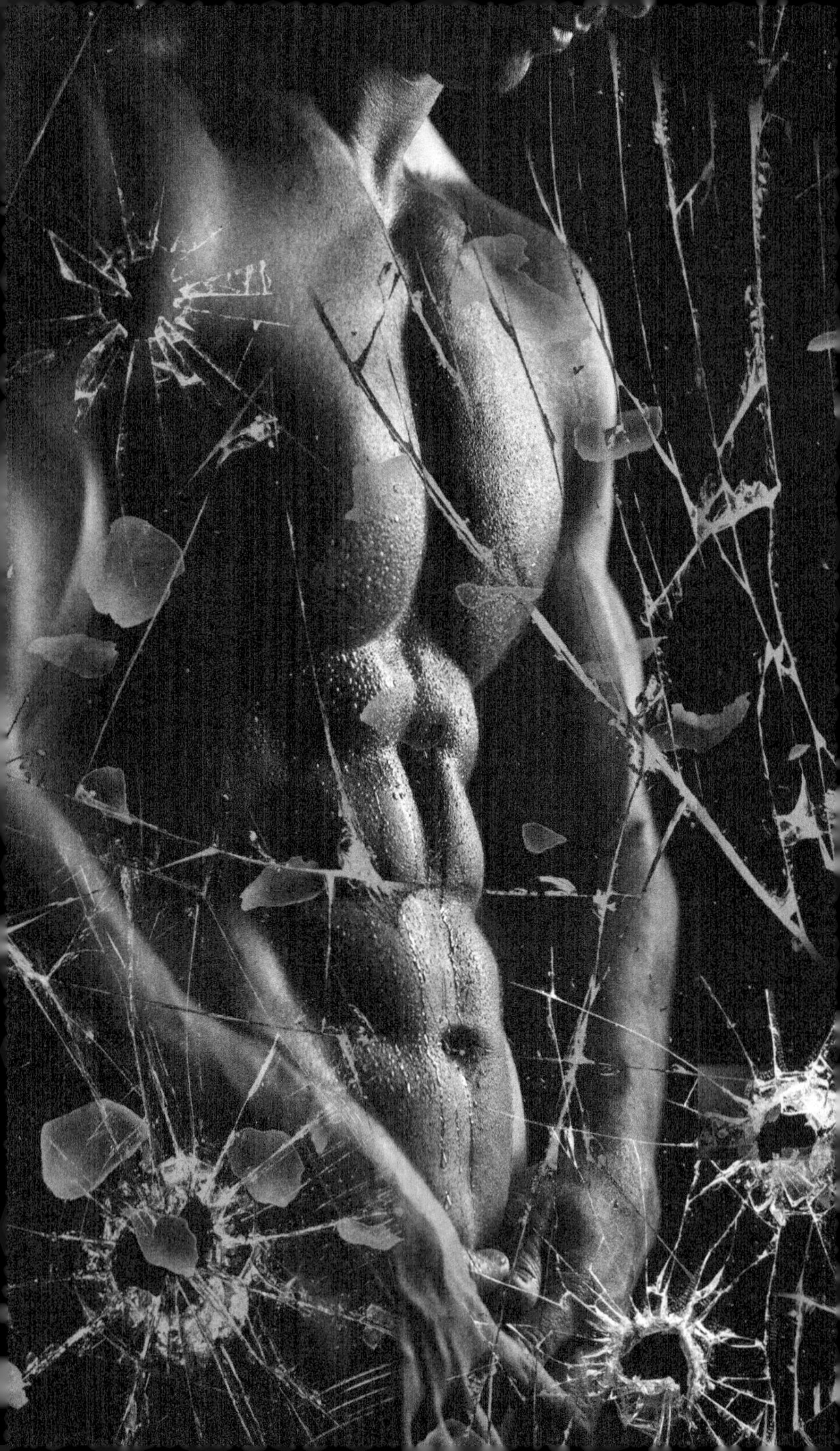

17

AURORA

It was raining. And I was sitting in my bed just staring out the window, not caring that someone on the other side of that camera was probably watching me in my misery right at that moment.

I'd gotten a letter from *him* this morning. The Demon. It had been shoved into the doorframe of my room so when I'd come back from getting some food, it had been waiting for me.

I would seriously love for whoever had planted this letter to teach me their ways, because I was still unable to get into this damn place without someone else opening the door for me.

They obviously didn't have that problem.

In the letter, he mentioned the collection of footage that he'd kept "for the memories."

He wanted me to come visit him. He missed me.

At first glance, the letter was innocent, or as innocent as a letter from a deranged serial killer could get. But it was easy for me to read the threat between the lines. I knew what was in that footage. I knew what it would show. There would come a point where the FBI would decide to renege on their agreement to absolve me of any alleged sins, and just decide to take me in.

I couldn't let that happen.

I'd rather die.

Hence why I was on my bed, struggling not to fall apart. Because as much as I didn't want that...I also didn't want to see him.

The last time I'd seen the Demon had been in the courtroom of his trial. I'd sat in the witness stand and told the judge and the jury a litany of my father's crimes. He'd stared at me the whole time, his face completely calm as if I wasn't hammering nails into his proverbial coffin with every word that I'd said.

He'd never shown any anger that day. Barely any disappointment either.

And that had been terrifying.

I talked a big game with the boys, but if there was anything that scared me shitless, it was him.

I closed my eyes and squeezed them shut, trying to think what to do. I didn't doubt he would follow through with his threat. But there was also no guarantee he wouldn't release the footage anyway even if I did come.

He was an asshole like that.

Okay. I was going to do it. I'd spent all this time running away from him, but obviously, he'd been tracking me. I could do this.

"We're a team, you and I," my father said as he began to pull out the small intestines of the guy on the table. "You'd never want to do anything to let the team down, would you, Delilah?" he murmured.

I was shivering in a chair in the corner of the room, trying to get lost in my imagination instead of watching the horror show in front of me. He'd never played with the intestines like this. The smell was...shocking.

"Delilah," he said in a sing-song voice as he gently chided me for not answering fast enough.

"No, sir," I murmured as I focused in on the Demon.

"I'd never want to hurt you, my sweet," he said as he continued to pull on the intestines slowly. The tissue ripped and brown sludge dripped out onto the floor.

I couldn't help but shiver from his threat, and the macabre display I was seeing.

There was no doubt in my mind that if I ever betrayed the Demon, the punishment he would give me would be worse than death.

I gritted my teeth as I dragged myself back to the present, already feeling like my defenses were caving in. The prison he was in was inescapable, or at least that's what the agents had bragged about when we'd set up the deal. There was no way for him to come for me.

I wondered if there was ever a time when I believed that, or if I was going to spend the rest of my life watching over my shoulder, expecting him to appear at any moment.

It took an hour, but I managed to drag myself off my bed and into my closet so I could get some clothes. I dressed simply--not too tight jeans and an oversized sweatshirt. I had to look modest for the Demon after all. I was only allowed to dress like a slut when I was luring in his next victims.

Would he be able to tell? That I'd lost my virginity and then continued on in a number of very unusual, dirty ways?

The question seemed ridiculous, but a part of me believed he really did have the satanic superpowers that people wrote about on the internet.

He'd always been able to see right through me, all the

way until the very end. He hadn't seen my betrayal coming. That had been the only thing I'd ever been able to hide from him.

I asked Jenna if I could borrow her car, and she agreed without even asking why. I was really starting to love that girl.

I drove in silence for the next couple of hours, spending the whole time shoring up the defenses in my mind so he couldn't slip through.

And then I was there.

Strongmoore Maximum Security Penitentiary.

I'd never been here before, but I was more than familiar with it. In the beginning, after his arrest, I hadn't just had nightmares...I hadn't been able to sleep at all.

I was convinced he was somehow going to escape, and if I slept, I would wake up with him standing at the side of my bed, just like when he'd first popped into my life. I would spend hours researching everything about Strongmoore that I could. My hacker friend had gotten ahold of the blueprint, and I'd studied it all, trying to think like him and plot out possible routes of escape.

But then time had passed, and he'd stayed put. And slowly...I'd started to sleep. Sleep filled with nightmares, but at least I'd slept.

My hands were trembling as I gripped the steering wheel and stared at the barbed wire fences. The oily slick of his evil felt like it was coating my skin already. And I hadn't even gone in.

I took a deep breath and turned off the car and got out, slowly approaching the entrance like I was marching towards my death.

Guards in dark blue uniforms watched me with suspicious eyes as I signed in. The secretary behind the glass, who looked like she smelled shit, took the clipboard and lazily stared at it before doing a double-take.

"You're here to see *him*?" she asked in shock. "He isn't allowed visitors."

"He's allowed one visitor," I whispered, dread dripping down my throat about what was inevitably going to happen next.

She typed something on her computer and then turned back to me with her lip curled up in disgust. "You're his daughter?"

I nodded, doing my best to keep my face blank and not show the hurricane of emotions swirling inside of me.

"ID please," she said shortly, and I was proud that my hand only trembled a little as I passed it to her. She grabbed the corner of it like she was afraid I'd taint her if our skin touched.

Look at me. One minute in the Demon's orbit and I'd lost all my fucking backbone. Evidently, I needed the guys to follow me around and torture me constantly or I turned into a scared little mouse.

She slid my ID back to me. "It will be a minute. He's in solitary at the back of the building."

I mean, that made sense. I wouldn't want to put a serial killer in with the general population of the prison either. Even if this was a maximum-security prison and most of the people in these walls were probably terrible people, I couldn't comprehend someone in here being more evil than the Demon.

I went and sat in the visitor's chair, ignoring the fact that the secretary and the two guards in the room were blatantly staring at me distrustfully like I was going to leap up and slit their throats at any second.

A while ended up being thirty minutes. Which was

terrible because my nerves only grew as the minutes ticked by.

I was a wreck when a beefy guard whose neck was as wide as his head barged through the door and called my name. I stood up and almost tripped...on air, before walking towards the guard. My head felt light-headed, like I was going to pass out any second.

This was a bad idea. I needed to leave. Right now. I stopped right before I got to the guard, and he looked at me, confused.

The footage that had been leaked splashed through my mind, and then a myriad of different kills and tortures followed.

And that was enough to get me moving again.

It was amazing how quiet the prison was as we walked through the hallways. I wasn't sure what I was expecting, maybe having to walk past prisoners' cells while they raged and gnashed their teeth in despair, but this area of the prison was clinical, almost like a boring office building.

We stopped abruptly outside of a door with a small window in it. I peered through and saw a glass wall with partitions every few feet. The room was completely empty, and I shivered as we walked in, wishing there was some kind of noise. Almost anything would be better than the complete silence of this place.

Maybe this was the punishment for prisoners. Silence so heavy that it drove them mad.

I'd once read about a room that had been built to be the quietest place on earth. Evidently, the longest anyone had been able to stay in it without going mad was forty-five minutes.

I was wondering if I'd somehow been transported to it.

I'd waited another ten minutes when a door on the other

side of the glass wall opened, making me jump out of my seat.

And then he was there.

The Demon.

His gaze sliced through me intently, and I did my best to hold his gaze right back. He'd bulked up since being put away, and his hair was a bit grayer. Everything else was the same though. Piercing blue eyes and tan skin that hadn't faded even locked up. Looking at him still made me feel like the devil was staring back at me from behind a handsome mask.

The two guards who'd brought him in let go of his handcuffed arms and then pushed him forward. He looked completely non-plussed at their rough treatment, but if I were them, I'd be watching my back. Who knew how he would make them pay for their disrespect.

He sat down in the chair across from me, and I was suddenly wishing the glass wall was a foot thicker.

"Delilah," he said in his smooth, polished voice. "This is a pleasant surprise."

I cleared my throat before answering. "I got your letter," I said simply.

"I've gained a new appreciation for writing letters while staying here," he mused lightly, like he was actually at a fucking resort and not the highest security prison in the country. His gaze darted across my face, studying me.

It took me a second to remember that he'd never seen this face before. "Still my pretty girl," he murmured.

"You got me here. What do you want?" I snapped, trying to mentally shake off the fear spiraling down my spine from just hearing his voice.

He made a tsking sound of disappointment and something inside me shriveled. I'd heard that sound quite a bit through the years, and it still rocked me even now.

"I see you still haven't learned to live in the moment," he said benignly. "And who says I want something. You should know me better now than to think that I wouldn't be missing my child. Even if that child completely and utterly betrayed me."

I remained quiet. Eventually, he would get to the point.

"You seem to be making friends at your new school."

I froze, wondering which "friends" he was talking about. Was it the guys...or Jenna? I couldn't ask him though; that would be like pouring blood into water and expecting a shark not to follow the trail.

"You have quite unusual housing arrangements. All men in that place, isn't it?"

I wanted to cry. I could tell he knew so much.

"Yes," I murmured, shocked that tears weren't threaded through my voice.

He hadn't even said anything yet. And I was a mess.

"When did you decide to start recording every awful thing you made me do? Was it when I was just a child?"

He chuckled, and the sound made me feel like throwing up. So many people had been lured in by that laugh. By that smile. By that handsome face.

And they'd all paid for it dearly.

"We don't need to have lies between the two of us, now do we? We both know that I didn't have to do anything."

"Now who's the one lying?" I spit even as I twisted uncomfortably in my chair. He was wrong. I knew he was wrong.

Except sometimes I wondered if I was the one whose memories had been twisted. Sometimes I wondered if my nightmares weren't actually closer to reality than I'd ever wanted to admit.

Fuck. Ten seconds in his presence and he was already twisting me up in knots. It was honestly a miracle that I'd stayed sane enough to get him put away.

"Five minutes," one of the guards barked, and the Demon's cheek twitched. I hadn't realized we only had ten minutes to talk.

It was a fucking miracle.

"I want you to start coming every week to visit," he said, and I stiffened in my chair.

"No," I spit out before I could think twice about it.

He cocked his head. Kind of like a raptor in *Jurassic Park*. Where you just knew he was studying every weakness you had. Even the ones you didn't know about.

"No?" he said silkily, sitting back in his chair.

"Thomas Danton. Remember him? He screamed so beautifully when you sliced his skin...and that blood spray. Seriously compelling."

My blood was freezing in my veins as an image of a bloated, shivering, pale man soared through my brain.

I could still hear his screams in my head.

"Margarite Placid. Ah, one of my favorites. I think one of her hands is still in a jar somewhere. That was quite creative."

"Okay!" I spit out, feeling like I was on the edge of bursting into hysterics. "I can't come every week though. It would be too hard to get here. And I don't have any money right now."

"Hmmm. I suppose we could do every month." He didn't ask about my *no money* comment. Maybe he assumed I'd burned all my cash on my useless plastic surgery.

"Every month," I repeated, my mind already churning

with how I could get my hands on that footage and rip his grip off my proverbial throat.

The guards were there then, tearing him out of his chair and yanking him forward so he was forced to stumble or fall on his face. He looked over his shoulder at me, and I had the crazy urge to shout for the guards to sleep with a gun in their hand. Or better yet...to not sleep at all.

I knew what that look meant.

Death.

Those guards would be lucky to last until dawn. Even with my father behind bars.

The ride home was like a dream. If you were having a dream laced with arsenic where you lost absolutely everything you'd ever loved.

I'd thrown up in the parking lot. Scratch that. I hadn't even made it to the parking lot. I'd thrown up the second one foot had left the building. The concrete by the front entrance of the prison was littered with pieces of my darkness. Pieces that only the Demon had been able to access.

There was a saying somewhere, one that talked about how villains were either born or they were made. The writer had asked which one you should be more scared of.

The answer was clear. You should be scared of both. Definitely both. Because the evil people who were born that way never had a soul to begin with, but the people who were made into villains...their souls were altered, corrupted. Made into something unrecognizable. And that was just as fucking scary.

I knew that from experience.

It felt like I was shedding a layer of skin the farther away from the prison I got. The switch from Delilah to Aurora was like an unexpected breath of fresh air.

When I got to campus, I parked Jenna's car and then went to return the keys.

"What's wrong?" she gasped when she saw me. I winced. I could only imagine how I looked. Probably more dead than alive. That's what spending time with a Demon did to you, it sucked the life out of you.

"Just tired," I said, trying to smile...unsuccessfully.

"Go to bed early, and then text me when you wake up," she ordered.

My throat felt clogged. "Thank you," I murmured, trying to thank her for a whole lot more than just letting me use her car.

Her face softened, and there was a slight sheen to her eyes as she looked at me. She just nodded and smiled brightly, and I said goodbye before walking as fast as I could back down the hallway.

It was amazing how tired emotional trauma could make you. The way it battered at your defenses until you were like half a person.

The trip to the Sphinx felt like a lifetime as everything inside of me shut down and I almost wanted to cry when I got to the door and remembered that I was at their mercy to reach my bed.

I sank to my butt and pulled my knees up to my chest, not caring how I looked to passersby.

One thing that I was a pro at, was pushing memories away, keeping all the unwanted ones locked in a box in my mind. That skill had always been necessary to my existence. My visit with the Demon had blown the lid of that box way open though, and there were so many faces crawling through my head, I could have screamed.

"Are you okay?" a deep voice hesitantly asked, and I looked up to see one of the pledges standing there.

"Peachy," I muttered as I struggled to my feet, feeling five years old at that moment.

He blocked the door with his body, and for a moment, I contemplated holding him at knife point so I could finally get the code.

But I decided against it. I was way too exhausted, and the guys would just end up changing the code anyway.

The pledge must have had the idiotic notion that I wanted to talk, because once we'd gotten inside the Sphinx, he followed me down the hall, chattering away. About what I couldn't tell you, I'd blocked it out. I got to my door and went to unlock it, and then I realized he was still hovering there.

"Listen Chris—" I began.

"My name's Derek," he pointed out unhelpfully.

I wasn't going to remember that. I'd taken to calling them all "Chris" in my head...and to their face. They may have been Sphinx members, but they were still what Cain referred to as "sheep." And "sheep" didn't need a name.

"Is there something you need?" I asked impatiently, way too tired for this conversation. My exhaustion was making me way nicer than I usually would have been.

"I was wondering if you wanted to hang out," he said, leaning against the wall and trying to look cool.

"Hang out," I repeated blankly. My mind not computing what he was saying.

"Like grab dinner or something." He had a cocky smile on his face, like I was a sure thing, and he was doing me a favor by asking me out.

"Are you stupid, pledge? Do you want her to bash your brains out?" barked Stellan as he came down the hallway.

Chris—I mean Derek, didn't look so cocky any more. In fact, he was cowering right now and I was pretty sure that he was shaking. I eyed Stellan, ignoring the pang of tired lust in my gut that always sparked up when he was near me.

I didn't think Stellan was that scary. But this guy looked like he was about to pee his pants. I sniffed the air gingerly. He might have peed a little already.

"I—" he squeaked, before he darted off down the hall without another word or look back.

I put my hand exaggeratedly on my chest. "I can't believe you just chased off my suitor," I said sarcastically.

Stellan rolled his eyes, but there was a ghost of a smile on his pretty lips.

"Seems like I already have enough competition. Wouldn't want to add anyone else to the list."

My mouth dropped as he leaned closer to me, his finger tracing the patch of skin between my shirt and pants, and sending tingles sparking across my skin.

His hand that wasn't on my waist came up and gently brushed against my lower lip. I couldn't stop the hitch in my breath.

If I wasn't so freaking tired, I might have been tempted to suck on his finger, or something else ridiculous like that.

But I was. So this conversation needed to be over. I didn't have the energy to be taken in the hallway.

Even though the idea of human touch to soothe my frayed edges sounded really fucking good at the moment.

I practically fell through the door as I abruptly unlocked it and ripped myself away from his touch.

"See you later," I called as I slammed the door in his stunned face. I leaned against it and listened, noting that he stood there for at least a minute more before he slowly walked away.

I was shaking from exhaustion as I stumbled to my bed, my body past the point of no return. I didn't bother changing, I just threw myself on top of the covers and almost immediately fell asleep.

"Inject just a little bit at first, Delilah. I want him to still be able to scream when we start," the Demon ordered. I tried to control the shaking of my hands as I did my best to push only a small amount of the poison in. The sweat on my hands wasn't helping the task either.

My stomach was hurting. It had been hurting all day. And having this man tied up, practically naked, was a lot for me to handle.

Especially because it was my birthday. And this...this was the Demon's idea of a birthday present. Like every girl dreamed of ending someone's life when they turned thirteen.

My hand slipped and the guy howled in pain as I accidently shoved the needle at least two inches into his skin. Hopefully I didn't hit anything important.

Or maybe I should hope that I had. That would help it to be over sooner.

"Get your head straight, darling," the Demon snapped, his hand suddenly on the back of my neck, squeezing slightly in warning.

I let go of the needle and it just stayed in place, stuck in his skin. I pulled away suddenly from my father's grip and stumbled away. "I don't want to do this," I sniffed, a tear running down my cheek as I stared at the floor, not wanting to look at his face and see the disappointment I knew would be there.

I heard his footsteps approaching and it was everything I could do to stay in place.

"Look at me," he said in a cold voice, and I forced up my gaze to meet his. I flinched when I saw the cold rage in his eyes.

"It's my birthday," I murmured as more tears fell down my face. *"I want to play with friends. I want cake. I want—"*

"I'm not good enough for you anymore?" he asked silkily as he grabbed my chin. *"Dear old dad lost his sparkle?"*

"No. That's not what I—"

"I've been too easy on you. You're not learning fast enough," he said in a calm voice as he cut me off.

He let go of my chin and then dragged me towards the man at the table. Grabbing a scalpel, he sliced across the man's chest, splattering blood all over both of us, and ensuring that he would die a slow death.

I was sobbing then as he dragged me over to the other side of the basement where there was a large cage where he would occasionally keep his playthings before he killed them.

"I'm going to show you what happens to the weak in this world, Delilah," he murmured as he forced me forward. It took me a moment to realize that he was going to put me in that cage.

"What are you doing? Please. I'm sorry!" I cried. But it didn't matter to him. He opened the cage and shoved me inside before closing it behind me and locking it. The Demon strode away towards the stairs on the other side of the room.

"I'm going to give you some time alone to reevaluate your priorities. A couple of days should do the trick," he told me as he flicked off the lights, leaving me in the dark with the gasping man as he walked up the stairs.

"Please," I screamed when the man began moaning. It was so dark that I couldn't see my hands in front of my face, and I was convinced that things were watching me.

"Please!"

"Aurora!" Paxton's voice pierced through the mindfuck I was stuck in, and my eyes shot open. Another scream ripped from my throat when I realized how dark it was. I was still in the cage.

"Aurora. Sweetheart," Paxton murmured as I sobbed and clawed the air around me. His warm body was suddenly on top of mine, completely covering every inch. "It's not real. It was just a dream," he said soothingly. His arms were on either side of my head and his hands were running through my hair. His comforting weight was like a dose of Xanax and my whole body began to relax almost immediately.

"It's not real," he whispered over and over again, until I could almost believe him.

Paxton's forehead met mine and he began to softly sing, his lips brushing across my skin.

"She's got a smile that it seems to me, reminds me of childhood memories," he sang gruffly. "Everything was as fresh as the bright blue sky. Now and then when I see her face, she takes me away to that special place. And if I stare too long, I'd probably break down and cry."

It took me a moment to realize that he was singing Guns N' Roses, and a hiccupped laugh burst out amid the tears.

"You're singing 'Sweet Child O' Mine'," I cried, tears still streaming down my face.

"Mmmh. My mother used to sing it to me as a child every time I had a nightmare. It was her favorite song."

"Sing it to me again," I whispered.

And he did. The whole song. Over and over again, until the bad dream seemed a world away.

Eventually my hysterics calmed, and the tears had gone from a torrent to a light drizzle. He slid off of me and gathered my body in his arms, tucking me right up against him.

I didn't understand how Paxton felt so...safe. He had asshole and heartbreak written all over him and yet, here, in the dark...he felt like mine.

"It was worse tonight," he murmured as he softly stroked

my hair. "I wasn't even in my room and I heard your screams."

I probably should have cared that a bunch of the Sphinx douchebags had heard me, but I couldn't find it in myself.

"Sometimes it's hard to remember what's real and what's just a dream. But this one...I know it happened. But I...I do everything I can not to think about it," I confessed.

"It was that bad?" he asked, his fingers tracing patterns on my skin.

I nodded, unable to answer because the tears were coming faster again.

"What do you think triggered it?"

I hesitated, not sure if I wanted to tell him where I'd been. That I'd seen *him*.

But they hated me already, right? And honestly...I just needed to tell someone. I needed to purge at least some of the poison out from under my skin.

"I saw him today." My voice was rough and scratchy from crying so hard.

He stiffened against me briefly before relaxing again.

"The Demon?" he asked. "Why?" I grabbed his hand off my hip and clenched it tightly in mine, pulling it against my heart.

"There's more footage," I whispered, my soul sounding broken even to my own ears. "And I just—I'm afraid that it will be too much."

He was quiet for so long, I almost thought he'd somehow fallen asleep.

"Did you ever want to do it?" he finally asked, and my whole body shuddered at the question.

Because sometimes, I wasn't really sure.

So I just didn't answer, and he didn't ask me again. He

just held me tightly there in the dark, and eventually, I fell asleep wrapped in his arms.

And the only dreams I had were of a little boy with dark hair and amber eyes, and a woman who sang rock songs to him to get him to sleep.

18

AURORA

I was lying on my stomach on my bed, trying to comprehend the math problem in front of me, when someone began pounding on my door, making me jump.

"Aurora! Open the fucking door," called Remington, banging again.

Hopping off my bed, I walked over to the door, a thread of worry pulling at my chest with the absolute panic in his voice.

I unlocked it, and it almost hit me in the face as he pushed it open the second he heard the lock click.

I opened my mouth to yell at him, but then I really took him in.

He looked like a mess.

"What's wrong?" I asked, feeling like I needed to grab my favorite knife and start cutting people.

"My aunt just called. My mother never made it to rehab. Which wouldn't have been so surprising...until I got this." He lifted up his phone to show me a grainy video of a woman with her hands tied behind her back and a gag in her mouth. Remington's hands were shaking as he held the phone.

"That's your mother?" I pressed softly, disgust curdling in my stomach.

I went around the side of the bed and kneeled down, pulling on the plank I'd loosened so I could store more of my stuff. I basically had things hidden all over the room at this point.

"What are you—Okay. Wow," he said as I pulled out a long, serrated knife and then hesitated for half a second before grabbing a gun as well.

"Alright," I said calmly, a familiar numbness spreading through my veins as I prepared myself for what was to come. "Do you recognize the room in that video?"

"No. Well—maybe." He shifted uncomfortably.

"Okay...where's the place it could be?"

"There's a club that my father and his buddies frequent. He's had me go with him a couple of times."

With how awkward Remy was being, it wasn't hard for me to imagine what kind of *club* this was.

"A sex club, I'm assuming. Because you rich pricks can't be anything but stereotypical in every way," I drawled.

Remington fucking blushed.

"Okay. An alien's inhabited your body," I told him as I checked my gun to see that it was loaded.

"It's moments like these that I know I'm fucked up," he commented. I glanced up at him, confused, only to be startled by the heat in his gaze where a sheen of tears was a moment ago.

"I would have guessed that guns would have been Cain's kink, but you learn something new every day."

Remington's phone buzzed again, and we both eyed it. When he lifted it up, I saw there was a video.

"Here, give it to me," I told him, reaching for the phone, pretty sure that whatever was in that video wasn't going to be good.

He clicked play before I could grab it, and I winced as I watched his mother being gang-raped by a bunch of old men. Every hole was being filled, and she was just lying there, a dead look in her gaze.

Remington dropped the phone and leaned over and threw up everywhere. I winced as it splashed onto my bare feet.

His eyes were red-rimmed and watery as he stood up and looked at me.

"I'm going to get dressed. While I'm doing that, can you use those computer skills of yours to try and find a blueprint of the club you think she's at? If that's really where he's keeping her, I don't want to walk in blind," I said, waiting for him to nod before I jogged to the bathroom to wash off my feet before changing.

When I came out a few minutes later, Remington was sitting on my bed with a computer in his lap, typing feverishly on the keyboard.

"Have you found it?" I asked as I headed into the closet to change.

He nodded, not looking up as he concentrated on whatever was on the screen.

After I'd slipped on some black leggings, a tight black tank top, a fitted black hoodie, and some black boots, I emerged from the closet. He glanced up at me and gave me a double-take. "That's quite the outfit, little devil," he murmured, before his gaze slid back to his screen.

I sat on the bed with him and went through the blueprints. It was pretty simple—a main floor with a large open area, women's and men's locker room type areas with showers and bathrooms, and then individual rooms along the perimeter of the building. The basement must have been where the really freaky things happened because the rooms were larger down there, like they were meant for multiple people to be using the rooms at the same time. The blueprints didn't show any secret passageways or anything like that, so hopefully they were accurate.

"Why haven't you called the others?" I asked, thinking we were most likely going to be really outnumbered.

"They're not here right now," he said vaguely. "They're working on a project."

Okay then. I'm glad that he was asking for my help with something important to him while still keeping me in the dark.

"You need to change," I told him with a frown as I realized he was dressed like he was going to the fucking country club instead of to commit murder.

"Right," he said, looking down at his dress shirt and slacks as if they'd offended him. "Be right back," he said before striding out of the room.

I grabbed a belt out of my nightstand that could hold my gun and my knife, and I fastened it around me before tucking my weapons into the loops...plus a few other things. Of course, I was better at all the up close and personal ways of ending someone, but the Demon had made sure I was at least decent with a gun.

Remington was already back when I finished, dressed in black gym pants and a long sleeve black shirt with a hood.

"Are you ready?" I asked, and he nodded, determination in his gaze. I followed him out of the room and we made our way through a few hallways and a set of stairs before getting to the underground garage I had such fond memories of.

Most of the garage was under construction, but there

were still scorch marks where Cain's McLaren had been. Which just made me freakishly happy even under the current circumstances.

Remington led me over to a new black BMW 8-Series Gran Coupe that looked very James Bond.

"How far is the club from here?" I asked, as I slid inside the cool leather interior.

"About thirty minutes," he answered, starting the car and then driving down the tunnel that led out of the garage.

Remington had sent the blueprints to my phone, and I studied them as we drove.

"Is there a possibility he could be tracking your phone?" I asked, staring at it in the cup holder like it was a snake that was about to attack.

Remington shook his head. "We all use special phones that are basically impossible to track or hack into. It's safe."

I wanted to ask why they felt the need to have special phones like that, but I decided not to press the issue...right now. The club was in the downtown district of the nearest city, perfectly situated so that all the businessmen could leave work immediately and head out for a night of debauchery.

Remington was obviously very familiar with this club. I wondered just how many times his father had taken him here.

The club was called "The Twisted Rose," and we parked a block away from it and got out of the car before heading down the sidewalk. Night was falling, and this area of the city seemed pretty empty, the rush of people headed home from work already past.

"Isn't the club open at night?" I asked, wondering if we were more off the mark than I'd thought in thinking that his mother would be here.

"It would normally be, which is why this is a 'maybe'. That room just looked really familiar to me." He cleared his throat. "I lost my virginity in one that looked very similar to that."

"I see," I snorted, and he shot me a wry look.

The plan was pretty simple. There was a back entrance that would be locked, but I was sure I'd be able to break into it. I hadn't found many things that could hold me back when I wanted to access them.

There were two sets of stairs that led down to the basement, one in the main area, and one off the back of the building that employees mostly used.

His dad was there; no doubt he was expecting us. I wasn't worried too much about that, though. I had a feeling that Senator Warren Taylor didn't give people the right amount of credit very often. He was obviously unaware of just how smart his son was, and he was gravely underestimating how dangerous I was.

Both of those things were going to change tonight if I had any say in it.

The area around the club was quiet, and there were no cars in the parking lot.

"Looks like it's closed."

"Probably for the special event," I said in disgust as we went around the back of the building. The door was in an alleyway filled with stinking garbage and a few stray cats. There were bags of trash outside the door, and I shivered just thinking of the grossness that was probably in them.

I slid my lock picking kit out of my harness and started to work on the lock on the door while Remington watched interestedly.

The lock clicked open and I smiled victoriously.

Remington pulled a gun out from under his shirt, and I nodded in approval. I guess he wasn't just a pretty face.

"Do you know how to use that?" I asked, making sure that he hadn't just grabbed a random one he'd found in the Sphinx.

He rolled his eyes and ignored my question. Fair enough. The more I learned about the guys, the more I learned just how much darkness was threaded around them. I was getting the suspicion there might be a lot of instances where they felt the need for guns. Which would be helpful tonight.

I opened the door as quietly as I could, just a crack, before pressing my ear to the space so I could try and listen. I was only met with silence, and I opened the door a little bit wider so we could slip into the dark hallway, lit by a row of red light bulbs along the ceiling. It kind of created a sort of hellscape feel, which was probably fitting for the situation I was anticipating we were about to walk into.

"Are we killing him?" I asked lightly, and he stutter-stepped as we walked. I knew from first-hand experience that even if your father was the epitome of evil, it still wasn't necessarily easy to pull the trigger that ends their life. It was hard enough to convince myself to get the Demon imprisoned even though killing him would have been far better... and safer, than what I'd done.

"I want him to die. But I want him to hurt first," he said, no hesitation in his voice.

My stomach clenched at the idea of torturing Remington's father. That was what Remington wanted from me, right? I just didn't know if I could actually do that in front of him, knowing that he'd never look at me the same way again.

Not that I should be caring what he thought about me.

But after freeing his little brother and sister, and defending him from his father, things had definitely done a 360. Or maybe it was a 180.

And that was why I was struggling with Physics class at the moment.

There wasn't anyone around, and it was completely quiet. More like a mausoleum than a sex club. *Fifty Shades of Grey* had definitely been exaggerating how much sexy music there would be at one of these places.

We passed a few empty rooms whose doors were open. There were all sorts of interesting equipment in the rooms, and I definitely had questions about what they all were used for. That one had spikes...definitely not sexy at all to me. But I guess to each their own.

But really, where did the spikes go?

We got to the staircase and paused at the top, another staircase from another time creeping into my memory until I finally pushed it away.

The last thing I needed right now was to be distracted by a flashback.

When we didn't hear anything, we crept down the carpeted stairs, which were excellent for noise control.

My breath started to come out in light pants the more we descended the stairs. I'd never thought that stairs would give me flashbacks, but here we were.

"Are you all right?" Remington whispered, his hand going to the small of my back as he looked at me, concerned.

Get your shit together, Aurora, I chided myself.

"Peachy," I told him, biting down on my tongue hard enough to make it bleed. The iron tang of blood was enough to center me.

Fuck, I was acting like a fucking vampire.

At the bottom of the stairs was another hallway, this one with luxurious black marble flooring, and dark red painted walls.

The decorator had definitely understood the assignment. It was all very sex dungeon-ish.

Also definitely not the vibe I would have wanted when losing my virginity. But maybe Remington hadn't cared.

I side-eyed him, wondering just how kinky he was, not that I should be surprised if he had some interesting tendencies. He had hunted me down in the dark, after all.

There were rooms lining the hallway, most of the doors propped open as they had been upstairs. There weren't any windows in the rooms down here, and since it was the basement, and the lights were off in all the rooms, I could only see the bare outlines of the "equipment" inside. There didn't seem to be anyone down here, and I was beginning to get concerned that his mom wasn't actually in this place.

Double doors flanked the end of the hallway, and Remington stopped me right in front of them.

"This is the room," he murmured, his face looking a little gray and his eyes pinched with worry and trepidation.

The floor plan hadn't shown another entrance into this room, which I knew from the plan was the largest on this floor, so we basically had to go in guns blazing because they would see us right away.

"Are you ready for this?" I asked him, and his eyes turned cold and hard, very unlike anything that I'd seen on Remy's face before.

He nodded.

As quietly as I could, I pushed down on the handle on one of the doors and it clicked open, immediately leaking sounds into the hallway that resembled a bad porno.

Remington was lightly trembling behind me, and I knew

it wasn't from fear—it was from fury. Taking a deep breath, I pulled the door open a bit wider and slipped into the room, immediately wishing that I had bleach for my eyeballs.

The scene in front of me was truly the stuff of nightmares. The same scarily thin woman that had been in the video his father sent to his phone was spread out on an enormous bed decked out in red satin sheets. She was completely naked, and her hands were hogtied behind her awkwardly. Surrounding her were three disgusting-looking pale men with almost identical fat, soft stomachs that told of a lifetime of fancy dinners and too much drinking. They were pounding in and out of her, filling every one of her holes, while Remington's father sat in a chair pulled up beside the bed. His hand was feverishly stroking his long cock.

Remington stumbled and cursed as he slipped in behind me. His father had seen us by then, and there was a wicked grin on his face as he took us in. He bit his lip as his attention moved from the top of my head to my feet, obviously mentally undressing me, and his hand began to move faster up and down his shaft. I struggled to keep the bile down, because fuck, that was disgusting.

The other three hadn't turned their attention to us yet, too busy trying to get off. Lifting up my gun, I aimed at the man who was choking her with his dick, and I shot him in the head. Blood sprayed everywhere as his body fell backward. Head wounds did always seem to bleed more.

Remy's mother was so beaten down, she didn't even flinch when it happened. Remington's father was stumbling out of his chair, though, darting for a pile of clothes I saw a few feet away from him laid out on a couch. He was an idiot, because he hadn't kept his gun right next to him even though he had to have known that Remington would come.

The other two assholes had pulled out of her body and were trying to struggle off the bed. Luckily for me, the bed was enormous, and with how large they were, they hadn't gotten far. I shot one of them in the throat and was about to take care of the other when a shot rang out from behind me. A bullet hit the third man in the chest, and he lurched backward.

By this time, Remington's father had made it over to the pile of clothes and was digging through them, I assumed looking for his gun. I shot at his hand, intentionally missing by just a few inches, and he roared as he sprang backward.

"You stupid bitch," he hissed through gritted teeth.

"I've been called worse," I responded sarcastically, walking towards him with my gun aimed at his chest. As soon as he took a step away from the couch and his clothes, I darted to the bed to check Remington's mother's pulse, knowing that Remington would have a gun pointed at his father.

My dark persona slipped for a moment when I saw just how badly she was ruined. Her eyes were staring up at me listlessly, and I could tell that her soul was broken, in a way that I'm sure it had never been before. Just by looking at her, I could see there wouldn't be a way back for her after this. She'd already been beaten down too much before tonight. She didn't have enough in her to get past the horror she'd been experiencing for who knows how many days.

His mother was so still that I actually wasn't sure she was still alive. But when I reached down to check her pulse, I could feel the faint flutter of her heart beating raggedly.

I'm sure she was wishing she was dead though.

I untied her hands and slipped the blanket over her so at least she didn't have to be exposed anymore, knowing she needed medical attention right away.

"I'm sorry," I murmured before the mask slipped back on, and all I could feel was the desire to make him hurt.

"Well, you got me. What are you going to do with me?" he asked calmly, not seeming afraid at all. Remington still had a gun pointed at his father, and I knew he was just itching to pull it. But this man deserved a far less easy death than a bullet hole.

He needed to suffer.

I just wasn't sure how far I could go in front of Remington. Once I showed that part of myself, there would be no going back. It would be hard to argue that I wasn't the monster that they said I was all this time.

Remington seemed to make the decision for me, though, because while keeping a careful eye on his father, and his gun raised, he strode over to the bed and grabbed some of the black rope that I hadn't noticed was hooked to the bottom of the bed.

"You're going to die, Senator," Remington said mockingly. "But we're going to make it hurt first."

Remington walked over to his father, presumably to tie him with the rope, and his father lunged towards Remington as soon as the gun was lowered. I huffed out a sigh of annoyance and then shot at his leg. Not enough for him to bleed out or anything like that, but enough to get his attention.

He howled like the pampered superstar that he was. You could guarantee that if I was shot, I wouldn't be crying. It was only getting publicly humiliated by the four guys I was starting to like that seemed to bring on the waterworks.

The Demon had made sure that physical pain didn't phase me.

While Remington's father was sniveling over his leg,

Remington quickly and efficiently tied his father's arms and legs and then threw him to the floor.

"You're pretty good with knots," I commented, a little bit of inappropriate heat blooming inside of me thinking about him tying me up.

He winked at me, a slight smile on his lips that disappeared when his mom suddenly groaned from the bed.

"Go help her," I told him softly, and he looked a bit torn. I understood that feeling. Revenge and vengeance were such powerful emotions that they often blocked out everything else.

"It's okay. I've got it," I told him. Remy had pulled out his phone and started to type on it.

"We have medical staff on call. They'll come straight here."

"Get your mom up there, and then you can come back," I gently told him, and he nodded and went over to the bed where his mother was now whimpering.

Remington's father was also whimpering, and honestly, it may have been one of the most pathetic things that I'd ever seen.

Remington scooped up his mom and headed out the door.

Me? I pulled out the knife tucked into my harness and slowly walked over to him, making sure his attention was on me the whole time. He was barely bleeding, so I knew the bleached white pallor he had going had nothing to do with blood loss, and everything to do with wondering what I was going to do next.

The Demon had taught me well. An important part of torture was the psychological factor. Your victims needed to be wondering the whole time what fresh hell you were going to bring upon them next.

With how heightened their emotions and adrenaline were while being tortured, it was most effective to be more exaggerated and slower in your movements. It just made it worse for them.

I crouched down next to him and then took the knife and trailed it down his cheek, nicking the skin along his jawline. He whimpered again.

"You know, Senator, you would think that a man in your position would've learned to stop underestimating people a long time ago. It really would've helped you out in this situation, wouldn't it have?"

"I have money," he cried out. "You can have all of it."

I chuckled to myself and pulled out my phone, using the link that I had to get into all of his hacked accounts. I turned the phone around and showed him all of his bank accounts and watched as he panicked even more.

"I think the correct statement is that *I* have all of your money," I told him with a dark chuckle.

"Please. I'll do better," he begged.

This was getting a bit ridiculous. I hadn't even done anything and he was begging like I'd just read him his last rites. Just as I was about to stab him in the hand, Remington walked back in. I froze, my knife hovering right above his father. I was just expecting to see that look in his eyes. That look that said he thought I was a monster.

"You'll have to walk me through this, sweetheart. I'm afraid that torture is more of Cain and Paxton's domain. I'm usually the pretty face of the deal," he said lightly, showing absolutely no signs of disgust.

If I hadn't known that I was already messed up, I would know it right now. Because I was totally getting off on the fact that Remington and I were about to torture his asshole father together. Another thing to talk about with that future therapist who I would eventually have to kill after I told them all my secrets.

Remington had his gun out again. "Alright, where do I shoot first?" he drawled.

I rolled my eyes. Rookie.

"You don't use guns in torture until the very end," I scoffed, recognizing the dark thrill in my voice that I'd always done my best to keep hidden. I took the knife and stabbed it into his father, about two inches into the skin, of course eliciting a loud scream because the man was a pussy. And then, I dragged the knife slowly across his chest, making sure that I stayed the same depth the entire time. This way I could rip at the skin and the muscle, but not hit any vital organs. And it hurt. A lot.

Remington was watching me, looking entranced when I glanced back at him.

I held out the knife to him while his father wriggled like a worm at my feet.

"Want a turn?" I asked.

He shook his head slowly and took a step forward. "I want to watch you, little devil," he said hoarsely.

It took me a second to realize what I was hearing in his voice.

It was lust.

Arousal.

He wanted me.

Badly.

These men really were as fucked up as I was.

I turned back to the sniveling fool, and this time I grabbed his bound wrists and latched onto his pinky finger.

"This is going to hurt," I said seriously before I began to rip every one of his fingernails off. His screams filled the room, sending shivers down my spine. I didn't want to look too closely at what kind of shivers they were.

I went to his feet next, and I took off every one of his toenails. He passed out, and I hummed in disappointment, reaching into my pocket for some of the smelling salts I'd grabbed before leaving.

"Holy fuck. You were prepared," Remington muttered, and I grinned at him, wondering if it was clear to him the madness that lay just under my skin.

I shook the salts under his father's nose, and he woke up with a gasp, tears falling down his face when he saw me leaning over him.

"Please," he croaked.

Evidently, that was enough to set Remington off, because he lunged forward and ripped the knife from my hands, and began to make long cuts all over his father's torso.

I was willing to bet that "please" had been offered to his father many a time over the years, without any sympathy, judging by the savage look on Remington's face.

There was blood everywhere, and I idly wondered if his father had any blood diseases with how nasty of a person he was.

Remington dragged his knife up his father's cheek, almost slicing into his eye, and the man howled.

He wouldn't die from anything that we were doing to him. I wondered how long Remington wanted this to last. There were three other bodies that needed to be taken care of before anyone randomly dropped by.

Just as I had that thought, Remington dropped the knife and it clattered to the floor. He lurched up and grabbed at his hair, letting out an animalistic scream that spoke to all of the pain and sorrow that this man had put him and his family through. His chest was heaving and he stared at me wildly.

"I'll finish him for you," I said, wanting to do this for him.

I pulled out my gun, just wanting to end it. I was about to pull the trigger when Remington's hand caught my arm.

I looked at him, confused.

"I don't want you to kill him. He's not deserving enough to have someone like you end his life."

"It's never good to leave loose ends," I told him, my finger about to pull the trigger again.

"He's going to die," Remington breathed. "I just don't want you to do it."

I froze, feeling the bloodlust bubbling under my skin. Taking a deep breath, I let it die and lowered my hand.

"Make sure he's taken care of," I said, checking once more that Remington was actually planning on ending this asshole's life.

"There's no way I'm sparing that fucker's life, but I will have one of the peons do it. That's about as much as he deserves. A nobody killing him."

I wondered what kind of peons they had that were up for murder, but at this point, I wasn't really surprised by anything they did or had access to anymore.

"Okay," I said, and Remington nodded, his gaze flaring once again. He typed something on his phone, and then took out his gun and slammed it down on his dad's head, immediately knocking him out.

"The cleanup crew will be here soon as well," he murmured, walking over to the couch and sitting down on it.

"Come here," he cajoled.

I grimaced and glanced at the couch.

"I can only imagine the germs on that," I told him. "No part of my body is going to sit on that thing."

He chuckled. "Come sit on my lap, little devil." Sparks threatened to set fire to my insides with the sex in his voice.

I'd never really thought that murder and sex went together; there had certainly not been anything sexual for me in the Demon's basements, but I was thinking I might be changing my mind now that Remington was in the picture...

I sauntered over to the couch and slid onto his lap, making sure not to touch the couch at all. He gathered me into his arms and hummed against my neck. "Cain was right," he murmured.

"About what?"

"About your scent. How is it that we're surrounded by death, and all I can smell is the coconut on your skin that I'm desperate to lick off?"

Whoa there.

"Let's wait to make my panties wet until after the dead bodies are gone," I joked, knowing full well that I was already soaked.

The smirk on his face told me that he knew it too.

Remington was hard underneath me, and when four men came in through the door, he didn't get up to greet them.

"Kill that one and take care of all the bodies," he ordered, gesturing to the four men on the ground.

"Yes sir," one of them said, and I resisted the urge to mock him.

But it was really fucking hard.

Remington cast one more hate-filled look at his father, and then he picked me up and stood, and then started towards the exit. We were both silent as we made our way through the building and out into the cool night air.

Remington set me down once we got outside. He stood there staring up into a sky whose stars were masked by the city lights all around us.

"Remington?" I asked hesitantly, wondering what he was thinking. He didn't respond to me for a long moment, and then he whirled around and pushed me against the outside of the building, his lips just a breath away from mine.

"We're going to go home, and then I'm going to take you in the shower and wash off my father's disgusting blood from your skin, and then...I'm going to fuck you."

My eyes widened at his words, and I swear my pussy fluttered.

I was up for that plan.

REMINGTON

It was hard to concentrate on the drive home. The need inside of me was all-encompassing. It was all I could do to resist touching her, but I knew as soon as I did, I'd end up trying to fuck her in this car, and I knew from experience that car sex made for an uncomfortable ride.

We were silent, but our silence was loud. Aurora was hard to read usually, almost impossible actually, but right now it was easy to know what she was thinking.

She was just as turned on as I was.

Maybe it was the adrenaline rush. Maybe it was the fact that the man who'd haunted me my entire life was finally gone. Maybe it was just her, but somehow I was able to push away the chaos I'd been feeling ever since I'd found out that my mom had disappeared.

Most would think I was a heartless monster for being

able to think about sex while my mother was in her current condition, but they obviously didn't know that, for all intents and purposes, my mother was a stranger to me. I didn't remember a time when she hadn't been drunk or out of her mind on whatever prescription drug my dad had supplied her with. She'd always been a shell of a person, one of the most self-absorbed people I'd ever come across.

Anything I did feel for her was because she had carried me into the world, and as far as I knew, she'd managed to pull herself together while pregnant with me and not use anything that would hurt me. And that...was about as much as my thoughts toward her extended.

Regardless of who she was as a person though, she hadn't deserved that. Not at all.

But although I would make sure that she got the best treatment possible, I wasn't going to waste a minute imagining a world where she was able to get her shit together. Some people were just impossibly broken, maybe from birth. And she was one of them.

So yeah, maybe most people would think I was a bastard for panting at the idea of fucking Aurora, but what we'd just experienced together...it felt like she'd taken my hand and dragged me out of hell. And I couldn't wait to reward her for that.

We finally got to the Sphinx what felt like a million fucking years later. And I didn't waste any time in the garage. As soon as we got out of the car, I picked her up and tossed her over my shoulder before trotting towards my bedroom. She squeaked adorably when I picked her up, but she didn't complain. It felt good to know that she wanted this as badly as I did. I walked straight to my shower and turned on the water, making sure the temperature was perfect before I walked us both in, still fully dressed. I set her down in front of me, just staring at her in awe. The black of our clothes had hid how much blood we'd gotten on ourselves, and I watched in fascination as the water on the shower floor ran red. I began to slowly pull off her clothes, prolonging the anticipation just like she had when she'd tortured my father—which, let the record show, was the hottest fucking thing that I'd ever seen. Well, maybe it wasn't the hottest thing; maybe having her naked in front of me right now, water running down her smooth skin in rivulets, was the hottest fucking thing I'd ever seen. My cock was fucking hard as a rock, but I let her have a moment in the water before I jumped her. Her eyes closed as she tilted her head back, sighing as the water washed over her skin.

Fuck, I loved her body. I'd had a lot of sex. And I wasn't going to apologize for that. Because as a result of all that sex, I knew exactly what I liked. I also knew that her body was the most delicious thing I'd ever seen. I found myself aching for her constantly.

I reached out and slid my fingertips over her breasts. Her head snapped up, and her breath hitched as she watched me tease her nipples until they pebbled.

"Do you like that, baby?" I growled. She nodded and bit her bottom lip. I loved how responsive her body was, more responsive than anyone I'd ever been with—like her body had been made just for me. "Here's what's going to happen," I rasped. "I'm going to mess with your perfect fucking breasts until you're panting for me. And then I'm going to get on my knees and eat your pussy until you scream loud enough for everyone in this fucking building to hear you. And after that, I'm going to fuck you against the shower wall until you black out. Sound good?"

My girl was watching me with a heavy-lidded gaze, and I

knew she was imagining every step of what I'd just laid out in her head right then.

I didn't think my cock had ever been so hard. I lost it then, the lust surging to the forefront of my brain so I couldn't think of anything else but getting inside of her. I grabbed her hips and yanked her forward, pressing my hardness against her soft stomach. Aurora purred, and that was all it took to make me snap. I pressed my lips against hers, my tongue pumping into her mouth with the same rhythm I was dry fucking her with.

The noises that came out of her mouth then—they made me feel like a fucking god. I began to massage her tits. Softly at first, then harder. I pinched, rolled, and tugged at her nipples until she was whimpering against me. Aurora was the kind of girl who liked a little bit of pain with her pleasure, and I could fucking get on board with that. She was moving against me in time with my hips, both of us desperate for more friction.

I've never been a possessive kind of guy, but Aurora made me want to own her. To fuck her until the only word she could say was my name. To mark her so that everyone knew that a piece of her would always belong to me.

I dropped to my knees, sighing as her hands moved against my skin. I pressed on her inner thighs, and she spread her legs wider for me. I'd never seen a prettier pussy. And I definitely didn't think that there was anyone that tasted as good as her either. I parted her folds with my tongue, loving the way she moaned when I began to suck on her clit. Pressure was building in my dick, and I wrapped a hand around the base to make sure I didn't embarrass myself. And then I went to work, licking, and sucking, and tasting like she was my last meal.

"Remington," she gasped, and honestly, that almost

pushed me over the edge just hearing her lust-filled voice murmur my name. I began to push my tongue in and out of her cunt, moaning as her taste filled my mouth. This was the drug that I wanted for the rest of my life. I needed to make a habit of making sure I tasted her like this every fucking day. She screamed as she came, and I continued to lick and suck until she was sobbing with pleasure. Giving her one last long drag of my tongue, I forced myself to my feet.

She looked confused when I grabbed my shampoo and started to wash her hair, relishing in the fact that my scent was going to be all over her skin. She sighed, and her shoulders relaxed as I worked on her hair.

And then I got to the fun part.

I grabbed some body wash and dumped it into my hand, and then I began to wash her with my hands, making sure to slide them over every part of her body in slow, worshipful strokes. She was trembling by the time I was finished with every part of her body except for her sweet pussy. I rolled my finger over her clit and then pushed in one finger. Her nails dug into my chest and I grinned, kind of wanting her to mark me all over. While my finger continued to go in and out of her, my other hand slid around her thigh and between her ass cheeks, and I began to softly massage her puckered flesh. She gasped as I pressed down on her asshole, and then I moved my thumb to her clit and began to play with that until she relaxed enough for my finger to slip past her tight ring of muscle.

"Remington," she sobbed as I thrust my fingers in and out of both of her holes simultaneously. Within seconds she gave me what I wanted, screaming as she came once again. I'd definitely accomplished my goal; there was no way that anyone nearby wouldn't have heard that. I especially hoped that the guys were in their rooms, dying because I had her in here and they didn't.

That was all I could take. I pulled my finger out of her ass and angled her hips up before I surged inside of her. Her tight cunt choked my cock, and I was the one groaning then. Her hands went up to my hair, and she pulled and tugged as I thrust into her savagely. I looped her right leg over my arm, a guttural groan tearing out of me at the new angle. I was a mindless beast in that moment, rutting inside of her until tears were streaming down her cheeks.

"Don't stop," she begged, I pressed my forehead against hers, losing myself and finding myself simultaneously in that moment.

"Never felt anything better," I gasped as she pulsed around my dick with a loud moan that sent me right over the edge along with her, my cock jerking inside of her until she drained me dry. I pulled her lips against mine and kissed her softly a few more times before I finally pulled out.

Her legs gave out and I caught her before she fell, gathering her into my arms and turning off the water before stepping out of the shower.

Her breath was coming out in gasps, and her head was against my chest, and for a moment, I could've sworn that I felt something I'd never felt before. I grabbed the towel and wrapped her in it before walking us into my bedroom where I grabbed one of my shirts and slipped it on her.

"Can we sleep in my room?" she asked tiredly, and I liked that, that she knew I'd want to be with her tonight. She was already completely out by the time I carried her to her room, and I pulled down her covers and set her gently in the bed before curling up behind her, my lips brushing against her neck before I enfolded her in my arms.

My name came out of her lips in a soft gasp, like she was

dreaming about me right then, and I was feeling like a sentimental fool because I would've done whatever she asked so I could hear her say my name like that again.

Sometime later I woke with a jerk when I felt a pinch on my arm, dragging me from the delicious dream I'd been having about what I'd done to Aurora in the shower.

It was Paxton.

"What's wrong?" I muttered sleepily.

"I need to sleep," he said quietly.

I raised an eyebrow. "Okay?"

"I can't do that without her," he admitted reluctantly.

I wanted to tell him to fuck off, but there was something desperate in his voice that had me reluctantly releasing that crazy, beautiful, perfect girl, and carefully sliding out of the bed so that she didn't wake up.

"You owe me," I told him as I stumbled sleepily towards the door.

He huffed. "No, you owe me after that soundtrack we were forced to fucking listen to for an hour earlier."

"You know it was closer to two hours," I snickered smugly before making my way out into the hallway and closing the door softly behind me.

I wasn't sure how I felt about the fact that it seemed like I'd just left a piece of my heart behind me in that room.

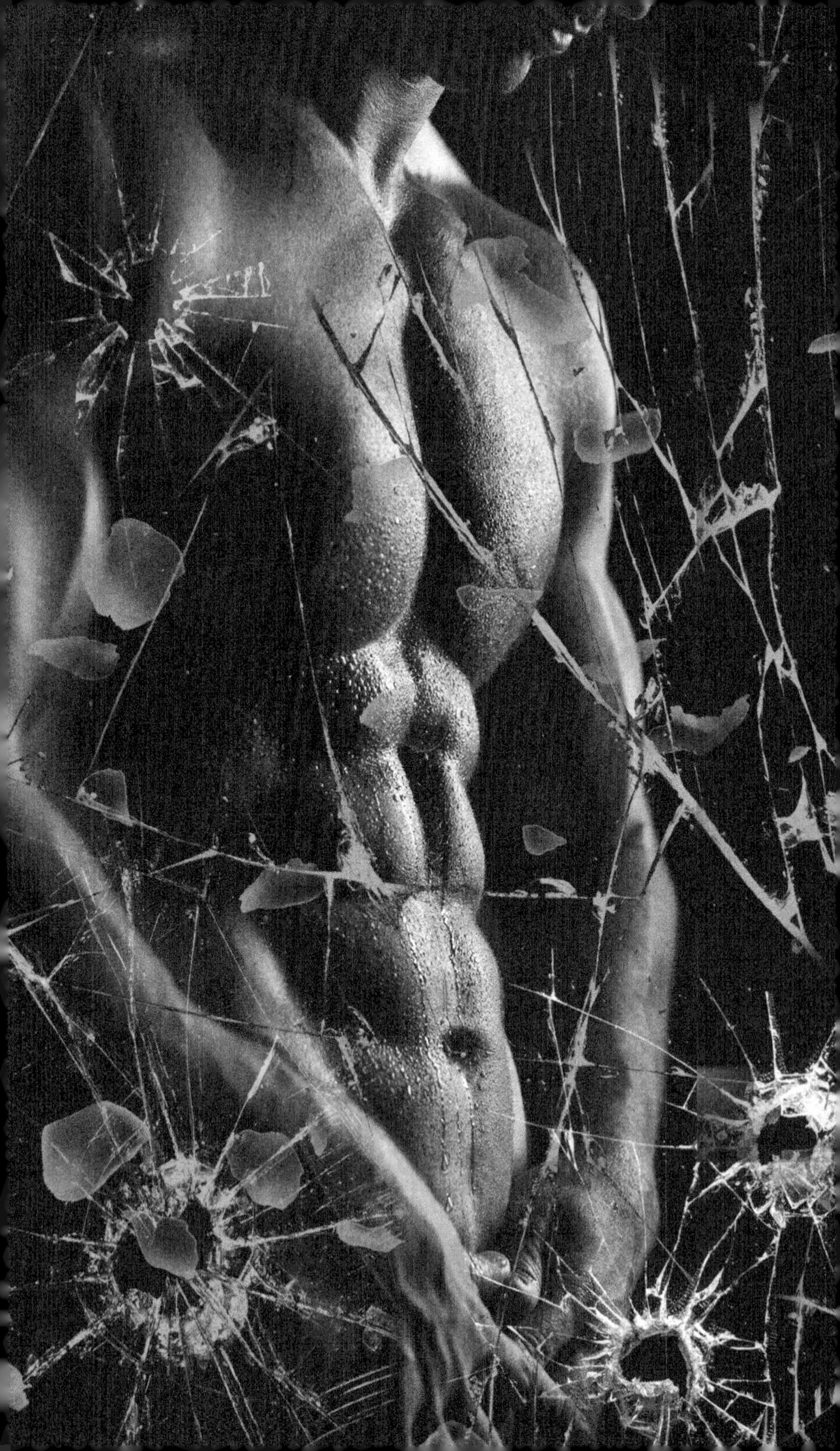

19

AURORA

I'd woken sometime in the night wrapped in Paxton's arms, Remington nowhere to be seen. And in the morning, Paxton was gone. Something I should have been getting used to.

I got dressed and went to get breakfast, and everything seemed so normal that the entire night before felt like a dream.

When I passed where the other Sphinx members ate and walked into the private breakfast room, Pax didn't even acknowledge me.

But breakfast was a bran-flake-free zone. Life was looking up.

Remington pulled me into his lap as I passed, which made up for the thrill of hurt I felt when Pax ignored me.

Stellan gave us a hard look, then picked up his cell phone and glanced at it as if we were irrelevant. Stellan's gaze sent a prickle of awareness washing over my skin, long after he'd looked away, as if the two of us were still tethered together.

Remington gripped my waist, his fingers absently

stroking along the bare skin where my t-shirt and my jeans gapped. One of the servants came in and placed a plate full of pancakes, bacon, and cut strawberries and blueberries in front of him. Remington speared a forkful of fluffy, perfectly sugary pancakes–and held it up to my mouth. When I took the bite, he smiled, as if he enjoyed feeding me.

"Aurora," Cain called, crooking his finger at me. "Come here."

"How can I resist you when you ask so sweetly?" I straightened to abandon Remington, willing to bet Cain was dying inside while Remington and I were so cuddly. Then I collapsed back against Remington's hard chest. His arm circled my waist, his lips nuzzling my throat, just below my ear. "Oh," I said in mock surprise. "It turns out it *is* easy to resist."

Cain sat forward with a frown. "Aurora. You burned my last toy. I think it's only fair you turn into my new one."

"Well, Cain, if there's one thing I learned from you and Remington in the labyrinth–it's that you can't handle me on your own," I said brightly.

There was something so wild and free about the way I acted when I was with them. I might have been warped and twisted, but I was a different girl than the Demon's daughter. I couldn't change how damaged I was–but that damage didn't seem so terrible when I was with these psychos.

Cain sat back in his chair, watching me with a glint in his eyes that told me our discussion wasn't over, but I stayed where I was and allowed Remington to feed me breakfast– even if it took longer that way and created a general air of simmering jealousy.

"Did you enjoy your breakfast?" Cain sat forward in his chair, when I'd taken my last bite. His gaze snaring me as if I were prey.

"I did," I purred back to him, resting my hand lightly on Remington's thigh. "Nicest meal I've had since I came to the Sphinx."

"Good." Cain stood from his chair and abruptly lifted me from Remington's lap, slinging me over his big shoulder. "Remington is welcome to feed you... but the only thing I care about putting in your mouth is my cock."

"What the hell?" I demanded, bracing my hands against the small of his back.

He smacked my ass. "Stop struggling."

"You can't just abduct me from breakfast!"

Cain let out a chuckle. "I think I can."

Remington had an amused look on his face–he seemed to be the only one of these men not plagued by jealousy– and he just shrugged at me.

Stellan buried his face in his hands. "Do you think Cain has ever considered not acting like a barbarian?"

"Doubtful," Pax observed.

Then the doors swung shut to the dining room behind Cain, and we were alone in the den the guys used–the one where Cain and I had done unspeakable things to the bartop.

Cain sat down in his club chair, re-angling me so I was sitting in his lap. I pushed my hair out of my eyes, trying to catch my breath–and my dignity.

"You and I have your punishment to discuss," Cain said.

"Don't ruin the surprise, you'll take all the fun out of it," I chided. "And besides, I was thinking you'd decided I'd actually done you a favor. I know how much you like my artwork on your skin."

He crooked one handsome eyebrow at me. Then he apparently decided not to comment on my brokenness and instead forged on. "I think you deserve a spanking, don't you?"

Always. I yawned dramatically.

Cain's lips curled up in a smile. "I know how you hate to be bored. This time it'll be a little different–since it will be in public."

I scoffed, an icy edge of fear entering my stomach, since Cain always had a plan and I had a feeling his plans were going to be hard to evade. "Exhibitionism is not my kink."

"Two counterpoints," Cain said, holding up two fingers to tick off. "One. You wouldn't know because you were a sad virgin when you came to us. Two. It *is* one of mine."

Cain's smile had a vicious edge that didn't in any way take away from his beauty. "After all, you publicly marked me... forever. I think it's only fair I show the world that you're mine too."

"Nope."

"Think about it today." Cain gently eased me off his lap, his hands on my waist. "Tell me what you think tonight. I was hoping to go to this sex club where I have a long-standing interest."

Sex club. Of course.

I'd bet his club was also called the Twisted Rose. The rich pricks all did seem to hang out in the same places.

But Cain never asked for favors. Cain never asked, period. "What kind of interest?"

"The club is a popular meeting spot for several...crime families with depraved interests, can you imagine that? And I really don't like the owner." Cain smoothed my hair with his hand, tucking a few strands back behind my ear, the expression fond. I caught his wrist to hold him still; the bastard was weaving a trap for me. Crime families. I was betting Cain's family fit into that category. Although I didn't know any specifics, I knew the guys had to be into more things that were illegal besides underground cage fights.

"You need me to get into this club?" I asked. *Easiest job ever since I'd already done it once.*

"Unless you want another girl to go with me," he said silkily. "Think about it. You can tell me what you think tonight."

The repetition of that phrase seemed wrong somehow. Was Cain really changing how he approached our–for lack of a better word that adequately described the crazy–*relationship*?

"I go tonight, and we're even?" I demanded, crossing my arms.

"For now," he said. "I imagine you're going to do something else to piss me off, sooner or later."

The entire idea of a sex club made me uncomfortable. And that sex club in particular–just getting a glimpse of all the equipment in those rooms last night...and seeing enough bloated rich guy sex to last me the rest of my life... sigh, I was in no hurry to return.

But I needed to find out everything I could about that place–and if there were no cameras to capture this spanking, I could humor Cain and help him with his, ah, business venture. I'd won Remington over; I wouldn't mind bringing the biggest psycho I knew onto my team.

"I'll consider it," I promised.

JENNA WAS WAITING FOR ME OUTSIDE MY CLASS. SHE GRABBED my arm and dragged me away. "You don't need to go to Physics today."

"I definitely do," I said. "For someone who knows how to

make a lot of neurotoxins, you'd think I'd be a science nerd. But I can't afford to miss a lecture."

"I figured out how to get you into the Sphinx." Her eyes glinted, and as my gaze snapped to hers, she nodded, grinning. "You can be a full-fledged member of the secret society. That would give you some leverage if you have to live in that house with them, wouldn't it?"

"It would make them crazy," I said. "I'm in love with this idea. But how?"

She dragged me off with her to the library. The deep silence of the shelves and carrels made me nervous now, after the note that had been left on my books. I should really ask Stellan if he'd left that for me, but it felt like a lifetime ago at this point. It felt different today though, walking in with a friend.

Especially if that friend was loud and bubbly and drew disparaging glances from librarians.

I shushed her as we sat down in chairs opposite each other. "It's a secret society. We're supposed to keep it a secret," I said with a laugh.

She paged through the requirements with me.

"Where did you find this?"

"Some stupid pledge accidentally returned his copy of their rule book in his stack of library books," she said with a laugh. "Look at this." She flipped to the front of the book. "It's been signed by every pledge who took possession of it–it's been in circulation at the Sphinx for sixty-three years."

I yanked my hand away from the book. "I can only imagine what's on the pages."

She pulled a face. "Well… look at the requirements. You're supposed to fulfill a certain number of hours of service to the Sphinx before you can officially become a member. Shed blood for them."

"Hours." I drummed my fingertips against the tabletop. "Does running for their entertainment count?"

She frowned. "Do I want to ask what's going on in the Sphinx? Do rich people have a treadmill kink?"

"You have to do a favor for at least two senior members."

She grinned. "I bet you've done them a lot of favors."

I thought of how I'd helped Remington, then Cain's request. "I think I can manage that one."

"There's a skill test on initiation day. And last but not least," she said, flipping to a thick section of the book. "You have to memorize all these rules and shit."

I groaned. *Killing someone to protect Remy's family was one thing. Going to Cain's sex club to help him out was one thing. But reading this whole fucking book...that was a lot of homework.*

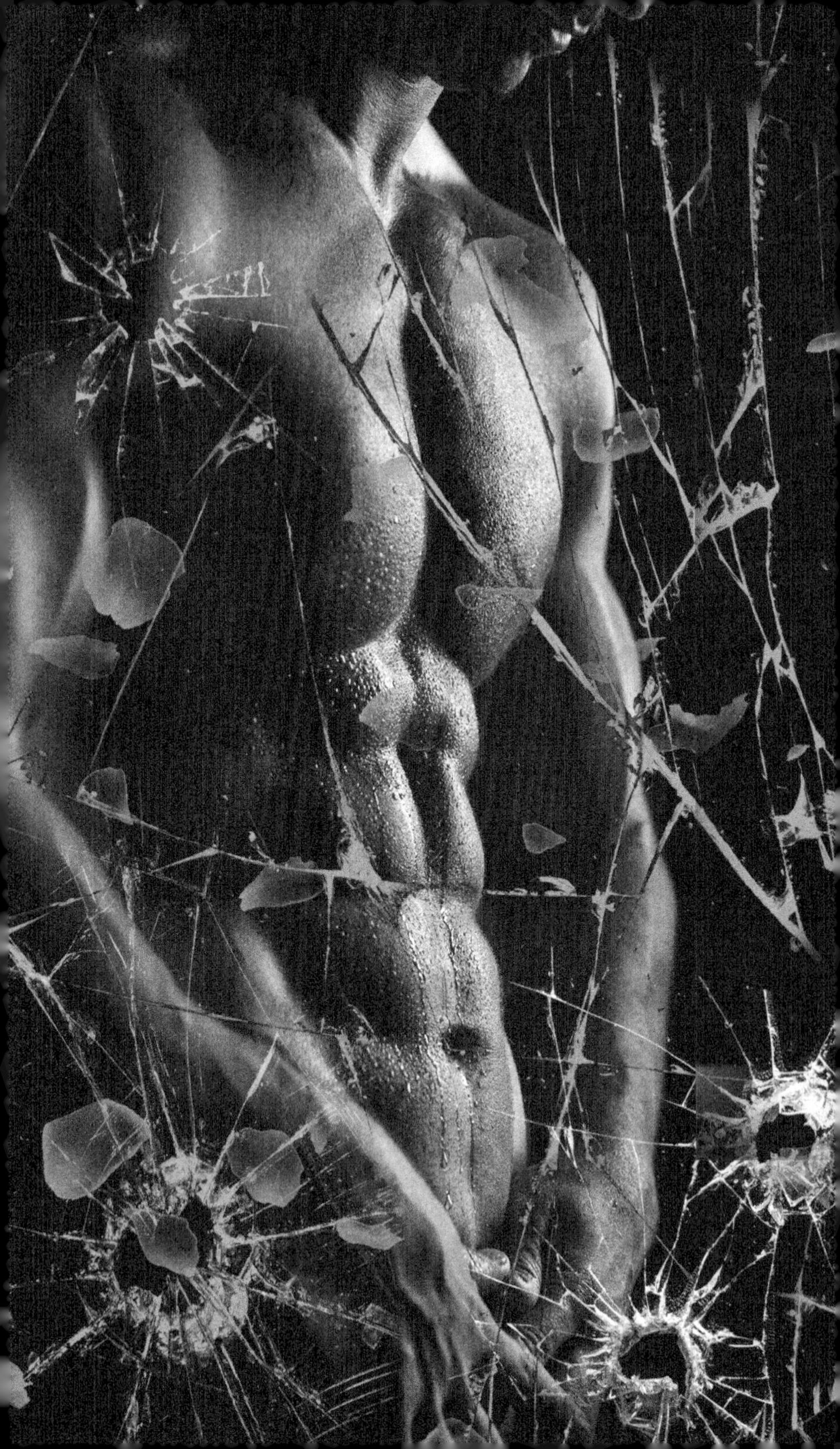

20

AURORA

That afternoon, I was walking back from class toward the Sphinx when Remington's Rolls-Royce Phantom rolled by. I almost raised my hand to wave like a dork, as if I actually was dating these guys.

The car stopped abruptly, as if Remy were picking me up. I caught a glimpse of Pax in the passenger seat, looking bored, as if he'd been dragged along on an errand.

But it was Cain who bounded out of the driver's seat, and before I could react with surprise, he slung me over his shoulder again.

Without fanfare, Cain dropped me into the trunk of the Rolls.

"What the hell is wrong with you?" I shouted, kicking out at him; I hit him square in the chest, but it didn't even rock his wall of muscle. I tried to scramble out of the trunk, but he was already closing it. The world suddenly went dark and muffled.

The next second, a cell phone rang. Cursing, I fumbled in the dark until I found it and answered. "You know I'm going to call 9-1-1, asshole. Even you can't just kidnap people from a college campus."

"Go ahead and try it. I'll wait." Cain sounded amused, and in the background, I heard the slam of his car door shutting.

I hung up on him and attempted to dial 9-1-1.

"9-1-1, what's your emergency?" Cain sounded even more unbearably satisfied with himself than usual.

"You're an absolute dickhead."

"You were right. Remington and I really do need to work as a team. I couldn't have set up a line for us to chat like this without him," Cain said mildly. "So, what do you think about that trip to the club?"

I'd been thinking about it all day, with a mix of trepidation and curiosity. I'd known even dragging me into a BDSM club wouldn't be enough for Cain, even if he needed me; there had to be some sort of special touch.

Apparently, that signature move was kidnapping.

"I was going to tell you I'd go," I was too pissed to even lie about it, "but apparently you decided you didn't care about my answer."

"Never did," he said pleasantly. "I just wanted you to know what you were in for tonight. It wouldn't be any fun to just stuff you into the trunk."

With mock-sympathy, he added, "Just so you know, the trunk of the McLaren was a lot more comfortable."

I was still telling him what an asshole he was when he cut in. "Just remember, I'm not going to let anyone else touch you. Just like you won't let anyone else touch me."

I wondered what Pax thought about that statement, since Pax had definitely touched me recently after his fight... and every night that he came into my room. Cain had said he considered Pax, Remington, and Stellan his only friends;

even though jealousy seemed heavy as smoke in the air whenever the others touched me, maybe they didn't count.

Or maybe I had the power to tear all four of them apart. The thought made me contemplate my potential for vengeance.

He'd hung up on me. I didn't feel my most empowered being trapped in this trunk. If only Jenna was here with her enormous purse of duct tape and tricks, I probably would've had an easy way to escape the trunk.

But would I escape? That was the question, and I didn't know the answer. I hadn't run from Cain yet.

The tires hummed loudly through the trunk as the beast carried me off to his lair.

When the trunk popped open, I was prepared to come out swinging.

But it had been opened remotely. I was alone in a big garage.

My phone chimed with a text message. *Look in the backseat. Time to dress the part.*

I tucked the phone into the back pocket of my jeans and swung open the door, hoping for weaponry. But no, just as I'd expected, it was just a black shopping bag.

I opened black-and-silver tissue paper to find a pair of black heels, a scarlet corset top with black laces, and a black mini skirt. True to Cain's usual style, apparently I didn't need underwear.

I rolled my eyes. Cain was so weird. If he needed my help, he could have just laid out the mission; if he wanted to see me in an outfit, he could just use his words. Seeing me like this would turn him on, and I loved having that power over the man who scared the Sphinx, the campus, the chunk of the world who knew Cain's vicious edge. I wasn't afraid to wield my power, even if I did that from my knees in a skimpy top, now and then.

The garage seemed drafty, so I crawled into the backseat of the car, and checked to see if there were keys. No luck. Then I gave in to my current fate and changed into the slutty outfit.

My cell phone rang.

"You're watching me, creep."

"Always."

A prickle of unease ran through my body, reminding me of that camera pointed at my bed. I'd dropped the wastebasket in front of it recently so I could have some privacy while I plotted.

I hoped it was Cain watching me, as sick as that was.

What if, somehow, the Demon had gotten his eye on my bed?

The thought made a shiver run through me.

"You're all right," Cain said confidently. He was definitely watching me–and misinterpreting me. "Remember what I said."

"You've said a lot of shit, Cain. Chatty Cainey, that's what everyone calls you behind your back."

He didn't dignify that with a response. "Walk down the hallway and go through the door straight at the end. I'm waiting for you in the room at the end."

"Great," I muttered to the dial tone, a bit incredulously. "Mysterious. Love it."

There's nothing someone raised by a serial killer loves like another fucking mystery, after all.

Shaking my head at myself, I followed the hallway, which ended in a T. The hallway branched to either side, but there was a room in front of me, so I pushed open the door.

The room in front of me was dark and small, and I frowned. Nope, not interested. I was still holding the door open in case it locked behind me when I felt a presence behind me and started to spin, just before someone shoved me. The cell phone skittered across the ground as I tried to catch myself, but it was too late.

I stumbled through the doorway and found myself in the narrow room, which was pitch black.

There seemed to be a real trend here of Cain keeping me in the dark.

Then suddenly, the lights came on.

And for the first time, I realized that I wasn't alone at all.

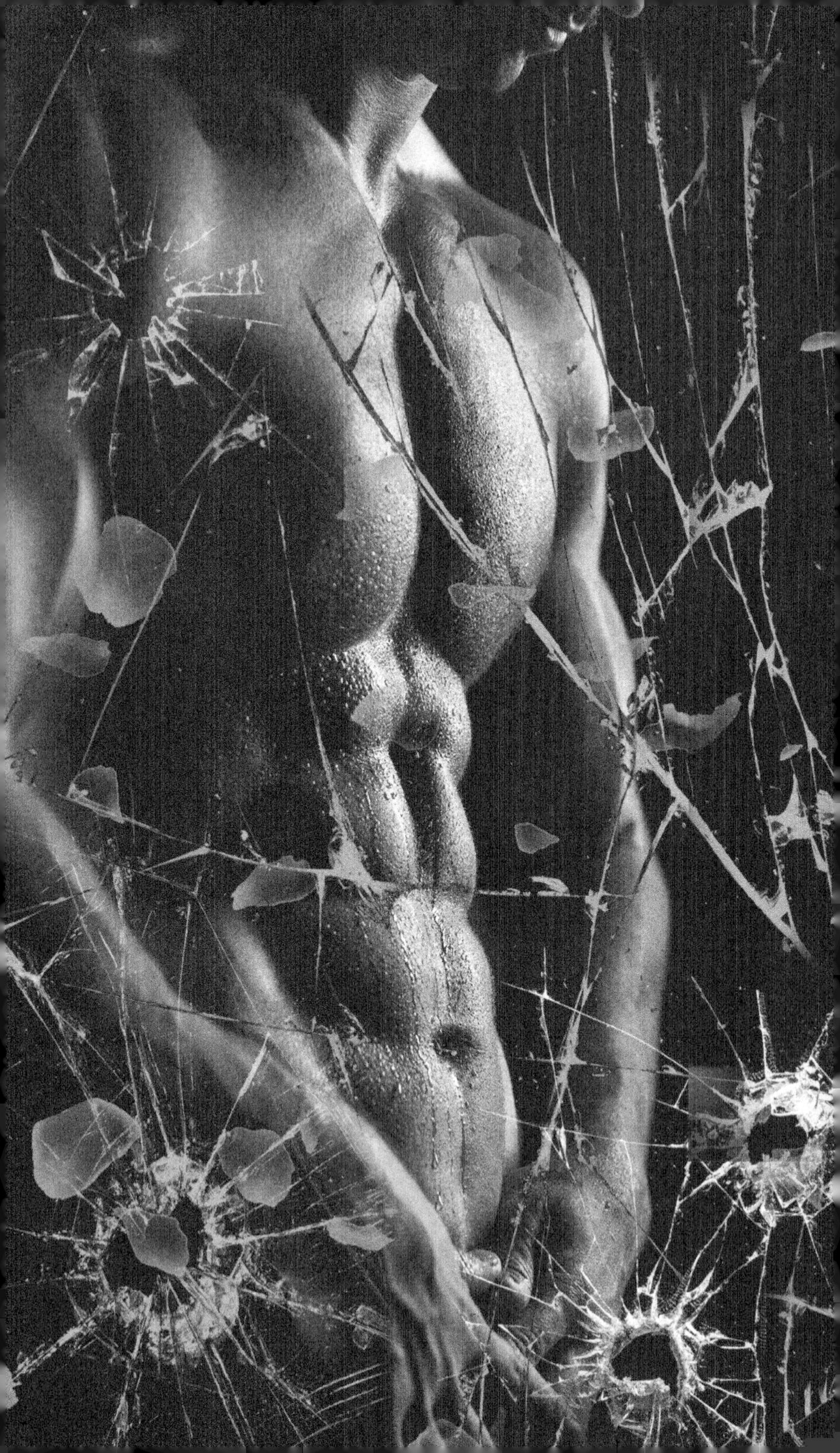

21

CAIN

Aurora was always gorgeous, but now her beauty was especially powerful. The flush of her cheeks as she stared out at the crowd, the way her skin looked dewy under the intense lights. Her white-blond hair, hanging in loose waves around her bare shoulders, glowed as if she were an angel.

She looked good in the outfit I'd wanted her to wear, and she looked good behind bars.

Her violet eyes flashed around, and she pressed closer to the bars, trying to get a good look around her. She didn't waste her time screaming or cursing at the world. She just tried to figure everything out. A wave of pride washed through me. She was so fucking perfect.

There were a dozen men facing her, each alone in their own box, each masked. I wondered if she would know me somehow, even from here.

"I'd like to start the bidding for an evening with this young woman at one hundred thousand dollars," the auctioneer said, and I adjusted my paddle in my lap.

I'd never been able to get close to Patrick Devine. There

was nothing he loved, though, like rough sex with virgins. He rarely attended events at his own club, but I knew he couldn't resist tonight.

Pax would figure out where he was without alerting security, I had faith in him. In the meantime, Aurora and I had a part to play. She'd done her first job as bait; everyone wanted to be the man who took the virginity of the Demon's daughter.

Okay, I'd pretended she was still a virgin. Virginity is just a social construct; sue me.

Now Aurora was on to her second job: forming a distraction.

Aurora chewed her lower lip, her nerves on full display. None of the other men here were smart enough to see her cunning too. She was fierce and fragile, vulnerable and vicious. Those men should be thankful that I'd saved them from being trapped with her, no matter how high they bid.

And bid they did.

The prices kept going up and up. Aurora cupped her hand over her eyes, trying to block the glare of the stage lights that blinded her and illuminated every inch of her perfect body.

I raised my paddle for eight hundred thousand.

Patrick would be getting desperate. He'd always wanted what I had, and even though this auction should have been anonymous now that we were vetted, I had no doubt that Patrick was taking advantage of being the owner. He knew who I was, and he knew what I wanted.

Aurora, always Aurora.

"One million," the auctioneer said crisply, and I knew Patrick had swallowed the bait.

I carried the paddle with me, humming, as I stepped into the gilded hall. Red curtains were draped around each door that led from this hallway; I was willing to bet it looked a lot nicer than Aurora's hallway.

I cupped my earpiece. "Remy."

That was all it took.

Somewhere, there were security guards watching a looped feed. Pax pulled open the door to one of the rooms, and I strolled inside.

"Patrick," I said, and he turned, his eyes wide and horrified.

"You stole from my father," I said mildly. "And therefore, from me."

I made a bored gesture with my gun, although I really did find the man abhorrent. "Also, there's the whole business where you've been trafficking girls. That kind of thing doesn't bother my father, but it annoys me, Patrick."

He made a sound of protest.

"The transfer already went through," Remy said into my ear. "Aurora's rate's been paid."

"Great," I said, right before I shot Patrick. The silencer on this gun was impressive, the sound of the gunshot barely louder than a dropped book, and I looked at it with admiration.

Pax and I dragged him out of the way. Then Pax straightened, wiping his bloody hands. "Quite the hostile takeover."

"They shouldn't have fucked with Remy," I said. My father had left this place on my to-do list for a while, but it hadn't been a priority for him–or me–until they decided to disrespect Remy's mother. They'd thought Remington's father was more powerful than I was.

They guessed wrong.

I sank into the chair that Patrick had previously occupied–which was more like a throne.

Tradition dictated the way the new club owners

cemented their position, by giving the members leverage over the owner. After all, by being the new owner of the club where all the mob families met and did business, I would have a lot of power.

I waited for them to bring me my Aurora.

Two of the club's bouncers dragged her into the room. She wasn't fighting–yet–she was obviously taking in everything around her, her eyes flickering around the room, then landing on me. Was she afraid? Or was she plotting?

One of the security guards shoved her down to her knees in front of me, all but throwing her to the ground. Pax, who had been leaning with his arms crossed over his chest, pushed off the wall abruptly. He was all coiled muscle and fury, but he stopped himself. I gave him a quick, hard glance. Not yet. None of the guards had noticed the way he'd rushed to bust some heads for Aurora's sake, and neither did she.

"Roll cameras," I said quietly to Remy. There was a faint hum of electronics and the light came on the video camera in front of me, transmitting to all the other guests in the other rooms. I rested my hand lightly on Aurora's head as I rose and faced the camera.

"I'm taking control of the Twisted Rose," I told the assembled guests, and the voice synthesizer in my mask distorted my voice, making me sound like a monster. "Patrick Devine has abruptly retired. And in accordance with tradition, I'm here to provide your leverage."

I could feel the rumble of tension through the club. One of the guards tried to walk back into the room, drawing his gun, and Paxton slammed into him, driving him back into the hall. There was a wet sound and a scream and then the door slammed shut, blanketing us in silence once again.

"I'm going to use you to christen my new territory," I told

Aurora with a smile, not that she could see it behind the ornate, faceless mask I wore. "Feel free to fight back. Everyone here would enjoy watching the Demon's daughter break."

If I weren't such an asshole, I would've told her what we were doing before we ever left. I was sure she would've agreed to help take down the Twisted Rose. She would've played the part I was forcing her into now anyway.

But this was so much more fun for me.

Especially if she figured out the game. Aurora looked up at me, and I wondered if she really saw me, even behind the mask.

The thought made something warm and strange surge in my chest, but I pushed it down.

Punishment first.

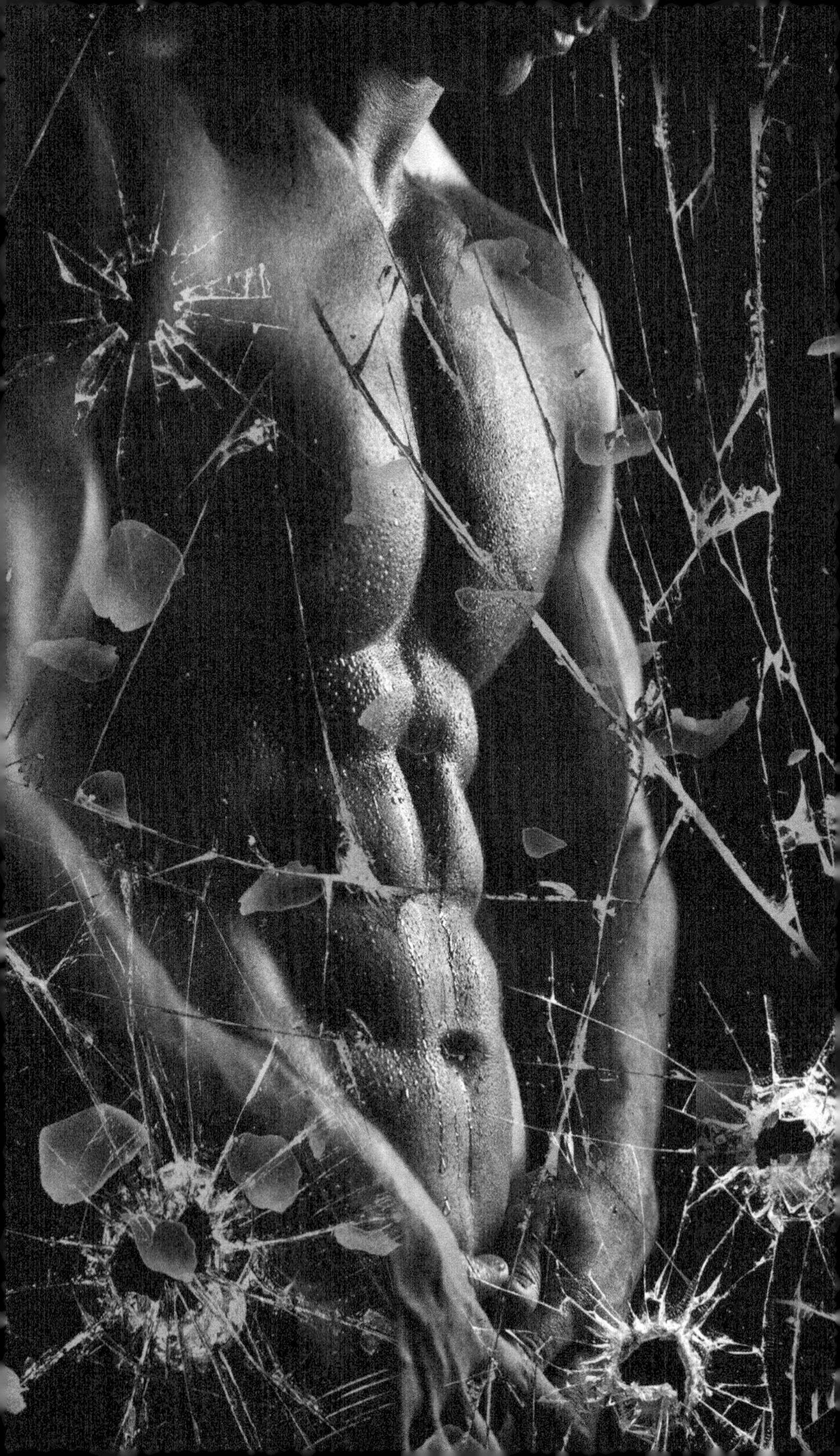

22

AURORA

For a minute when the lights first came up, I'd been terrified. I knew, thanks to the internet, how much some people out there prized the idea of taking my innocence—as if there was any of that left after the Demon was through with me. They thought since I'd done terrible things, they had the right to do terrible things to me.

But that fear faded in seconds. Cain had been so obvious: *I'll never let anyone else touch what's mine.*

He'd win the auction. I should just make it look as if it weren't a foregone conclusion.

Also, I was going to murder him later. This nightmare *more* than paid me back for the tattoo... especially since the weirdo wouldn't even talk to me about what was happening. He needed so much therapy. He had to know I'd be happy to take down the Twisted Rose after what they'd done to Remington's mom.

Was Cain trying to torture me, forcing me into the role of a victim like other girls who had come through here, like girls who had been stolen by men like my father? Or was he trying to test me—to see if I figured out what was happening and kicked ass as part of the team, even if it made me look weak and vulnerable?

Disquiet hummed beneath my surface–because Cain seemed boundlessly confident in himself, but I wasn't so sure that arrogance was justified–and I let it all show on my face.

Two of the guards came in, opening the door to my tiny cell. "You're being taken to the owner," one of them said with obvious satisfaction. He had tattoos running up his neck, the kind of neck that made a man look like a thumb. I was going to call him "Neck."

The second one, tall and dour-looking, held out an arm to usher me out of the tiny room, but Neck grabbed my arm and yanked me roughly forward. Into my ear, he said, "The owner is going to use you up, fill all your holes with his cum, break you, and I get what's left."

"Wow," I said, my voice flat and bored. I couldn't help myself. "That's the saddest brag I've ever heard."

He dragged me along, his fingers bruising deep into my skin, purposefully trying to make me stumble. I did my best to both keep my balance and stifle a yawn. These men were the most boring kind of evil, and I knew they couldn't hurt me, not when Cain and Pax claimed that pleasure.

If it had been anyone else, I would've felt degraded by Cain's threats; even though those dark words were for the benefit of the crowd. But when I was close to these men, I would never break. Somehow, the struggle between us made me stronger, different.

Cain wrapped his hand around the back of my throat and steered me ahead of him from the small room. "Let's go inspect our new territory," he said, his voice low pitched, distorted. He still absently carried his auctioneer's paddle, tapping it lightly against his other leg.

I missed the way sarcasm and sex usually dripped from his every drawled syllable.

The two of us walked through red curtains and down a dark wood-paneled hallway. We emerged into a cavernous room with many smaller rooms branching from it. I still didn't know where the spikes went, and now I didn't want to.

The men in masks had moved quietly into the room and stood in various places, gripping drinks. Pax came in over the announcements. "It's the night for leverage, gentlemen. The usual no-cameras policy has been temporarily lifted. If you are in the circle, expect to be recorded."

"The circle?" I started to wonder, but then the room's lights dimmed and a circle was illuminated. At the center of the circle was a simple black bench–which looked out of place given all the strange equipment dotted around the club.

I caught glimpses of Stellan, then Remington, in the crowd. I guessed that was no surprise. They were all so close to Cain there would be no way they wouldn't be involved in his "mob" business if Cain was a part of it. There were members of the Sphinx here too–enough of them to seem like an army.

And for better or worse, I seemed to be involved in their business now too.

Cain bent me over the bench backward, fastening one wrist to the cuff. "You're all mine, princess."

His voice was mocking.

"Call me little devil," I whispered huskily.

The mask stared down at me, unblinkingly, then he reached up and pulled it away. Icy blue eyes met mine. There had been the smallest needle of cold doubt in my stomach, then suddenly it warmed and was gone. He set the mask on top of my heaving chest, as if it were a barrier between us–a small and temporary one.

"How did you know?"

"I can smell your jealousy from a thousand feet away," I whispered, his lips close to mine. I writhed against his body, knowing I'd look desperate to escape to the men who watched us, but really, I ground my hips up against his. "You'd never let someone else touch me like this."

Pride sparked in his gaze. "I'm going to have you on every piece of equipment in this club, Aurora. In time."

I bit my lower lip as his lips skimmed over my throat to the swell of my breasts above the corset. I'd thought he wouldn't want anyone to see me, that he would feel the same way as Stellan when Stellan had fixed my clothes–but in Cain's twisted logic, I could see how this would make sense.

He was showing *his* world that I belonged to him.

The sudden realization of how much safety came with that struck me like a blow, accompanied by a hollowing in my stomach as I realized my true vulnerability. It wasn't being naked. It was getting used to being protected–letting myself feel warm and safe, relaxing for the first time in my life.

And the next second, I was pissed off. Rage swelled in my chest, and I wasn't sure it was even for Cain. I was just so sick of my life–of having to look over my shoulder for the Demon, his followers, his enemies.

The Demon would be so pissed off about this video too, about me losing my precious virginity that mattered to him so much, in such a public place–if he hadn't already seen me lose it, thanks to cameras in the Sphinx.

I reached out and punched Cain in the face, surprising him with my left hook. His chiseled, clean-cut jaw jerked to one side, just before I nailed him in the chest with my high-heeled shoe. It fell off under the impact, which was probably for the best, because Cain grabbed my ankles in either hand, his face suddenly set.

Unceremoniously, Cain flipped me over so I was half-hanging off the bench, my one wrist still anchored in the chains.

"I love the spirit," he deadpanned, right before he slapped my ass with his hand. He pushed my skirt up, his touch sending sparks flying down my spine. "This is quite the slutty outfit for the Demon's virginal daughter. I like it…a lot."

His short fingernails raked over the skin he'd just reddened, sending a shiver up my spine, before his tip pressed against my core. I caught glimpses of the guys and of familiar faces in the crowd from the Sphinx, but I was too distracted by the heat coursing through my body, between the connection between Cain and me, to pay enough attention to read their expressions.

I should have been angry at having anyone watch us.

But I loved having Cain grip my throat and turn me over again, the way his eyes went heavy-lidded as they swept my breasts in the corset. He straddled me, his hands gripping my wrists, harder than any restraints.

Cain's lips swept over my throat, rousing desire everywhere he touched. I tried to shrink into the bench, to pull away from him, but I couldn't force myself away, even knowing I should look unwilling for the crowd. For Cain, most of all.

But I wanted him, and my hips rose, and there was no denying the connection that sizzled between the two of us, dangerous, fiery bonds that seemed like they could burn the whole world. His tip brushed against my wet heat, and he groaned in my ear, the sound private even though nothing else about this was.

He shoved inside me, rough and brutal despite his size, and I wrenched back against him as he set a punishing pace. His tip seemed to slam home deep inside me, and he filled me so much that I burned in both good ways and bad.

There could have been no one else in the room, because all I could see was him; he filled my senses, with the spicy scent of his cologne, the heat of his body against mine, the sense of him filling me and surrounding me and pinning me down. His blue eyes bore into me, but they weren't icy anymore; they were bright and blue as the sky, no matter how dark everything was around me.

My channel began to pulse around him, so hard that it hurt when he was already so big, and I let out a moan that was half a scream. "Cain..." I begged, not knowing what I even wanted. I wanted him to stop and I wanted him to keep going forever.

"Mine," he answered with a faint smile that no one else could see, his handsome face close to mine. "Now everyone will know."

"Good," I managed, my voice ragged. "Hopefully I won't have to beat any other girls senseless."

"Oh, I hope the fun's not ending now." Despite the banter, his lips were tight, a faint tick starting in his cheek, as if he were holding himself back.

Then he exploded inside me, following me over the edge.

I fell back against the bench.

"Party's over," Pax called to the crowd. "You'll have your video proof delivered within the next few minutes. Tell your friends about the change in management."

Cain walked away from me as if I were nothing. It was probably for the sake of his reputation.

But maybe it wasn't.

It was Stellan who gathered me up in his arms and carried me away to the back. I let my head rest on his shoulder and tried to conjure up the exact sensory details of the man who carried me in the labyrinth. Had it been Stellan?

"Just so you know," Stellan said quietly, "the cameras only captured Cain's face. For their leverage. But from the angle... no one will know it was you. Since Cain only pushed your skirt up, his body hid yours, too."

His kind tone surprised me.

"It's not like my reputation matters anymore," I said breezily.

Stellan cocked his head to one side, studying me. He looked at me as if he looked right through me. Cain did too, but it was different with both of them. Cain studied me as if he could see through to my soul because it was the mirror image of his. Aurora, chasing the same darkness he did. Stellan looked at me as if he saw right through all my jaded edges to the girl I'd been—as if she were still alive at the core. Delilah, kissing him in the rain.

"It matters to me," Stellan said. He leaned in and kissed my forehead, and something about that felt more intimate—and angered me more—than Cain's public display.

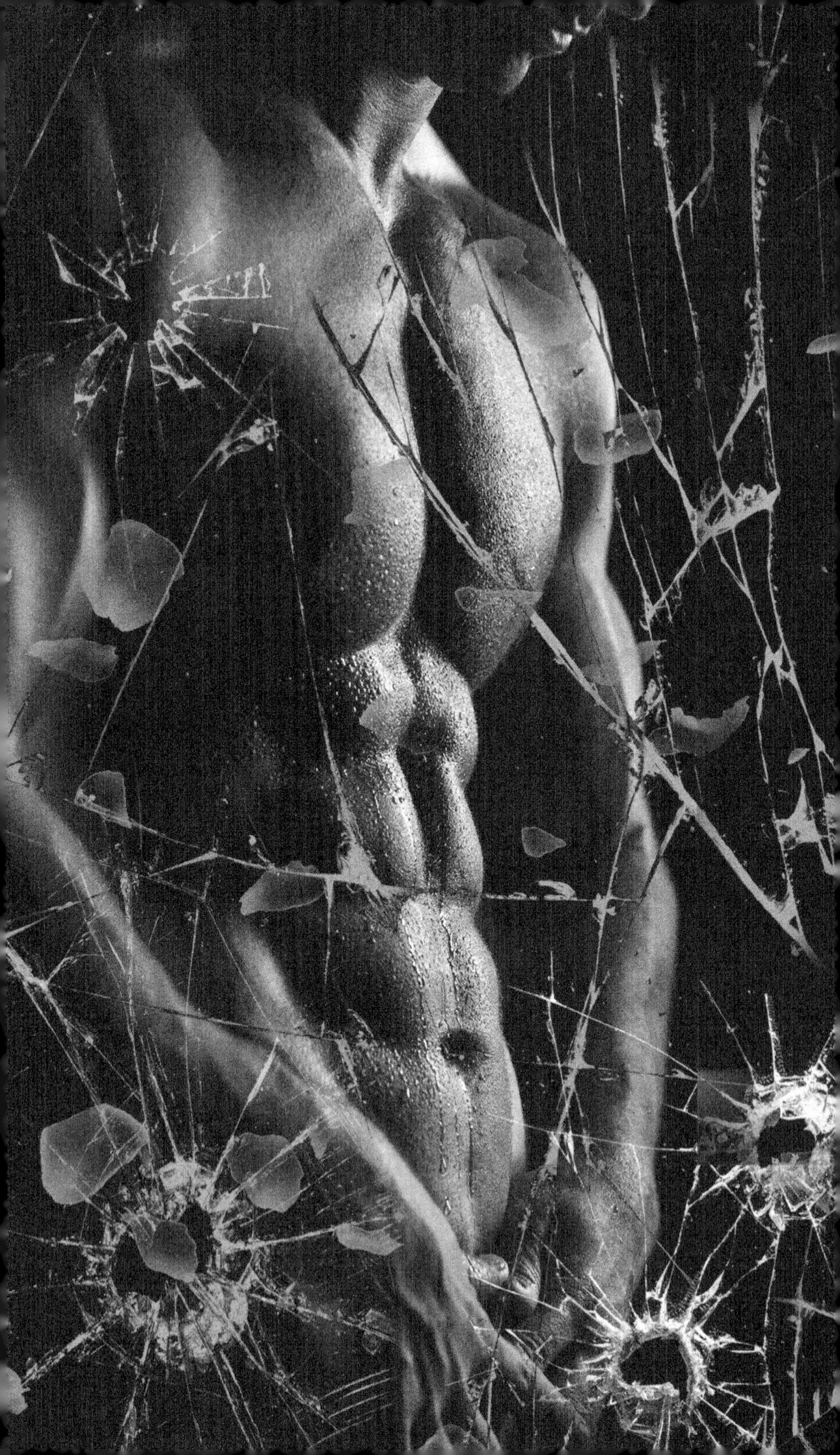

23

AURORA

The next day, I lay in bed still thinking about that kiss, and how one tender kiss from Stellan could leave me feeling shattered in a way that rough sex strapped down never could. Cain's rough handling made me feel as fierce and vicious as he was; Stellan's kisses burned straight to my soul and reminded me of the tender, tongue-tied girl I used to be with him.

I'd gotten revenge on Cain and Pax and Remington–as complicated as revenge had grown in all those cases–but I hadn't punished Stellan.

And he was the one who had started this all.

I made an impulsive decision and flung the covers to one side, getting out of bed to search the closet. I pulled out a pale pink summer dress that reminded me of Delilah, who was dark-haired and shy. When I pulled it on and glanced in the mirror, I could catch glimpses of my old self, even with all the plastic surgery–the way I caught my lower lip with my teeth and worried it, the way I played with my hair. The memory of the way I'd fallen back into my old ways around the Demon, growing ragged and eager to please, made me want to murder Delilah and bury her deep.

Knowing that Stellan couldn't get it up for any other girl was oddly satisfying, and not just because Stellan made me feel sad and vicious in equal measure. The way he'd rejected me hurt worse than being rejected by anyone else. And it hurt worse than anything Cain, Remington, or Pax could ever do to me.

I'd searched Cain's and Remington's room. But maybe Stellan was the one who had been watching me.

I waited until he went to breakfast, then slipped down the hall and let myself into his room, then slid my lock picks back into my pocket.

I searched his room trying to find the news feed for the hidden cameras. Maybe it made sense Stellan would be my stalker. Supposedly he had this intense secret obsession if he couldn't even be attracted to another girl, but I couldn't find anything on his laptop or in his room.

And yet, I doubted one of these guys was keeping secrets from the others, at least I doubted they'd keep those kinds of secrets about me. I could imagine the way the other three would react if they discovered one of them was peeping on me, and I imagined the rest of them being dangerous in their fury.

Yet at the same time, I could easily imagine all four of them agreeing that keeping a constant electronic eye on me was a good idea. If just one of them was stalking me, their anger wouldn't be because they were white knights. It would be because someone had left out someone else, and they all seemed to feel like they shared ownership.

I caught a glimpse of a journal in a drawer, and I picked it up curiously, then was horrified to realize it was Sophia's. I hastily closed it and set it back in the drawer, my heart pounding. Seeing my best friend's handwriting, I'd heard the sentence she'd written in my head, as close as I'd come to hearing her voice in years. My chest ached, and my hand trembled as I forced myself to close the drawer.

I wanted to read it all. I wanted to be close to her again. But Sophia couldn't exactly give me her permission.

Had Stellan been reading these?

Sophia would have been pissed. My anger pulsed as I paced his room, debating what to do next.

His dark gray sheets and plain white comforter spilled off the bed, so different from when we were in high school. I used to peek in through his doorway when I followed Sophia toward her room, doing my best not to be caught because she always teased me about my crush on Stellan. Once when I'd started to get annoyed, she'd tucked her arm over mine and promised, "I want you to be my sister, believe me, I hope you marry that moron even though I think you deserve better." I remembered there being a look in her eye I didn't understand as she said it, but then she'd smiled, and everything had been okay.

The memory made a smile cross my face, then I thought about how Stellan couldn't stand to have sex with anyone else, and my smile darkened. I crossed to his bed.

And that was why, when Stellan walked into his room, I was lying back on his pillows. He didn't seem as excited to find me on his bed as Cain had been.

Stellan stared at me for a few long seconds. "What are you doing in here, Aurora? And how did you get in here?"

He sounded tired, but his nostrils flared. His eyes were drawn toward my thighs.

I'd been playing with myself on his bed, replaying the day dreams I used to have about Stellan when we were young. All the girls in our high school had a crush on the tousle-haired star athlete with the easy grin. It sounded stupid now, but when I was a teenager, I'd loved all those stupid rom coms set in high school, where the geeky outcast girl and popular high school jock fell in love.

In high school, we traveled in different circles. I hung out with Sophia and her artsy friends. But even then I thought there'd been something about the way he looked at me, like he was drawn to me. I hadn't been sure if it had been my imagination or not when I was young and innocent.

Now I knew that I held that power over him for real. I'd been replaying those daydreams I used to have about Stellan kissing me. I'd never even let myself daydream about him when I was around the Demon; I was so desperate to protect Stellan and Sophia from the Demon, and just as desperate to stay.

But at night, I used to imagine what it would be like if Stellan kissed me openly in the halls, if he held my hand. I used to imagine my body pressed against his in the shadows of a high school party, the kinds where I was never invited. I used to imagine Stellan's hands on my hips, the way his gaze would spark with lust when he looked at me.

Stellan's eyes sharpened. "What are you doing?"

I stretched languidly, letting my skirt slip up. I hadn't bothered to wear underwear. Cain certainly seemed to hate when I did–except for the opportunity it gave him to steal it.

Stellan's reaction to catching my hands between my thighs was instantaneous, his cock stiffening, his eyes dilating.

"Aurora," he said, and I couldn't read his tone. Anger? Desire? Desperation? "What the fuck are you doing in my room?"

"There's nowhere that I'm safe from you, Stellan. I don't think there should be anywhere that you're safe from me." I let my thighs fall apart, his gaze drawn to me so intensely that I felt it through my core. "I want you to think of me every time you lay down on this bed. Think about what you could've had."

His gaze rose to meet mine, his brow furrowing angrily. "You're always safe with me."

I let out a laugh. "You have got to be kidding me, Stellan. Or are you just lying to yourself?"

His jaw tightened. "What do you want from me? Am I supposed to be sorry that I've tried to push you so I could find the truth about my sister?"

"I want the truth about what happened to Sophia as much as you do!"

"Really?" His gaze met mine. "Then if you really weren't involved... did you ask about her when you went to see the Demon?"

My stomach hollowed out.

"How do you know?" I demanded. I didn't want these men to ever see the girl I became around the Demon. I was ashamed of my weakness.

Stellan didn't deign to answer that question. I retraced my memories, trying to figure out how he could have tracked me down. I didn't think that anything in the camera feed had given me away. Was Paxton that much of a blabber mouth? Or were they all tracking me?

Or maybe they just always had someone tailing me. Maybe *they* were always tailing me. But if that were true, I wouldn't have been able to break into Remington's room and hide under his bed...unless the bastards had known I was there and been playing their own game. As I absently stroked my hand between my thighs, toying with my clit, I replayed everything, debating what could have been just another lie between these men and me.

"Aurora," Stellan groaned. His face looked as if he were warring with himself, then he suddenly sat on the bed beside me, his gaze sharp and hungry. He twitched my skirt completely out of the way, watching my fingers work against my clit.

Then he leaned over and pressed a tender kiss to my thigh, his hands wrapping around my thighs. He looked up at me with the worshipful look I'd always longed to see, and my heart stuttered in my chest.

When he reached to touch me, my hips were already rising to meet his touch.

And I lashed out and kicked him.

Stellan grabbed his shoulder, a hurt look crossing his face. "What the fuck is your problem?"

"I don't want you to touch me until you stop being a moron!"

Stellan straightened, wariness coming over his face. "You hate me more than you hate the rest of them. Why? If you don't know what happened to my sister, if you don't feel guilty, then why is it that you hate me so much?"

"I don't hate you more than them," I said, only to feel a thrill of hard, bitter rage at the sight of his face–and to realize he was right. If I hated him like I hated them, I would have punished him the way I had gone after Cain, Pax, and Remington.

I went on, my voice cool. "I feel sorry for you. I feel sorry about your sister."

"Oh bullshit," he said, his voice a controlled explosion. "I mean, I don't doubt that's true on some level. I know you miss Sophia too. Although maybe you miss her even though you helped hurt her. I don't know, Aurora. Maybe you felt like you were trapped. Maybe you felt like it was her or you."

"Would you listen to yourself?" I demanded. "You're right Stellan, I do hate you. Because those men out there are trying to protect you and help you, because of your weird brotherhood of bullshit."

I scrambled up to my knees on the bed. Hopefully Stellan would continue to think about me at night. Hopefully he'd be tormented by the memory of finding me on his bed but knowing I wouldn't be his. I leveled a finger at his chest.

"They're assholes because of you. For you. And you dare try to fucking kiss me, when you won't just believe that I loved Sophia too, that I would never have hurt her?"

He stared back at me, his eyes blazing. "You didn't love her like I loved her. Or like she loved you."

"If you don't trust me, then you're not just being a dickhead to me when you kiss me anyway. You're betraying her memory," I said tightly.

"Do you think I don't fucking know that?" he demanded, his voice ragged. He ran his hands through his hair. "Christ, Aurora. Half the time, I know you didn't, I know you couldn't have. Then you seem like the only piece of her I have left. But sometimes, I wonder, and I can't stand to look at you..."

He sounded so anguished that it tore open something in my chest, but anger lashed into its place a second after.

I stared at him, crossing my arms over my chest. "There is no way for me to prove to you that I didn't hurt Sophia. Unless we find Sophia and what really happened to her."

"Then let's do that," he said abruptly. "If you really care, Aurora, then let's go home. Let's find out what happened to Sophia."

He stared at me, something hard and flinty coming into his eyes. "But I swear to God, Aurora, if I trust you, that you're on my side. If I trust you, because she trusted you... and you did hurt her. I'm going to kill you."

"That's fine." I said crisply. "Because I know that I didn't have anything to do with her death and that you are a moron."

"I want to be proven a moron in this case, believe me." He studied me curiously. "You have all that hate sex with the others. Did you come into my room trying to get my attention?"

The connection between us that seemed to transcend time and reality burned brighter and hotter than ever. I could've been dark-haired, wide-eyed Delilah or cool, blond Aurora. Then I snapped back into reality.

"I already know I have your attention, Stellan. I'm just waiting for you to be worthy of mine."

For a second, my crisp words seemed to land like a lash. Then he said confidently, "it seems like you're paying attention to me now, Delilah."

When he used my old name it always sounded full of emotion. His hands fell on my hips, and his lips brushed my cheek. He tilted my chin up to his, and he stared down at me with feeling in his gaze.

Stellan's tender kiss devastated me in a way that rough sex with my monsters couldn't. The others made me feel empowered; they hurt me, and I hurt them back. When Stellan kissed me, I wanted to kiss him back, to lose myself in him.

The new Aurora shoved him away. "I can't do this with you, not until you're ready to give me all of you. Not until you can come to me with no reservations. If you really think that I can be close to you knowing that you think I could have hurt Sophia..." I shook my head.

"Everyone else in the Sphinx thinks you're a monster." His voice had gone cool, his eyes shuttering. He crossed his arms over his powerful chest. "Why is it so terrible if I wonder about it too?"

"Because you were supposed to be the one who knew me! You recognized me despite all those surgeries! You knew me before! When you figured out I was the Demon's daughter, you should've known I left to protect you!" I exploded back, and suddenly I realized how true my disappointment was.

I'd always wanted Stellan to be the one who knew what I'd done and who loved me anyway. That had been a dream I'd had when I was younger, a dream that seemed ridiculous now.

"You did?" Stellan asked. He was frowning again. "So you knew the Demon might hurt my sister?"

"No. I thought the Demon would hurt you."

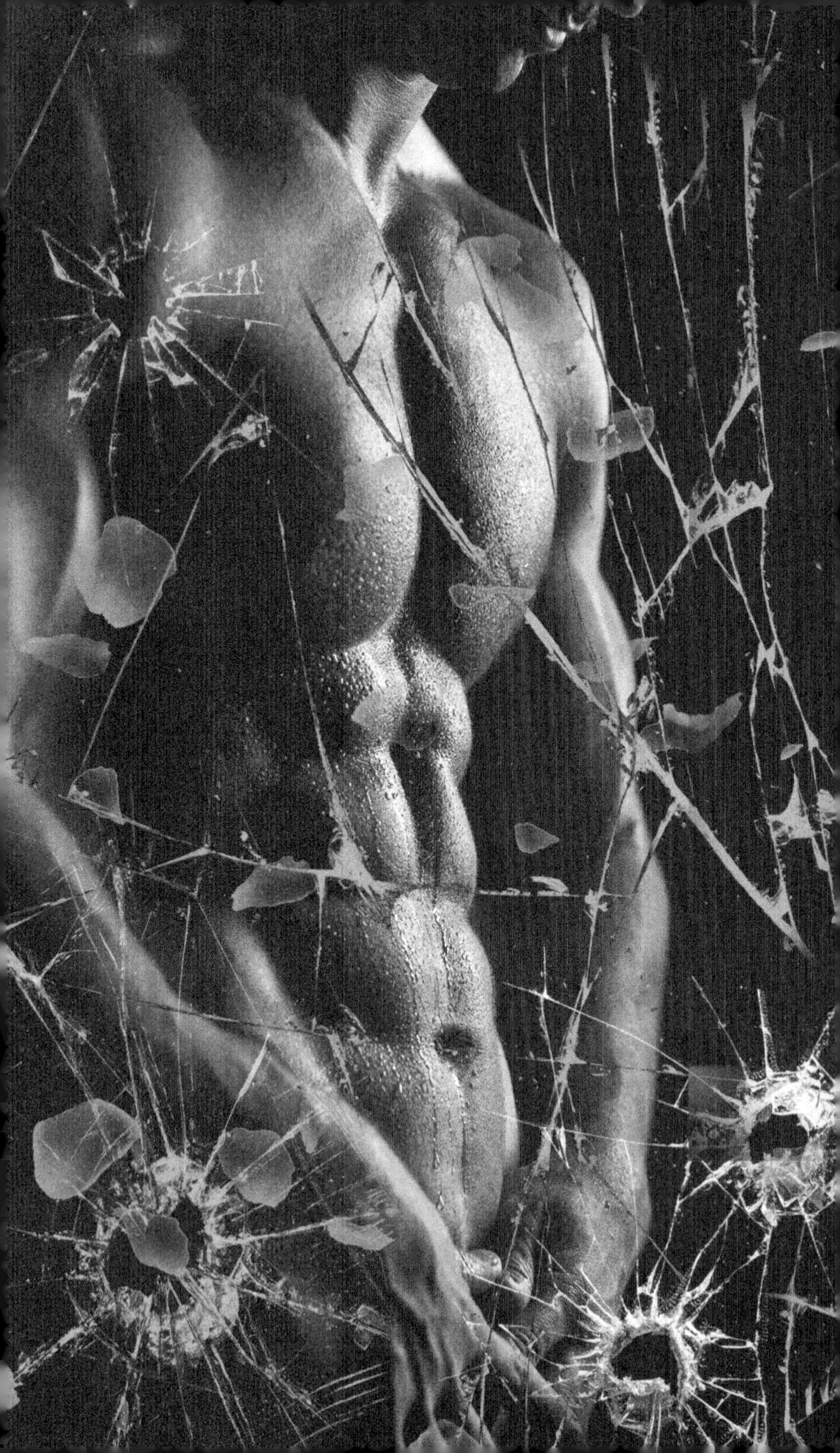

24

AURORA

I'd left Stellan with that thought and went back to my room for the afternoon. And now Remington and I were headed toward dinner. He swept his hand up the curve of my ass to rest lightly at the small of my back. "Unfortunately, we have to leave for a while tonight. You should invite Jenna over and lock yourselves up in the house, because the Sphinx will be empty."

"I'm used to being alone, Remington," I reminded him.

"I don't like it," he disagreed. "I like to know you're safe. That's why I'd even let you break the no-strangers in the Sphinx rule for tonight. I'll argue with the guys."

"If you just want to know I'm safe, I don't know why I'm still here with you all," I said lightly. "I didn't exactly feel safe when you and Cain did your very best minotaur impressions and chased me through the labyrinth."

Remington looked at me skeptically, his hands resting lightly on my shoulders. "You knew it was us."

"You're not safe, nice men."

Remington scoffed, then slung his arm over my shoulders for the two of us to head through the den and into the dining room. "You don't like safe, nice men. Leave that type to sweet girls like Jenna."

At dinner, I declined Remington and Cain's forceful invitations to sit on their laps. As I waved them off and draped my napkin in my lap, I reminded them, "You're all very cute, but I don't like for anyone to get between me and my dinner."

"So, tonight is initiation night for the Sphinx members," I said.

Pax pointed his fork at me. "Yes. You'll be unattended. Try to stay out of trouble."

"It's not my fault that trouble always finds me. I tried." I mimed a circle around my face; I'd done everything I could to start over. "But don't worry. I'll stay close."

Cain cocked his head to one side.

"You'll need to stay here," Remington said. "It's all Sphinx business. Just like at the Twisted Rose, rich people are weird about their traditions."

"I would like to join the Sphinx," I said calmly, pulling the worn book out from under my napkin and dropping it on the table.

They all seemed shocked for a second.

"It's a long process," Pax said. "And girls aren't allowed."

"Girls aren't officially forbidden," I argued, tapping the book with my long red fingernails. Jenna and I had gone through their possible objections, and given the general faint Axe-body-spray stench of much of the Sphinx, we'd figured that might be one of them. "And Clause Eight says that there's not to be additional prescriptions added to any incoming class at the Sphinx, *unless* by unanimous agreement of all its senior members. Who happen to be sitting at this table." *And owing me.*

"No," Stellan scoffed. "I'm sorry, Aurora, but you'd ruin

the Sphinx's reputation. And you haven't done any of the requirements."

I held up a finger. "One. Two significant favors for two existing members. Remington, was it *significant* that I helped rescue your mom and siblings?"

Cain sat back, the look on his face amused, and he seemed to expect my next words as I turned to him. "Was it significant that I acted as bait for your takeover of the Twisted Rose? Because I feel like an accessory to murder."

"As well as my favorite fucktoy?" Cain asked.

"Your only," I reminded him with a tight smile. "No other girl's ever going to see your cock without laughing their asses off at my finest handwriting."

"You're supposed to be trying to win him over," Remington muttered under his breath to me as Cain's eyes narrowed.

"I just need one person to nominate me," I said.

Remington was avoiding my gaze, drumming his fingernails on the tabletop. Stellan gave me a short, sharp shake of the head; maybe I shouldn't be surprised he was pissed at me at the moment.

"Sorry, Aurora," Pax said. "We've got plans for the Sphinx. Even if we successfully made you a member, well... The alumni network is pretty important to us, and they would not be impressed."

I couldn't believe I still had the capacity to be disappointed by them. But as I was leaving dinner, Remington slung his arm over my shoulders again. I was about to shrug him off when he hip-checked me abruptly to one side, shoving me into a room as we passed.

"What?" I demanded.

He held his arms out with a flourish, giving me a cocky grin.

We were in a walk-in closet, where dark robes were neatly folded.

"This is going to be so much more fun if we surprise them," Remington said, and I felt a grin come out over my face before I jumped to hug him.

Tonight was going to be full of surprises.

Dressed in a black robe and a gold mask that hid my face, I followed the other acolytes down the steps of the Sphinx and into the night. Tonight was the night we took our places. I'd heard that other students hid inside because, sometimes, the Sphinx initiates took revenge on various people who had wronged the Sphinx as one of their tests. Jenna claimed it was probably all made up in past years, but I wouldn't put it past these men of mine to make it a reality.

"Tonight," Cain said, "You all are supposed to be initiated into the Sphinx. For the past few months, you've tried to prove your worth, and your ranks have been decimated as some of your peers have been found unworthy."

"But there is one last night of testing. Tonight you all have your missions." Pax spoke up, and even though his face was hidden behind a mask, I'd know his voice anywhere. I felt it through my bones, deep and bass.

"You'll meet us back here tonight when you've collected your tithe to the Sphinx," Remington added. They had a different requirement of each pledge, something that would hurt, that would take a sacrifice no matter how rich they were. Some of them needed to steal something, some of them needed to provide leverage, some of them needed to bring a chunk of the family fortune to the table. Nothing was easy.

Remington had pointed out that, when the moment of challenge came, my price had to look the same as anyone else's.

So tonight, I was digging up a corpse.

The thought made my stomach tense, bile climbing up my throat. Was it worth it, to disturb the Demon's old graves? There were corpses no one ever found, buried with proof of their sins.

Like Carrie Hayward.

Remington thought it was nice symmetry to provide the grave to the Sphinx, but then, he wasn't the one who was likely to break a nail digging up the box buried with Carrie. Remington knew they'd all appreciate having the dirt on Carrie to hold over his family.

I headed around the Sphinx to the car. Once I'd locked myself in the driver's seat, I tore the mask and hood off, because if I was a police officer, I'd one-hundred-percent pull someone over if they wore a depraved-sex-club mask when it wasn't even Halloween.

Maybe the masks were supposed to be dignified and mysterious, but I'd never see a mask again without thinking, *sex club.*

I started up the car I'd borrowed–i.e. stolen–from Paxton, BANKS blasting through the cabin. I didn't bother to turn it down, grateful to peel out onto the open road.

It started raining as I was driving, and it felt like I was going home, but not to a home where I belonged, not somewhere I wanted to be. The rain lashed the windshield, almost blinding, and a sheet of water coated the road with a silver shine. The fog rising into the air made the world look supernatural and unreal.

All the acolytes must be getting soaked by now. I tapped my fingers on the steering wheel, knowing that my time was coming. There was a shovel in the trunk. I'd bring them the box, then I'd give them the coordinates to the grave.

When I pulled off the road and bumped slowly down the gravel lane, the rain beat against the trees overhead. Even my headlights seemed too dim to penetrate far into the night.

I opened my car door and pressed the button to pop the trunk, taking a deep breath to steady myself. The scent of ozone and wet greenery filled the air.

I should've gone further away from the Demon when I picked my college, not someplace where I could reach one of his favorite burial sites. Except there were so many graves. It seemed there was nowhere I could outrun him anyway.

But it would be worth it to stand as a member of the Sphinx–no longer trapped there, but choosing to become one of them. I'd be standing as their equal when the sun rose on the new secret society.

I blew out a breath, determined, and moved quickly to the trunk. The wind tugged at my hair, and I shivered through my hoodie, but I knew the effort of digging would warm me up soon. I lifted the hatch.

A face stared up at me. For a second, I thought there was a corpse in the trunk; the man was so still, his eyes staring up into nothingness.

Then abruptly, he lunged toward me.

25

AURORA

I screamed in surprise and tried to slam the trunk back down again on the man who'd attacked me. But it was too late and I stumbled back, scrambling to grab my knife.

My attacker thrust something against my body, and I realized it was a taser as I was trying to get away from it, but I was too late. The taser connected with my arm and pain jolted through my body. My legs stopped working. My whole body twitched as agony coursed through me; my body jerked against the ground, my view suddenly filled with twigs and dirt.

My attacker scrambled out of the trunk and got down on top of me. He started to yank my hands together, securing my wrists with a zip tie.

My body stopped jerking only to find myself being loaded into my own trunk.

"Who are you? I demanded weakly, because exactly what enemy I faced now mattered. There was a big difference between escaping my father's elaborate, poison-laced traps and escaping some random off the internet. Maybe

Remington hadn't managed to sweep the internet for all traces of me as well as he thought.

"Remington's father sends his regards," he snarled. "Think about that and what you can look forward to now, bitch."

Fuck. I knew what a monster Remington's father was. He must have survived after all...then a beat of doubt made me pause. Remington's rage at his father had seemed real. But what if Remington had left his father alive instead of having him killed?

I wondered for a second if this guy might take me back to the club where Remington's mother had been. But Cain had control of the club now. It was hard to imagine Remington's father would ever use it like that again.

The door slammed shut, giving me plenty of time to piece through every faint clue and think through every dark possibility. The hours hummed by, carrying me further away from my earlier mission to retrieve Carrie Hayward's hand and files.

I'd been dreading digging in the woods, but now I felt nostalgic about the idea.

The car finally came to a stop, and I tensed, ready to fight even with flexicuffs cutting into my wrists. My body was one aching knot, and I tried to ease myself from side to side, limbering my muscles. I wouldn't go down without a fight.

When the hatch was opened, I found myself facing three men. One was the man who had kidnapped me. One was Remington's father. And the third I didn't recognize at first.

Slowly, I realized that we were in that same garage once more. I stared around at them, wondering if they had chosen to do this here because they wanted to hurt the guys, or if...I didn't want this terrible dark idea to be true, but I had to confront the possibility the guys had given these men their blessing to hurt me like this. Maybe the entire situation with Remington had been set up. The thought made me feel not just rage, but a sudden surge of grief and loss that burned through my veins.

I didn't want the men of the Sphinx to be my villains anymore.

And I didn't want to be a villain to them.

But if Pax, Remington, Cain, and Stellan created this situation, and these men hurt me, then I would have to kill them.

The realization was hard and brittle in my chest.

"Leave her here for them to find," Remington's father said. He wasn't looking very good, the only silver lining to this situation. The slash on his face looked infected and there were bandages on his fingers. I was sure that underneath his shirt wasn't looking too good either.

"And we'll make sure they think the Black Wings gang did it," the third man said, the one I didn't recognize. "Fighting that war should keep them busy for a while. Get these boys to do some work for us and grieve this bitch."

Relief swept through me. They were planning to lie to my men; that meant at least the guys weren't in on the situation.

"Let's do this and get it over with, then," the third man said. He seemed bored and impatient about the whole thing. He was a tall hulking man with shaggy brown hair and tattoos crawling up his arms and neck. "We can have her carved up afterward. There's no reason to waste time here. If Cain discovers we were involved...We don't need that kind of war. Not when the boys can do so much good for us."

"Think this through." Remington's father's eyes glittered

with lust... lust to hurt me. "If the worst is true and they really do give a fuck about her, then they're going to do an autopsy. And an autopsy is going to show that she was mutilated after she was killed."

The third man eyed him as if he could read right through Remington's father's bullshit and see that he was just eager to hurt me. "No, because I'm the one they'll go to for an autopsy."

"They don't have those kinds of resources. Not yet. Not without going through me."

The big one gave Remington's father a look. "That's why you're alive, after all."

I thought of how Remington had called in help to deal with his father and felt a sudden surge of bile in the back of my throat.

The big dark blonde man was Cain's father. The head of the mob.

"Why did you insist on coming here then?" Remington's father asked impatiently. "There are so many other places we could have gone."

"Yes, but we've got people increasingly loyal to Cain and his boys. We have to be careful about where we do certain things. Any place else would be obviously tied to us. But seeing her blood splattered here, they'll think it could have been anyone who was angry about the hostile takeover."

The man looked self-satisfied. "And it should blind them with rage."

"I'm not losing my chance to torture her like she tortured me," Remington's father ground out.

"You'll do what I tell you," Cain's father answered. He looked me over, then seemed to relent. "Fine. It'll be easier not to doctor the autopsy. And we have some time. My guy said the boys won't be expecting her back from her initiation until it's close to sunrise."

Of course he would have a mole in the Sphinx.

I thought about how long the drive had taken me to the site, and how long it must have taken to drive back here, and I wondered how much torture I'd have to endure before the boys missed me. There was no reason they should even think of coming here, anyway.

Confirming my fears, the third man said, "All the security cameras are off. Looped, I should say, because anything else would certainly raise alarm bells. We just have to make sure you get out of here before they realize their security systems have been fucked with."

"I'm on it," Remington's father promised impatiently.

Cain's father scoffed. "Your obsession with this girl is fucking your judgment, but fine. Cleveland, you stay here and make sure he gets out of here in time. But if Cain comes, make sure you kill the girl and get out of here without him seeing you. He'll tie you back to me."

Remington's father was staring at him, obviously still stuck on sentence one. "You should talk. Your son is obsessed with her."

"He'll get over her once she's been removed from the equation." The mob boss looked at me curiously. "I wonder what made you Cain's one weakness. I'd love to know and be able to take advantage of that. But alas, you'll be dead soon." He shrugged. "Some things must remain a mystery."

Cain's father walked away toward his car, also parked in the garage.

Remington's father turned to face me with manic glee written across his face.

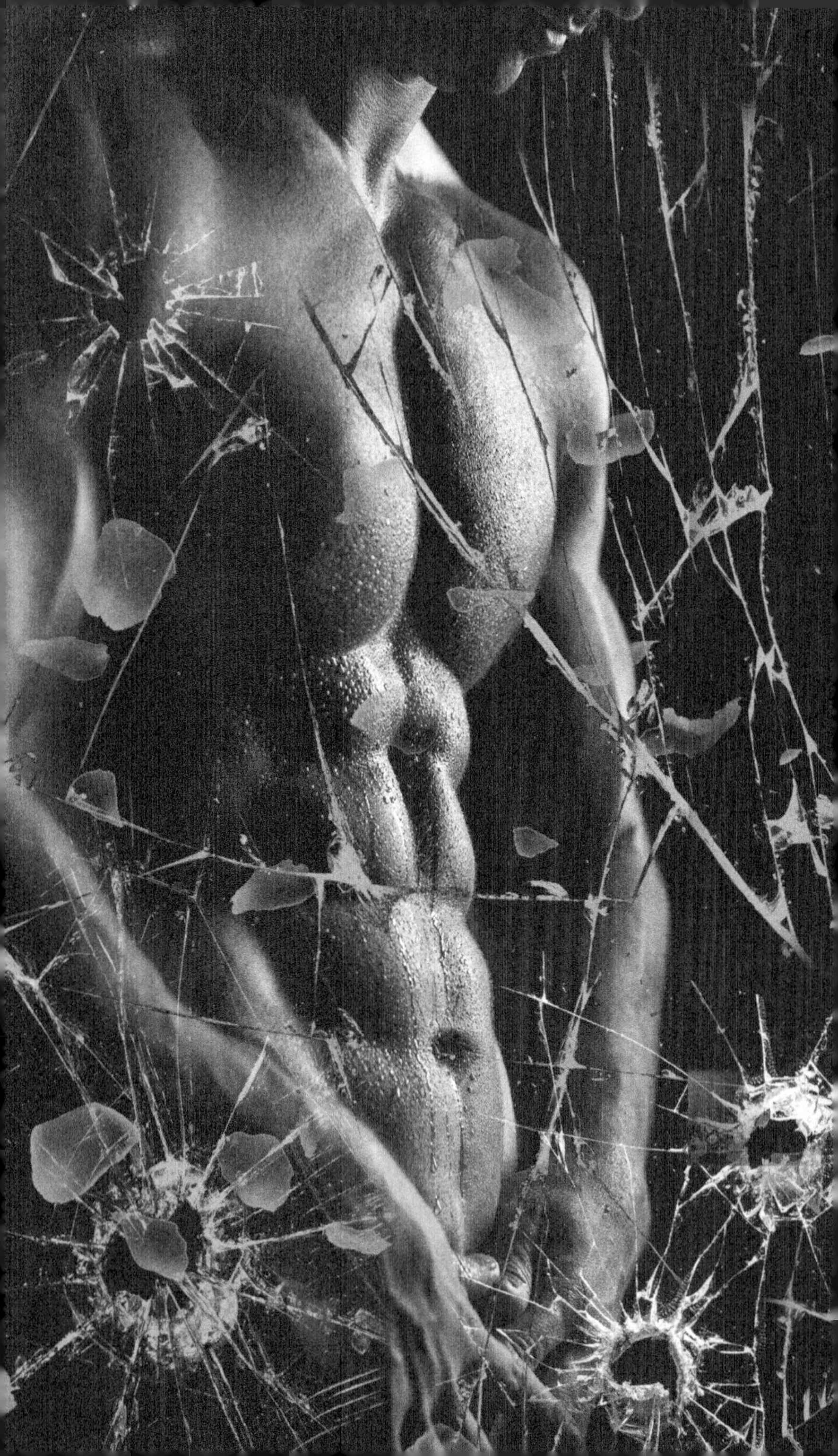

26

REMINGTON

Not long before sunrise, the Acolytes began to gather again. Pax, Cain, Stellan, and I sat like kings abiding over the temple at the Sphinx. They came in from the cold rain outside, drenched and carrying their tithes. It was the first time any of them had been allowed in this room, which was normally kept locked. The other full members of the Sphinx ringed the room, dressed in black.

Acolytes lay down their treasures at the altar to the Sphinx. It was a stone slab set between two enormous recreations of the monster. There were stories about people being sacrificed on that altar as sacrifices to the Sphinx, when members had greatly wronged the community. I wasn't sure if any of them were true. I was happy to spin stories and hype things up when it suited me, but I was very reluctant to believe anyone else's bullshit.

Including the bullshit that women weren't capable of doing the Sphinx's business. I knew a girl with bloody hands, a dirty mouth, and a bright heart. My gaze scanned the crowd of acolytes in dark robes and gold masks, but I didn't see one particular slight figure.

My heart seized in my chest. Aurora wasn't here. Where could she be? I thought back to how I had injected that tracker under her skin, covering the violation with my bite. I'd been so proud of myself for thinking to bury my secret beneath her skin, as we stalked her in the dark.

I'd tasted her salty blood in my mouth. Cain had been gleeful, or as close to any excited emotion as Cain ever came; he marked her back and she didn't even know that he'd won. The thought filled me with satisfaction, just because it meant that now I had a way to find out where my girl had gone. My first impulse was that she'd run from us.

I didn't know how I felt about Aurora running.

It was probably wise of her. But I couldn't stand the idea of never seeing her again.

She woke dark, complicated emotions in me that I couldn't make sense of. And there were the lighter, brighter emotions–the thrill of excitement I felt when she walked into a room, the way her beauty lit something in my chest–that were scarier than the darkness. She shouldn't love any of us.

If there was any goodness left in me, maybe I should help her get away from us all.

Maybe she had used the quiet of the night to escape the four of us, and if so, maybe I should delete our ways of tracking her so that the little electronic chip pinging under her skin wouldn't mean anything. First, I just had to know because part of me hoped Aurora would still come struggling through the doors of the Sphinx, carrying that box.

I could just imagine her kneeling at my feet....and then rising, taking off her mask, a full member of the Sphinx.

But most of all, it wouldn't just be a sign that she belonged to the Sphinx. It'd be a sign that she belonged with us. We had changed the rules, rewritten them to include her.

When I pulled up the tracker, there was no sign of Aurora on campus. I scrolled outward on the map, looking for her location.

She was at the old club. What the hell was she doing there? I glanced at my friends, wondering if she was doing more than a mission for me. Maybe she'd secretly won over each of the guys. It wouldn't have surprised me.

And it wouldn't surprise me if she'd kept that a secret for her own amusement either. She played her games too.

"What do you think Aurora is doing right now?" I asked Pax. He froze, then glanced at me at first as if he'd been lost in thought.

His fingers tightened on the edges of his throne. "Is there any chance we could go a day without talking about Aurora?"

"Not very likely," I admitted. I went back to watching the acolytes mill around, checking in with each other. One of them announced they were all present and ready.

"I hope so," Cain said, that subtle threat in his voice that made them all quiver. Cain leaned forward, about to start the presentation of the gifts to the Sphinx and us, but I stopped him with a hand on his forearm. Cain cocked an eyebrow as he turned to face me.

"There's something wrong with Aurora," I said.

"What else is new?" he muttered.

"I mean it," I said. "She's back at the Twisted Rose."

Cain sparked with instant fury. "I thought she was locked safely in her room tonight."

"I was never going to actually lock her in." Stellan seemed surprised by the idea. "You know how much she would hate being trapped after her time with the Demon."

Cain rolled his eyes. "It's different when she's in the Sphinx. She knows she's safe here... otherwise, I wouldn't have found her ass on my bed eating popcorn."

"Is it different?" Stellan asked skeptically. Then he added, "After tonight, I'm taking Aurora back to our hometown. I need to know what happened. One way or another, the two of us need to figure it out."

"Good," Pax said shortly. "We've all been waiting for you to get your head out of your ass."

"Hopefully we get the chance for Stellan to resurrect his head from his rectum," I said, "but I'm not sure because, like I just said, Aurora is at the Twisted Rose. Did anyone else send her on a mission?"

"On a mission? What the fuck are you talking about?" Pax demanded, then understanding dawned over his face. "You were working with her on this first-girl-in-the-Sphinx nonsense."

"If none of you sent her on a mission, then I don't know why she would be there, because she went to get Carrie Hayward's hand and his files. The files, as her tithe. The hand, mostly for my own amusement."

"We're going to the Twisted Rose." Cain rose suddenly, his voice rolling through the temple when he said, "The initiation will continue after you have faced your next task."

I was amazed by how quickly he could improvise, making it seem as if everyone should have expected this task all along.

Cain made up some bullshit tests for our initiates and told them to be sure to keep their phones ready and available for the next phase of initiation. Then once he'd sent our acolytes running off, we headed to the Twisted Rose.

When we reached the Twisted Rose, we found Paxton's car parked in the big underground garage, the one used for transport and workers, not clients. I went over to check the trunk. It was empty, with no sign of the box or a dirt-crumb-covered shovel. Anxiety twisted through my gut.

"You never should have done this without talking to us." Cain sounded furious. "Is your loyalty to us or to her?"

It was funny that he was accusing me of being disloyal for his sake when his fury was obviously protective towards her. Sometimes psychopaths weren't very self-aware. Even though Cain seemed to understand everything about the rest of us with a glance. Sometimes it seemed as if, while he was learning how to imitate a normal human, he'd become better than the rest of us at understanding what was happening in the human head.

Just then, a scream seemed to echo through the building. A building the was well sound-proofed. It took me a second to realize that someone had to be projecting the sound through the loudspeakers.

Aurora. I knew in my heart it was Aurora already, and protective rage tightened every muscle. I was ready to kill for her.

"What the fuck is going on?" Cain demanded. But he was already running toward the sound, his gun pulled out.

As always, the rest of us plunged in after him.

AURORA

"Let's see. I'm trying to think what I should do first," Warren mused. He began humming to himself as I glared at him, wishing I could just reach out and stab him in the eye.

It better not be the end for me, because having Senator Warren Taylor be the person that killed me off would frankly be gross. And really disappointing.

Even though I'd understood the romanticism of Remington not wanting me to kill his father, I was deeply regretting going along with it. The next time that I felt like someone should die, I was just going to do it no matter what anyone else said.

New life goal.

"Oh, I know what needs to happen," he finally said, grabbing a huge butcher knife from a drawer nearby. I hoped that one of them had put that in there, because I couldn't think of a single reason that a sex club would need a large butcher knife for its activities. Although as Cain had pointed out many a time, I had just recently been de-virginized. So there were probably lots of things that I didn't know.

He practically ran towards me with the knife, and I inwardly rolled my eyes, realizing how he hadn't learned anything when I'd tortured him.

I was expecting him to stab me right then, but he stopped right in front of me, frowning when I didn't flinch or jump.

"I wonder what it takes to make the Demon's daughter scared?" he crooned as he lifted my chin with the flat part of the knife.

I could easily answer that one. It took the Demon himself.

He gritted his teeth, grabbed my shirt, and then began to saw at the fabric with the knife until it split open in front, revealing my sports bra. At least I didn't have a little lacy number on; I hadn't wanted to unearth a body in lingerie.

Although props to whoever could manage to do that.

Warren took the knife and sliced at my leggings next.

And that's when my stomach began to hurt.

Being able to handle pain was one thing, but I hadn't mastered sexual assault, so this was probably not going to end well.

I was definitely going to be screaming if any part of his body entered any part of mine.

I made a vow to myself that I wouldn't cry though. The last thing that Warren Taylor deserved was my tears.

I was, unfortunately, wearing a thong, so when the leggings split open, he got an eye full of...a lot.

While he stared at me, lust dripping out of his eyeballs, I tried to work on the knots on the rope around my wrists, but they'd done a good job. They were extremely tight, and I couldn't get them any looser.

Warren dropped the knife and then grabbed the straps of my sports bra, yanking them down so my breasts popped free. I bit my lip and stared at the ceiling while he grabbed my breasts and brutally squeezed them. One thing that the Demon had taught me was how to disassociate from my surroundings. And even though I'd used it mostly to protect my mind from pain in the past, I definitely needed it in this situation.

I tried to picture myself floating above my body, trying to convince my mind that I couldn't feel what was happening to me. And it worked, a little. He bent over my body and bit one of my nipples, and I didn't scream.

It was only when he ripped down my panties and forced two of his bandaged fingers roughly into me that I shrieked, the sound filling the room.

This wasn't happening, this wasn't happening, I tried to tell myself, continuing to think about floating above my body and leaving it behind.

But the way that he was trying to break my vagina made it impossible. A scream almost burst my eardrums, and it took me a second to realize that it was coming from me.

All of a sudden the door to the room burst open and an animalistic growl joined my screams. The Senator pulled his fingers out of me and lurched backward, terror filling his features. He'd obviously thought that he would have more time before he was discovered.

I didn't bother trying to look behind me to see who'd entered the room; I knew who it was. Their dark energy was filling my lungs.

Unfortunately, their presence didn't take away the fact that I'd just been extremely violated, and I turned my head to the side and began to throw up violently.

But at least there weren't any tears.

Paxton came into view and threw himself at Warren, knocking him to the ground as he began to pummel him ferociously with his fists.

"Little devil," Remington's voice said from next to me, and I blinked up at him, trying to get a hold of my emotions. At least he wasn't looking at me with pity; I didn't think I could've handled that.

Despite the gentleness of his voice, the only look on his face was one of rage.

He made quick work of my ropes, then pulled his shirt off and slipped it over me so that my parts were covered.

I was shivering violently, and Remington was saying something else, but my attention had gone back to where Paxton was tenderizing the Senator's face.

"Stop," I croaked. I must've screamed a lot because my voice was rough. "Stop," I said again.

Stellan heard me and strode over to Paxton and yanked him off of Remington's father. Paxton had evidently found himself in some sort of rage blackout, because he punched Stellan in the face after he pulled him off.

"Fuck," roared Stellan as he tried to get Paxton to calm down. Cain was there then, and together, the two of them managed to calm Paxton's beast enough that he wasn't trying to kill everyone around him.

"How are we killing him?" growled Cain. I struggled to sit up, trying to ignore the ache between my thighs that was already starting to develop.

"*I'm* going to kill him," I snapped.

Maybe this was what would tip me over the edge, finally sever the frayed thread that had kept my humanity present. There was only so much a girl could take, after all. And being violated like that by one of the scum of the earth who'd been allowed to lord over everyone for far too long was too much.

As I struggled to my feet, I found myself throwing up again. I wiped off my mouth with the back of my hand and walked over to where Warren was writhing on the floor in pain. If Paxton had been allowed to continue for very much longer, he would've been dead soon, and that would've been a true shame.

I felt Cain's presence behind me, and then he wrapped his arms around my waist, nuzzling against my neck even though I must've smelled awful. That was oddly sweet for him.

"How are you going to do it?" he purred.

"I'm going to rip off his dick, and then I'm going to give

him a poison that will literally eat away at his insides for over two hours before he'll die."

Cain pulled me into an even tighter embrace, and I realized he was fucking hard.

We all definitely needed to get our heads checked.

"Can we do this back at the Sphinx?" I asked tiredly. I wanted to be able to slip into bed after watching him die.

"Of course, little devil," said Remington quickly, walking over to his dad and kicking him in the head so that he fell unconscious.

Paxton gave him another kick in the ribs for good measure, and then he and Remington heaved him up and began to drag him towards the door. Cain let me loose from his octopus hold and began to walk after them.

I was surprised when Stellan came up beside me and grabbed my hand. "Are you alright?" he asked quietly.

"No," I admitted, unable to look him in the eyes. Out of all of them, Stellan knew me best. I was afraid if I looked at him, he'd be able to see how much what happened had fucked with my head. And I wasn't ready to show that much vulnerability to them, especially not to him.

When we got outside, I saw Paxton and Remington tossing Warren into the trunk. I let Stellan lead me towards the car, but then I pulled my hand away from his, slid into the car, and let Remington pull me into his lap.

"I'm sorry, little devil," he murmured to me as I laid my head against his shoulder.

I nodded but didn't say anything, and we were all quiet for the whole ride to the Sphinx. We pulled into the underground garage, and I mentally steeled myself for the next few hours.

I stopped by my room to grab some of the poison I had stashed, making sure that the guys stayed in the hallway while I did so. Not that I was sure that the camera hadn't already caught everything. But I could at least pretend I had secrets in my room.

Note to self: Remember to get one of those things that scanned for bugs and cameras in rooms. I already had a program on my computer that did that, but I needed one for everything else.

When I came out, the guys dragged Warren to a room I'd never gone in before, one that suspiciously had a tile floor and a drain in the middle of it.

I didn't question it, I just leaned against the wall and watched as they threw him in the middle of the room, his head crunching down on the tile in a way that really boded well for a traumatic brain injury.

"He's all yours," Cain drawled. Paxton was even quieter than usual, staring at the floor as if lost in thought. Stellan's attention was directed at me, the concern in his eyes all too visible.

And Remington...he was staring at his father, an icy blankness to his face. "Remy," I hoarsely whispered, and he jumped like he'd forgotten the rest of us were in the room.

"Do you want to be the one that does the honors?" I asked. Although what I'd been through with him was obviously awful, he'd endured a whole lifetime of his father's particular brand of cruelty.

"No," he said before striding out of the room without another word.

Cain opened a drawer and pulled out what suspiciously looked like an all-inclusive torture set. Or it could've been a toolkit, if you were a sane person. There were screwdrivers and wrenches...and knives. There was even a large lighter. Everything that I needed to work with.

"We'll leave you to it," Cain said with a cheery wink,

before heading towards the door. Paxton followed him, his attention still on the ground, and of course, Stellan was the one to lag behind.

"You don't have to do this," he said, and I wondered how we got to the point where he couldn't see what was right in front of him. One of the biggest problems between us was that he was holding onto a ghost, a memory of a girl from the past.

She didn't exist anymore.

She'd never exist again.

"Stellan," I mused, brushing some hair out of my face. "Delilah's dead. You're wanting to take all the good parts of Delilah one minute, and then doubt there's any good in Aurora. It doesn't work like that. Both of those people have monsters inside of them."

Stellan shook his head in frustration and marched out of the room, slamming the door behind him.

"Guys are idiots," I told myself as I went over to the toolkit and grabbed a small steak knife. I didn't want to cut *it* off too quickly; I wanted to have to saw my way through his dick for the maximum pain effect.

After grabbing the knife I walked back over to Warren Taylor and crouched down beside him. "Wakey, wakey," I sang, and somehow, that got him to wake up. Or maybe it was the fact that I stabbed him in the leg at the same time.

His eyes were dilated, and he definitely wasn't seeing straight. I clenched his jaw, making sure my nails dug into his skin, and then dropped a syringe full of the poison into his mouth. It only took one minute before it began to work. He started sweating and frothing at the mouth, and I knew my smile must've been horrific in that moment. I held up the knife in front of his face.

"Not that you're going to get another chance, but I hope you enjoy losing your pathetic manhood," I smiled.

Without waiting any longer, I pulled down his pants and went to work, his screams a beautiful lullaby for my aching soul from his violation.

When it was done, I opened his mouth and stuffed his dick inside before using the lighter to cauterize the wound between his legs so he didn't bleed out immediately. A little trick the Demon had shown me once.

And then I decided I didn't feel like watching his death. One of the other guys could do that. I set the knife on the counter and washed my hands in the industrial sink built into the cabinet, only then remembering that all I had on was Remington's shirt.

I didn't look back as I walked out of the room, and I wasn't surprised to see Cain leaning against the wall in the hallway.

"Will you take care of the body?" I asked. He nodded and went to walk past me, but before he did, he grabbed me around the waist and laid a savage kiss on my lips. It was a kiss between two monsters...and I didn't hate it.

After letting me go, and disappearing through the doorway, I trudged down a few hallways until I got to my empty room. I stood there, just looking around, wondering why, after everything I'd been through in my life, this was what was really hurting me. I wished there was a way to scrub my brain of all the baggage that was stored there, starting with the feel of his bandaged fingers scratching my insides, a sensation I swore I could still feel right that very minute.

I hurried over to the shower, desperate to scrape the memory of his touch off my skin. The water was hot enough that it stung as it splashed against me, but I savored the pain, scrubbing my skin until it was red and raw looking.

After deeming myself clean enough, I crawled into bed, wondering if it was even any use trying to sleep. I was beyond physically and mentally exhausted, but I could already feel the nightmares lurking, just waiting to have their fun.

Just as I'd laid my head on the pillow, the door to the bathroom I shared with Paxton quietly opened, because of course the locks never worked against these guys.

Paxton appeared in the doorway and walked over to my bed.

"I was hoping you'd come," I whispered.

"I knew the nightmares would be bad after what happened today," he murmured, reaching his hand down to stroke my face, his eyes glittering in the moonlight streaming from the window.

I closed my eyes and savored his touch, the rough calluses on his hands from fighting, and whatever other crazy shit he got up to, feeling like perfection against my skin.

He didn't ask permission, and he didn't need to, before he crawled into my bed and turned me around so that our foreheads were touching and his arms went around me.

"I—I can't stand that I let that happen to you," he whispered after a long moment of silence. I thought of the truth he'd given me that first night he'd come in, when he'd told me about his mother. He was probably struggling almost as badly as I was over what had happened today.

"You don't even like me," I answered, because sometimes I was a stupid bitch. Especially when I was traumatized.

His arms tightened. "You know that's not true." His response felt like a confession, and my mouth dropped open in shock because I hadn't expected Paxton to ever admit that he didn't *not* like me.

Paxton's hand moved from my waist into my hair, a soothing caress that had a needy whimper floating from my throat.

I hadn't thought I was capable of feeling any arousal any time soon after what had happened today, but between the feel of him, and the fact that he was shirtless, showcasing all that perfect rippling muscle under smooth skin—it would have been a temptation for anyone. I forced myself to move my gaze away from his chest, but the sight of his beautiful face did me in. I found myself sliding on top of him, straddling his legs as my hand came to his face. Even in the dim lighting of the room, I could see the emotion pouring from his gaze. And the look inside of them—it almost looked like...

Paxton cradled my cheek in both of his hands as I continued to stroke his face with my thumb. Without saying anything, he pulled my head down and brushed his lips gently against mine.

That moment of softness from him suddenly had tears falling from my face. I slipped my arms around his neck and held onto him, needing him to ground me.

"It's okay, baby," he whispered over and over as he began to kiss every inch of my face, finally resting his lips against my forehead and breathing into my hair.

Paxton rolled me to my back so that he was on top of me. As if my fingers had a mind of their own, they slid from his neck to his back and I began to trace the muscles flexing as he held himself over me. I pushed my face into his neck, dragging in huge gulps of his delicious scent. I began to lick and suck the skin on his neck, until he was moaning and pressing me into the bed.

We became wild and needy then, rolling around the bed together, lips, tongue, and teeth clashing as we moved together. He pulled my shirt down and began to suck on my nipple, causing electric sparks to cascade all the way down my body to my clit, which began to pulse with need.

Yes. I wanted this. I wanted him to make me forget. I arched into him, rolling my pussy against his hard length. I closed my eyes as he let go of my nipple with a pop and then began to make his way down my skin, his hand reaching down to massage my clit.

I was close to euphoria one second, and then his fingers pressed into me, and that was it.

I screamed as I was back in that room, the senator over me, viciously fucking me with his fingers. The scene flashed violently through my mind, over and over again, until I didn't know what was real and what wasn't anymore.

I didn't know how long it took to come back to my bedroom, but when I finally did, it was to Paxton's worried gaze. He was stroking my hair and whispering words that my fragile mind couldn't seem to comprehend. But I could hear his deep, smooth voice, and as the sound of it washed over me, my heart rate began to come down.

"I–I'm sorry," I finally said, feeling completely embarrassed that I had just fallen apart like that as we were—

"Don't say sorry. Don't ever say fucking sorry to me again," he ordered. "None of that should even have happened. Of course you wouldn't be okay with me touching you after he..." His face flooded with anger, and I knew it wasn't against me; he was chastising himself. He slid to the side of me, and I rubbed my face with my hands, wishing I could cut today from my life.

Paxton slid his arm under my head so I was completely cradled in his embrace.

Then he began to sing again, his voice lighting up my insides and pushing away the dark.

I wondered, not for the first time, how significant it was that he was giving me that piece of him, one of the only things that he'd kept from his mother.

I drifted off to sleep with his voice, scent, and body completely surrounding me in a protective cocoon that I never wanted to leave.

How was I ever going to sleep without him again?

And even though the nightmares still came, with Paxton's steady presence somehow enveloping me even in my dreams...they didn't seem so bad.

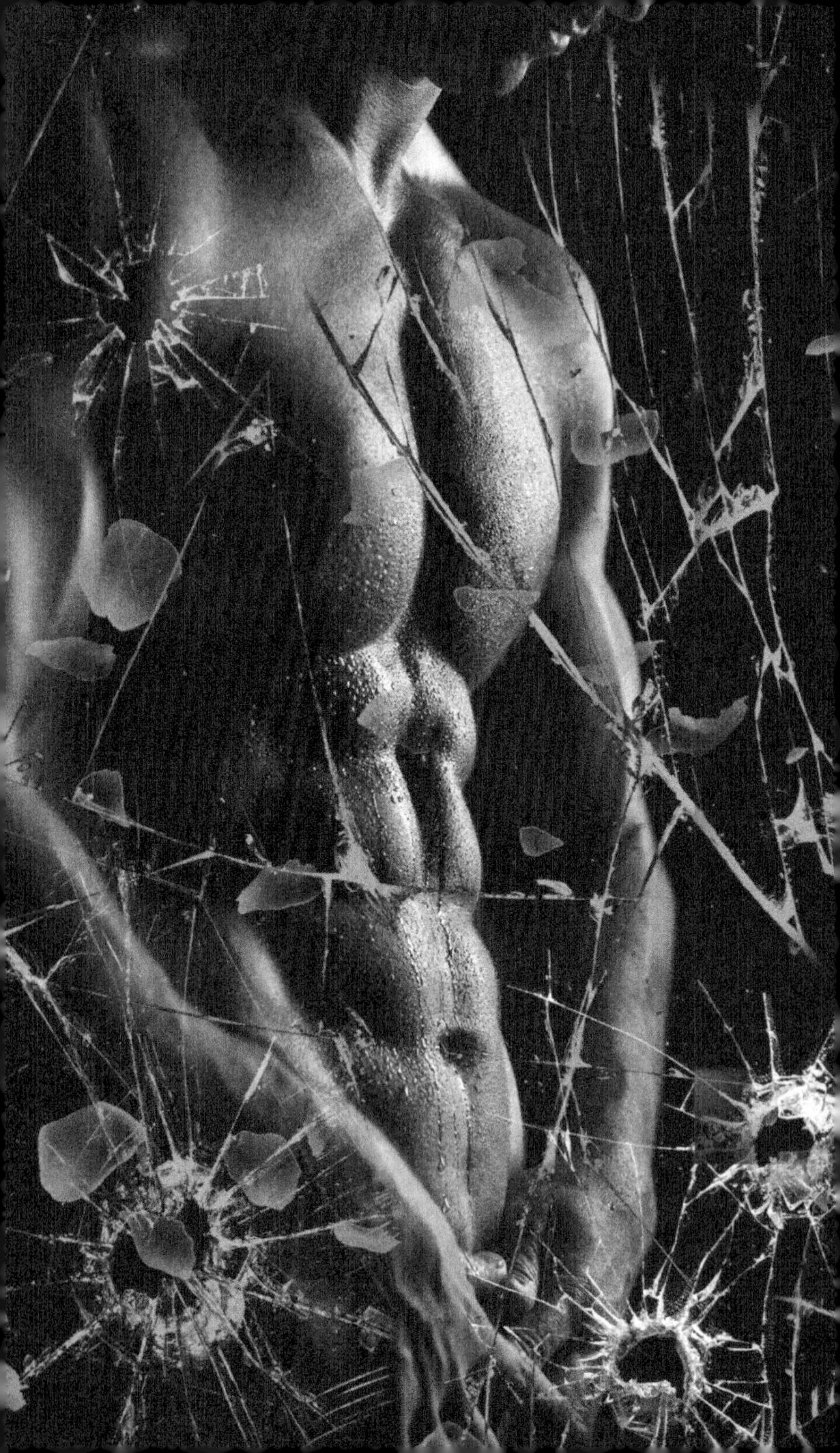

27

AURORA

To my surprise, Paxton was still wrapped around me in the morning...and it honestly kind of felt weird.

But weird in a good way, like I wouldn't mind doing it every morning. He was cuddly, and he helped me make my bed...and it was just really fucking domestic considering we were enemies.

Or kind of enemies. I was a bit confused at the moment.

He brushed his lips against mine. "I'll see you at breakfast," he murmured, before walking through the bathroom to his room and closing the door behind him.

Suddenly, I didn't want to go to breakfast. I didn't think I could stand it if he was back to hating me in front of all of them. Since he'd started to come into my room, the nights had been our neutral ground—the only time where we let down our walls and pretended like *we* didn't hate each other during the day.

But after last night...it felt like the carefully constructed barriers we'd created between the night and the day were crashing down around us.

And the bad part was, I didn't know if I wanted to rebuild them.

Something inside of me was begging him not to break my heart.

I hated that.

Deciding I would just grab something in the cafeteria before class, I got dressed and then headed out into the hallway...where Paxton was waiting for me.

"What are you doing?" I asked suspiciously.

"Taking you to breakfast," he replied innocently, looking far too hot in his white henley and black jeans. I mean, he took the hot bad boy look to new extremes.

"Okayyy," I answered, and he freaking grabbed my hand and took me down the hall to the dining room.

Had I hit my head yesterday and entered an alternate reality where Paxton had turned into my dream boy? Because this didn't feel right.

I stopped him in front of the door that led into the dining room where I was certain that the other guys were waiting.

"What's the catch?" I said, ignoring how cute his "confused" look was.

"What catch?"

"I mean, are you going to throw a bucket of blood on me instead of punch this time, just when I've let down my guard?"

"I never liked that movie," he drawled before opening the door and dragging me inside where the others were indeed sitting around the large table.

He didn't let my hand go, not until I was settled in his fucking lap at the table, with everyone staring at us like Paxton had lost his mind.

Which I was pretty sure he had.

"Found a new breakfast buddy?" Remington teased, relaxing back against his chair. As usual, he was the first one to get used to new dynamics between the guys and me.

Cain and Stellan did not look relaxed at all, and when my eyes clashed with Stellan's, he abruptly stood up, his chair crashing to the floor as he strode away.

"What's eating him?" asked Paxton lightly as he held up his fork to my lips. It was waffles this morning, and I immediately opened my mouth and moaned as I savored the buttery dough and the sweet maple syrup.

And Paxton was definitely getting hard underneath my ass.

Okay...I'd never thought I'd be into the whole baby bird thing with men feeding me, but after Remington...and now Paxton—I could affirmatively say it didn't suck.

"Did you lose your mind during the night?" Cain asked silkily, the danger in his voice sending shivers catapulting against my skin.

He sounded like a douche, and I thought about telling him then that his dad had been involved yesterday, just to piss him off. But I wanted to look into that situation a bit closer myself. It felt like there was so much about what had happened that I was missing.

Paxton deliberately stuffed a huge bite of waffles into his mouth, chewing for what felt like ten minutes before he answered. "I have no idea what you're talking about," he finally said innocently.

Cain dropped his fork with a clatter, and he crossed his arms in front of him, looking...jealous? "So this is a thing we're doing now?" he growled, nodding his head at Paxton and me.

"Personally, I kind of like having the little devil around," Remington said, throwing me a wink that made my insides stir. "But I'm claiming her tomorrow for breakfast. I feel it's only fair that if I have to hear her moaning like that, at least she can do it on my lap."

I squirmed on Paxton's lap–not on purpose, of course–and Paxton's arm tightened around my waist.

"Be good," he whispered in my ear as he put another bite of waffle, dripping with syrup, up to my lips.

I grinned as I opened my mouth and took the bite, moaning exaggeratedly as I did so.

"Fuck," Cain cursed before jumping up from his chair, knocking over his juice, and practically running out of the room.

Remington cackled, but it sounded a bit forced. I wondered how he was doing after everything that had happened yesterday. I decided to ask later, not wanting to bring the senator into what was turning out to be a nice morning.

After breakfast, Paxton turned all moody again, telling me he'd see me later and stalking away the second I was off his lap.

I was never going to understand what was going on in that guy's head. But at least he hadn't been cruel. That was an improvement.

"And then there were two," Remington announced dramatically, like he was telling a story to a crowd of people.

I shook my head in mock exasperation.

"What do you say, little devil? Should we go to class?"

"If we have to," I groaned and followed him out of the dining room and back to my bedroom, where I grabbed my bag from the chair it had been lying on. As soon as I picked it up, a folded piece of paper dropped to the floor. I frowned as I bent over to pick it up before unfolding it.

I See You.

The letters had been cut out from newspapers and then glued onto the page.

"What's that?" Remington asked.

"Just some notes I took," I said quickly, not exactly sure why I was lying.

Or maybe I did know why. I still didn't know if they were the ones behind the camera in my room.

This could just be an extension of that.

After you'd been publicly humiliated by men you thought you were becoming close to...it took a while to trust again.

If that was ever even possible.

We walked to class, everyone giving us a wide berth. I examined Remington out of the corner of my eye. He did look less...welcoming than usual. His hands were in his pockets and his eyes were glued to the ground, and he wasn't doing that annoying whistling thing he did all the time when he was following me around campus.

One guy was daring enough to say hello to him as we passed, and honestly, I was surprised that the guy didn't drop dead from the look Remington gave him in return.

We'd almost gotten to the building where my physics class was located when Remington suddenly grabbed my arm and pulled me to the side of the building where no one else was.

"Remington?" I asked carefully, not able to read the wild look in his eyes.

"I'm sorry," he said in a low, gruff voice shot with something that sounded almost like...regret? "I'm so fucking sorry. It was my fault that yesterday happened. I should have killed him when you said to. I—fucked up."

I bit my lip, feeling a bit uncomfortable at his apology.

And then it got even worse.

Remington Taylor. The senator's son and one of the "kings" of this college--and probably the world in the future—got down on his knees.

Right where he belonged.

"You said I would get on my knees, and I didn't believe you. But here I am, little devil, begging you to forgive me," he said solemnly. "I'm completely obsessed with you, and I'm never going to hurt you again."

Normally, if Remington Taylor said something so corny, I would assume he was mocking me. But there was nothing in his eyes to tell me he didn't mean every word coming out of his mouth.

One down, three to go.

The words flashed in my mind, and honestly, it was all I could do to keep the triumph off my face. I'd do that privately, because I was a fucking grownup and not petty like that.

Or at least that's what my story was today.

I pretended to think about it for a long time while he looked miserable kneeling down on the cold, muddy grass we were on.

Crouching down so that our faces were even, I took his chin in my hand. "I forgive you, Remington. But if you ever hurt me again, I'm probably going to kill you," I said lightly.

His eyes lit up, fire racing through them.

"Holy fuck, I'm in love," he breathed, and I rolled my eyes as I straightened up, pretending to ignore the thrill racing through my veins.

Because I was pretty sure he meant it.

"Save your love, pretty boy. All I want from you, is for you to listen to me next time I tell you someone needs to die. Oh...and for you to repeat this little show in the middle of the green like you promised when we made that bet about Paxton's fight."

He stood up and abruptly pulled me towards him, claiming my lips in a hard, possessive kiss that had my pussy throbbing. His tongue slipped into my mouth with long, aggressive licks, and I kissed him just as roughly back.

When he let me go, Remington's hand landed on my ass with a hard smack. "Let's go to class, little devil," he said, looking far happier than he had on the walk over. "I wouldn't want to contribute to your path to failure in physics."

"And he's back, ladies and gentlemen," I drawled, unable to hold back the smile shining from my fucking face. He grabbed my hand and led me back towards the building, and yesterday's horror fest seemed just a little bit farther away.

Fuck. I was falling for Remington Taylor.

CLASSES SEEMED TO DRAG ON FOREVER THAT DAY, EVEN WITH Remington shadowing me throughout all of them. I breathed a sigh of relief when my final class ended for the day and I could finally go back to the Sphinx and watch some trash television or something.

As soon as we got into the hallway, I knew something was wrong. The hallway was filled with people, but it was quiet. Everyone was whispering softly to each other, and as soon as I came into view, every fucking eye was on me.

"What the fuck is happening now?" questioned Remington exasperatedly.

A girl that looked vaguely familiar came rushing up to us.

"I'm so sorry, Remington," she said with real fucking tears in her eyes as she tried to grab his hand.

Ah, now I remembered where I knew her from. She'd been one of the groupies at Paxton's fight. Another girl desperate to ride Remington's dick.

Remington looked at me confused as he pulled his hand away from her and put it around me. "Um, what exactly are you sorry about?"

Her hand flew to her mouth. "Oh my gosh, you don't know!"

I rolled my eyes, done with the show. "Can you please get on with it, or get out of the fucking way."

Hate flashed in her eyes before she quickly shuttered it. "Remington, they just found your dad's body," she said sympathetically.

I froze, and Remington and I both gazed wide-eyed at each other, twin looks of surprise on our faces. How the crap...

"Thanks for that, Bailey," he said, quickly leading me around her and towards the exit.

"My name's Tabitha," she yelled behind us, but neither of us bothered to glance back.

"I thought Cain would've taken care of the body himself," I whispered through gritted teeth when we were almost to the door.

"He did," growled Remington. "Cain even buried it himself."

Remington stepped out the door first, and I followed. He almost knocked me to the ground when he came to a screeching halt and I ran right into him. I looked around him to see what the holdup was, and my insides froze when I saw that there were a hundred people dressed in white standing in front of the building, all of them completely still.

"There she is!" one of them cried, and they began to run towards the door like the maniacs they fucking were.

"Delilah!" they called to me.

"Demon's Daughter!"

"We pledge our lives to you!"

"We live to serve you!"

"Fuck," I hissed as my pulse began to race. I grabbed Remington's shirt and pulled him back inside, slamming the door shut before they had reached the steps. I just hoped that they had enough sense not to try and come into the school buildings.

Although they worshiped a serial killer called The Demon...how much sense could they have?

I belatedly realized that Remington had pulled me behind him as we both stared at the door, ready for it to burst open and a herd of crazy people to start running at us.

But the door remained closed. I could hear people talking behind us, but they definitely didn't matter compared to the demon-worshipping horde right outside these doors.

"Friends of yours?" Remington murmured, his shoulders relaxing a bit.

"Friends of my dad's, actually," I answered, a false brightness to my voice.

Remington's phone went off and he pulled it out of his pocket. He tensed when he read whatever message was on his phone.

"Problem?"

He looked up from the screen. "You could say that..."

I held out my hand for his phone, and to my surprise, he gave it to me.

I glanced down at the screen, and as soon as I saw the picture on it, I immediately dropped it. It felt like all the blood had drained from my face, and I was lightheaded, nauseous...all the bad things.

The picture was of the senator's body, naked and sprawled out in a dirt pile. And maybe to most people, that would have been bad enough, but the fact that his chest was cut open and the skin flaps were spread out beside him like angel wings...made it a hundred times worse.

That was the Demon's calling card. It was what he left on every single one of his victims.

The Demon who made his victims into angels.

And since I knew that the Demon hadn't escaped from the maximum-security prison in the last twenty-four hours, that meant there was another psycho out there who was watching us...closely.

However, judging by the cult outside waiting for me to emerge, they didn't know about the copycat.

They thought I'd done it, and they were eager to pay homage.

"They think I did that," I said aloud, although I was sure that Remington had already thought of that. "I mean, I did do that, but not the whole skin flap thing. Obviously."

"You know I thought I was going to have a dull life filled with drinking and debauchery, and you've shot that all to hell, little devil."

I rolled my eyes, but couldn't help but smile. I'd had a flash of doubt when I first saw the picture, like he was going to immediately think that I'd done it and we'd be right back to him trying to ruin my life.

Maybe he had actually meant what he'd said on his knees after all.

"Drinking and debauchery, huh? Yeah, I would imagine

that wouldn't compare to murder and pretending to be a minotaur."

He snorted. "It's a good thing I'm an expert in all things Greek mythology, or that joke would be meaningless." Remington crouched down to pick up his phone, the picture still displayed on the screen. He clicked it off and began to lead me away from the door, I assumed to the exit on the other side of the building. Everyone was staring at us as we passed, even more so than usual.

"Nothing to see here, ladies and gents. And if you value your social status at all…I would look away if I were you," Remington announced as we walked.

As if they'd been ordered by God himself, everyone immediately turned away from us.

"It's kind of creepy how everyone worships you here," I muttered.

Remington snickered. "Says the girl who has a cult waiting outside that actually does worship her."

Instead of heading to the back door, Remington turned down a hallway to the right where I saw another exit I hadn't known about.

Remington peeked through the small glass window. "Pax is here. Thank fuck."

He threw open the door, revealing a narrow alleyway where Pax was waiting in a car I'd never seen before.

They must have another garage they hadn't told me about.

Homework for another day.

We jumped into the car and Paxton raced forward. He was lucky there wasn't anyone standing in the roadway because we definitely would have killed them.

"Any ideas on who dug up the body?" Remington asked Paxton.

"Cain has some ideas, none of them good."

Here they went again, alluding to something mysterious and leaving me out of it.

Fucking bullshit.

As we pulled onto the main road, I saw that the campus police had arrived, and they were currently trying to herd the maniacs off school property. I ducked my head down as we passed so none of them could see me.

We pulled in front of the Sphinx, and Paxton and Remington looked back at me.

"What?" I asked as I opened the door and neither of them made any move to join me.

"Go ahead and get inside. I have to deal with the fact that the senator's body has just been discovered. Time for me to play the mourning dutiful son and get all the assets transferred," said Remington. I hated that the senator would no doubt be remembered as a pillar of the community to the sheep in the country who didn't know the monsters that lurked under their leaders' skin.

Honestly, I should win a fucking Oscar for the fact I was able to keep my face entirely blank. He was so going to freak when he realized how much of his money had been transferred to my accounts.

But he did owe me.

"No problem," I said cheerily, and Paxton and Remington both shot me a weird look.

Right. I didn't do cheery. Maybe cancel the Oscar.

I got out of the car before I gave anything away, and then I remembered something. Remington's window was down and I leaned in close.

"Remington. What's the code to the door?" I asked sweetly.

"Demon's daughter," he said with a laugh as the car suddenly sped away, barely missing taking my head off.

Assholes.

I darted to the door, just in case there were any demon worshippers walking around, and typed in the code Remington had given me.

It was shocking when the door actually opened.

Miracles really did happen.

I walked towards my room and froze when I saw that my door was cracked open. I definitely remembered locking it before I'd left the room. Cautiously, I pushed the door open, keeping my body plastered behind the doorway just in case there was a psycho in there ready to attack.

When I peeked in, though, it was just Stellan. Sitting on my bed and staring at a piece of paper he was holding.

"I think I've told you boys I'm not fond of breaking and entering, especially when it's in my room," I said sarcastically as I walked in.

Stellan looked up, his face a blank mask that had me stopping in my tracks.

"Oh, for fuck's sake, if you honestly think I did that to the Senat—" My words were cut off when he thrust the piece of paper he'd been looking at into my hands.

Nausea exploded in my stomach when I realized it was a printout of a picture, one that I'd never seen before but clearly remembered someone taking. In the picture, Sofia and I had our arms around each other, and we were giving the camera huge smiles.

It would have been a nostalgic, perfect photo if not for the face peering out of the window of Sofia's house behind us.

It was the Demon, and he was smiling widely. Fuck.

"Stellan—" I felt a prick in my neck, and I turned around

to see Stellan with a syringe in his hand.

"What are you?" I slurred, whatever he'd injected me with spreading through my veins like a wildfire.

"I'm going to find out the truth no matter what, Delilah," he murmured as I stumbled towards him. I fell forward and he caught me, smoothing my hair away from my face. "And you're going to help me."

Then everything went black.

Continue the Rich Demons of Darkwood series in Make Me Wild

Get Make Me Wild here.
http://books2read.com/demonsofdarkwood3

The Delilah

1/4 cup Pomegranate juice
1 1/2 ounces bourbon
1/2 ounce raspberry liquor
and juice from 1/2 lemon

Make Me Lie

AUTHOR'S NOTE

Is your Kindle still working? Or did you shatter it in a million pieces with that ending? #sorrynotsorry

We are having so much fun with this series. There is still so much to come. The Rich Demons just can't seem to stay out of trouble. Thank goodness they have Aurora.

A huge thanks to our betas on this one: Summer and Caitlin. Thank you for taking the time to make this book so great!

Another thank you to Jasmine for proofing our baby and making her shine.

Thank you to Victoria for creating two beautiful covers... can't wait to see the next one!

And last but not least...thank you to you, our readers. We couldn't do what we loved without you.

XOXO,
    C.R. & May

PREVIEWS

Keep reading for a preview of other works by C.R. Jane and May Dawson...

I was sold to my enemies. And not just my enemies. I was sold to monsters. I should know all about how to survive monsters though, I come from a family of them. We aren't Butchers in name only, after all.

I'm shipped away to New York City to the powerful head of the Costa Nostra, the Rossi Family.

My first meeting with them is bloody and wild, just like they are.

Lucian, Raphael, and Gabriel Rossi...they own me now. And they won't let me forget it.

A dahlia has always bloomed best in the light, but they're determined to keep me in the dark.

The thing they don't realize is that I'm more than what I seem.

It's a race to the ending, me against them.

They want to ruin me. And I'm afraid I just might like it.

Ruining Dahlia Copyright © 2022 by C. R. Jane

Cover by Maria Spade

All rights reserved.

No portion of this book may be reproduced in any form or by any electronic or mechanical means, including information storage and retrieval systems, without written permission from the author, except for the use of brief quotations in a book review, and except as permitted by U.S. copyright law.

For permissions contact:

crjaneauthor@gmail.com

This book is a work of fiction. Names, characters, businesses, places, events, locales, and incidents are either the products of the author's imagination or used in a fictitious manner. Any resemblance to actual persons, living or dead, or actual events is purely coincidental.

Proof: Jasmine Jordan

1
DAHLIA

It was dark.

Isn't that how all these tales go?

Maybe everything had always been dark for me though, since the moment I took my first breath as a baby. Always somber. Always sad.

An ache inside of me that the doctors and the medicine could never fix.

I laid in bed that night, listening to the sounds of the party that my parents were throwing to celebrate some deal that The Firm had managed to enter into.

There was a nightlight across the room, its light a beacon that I would stare at every night until finally I drifted off to sleep.

I had always been scared of the dark. Which was a strange thing in itself since I just confessed to living in it.

But ever since I could remember, I'd needed a light on.

At first, I'd been allowed to have the closet light on, but then my father had insisted that "no child of his was going to be afraid of the dark," and from that moment on, it wasn't allowed. He'd gone so far as to unscrew my lightbulb at night so I could "get over my fears." It was only my continual screaming at night that got him to allow me a small nightlight. When I was away at school, I always kept the light on in my room, but here I was, back home on holiday, the nightlight my only saving grace.

A small creak sounded in the room. I flinched at the noise, my eyes desperately searching the darkness to see what monster was waiting in the dark corners of my room. I watched in terror as the door to my closet inched open, the sound of its creaking scraping down my spine, and a massive form stepped out from its depths.

I opened my mouth to scream, just praying that the music wasn't too loud and that someone would be able to hear me before it was too late.

"It's just me, pet," my uncle's voice whispered in the darkness.

I trembled beneath my blankets, sliding farther away from him until I hit the wall, because I knew even at eight there was no good reason for my uncle to be hiding in my closet.

His footsteps were soft as he ambled towards me, his features becoming clear as he walked into the nightlight's purvey.

"Please get out," I hoarsely begged, not sure what to do. My Uncle Robert was my father's right hand. A skilled killer whose name was synonymous with The Firm.

My father would never believe me over him.

"Don't be afraid, Dahlia," he whispered as he reached my bed.

I whimpered and pulled the covers up closer to my chin.

I cried when he slid into the bed with me, his hands traveling over my skin.

I shattered into a million pieces when he first stroked his

finger across my knickers. The darkness that lived inside me spread through my veins, until any light that had been trying to survive was extinguished, leaving me an empty husk.

But I didn't cry after that.

Or the time after that.

Or the time after that.

I didn't cry ever again.

Twelve Years Later

"Bollocks," I murmured as a busy passerby shoulder-swiped me as they walked past, the white chocolate mocha in my hand going flying all over the pristine white blouse that I'd mistakenly chosen for this flight. For some inane reason, I'd thought that getting all dressed up before my eight-hour flight made sense.

Not that the man waiting for me at the end of the flight would care if I was dressed up or not. He probably wouldn't care if I showed up in a paper bag...or if I showed up at all.

Butterflies swarmed inside me just thinking of what lay ahead. I'd stopped in the middle of the walkway to assess the damage, so it wasn't a surprise when someone knocked into me again, spilling the rest of my drink.

"Fuck," I griped as I finally did the sensible thing and scurried out of the way of the thousands of people milling around in the Heathrow airport today. I'd never been in a public airport before. I'd always been on a private plane courtesy of the wealth of my father, Trevor Butcher. But he was gone now, and my brother...along with my new fiancé had apparently thought that commercial was the way to go.

For a moment, I imagined melding into the crowd and

setting off for some exotic locale to be lost in. I imagined golden beaches, and drinks with the little umbrellas in them...or maybe an idyllic lake setting where I'd spend my days on a dock, watching wisteria grow over my bare feet, writing the next great novel which would never see the light of day.

I would have thought them all foolish to send me on my own. A girl even an ounce braver than me would be running for the hills, desperate not to marry a perfect stranger. After all, they didn't know the nightmares that waited for me here in England were far worse than anything I could comprehend waiting for me in New York. They didn't know how close I'd been to trying to get away...permanently.

Or maybe they did. My stomach clenched at the thought. Maybe they saw the ruin in me. Either way, my warped, damaged self somehow held some loyalty to "The Firm"...so here I was, the obedient daughter to the very end.

I shook my head, trying to push away the memories and images that seemed to be permanently etched into my mind.

That was all behind me now. This was my fresh start. I threw my now empty cup away and looked around to see if there were any airport shops I could get a new shirt from, since my bags and belongings were all either checked already or shipped to New York ahead of me. I wandered through the airport, glancing at the stores, searching for anything that might sell clothing, until I stopped and turned around, not wanting to get too far from my gate.

See...the perpetual good girl to a fault.

I weighed my options as I spotted a shirt sporting the Union Jack in one of the gift shops. Which was worse, meeting my future husband with a brown stain that resembled shit all over my shirt...or wearing that?

Union Jack it was.

My hand reached for the shirt at the same time another hand did, and our skin brushed against each other, until I yanked my hand away like I'd been burned.

I turned my head to apologize, but my words got lost at the blond Adonis standing next to me.

Everyone was looking at him. It was impossible not to. He was beautiful. Like Chris Hemsworth and Henry Cavill had merged into one being and then been touched by Midas.

And that description wasn't an exaggeration.

It was his eyes that caught me first. They were the color of a thousand dancing waves, the exact color of pictures I'd seen showing the Caribbean. Or maybe not the Caribbean. They seemed to change the longer I stared. Maybe they were more like the hot blue flicker of a flame, burning my insides until a warm, achy feeling overtook me. Something I'd never experienced before, not even with Leo.

The color was startling against his golden features. Golden skin. Golden hair that reminded me of a field of golden wheat in the peak of the summer, right before fall hit and it was ready to harvest. His aristocratic nose would have had Prince William weeping with envy. And those lips...I knew a thousand women who would give their left ovaries... or both ovaries...to get a pair.

"I'm sorry, what did you say?" I asked, realizing that the beautiful stranger had just spoken.

He looked at me, amused and unimpressed at the same time.

I blushed furiously under his gaze, feeling like an errant school girl who'd never seen a man before.

I quickly yanked my gaze back to the offensive-looking

shirt in front of me, wondering idly why this perfect creature would be wanting anything to do with this shirt.

"I was saying we seem to have the same taste in horrible clothing," he said with a practiced grin that melted my insides. His accent was American, and the timber of his voice was like honey, like he'd been biologically made to attract a mate in any way possible.

I could only imagine his scent. I resisted the urge to lean forward and try and capture it.

That would be too much, right?

He looked amused again and I belatedly gestured to my ruined shirt, only then realizing that not only was it stained... It was also see-through. When I quickly crossed my arms in front of my chest to try to hide the fact that my nipples were standing at attention, I almost missed the flash of heat in his gaze, followed by a surprised expression that looked out of place on his face. I'm sure a guy like him had seen a million boobs.

And with that thought, I turned my attention back to the shirt, dismissing whatever errant thoughts I'd had about him.

But a piece of me wondered...could a man like him make me feel?

"I'm sorry if I offended you. I'm sure the shirt would look amazing on you," he said quickly, blinding me with another perfect grin.

"I know why I'm buying this blight of patriotism, but why are you?" I asked, examining the expensive-looking black dress shirt and slacks he was sporting, the dark color making his golden appearance even more noticeable.

He brushed his hand through his hair, almost sheepishly. "It's a thing I do. Well, a thing I collect," he explained. "I try to get a trashy t-shirt from every country I visit."

"How many do you have?" I asked, giggling at the thought of this veritable god having a closet somewhere stuffed with corny t-shirts. I tried picturing him in one, but my mind couldn't quite wrap around the thought.

He chuckled, probably at the look on my face. The sound reverberated right through me, stoking the flames inside that I was trying desperately to suppress. I didn't want to jump the man after all, and I was really close to that.

"Fifty-three?" he mused, stroking his lips with his thumb as he thought about it...I found myself strangely jealous of that thumb. "Well, I guess fifty-four as soon as this piece of art is paid for."

"Well, your reason for buying this shirt is far better than my clumsiness."

I rifled through the shirts, looking for my size. Once I found it, I turned around and almost dropped it when I found him staring at me intensely, all the earlier lightheartedness completely gone. He was studying me closely...clinically, like he was tearing off the layers of my skin to see what was inside.

I hoped he didn't venture too far down, he would only be disappointed when he got to my insides and found there was nothing but empty space.

What did it say about me that this small glimpse of the darker side of him only made me more attracted?

"Well," I began awkwardly. "Enjoy your shirt," I finished lamely, wanting to slap myself in the face for not being able to come up with something wittier.

"I hope you can find another coffee before your flight," he said charmingly as he reached past me and began to look through the shirts.

I was far more reluctant to leave his side than I would've liked as I headed towards the cashier stand to pay for my shirt. The bored-looking clerk quickly rang up my purchase, snapping her gum loudly as she did so. I forced myself not to wince. I'd always hated the sound of chewing. Chewing gum. Chewing food. It all drove me mad. Just another one of the little idiosyncrasies that set me apart from the rest of society.

I grabbed the shirt, not bothering to have her bag it since I would just be putting it on, and strode towards the exit, furtively looking around to see if I could get one more glimpse of him. He was still by the shirts, and he didn't turn around when I strode past him.

That was really okay, though; the backside of him was almost as good as the front.

As soon as I stepped out of the store, it all came rushing back. Where I was going. The fact that technically I was an engaged woman... It would take a minute to get used to that. I waited for the rush of guilt to hit me, since I'd spent the last two weeks after finding out about this whole arranged marriage trying to wrap my mind around the idea of becoming a stranger's wife.

Nope. Nothing. Not a flicker of guilt that I was just lusting crazily over a stranger.

My mum would be so disappointed, God bless her distracted, oblivious soul.

Rosemary Butcher was a lot of things, but oblivious was probably the most apt description for her. Oblivious to my father's sins, oblivious to my brothers following in his footsteps, oblivious to her daughter's pain.

I stepped into the bathroom stall, thinking of how excited she'd been for me as we said our farewells. She'd thought that this was the most amazing thing that could have happened to me. It would've been amazing if she was actually right.

But Rosemary Butcher was never right.

About anything.

I shook my head and pulled off my blouse, trying to push away the memory of that last hug she'd given me before she'd "spotted out for tea." It was amazing how someone could love you so much, and at the same time, not see you at all.

I should've just stuffed my shirt in my bag. I'm sure someone could have gotten the stain out, but instead, I impulsively threw it into a trashcan in the stall. I tore off the tag to the Union Jack shirt and slipped it on, immediately realizing that I'd somehow managed to get a size too small. I blamed it on being distracted and cringed as I pictured showing up to New York in a skin-tight t-shirt sporting the Union Jack flag.

Deciding I didn't have a choice but to buy another size, I peered into the trashcan to see if I could grab my blouse so I could take this one off and exchange it.

Of course, I muttered to myself, when I saw that I'd managed to throw the blouse right into an open diaper filled with poop.

I guess I was about to be the proud owner of *two* Union Jack shirts. Maybe there were better ones in there that I could find.

Continue reading Ruining Dahlia (a dark mafia STANDALONE) HERE.

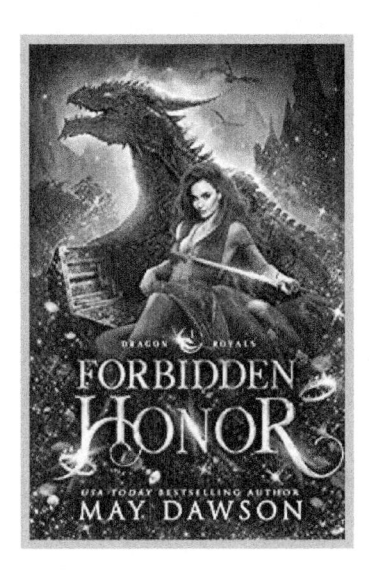

In my world, dragon shifters rule. Dragon shifters are always royals. They're always male. They're always assholes.

An orphaned servant like me? Everyone assumes on first shift, I'll turn into a squirrel.

Instead, I grow wings. Breathe fire. Throw the world into chaos.

No one wants a girl in the Royal Dragon Guard. So I'm disguised as a man and sent off to military training.

The Dragon Royals are not a welcoming bunch. These princely scions of the four ruling families have been training to fight the plague-crazed Scourge since they were toddlers. Every girl in the city dreams of winning the heart of one of the dragon nobles, but they only care about each other.

Jaik, the cold-hearted hero who never smiles and never falters. Arren, who kills without mercy and guards his friends fiercely. Lynx and Branick, the twin spymasters with deadly swords. Talisyn, with the beautiful cruel mouth and endless bravery.

By night, I'm the servant they flirt with. I'm the one stealing Jaik's heart and kissing Talisyn and antagonizing Arren. All the while, Branick and Lynx fret that I'm a spy, sent to destroy the Royals.

By day, I'm Lucien Finn, the man they despise and the dragon shifter they have to fight alongside.

These royals are determined to make me fall, and the princes play dirty. Can I ignore the pull they have on my heart and kick them off their thrones?

Will they break the maid... or kill the man? What will it do to us all when they finally discover the truth about who I truly am?

If cocky dragon shifters, steamy scenes, and snarky heroines who refuse to choose anything less than ALL their heart's desires offend...then back away. Otherwise, scroll up and dive into the adventure alongside Honor.

Forbidden Honor Copyright © 2021 by May Dawson

All rights reserved.

No portion of this book may be reproduced in any form or by any electronic or mechanical means, including information storage and retrieval systems, without written permission from the author, except for the use of brief quotations in a book review, and except as permitted by U.S. copyright law.

For permissions contact:

Maydawsonauthor@gmail.com

This book is a work of fiction. Names, characters, businesses, places, events, locales, and incidents are either the products of the author's imagination or used in a fictitious manner. Any resemblance to actual persons, living or dead, or actual events is purely coincidental.

I n my world, dragon shifters rule. Dragon shifters are always Royals. They're always male. And they're always assholes.

I have to obey if I want to survive.

But I don't have to like it, and I don't have to like *them*.

It was lunch time, and I was thinking about just how much I disdained the royals as I watched them from the balcony of Prince Jaik's room. I'd been cleaning his room when the noon bell tolled, and I hadn't hesitated to dump his dirty laundry in a pile by the door and head outside.

Red strands lashed my face until I raked them back into a ponytail, tying them with a leather thong from around my wrist. I needed that breeze after being up-close-and personal with the prince's laundry.

Prince Jaik was sword-fighting with one of the young dukes, Arren. Arren moved impossibly fast for a man so tall and muscled, his dark hair pulled taut from his chiseled features. Jaik's gorgeous cheekbones, wavy dark hair and tall posture in his dark uniform made him look impeccable.

But I knew better. The man's armpits stunk like any other's when he was done with a day of training.

That was what he—and the other dragon royals—were up to at the moment. The rest of the shifters at the academy had already melted away to lunch, but the five of them continued to banter and fight. Their swords rang against each other's, their muscles rippling and flexing under tanned skin. They seemed to coordinate without ever saying a word, two of them attacking the other three, moving in fluid tandem.

They should stay shirtless like that forever.

And not just because it was easier on the laundry.

"Honor." My friend, Calla, leaned across the opposite balcony, waving to catch my attention. "How did I know you'd be watching them?"

"I wish we could train too," I said, before she could accuse me of having too much fun watching them.

I could enjoy the sight of the pretty men even if I didn't have any respect for them. Not that they needed my respect; they had the adoration of an entire nation, because they stood between us and the Scourge.

"I know, I know. Come over here, I've got cake."

I threw my sandwich back into my bag and tossed it over my shoulder, just as Calla hurriedly said, "Use the *door*, Honor. The hallway is your friend."

I grinned back at her as I backed up and ran toward the balcony ledge. Calla backed up, shaking her head, until her back pressed the stone exterior of the building.

I jumped, got my balance on the edge of the railing, and leapt easily from one side to the other. In a second, I was beside Calla.

She sighed. "You scare me."

"You're still afraid of heights."

She leaned over the railing, taking in the training yard far, far below. She was silhouetted against the shimmering lake and the blue outline of the mountains in the distance. "You don't have to be afraid of heights to know that jumping balconies is a bad idea if you want to live until our first Shifting Moon."

She was excited for our first shifting. I imagined that would be nice.

"Mm," I said. "Maybe I don't want to live long enough to find out my soul-creature is a field mouse."

"What's wrong with being a field mouse?" She raised both eyebrows at me, reminding me—too late—that Calla was from a proud family of chipmunks. Perhaps field mice and chipmunks were cousins in her eyes.

"Nothing," I said, too late to be convincing.

"You want to be something fierce." She put her hands up beside her face and imitated claws. It was adorable. It was charming. It was not remotely fierce.

"Hey, when you're an orphan, the first shifting moon is an exciting gamble." Although our soul-creatures were supposed to be manifestations of who we truly were, most times, they ran in families. Only males shifted into dragons, the highest of creatures, but their royal sisters tended to shift into lions or wolves.

And servants like Calla and me tended to be smaller, meeker, and far more edible.

"It's an exciting gamble for everyone," Calla reminded me. "Greta Sandstone discovered her real father was a hawk."

I groaned. "What a terrible day."

Calla had squawked and run away from the temple as if her true soul creature were an angry chicken.

One of the Royals whirled, throwing his sword—and a

long, horned head and a powerful tail whipped out of his body as he grew long and scaled. The next second, his transformation was complete and he was an enormous dragon. He let out a long, blast of fire at the other royals, who threw up magical shields to block the attack and jumped over his wicked tail.

Their power was incredible, I had to admit. The Scourge had recently surged right outside the gates of the city. The royals had stopped them as the rest of the city cowered in their houses.

Calla propped her chin on her hand, forgetting to eat as she gazed at the royals. "You know, Lara got her hands on this *amazing* story being passed around about the dragon royals."

"A true story?"

"No, it's a fantasy. A romance. One of Lara's cousins wrote it."

I groaned. "Look at those men down there. They might be the heroes of the kingdom, but they are wildly arrogant. They're probably terrible in bed."

Calla looked considering. "They're really good with those swords."

"Don't tell me you've fallen victim to their fan club, too." I had regrets about being so condescending about the Royals' fan-fiction now, because part of me was a little curious. Did they always have tails? Some Fae did, although our race of shifters looked more mortal than the Fae in the storybooks I'd read.

Ever since the Scourge began, our island had been sealed away from the rest of the Fae world. Storybooks were the only glimpse I'd had of the bigger world beyond.

"Come on," Calla swept her arm toward the door. "We

should get out of here. We're not supposed to linger in their rooms once we're done."

The military students training here were apparently too precious to wash their own laundry or scrub the hallway floors. Worst of all, though, were the royals, who were too important to even clean their own rooms.

"But I like the view," I pouted, then added, "of the mountains."

I glanced down at the empty yard only to realize the royals had left the yard as we were chatting, and sudden disappointment dropped like a stone.

"Mm-hmm." Calla gave me a knowing smile.

Maybe every girl in Rylow secretly dreamed of winning the heart of a dragon prince.

Maybe that was even true for me, even if I also fantasized about kicking their asses.

They were a pretty fine-looking group of men.

A voice in the hall called for Calla, summoning her out of the room, and Calla scrambled toward it. I grabbed half her handful of cake before she could go.

"You're going to get in trouble," she hissed at me.

"Is that a promise? Because I'm so very bored," I answered, even though the truth was, I needed the money. Which meant I needed the job.

But that didn't mean I wouldn't defy the head housekeeper behind her back. I was an *uppity orphan*—as she'd informed me. Now I had a reputation to live up to.

"I'm going to work right through my lunch break because I'm such a diligent employee," I added, and even though Calla's back was to me as she bustled through the room toward the door, I could feel the eye-rolling vibe.

Carrying my cake in one hand, I leapt onto the balcony,

then across. I strolled into the prince's room, scattering crumbs as I ate my cake. I still had to mop the floors anyway.

Then the connecting door to the bath swung open.

Prince Jaik stepped out, wearing nothing but a towel wrapped around his waist. Beads of water trickled from his spreading shoulders down the most beautiful set of abs I'd ever seen.

He stopped dead, staring at me, now wearing both a towel *and* a frown.

"Hi, just finishing up tidying your room," I said, flinging my arm to encompass the room—and flinging crumbs along with it.

A bit of frosting landed on the prince's cheek. Pink frosting. It complemented his dark hair and furious amber eyes quite nicely.

"What are you doing in here?" he demanded. "Haven't I requested my privacy?"

I was momentarily flummoxed. "Did you think the towels picked themselves up by magic? That the dirty clothes turned sentient at night and walked themselves to and from the laundry?"

"Oh, you're a smartass, aren't you?" He leaned in the doorway. "I'm sure the head housekeeper would love that."

"And I'm sure no one loves a tattle tale." I tapped my cheekbone with two fingers. "You've got a little something right there."

He swiped and his fingers came away covered in pink frosting. "You're not a very good housekeeper, are you?"

Funny, I'd heard some variation on that—usually with a lot more swearing—several times from the Head Housekeeper since taking this job. "Maybe I'm meant for something more."

"Mm. What's your name?"

Giving him my name seemed like a very bad idea. "Aren't you supposed to be in class? I can take care of the floors while you're off. It's no trouble."

His eyes blazed. "I don't need you to tell me where I'm supposed to be."

Oh god. Even those abs wouldn't make up for his anger problems. Why are the beautiful men so often such bitches?

The bit of cake still in my hand was becoming a sticky distraction, and I didn't know how else to get rid of it, so I stuck it in my mouth. I backed away from him, still chewing.

"What is wrong with you?" he demanded.

I had an awesome snarky response for that, but the words came out a bit jumbled and with a spray of crumbs.

"I'm sorry, what did you try to say to me?" He took a step forward to match each step I took backward, as if we were dancing.

I've never liked dancing.

I swallowed just as I stepped out onto the balcony. "Honestly, you'd think with all that power you wield, all the reverence you get from the common people, you wouldn't be so *touchy*. How do you get your feelings hurt so easily?"

He took the next step forward a bit faster, and I turned and leapt onto the railing, then over to the next balcony.

We rotated who cleaned the princes' rooms. I wouldn't come up in the rotation for a week or two, and hopefully I'd embarrassed him enough that he wouldn't *tattle* to the Head.

But probably, I was going to end up fired in the next hour.

I stopped and turned toward him. His eyes still blazed with anger, but he leaned against the railing opposite me.

"You're awfully sure-footed for a servant."

"And you're awfully tender-feeling for a king," I shot back.

I stuck my tongue out at him and sauntered into his friend's room.

The second I was out of his sight, I ran through the room and careened out into the hallway.

But the prince didn't chase me.

Read the rest of Forbidden Honor now....

BOOKS BY C.R. JANE
WWW.CRJANEBOOKS.COM

The Sounds of Us Contemporary Series (complete series)

Remember Us This Way

Remember You This Way

Remember Me This Way

Broken Hearts Academy Series: A Bully Romance (complete duet)

Heartbreak Prince

Heartbreak Lover

Ruining Dahlia (Contemporary Mafia Standalone)

Ruining Dahlia

The Fated Wings Series

First Impressions

Forgotten Specters

The Fallen One (a Fated Wings Novella)

Forbidden Queens

Frightful Beginnings (a Fated Wings Short Story)

Faded Realms

Faithless Dreams

Fabled Kingdoms

Fated Wings 8

The Rock God (a Fated Wings Novella)

The Darkest Curse Series

Forget Me

Lost Passions

Hades Redemption Series

The Darkest Lover

The Darkest Kingdom

Monster & Me Duet Co-write with Mila Young

Monster's Plaything

Academy of Souls Co-write with Mila Young (complete series)

School of Broken Souls

School of Broken Hearts

School of Broken Dreams

School of Broken Wings

Fallen World Series Co-write with Mila Young (complete series)

Bound

Broken

Betrayed

Belong

Thief of Hearts Co-write with Mila Young (complete series)

Siren Condemned

Siren Sacrificed

Siren Awakened

Siren Redeemed

Kingdom of Wolves Co-write with Mila Young

Wild Moon

Wild Heart

Wild Girl

Wild Love

Wild Soul

Stupid Boys Series Co-write with Rebecca Royce

Stupid Boys

Dumb Girl

Crazy Love

Breathe Me Duet Co-write with Ivy Fox (complete)

Breathe Me

Breathe You

Rich Demons of Darkwood Series Co-write with May Dawson

Make Me Lie

Make Me Beg

Make Me Wild

BOOKS BY MAY DAWSON

The Lost Fae Series

Wandering Queen

Fallen Queen

Rebel Queen

Lost Queen

Their Shifter Princess Series

Their Shifter Princess

Their Shifter Princess 2: Pack War

Their Shifter Princess 3: Coven's Revenge

Their Shifter Academy Series

A Prequel Novella

Unwanted

Unclaimed

Undone

Unforgivable

Unstoppable

The Wild Angels & Hunters Series:

Wild Angels

Fierce Angels

Dirty Angels

Chosen Angels

Academy of the Supernatural

Her Kind of Magic

His Dangerous Ways

Their Dark Imaginings

Ashley Landon, Bad Medium

Dead Girls Club

The True and the Crown Series

One Kind of Wicked

Two Kinds of Damned

Three Kinds of Lost

Four Kinds of Cursed

Five Kinds of Love

Rich Demons of Darkwood Series Co-write with C.R. Jane

Make Me Lie

Make Me Beg

ABOUT C.R. JANE

A Texas girl living in Utah now, I'm a wife, mother, lawyer, and now author. My stories have been floating around in my head for years, and it has been a relief to finally get them down on paper. I'm a huge Dallas Cowboys fan and I primarily listen to Beyonce and Taylor Swift...don't lie and say you don't too.

My love of reading started probably when I was three and with a faster than normal ability to read, I've devoured hundreds of thousands of books in my life. It only made sense that I would start to create my own worlds since I was always getting lost in others'.

I like heroines who have to grow in order to become badasses, happy endings, and swoon-worthy, devoted, (and hot) male characters. If this sounds like you, I'm pretty sure we'll be friends.

I'm so glad to have you on my team...check out the links below for ways to hang out with me and more of my books you can read!

Visit my **Facebook** page to get updates.

Visit my **Amazon Author** page.

Visit my **Website**.

Sign up for my **newsletter** to stay updated on new releases, find out random facts about me, and get access to different points of view from my characters.

ABOUT MAY DAWSON

May Dawson lives in Virginia with her husband and two red-headed wild babies. Before her second career as an author, she spent eight years in the Marine Corps and visited forty-two countries and all seven continents (including a research station in the Antarctic). You can always find her on Facebook in May Dawson's Wild Angels or on the internet at MayDawson.com

Printed in Great Britain
by Amazon